In the Royal's Bed

MARION LENNOX

Published in Great Britain 2015
by Mills & Boon, an imprint of Harlequin (UK) Limited,
Eton House, 18-24 Paradise Road, Richmond, Surrey, TW9 1SR

Wanted: Royal Wife and Mother, Cinderella: Hired by the Prince and *A Royal Marriage of Convenience* were first published in Great Britain by Harlequin (UK) Limited.

ISBN: 978-0-263-25215-6
eBook ISBN: 978-1-474-00394-0

05-0515

Harlequin (UK) Limited's policy is to use papers that are natural, renewable and recyclable products and made from wood grown in sustainable forests. The logging and manufacturing processes conform to the legal environmental regulations of the country of origin.

Printed and bound in Spain
by CPI, Barcelona

Marion Lennox is a country girl, born on an Australian dairy farm. She moved on—mostly because the cows just weren't interested in her stories! Married to a 'very special doctor', Marion writes for Medical Romance™ as well as other Mills & Boon® series. She used a different name for each category for a while—if you're looking for her past Mills & Boon® romances, search for author Trisha David as well.

In her non-writing life Marion cares for kids, cats, dogs, chooks and goldfish. She travels, and she fights her rampant garden (she's losing) and her house dust (she's lost). Having spun in circles for the first part of her life, she's now stepped back from her 'other' career, which was teaching statistics at her local university. Finally she's reprioritised her life, figured out what's important, and discovered the joys of deep baths, romance and chocolate. Preferably all at the same time!

WANTED: ROYAL WIFE AND MOTHER

BY
MARION LENNOX

With love and grateful thanks to the Maytoners.
True friends are gold.
Or should that be opals?

CHAPTER ONE

IT WAS the end of a long day in the goldfields, and Kelly had personally found almost a teaspoon of gold. The slivers of precious metal were now dispersed into scores of glass vials, to be taken home as keepsakes of a journey back in time.

Her tourists were happy. She should be, too.

But she was wet. She was dressed in period costume and raincoats hadn't been invented in the eighteen-fifties. As the day had grown colder Kelly had directed her tour groups down the mines, but she'd been wet before she'd gone down and the cold had stayed with her. Now she emerged from underground, desperate to head to her little cottage on the hill, strip off her dungarees and leather boots and sink into a hot bath.

She might be a historian on what was the re-creation of a piece of the Australian goldfields but, when it came to the offer of a hot bath, Kelly was a thoroughly modern girl.

The park horses—a working team that tugged a coach round the diggings during the day—lumbered up the track towards the stables and she stood well back. Horses… Once she'd loved them, but even now, after all this time, she hated to go near them. She waited.

Once the horses passed she expected her way home to be clear, but there were always one or two tourists lagging behind, as eager to stay as she was eager to leave. She had to manoeuvre her way past a last couple. A man and a child. They seemed to have been waiting for the horses to pass so they could speak to her.

Who were they? She hadn't seen them on the tour and she'd surely have noticed. The guy was strikingly good-looking: tall, tanned, jet-black hair—aristocratic? It was an odd description, she thought, but it seemed strangely appropriate. He was lean and strongly boned. Almost…what was the word…aquiline?

The little boy—the man's son?—was similarly striking, with olive skin, glossy black curls and huge brown eyes. He looked about five years old, and the sight of him made Kelly's gut clench as it had clenched countless times over the past five years.

How many five-year-old boys were there in the world?

Could she ever move on?

Could this be her?

Rafael stared across the track at the slip of a girl waiting for the horses to pass. Princess Kellyn Marie de Boutaine of Alp de Ciel? The thought was laughable.

She was wet, bedraggled and smeared with mud. She was dressed like an eighteen-fifties gold-miner, only most eighteen-fifties gold-miners didn't have chestnut curls escaping from under their felt brimmed hats.

He'd read the report. This had to be her.

But this was harder than he'd thought.

Back home it had seemed relatively straightforward. He'd been appalled when he'd received the investigative report. Like the rest of the population of Alp de Ciel, he'd thought this woman was a…well, no fit mother for a prince. He'd thought she'd left of her own free will, as unwilling to commit to her new baby as her royal husband had been.

But what the report had told him…

He cast a glance down at the child at his side. If the report was true… If she'd been forced away…

He had to step forward. If he did only this one thing as Prince Regent, it had to be the righting of this huge injustice.

Mathieu was gripping his hand with a ferocity that betrayed his tension. They'd come all this way. The child couldn't be messed around.

The woman—Kellyn?—was about to leave. The park was about to close.

This had to be done now.

The horses were gone and yet they were still here. Man and child. Watching her.

'Can I help you?' Kelly managed, forcing forward her stock standard I'll-make-you-enjoy-your-experience-here-or-bust smile that most of the staff here practised eternally. 'Is there anything you need to know before we lock up for the night? I'm sorry, but we are closing.'

The rest of the group were moving away, making their way towards the exit. Pete, the elderly security guard, was leaning on the gates, waiting to close.

'I can give you a booklet with pictures of the diggings if you like,' she offered. She smiled down at the child, trying really hard not to think how like…how like…

No. That was the way of madness.

'I see you came late,' she said as the child didn't answer. 'If you like, we can stamp your tickets so you can come back tomorrow. It's not much extra.'

'I'd like to come back tomorrow,' the child said gravely, with the hint of a French accent in his voice. 'Can we, Uncle Rafael?'

'I'm not sure,' his uncle replied. 'I'm not actually sure this is who we're looking for. The guy on the gate…he said you were Kellyn Marie Fender.'

Her world stilled. There was something about this pair… There was something about the way this man was watching her…

'Y…yes,' she managed.

'Then we need to talk,' he said urgently and Kelly cast a frantic glance at Pete. She was suddenly terrified.

'I'm sorry,' she managed. 'The park's closing. Can you come back tomorrow?'

'This is a private matter.'

'What's a private matter?'

'Mathieu is a private matter,' he said softly, and he smiled ruefully down at the little boy by his side. 'Mathieu, this is the lady we've come to meet. I believe this lady is your mother.'

The world stopped. Just like that.

Death was the cessation of the heart beating and that was what it felt like. Nothing moved. Nothing, nothing, nothing.

She gazed at the man for a long moment, as if she were unable to break her gaze—as if she were unable to kick-start her heart. She felt frozen.

There'd been noises before—the cheerful clamour of tourists heading home. Now there was nothing. Her ears weren't hearing.

She put a hand out, fighting for balance in a world that had suddenly jerked at a crazy angle. She might fall. She had to get her heart to work if she wasn't to fall. She had to breathe.

The man's hands came out and caught her under the elbows, supporting her, holding her firm, forcing her to stay upright.

'Kellyn?'

She fought to get her next breath.

Another. Another.

Finally she found the strength to stand without support. She tugged away a little and he released her, watching her calmly as she took a couple of dazed steps back.

They were both watching her, man and boy. Both with that same calm, unjudging patience.

Could she see…could she see?

Maybe she could.

'Mathieu,' she breathed, and the child looked a question at the man and nodded gravely.

'Oui.'

'Parlez-vous Anglais?' she asked for want of anything more sensible to ask, for she'd already had a demonstration that he did, and both man and boy nodded.

'*Oui*,' the little boy said again. He reclaimed his uncle's hand and held tight. 'My Aunt Laura says it's very important to know *Anglais*.'

'Mathieu,' she breathed again, and her knees started to buckle again. But this time she was more in control. She let them give, squatting so she was on the child's level. *'Tu est Mathieu. Mon…mon Mathieu.'*

The little boy hesitated. He looked again at his uncle. Rafael nodded—gravely, definite—and the little boy looked again at Kelly.

He kept on looking. He was taking in every inch of her. He put a hand out to touch her dungarees, as if checking that they were real. He looked again at her face and his small chin wobbled.

'I don't know,' he whispered.

'You do know,' Rafael said gently. 'We've explained it to you.'

'But she doesn't look…'

Kelly had forgotten to breathe. It seemed the child was as terrified as she was. And as unbelieving. He blinked a couple of times and a tear rolled down his cheek, unchecked.

She had an urgent need to wipe it away. To touch him.

She mustn't. She mustn't even breathe. She had to wait.

And finally he came to a decision. He gulped a couple of times and gripped his uncle's hand as if it were a lifeline. But the look he gave her… There was desperate hope as well as terror.

'Uncle Rafael says you are my mama,' the child whispered.

And that was the end of her self-control. She, who'd sworn five years ago that she was done crying, that she'd never cry again, felt tears slip helplessly down her cheeks. She couldn't stop them—she had no idea how to even try. She couldn't think what to do, what to say. She simply squatted before her son and let the tears slip down her cheeks.

'Oi! Kelly.' It was Pete on the gate, concerned at her body language, concerned to get these stragglers out of the park. 'It's five past five,' he yelled.

Rafael glanced down at Kelly, who was past speaking, and then called to Pete, 'We're not tourists. We're friends of Kellyn's.'

'Kelly?' Pete called, doubtful, and Kelly somehow stopped gazing at Mathieu, gulped a couple of times and found the strength to answer.

'Lock up, Pete,' she called unsteadily. 'I'll let them out through the cottage.'

'You sure?' Pete sounded worried. The head of security was a burly sixty-year-old who lived and breathed this park. He also treated the park employees as family. Any minute now he'd demand to see Rafael's credentials and give Kelly a lecture on admitting strange men into her home.

'It's okay,' Kelly called, straightening and forcing her voice to sound a lot more sure than she felt. 'I know…I know these people.' Her voice fell away to a whisper. 'I know this child.'

The park—a restoration and re-enactment of life on the gold-fields in the eighteen-fifties—had mine-shafts, camps, shops, hotels and also tiny homes. As much as possible it was a viable, self-supporting community and the homes were lived in.

Kelly's cottage was halfway up the hill. There were ten of these cottages in the park, and Kelly felt herself lucky to have one. It might not have mod cons but it had everything she needed and she could stay steeped in history and hardly ever step out into the real world.

Which was the way she liked it. She didn't think much of the outside world. Once, a lifetime ago, she'd ventured a long way out and been so badly hurt she might never venture out again.

Now she stepped through the front door of her cottage feeling as if her world were tipping. The warmth of her wood-stove reached out to greet her, and it was all she could do not to turn round and slam the door behind her before these strangers followed her in.

For the more she thought about it, the more she thought this must be some cruel joke. Fate would never do this to her. Life had robbed her of Mathieu. To hand him back… It was an unbelievable dream that must have no foundation in reality.

But here they were, following close on her heels, allowing her no time to slam the door before they entered.

The child's gaze was everywhere, his eyes enormous, clearly astonished that behind the façade of an ancient weatherboard hut was a snug little home. There was no requirement by the park administration that the interiors were kept authentic but Kelly loved her ancient wood-stove, her battered pine table, the set of kangaroo-backed chairs with bright cushions tied to each and the overstuffed settee stretched out beside the fire.

She had soup on the stove—leek and potato—and the smell after a cold and bleak day was a welcome all by itself.

Now they were inside, she didn't know where to start. The man—Rafael—was watching her. She watched the child. Mathieu watched everything.

'Is this where you live?' the little boy asked at last. He was backing away from eye contact with her now. The mother-child thing…neither of them knew where to start.

'Yes.' She couldn't get enough of him. She didn't believe—yet—but she wanted to, oh, she wanted to, and for this tiny sliver of time she thought what if…what if?

'Do you have a real stove?'

'This is a real stove. Do you want to see the fire inside?'

'Yes, please.'

She flicked open the fire door. He stared at the pile of glowing cinders and frowned.

'Can you cook on this?'

'You can see the pot of soup.' She lifted a log from the

hearth and put it in. 'My fire made my soup. It's been simmering all day. Every now and then I've had to pop home to put another log on.'

'But you must have a stove with knobs. Like we have in the palace kitchens.'

The palace kitchens. Alp de Ciel. Maybe…maybe…

'I do have an electric stove,' she said cautiously, feeling as if she were buying time. She opened a cupboard and tugged out a little electric appliance—two hotplates complete with knobs. 'In summer when it's really hot I cook with this.'

'But in winter you cook with fire.'

'Yes.'

'It's very interesting,' Mathieu said, while Rafael still watched and said nothing. His gaze disconcerted her. She wanted to focus exclusively on Mathieu but Rafael had unnerved her.

'Does it cook cakes?' Mathieu asked.

'There's a cake in the pantry,' she said. She'd been miserable last night and had baked, just for the comfort of it. There'd been a staff meeting planned for this morning and she'd intended to take it along, but then one of the guides had called in sick and she'd had to take his place. So the cake was intact.

She produced it now while the child watched with wide-eyed solemnity and the man kept watching her.

'It's chocolate,' Mathieu breathed.

'Chocolate's my favourite,' Kelly admitted.

'Uncle Rafael says you're my mother,' Mathieu said, still not looking at her but eyeing the cake as if it might give a clue to the veracity of his uncle's statement.

'So he does.'

'I don't really understand,' Mathieu complained. 'I thought my mother would wear a pretty dress.'

It was too much. Kelly stared at the child and she thought she was crazy, this was crazy, there was no way this was real.

I thought my mother would wear a pretty dress.

This little one had a vision of his mother. As she'd had a vision of her child.

'I feel like crying,' she said to the room in general, thinking maybe that saying it might ward it off. But shock itself was stopping her from weeping. Every nerve in her body was focused exclusively on this little boy.

'I don't understand either,' she said at last as both males looked apprehensive. They were also looking a little confused. No, she wasn't wearing a dress. She was wearing dungarees and a flannel shirt and leather boots. She was caked in mud. She was no one's idea of a mother.

She hadn't been a mother for five years.

'You know Mathieu's father is dead?' Rafael said gently, and her eyes jerked up to his.

'Kass is dead?' She stared wildly at him and then looked down at the little boy again. 'Your papa?'

'Papa died in a car crash,' Mathieu said in a matter-of-fact voice.

'Matty, I'm so sorry.'

Matty. The name Mathieu had been chosen by his father. It had seemed far too formal for such a scrap of a baby. Matty was what she'd called him for those few short weeks…

'Aunt Laura calls me Matty,' he said, sounding pleased. 'Aunt Laura says the nurses told her my mama called me Matty.'

'But…' Her head was threatening to explode. She sank on to a chair because her legs wouldn't hold her up any more. 'But…'

'Matty, why don't you do the honours with the cake?' Rafael suggested. With a sideways glance at Kelly—who was far too winded to think about answering—he opened the cutlery drawer, found a knife blunt enough for a child to handle, found three plates and set them on the side bench. 'Three equal pieces, Matty,' he said. 'You cut and we'll choose. As wide as your middle finger is long.'

Matty looked pleased. He crossed to the bench and held

up his middle finger, carefully assessing. Clearly cake-cutting would take a while.

Rafael pulled out a chair and sat on the opposite side of the table to Kelly. He reached over, took her hands in his and held them. He had big hands. Callused. Work worn. They completely enclosed hers. Two strong, warm hands, where hers were freezing. She must be freezing, she thought. She couldn't stop shivering.

She'd had the flu. She wasn't over it yet. Maybe that was why she was shivering.

'I should have phoned,' he said ruefully. 'This has been too much of a shock. But I was sure you'd have heard, and I didn't understand why you didn't contact us.'

'It's me who doesn't understand,' she whispered.

'You don't read the newspapers?'

'I…not lately. I've been unwell. This place has been hopelessly understaffed. What have I missed?'

'Alp de Ciel is only a small country but the death of its sovereign made worldwide news. Even right down here in Australia.'

'When?' What had happened to her voice? It was coming out as a squeak. She tried to pull her hands away but failed. She couldn't stop this stupid shivering.

He was still holding her. Maybe he thought she needed this contact. But he was a de Boutaine. Part of her life that had been blocked out for ever.

Matty was a de Boutaine. Matty was in her kitchen cutting cake.

'I've had flu,' she whispered, trying to make sense of it. 'Real flu, where you don't come out from under your pillow for weeks. The whole park staff's been decimated. For the last couple of months, if we haven't been sick we've been run off our feet covering for those who are.'

'Which is why you're trudging round in the mud,' he said softly. 'My informants say you're a research historian here.'

His informants. That sounded like Kass. 'What I do is none of your business,' she snapped.

'The woman who is responsible for Mathieu is very much my business.'

She stared at him. Staring seemed all she was capable of. There was nothing else to do that she could think of.

'Who…who are you?' she whispered.

'Kass was my cousin.'

She moistened her lips. 'I don't think…I never met…'

'Kass and I didn't get on,' he said, with a sideways warning glance at Matty. There were things that obviously couldn't be said in Matty's presence. But Matty was doing his measuring and cutting with the focus of a neurosurgeon. These cake slices would be exactly equal if it took him half an hour to get it right.

'My father was the old prince's younger brother,' Rafael said. 'Papa married an American girl—my mother, Laura—and we lived in the dower house at the castle. My father died when I was a teenager, but my mother still lives at the castle. She and my father were very happy and she never wants to leave, but I left when I was nineteen. For the last fifteen years I've spent my life in New York. Until Kass died. Then I was called on. To my horror, I've discovered I'm Prince Regent.'

'Prince Regent.'

'It seems I'm the ruling Prince Regent of Alp de Ciel until Matty reaches twenty-five,' he said ruefully. 'Unless I knock it back. Which I don't intend to.'

So the Prince Regent of Alp de Ciel was sitting at her kitchen table. Unbelievable. She didn't believe it. She was fighting a mad desire to laugh.

How close to hysterics was she?

'So you're Prince Regent of Ciel.'

'Yes.'

'And you've come to Australia…why?'

'Because Matty needs his mother.'

That was enough to take her breath away all over again.

'Kass decreed he didn't need his mother five years ago,' she whispered. She shot Matty a quick glance to make sure he wasn't a figment of imagination. She'd been delirious for twenty-four hours with influenza. She was still as weak as a kitten. This was surely an extension of her illness.

But no. Matty was here. He was evening up his slices, taking a surreptitious nibble of an equalizing sliver.

'My cousin,' Rafael was saying, softly so the words were for her alone, 'had the morals of a sewer rat. I heard what he did to you. You were a kid; he married you and then you were in no man's land. Mother of a future Crown Prince. Only of course you'd signed your rights away. As a commoner marrying into royalty, you had to sign an agreement saying if the marriage ever broke down full custody of any children would stay with the Crown. So when you had an affair…'

'I had no affair,' she said, dragging desperately on to truth as a lifeline.

'It seems now that you didn't,' Rafael said grimly. 'It was the only thing that made it palatable to the world. That there were men who claimed to be your lovers. That you were proven to be immoral. Everyone knew Kass never had any intention of being faithful to a wife—he only married you to make his father furious. But…'

'I don't want to talk about this.'

'No, but you must.' His hands were still holding hers. She stared down at the link. It seemed wrong but it was such an effort to pull away. Did she have the strength?

Yes. This man was a de Boutaine. She had no choice. She tugged and he released her.

'The story as I knew it,' he said softly, 'is that Kass married a commoner who was little better than he was. Together you had a child, but the only time you came to the castle was in the last stages of your pregnancy. By the time you had the child, the word was out. Your behaviour was said to be such that the marriage could never work. Kass's public portrayal of your character was so appalling he even insisted on DNA testing to prove Mathieu was his son. Then, once Mathieu was proven to be his, he sent you out of the country. He cancelled your visa and he didn't allow you back. The terms of the marriage contract left you no room to fight, though the people of Alp de Ciel always assumed you were well looked after in a monetary sense. You disappeared into obscurity—not even the women's magazines managed to trace you. You weren't a renowned beauty looking for publicity. You weren't flying to your lawyers to demand more money. You simply disappeared.'

'And Matty?' she whispered. For five years…every minute of every day he'd stayed in her heart. What had been happening to him?

But Rafael was smiling. Matty had the three slices even now, but there'd been a few crumbs scattered in the process. He was carefully collecting them, neatening the plates before he presented his offering to the adults.

'Matty's been luckier than he might have been,' Rafael told her. 'Kass couldn't be bothered with him and abandoned him to the nursery. My mother had been in the US with me for the few weeks while you were at the castle—she knew nothing about you, and as far as she was concerned the reports about you were true—but when she returned there was a new baby. He had no mother and a father who didn't care. My mother loves him to bits. Every summer when Kass closed the palace and disappeared to the gambling dens in Monaco or the South of France, she brought him to New York to stay with me. Kass didn't care.' He smiled. 'My mother cares, though. Which is where I come into the picture.'

There were too many people. There was too much information. 'My head hurts,' she managed.

'I imagine it must,' he said and smiled again, a gentle smile of sympathy that, had she not been too winded to think past Matty, might have given her pause. It was some smile.

'My mother took Kass's word for what sort of woman you were,' he said. 'We knew Kass had married to disoblige his father and that he'd married a...well, that he'd married someone really unsuitable seemed entirely probable. When Kass told the world how appalling you were he was believed—simply because to marry someone appalling was what he'd declared he'd do. You disappeared. The lie remained. Then, when Kass died, his secretary finally told me what really happened.

'Crater...'

'You remember Crater?'

'Yes.' All too well. An elderly palace official—the Secretary of State—with an armful of official documents, clearly spelling out her future. He'd sounded sympathetic but implacable. Telling her she had no rights to her son. Showing her the wording of the documents she'd signed in a romantic haze, never believing there could be any cause to act on. Telling her she had no recourse but to leave.

'He's felt appalling for five years,' Rafael told her. 'He said that six years ago Kass left the castle, furious with his father, and met you working on site on an archaeological dig. He said you were pretty and shy and Kass almost literally swept you off your feet. He could be the most charming man alive, my cousin Kass. Anyway, as far as Kass was concerned you fitted the bill. You were a nobody. You had no family. He married you out of hand, settled you in France and made you pregnant. Only then, of course, his father died. Kass was stuck with a wife he didn't need or want. So he simply paid his henchmen to dig up dirt on you—make it up, it now seems. Crater had doubts—he was the only one who'd met you before you were married when Kass had called on him to draw up the marriage documents—but there was little he could do. The prenuptial contracts were watertight and you were gone before he could investigate further.'

'Yes…' She remembered it every minute of her life. A paid nanny holding the baby—her baby. Matty had been four weeks old. Kass, implacable, scornful, moving on.

'I'm cancelling your visa this minute, you stupid cow. You won't be permitted to stay. Stop snivelling. You'll get an allowance. You're set up for life, so move on.'

She'd been so alone. There had been a castle full of paid servants but there had been no one to help her. She remembered Crater—a silver-haired, elderly man who'd been gentle enough with her—but he hadn't helped her, and no one else had as much as smiled at her.

She had to go, so leave she had. And that had been that. She'd gone back to France for a while, hoping against hope there'd be a loophole that would allow her access to her little son. She'd talked to lawyers. She'd pleaded with lawyers, so many lawyers her head spun, but opinion had all been with Kass. She could never return to Alp de Ciel. She had no rights at all.

She'd lost her son.

Finally, when the fuss had died—when the press had stopped looking for her—she'd returned to Australia. She'd applied for the job here under her mother's maiden name.

She'd never touched a cent of royal money. She'd rather have died.

And now here he was. Her son. Five years old and she knew nothing of him.

And Matty? What had he been told of his mother?

'What do you know about me?' she asked the little boy, while the big man with the gentle eyes looked at her with sympathy.

'My father said you were a whore,' Matty said matter-of-factly as he carried over the plates, obviously not knowing what the word meant. 'But Aunt Laura and Uncle Rafael have now told me that you're a nice lady who digs old things out of the ground and finds out about the people who owned them. Aunt Laura says that you're an arch…an archaeologist.'

'I am,' she said softly, wonderingly.

'My mother and I have told Matty as much of the truth as we know,' Rafael told her. The cake plates were in front of them now, and they were seated round the table almost like a family. The fire crackled in the old wood-stove. The rain pattered on the roof outside and the whole scene was so domestic it made Kelly feel she'd been picked up and transported to another world.

'Kellyn, my mother and I would like you to return,' Rafael said, so gently that she blinked. Her weird little bubble burst and she couldn't catch hold of the fragments.

'Return?'

'To Alp de Ciel.'

'You have to be kidding.' But she couldn't take her eyes from Matty.

'Mathieu is Crown Prince of Alp de Ciel.'

She couldn't take this in. 'I…I guess.'

'I'm Prince Regent until he comes of age.'

'Congratulations.' It sounded absurd. Nothing in life had prepared her for this. Matty was calmly sitting across the table eating chocolate cake, watching her closely with wide brown eyes that were…hers, she thought, suddenly fighting an almost irresistible urge to laugh. Hysteria was very, very close.

Matty was watching her as she was watching him. Maybe…maybe he even wanted a mother. He wanted her?

This was her baby. She longed with every fibre of her being to take him in her arms and hug him as she'd dreamed of holding him for these last five years. But this was a self-contained little person who'd been brought up in circumstances of which she knew nothing. To have an unknown woman—even if it had been explained who she was—hugging and sobbing, she knew instinctively it would drive him away.

'I'll never go back to Alp de Ciel,' she whispered but she knew it was a lie the moment she said it. She'd left the little principality shattered. To go back… To go back to her son… Her little son who was looking at her with equal amounts of hope and fear?

'It would be very different now,' Rafael said. 'You'd be returning as the mother of the Crown Prince. You'd be accepted in all honour.'

'You know what was said of me?'

'Kass said it over and over, of all his women,' Rafael said. 'The people stopped believing Kass a long time ago.'

'Kass was Matty's father,' she said with an urgent glance at Matty, but Rafael shook his head.

'Matty hardly knew his father. Matty, can you remember the last time you saw Prince Kass?'

'At Christmas?' Matty said, sounding doubtful. 'With the lady in the really pointy shoes. I saw his picture in the paper when he was dead. Aunt Laura said we should feel sad so I did. May I have some more chocolate cake, please? It's very good.'

'Certainly you can,' Kelly whispered. 'But Kass...Kass said he intended to raise him himself.'

'Kass intended nothing but his own pleasure,' Rafael said roughly. 'The people knew that. There's little regret at the accident that killed him.'

'Oh, Matty,' Kelly whispered, and the little boy looked up at her and calmly met her gaze.

'Ellen and Marguerite say I should still be sad because my papa is dead,' he said. 'But it's very hard to stay sad. My tortoise, Hermione, died at Christmas. I was very sad when Hermione died so when I think of Papa I try and think of Hermione.'

'Who are Ellen and Marguerite?'

'They're my friends. Ellen makes my bed and cleans my room. Marguerite takes me for walks. Marguerite is married to Tony who works in the garden. Tony gives me rides in his wheelbarrow. He helped me to bury Hermione and we planted a rhod...a rhododendron on top of her.'

He went back to cutting cake. Rafael watched her for a while as she watched her son.

'So you're in charge?' she managed at last.

'Unfortunately, yes.'

'Unfortunately?'

She gazed across the table at his hands. They were big and strong and work-stained. Vaguely she remembered Kass's hands. A prince's hands. Long and lean and smooth as silk.

Rafael's thumb was missing half a nail and was carrying the remains of an angry, green-purple bruise.

'What do you do for a living?' she asked. 'When…when you're not a Prince Regent.'

'I invent toys. And make 'em.'

It was so out of left field that she blinked.

'Toys?'

'I design them from the ground up,' he said, sounding cheerful for a moment. 'My company distributes worldwide.'

'Uncle Rafael makes Robo-Craft,' Matty volunteered with such pride in his voice that Kelly knew this was a very important part of her small son's world.

'Robo-Craft,' she repeated, and even Kelly, cloistered away in her historical world, was impressed. She knew it.

Robo-Craft was a construction kit, where each part except the motor was crafted individually in wood. One could give a set of ten pieces to a four-year-old, plus the tiny mechanism that went with it, and watch the child achieve a construction that worked. It could be a tiny carousel if the blocks were placed above the mechanism, or a weird creature that moved in crazy ways if the mechanism was in contact with the floor. The motor was absurdly strong, so inventions could be as big as desired. As kids grew older they could expand their sets to make wonderful inventions of their own, fashioning their own pieces to fit. Robo-Craft had been written up as a return to the tool-shed, encouraging boys and girls alike to attack plywood with handsaws and paint.

'They say it encourages kids to be kids again,' Kelly whispered, awed. 'Like building cubby houses.'

'Uncle Rafael helped me build a cubby house in the palace garden,' Matty volunteered. 'We did it just before we left.'

'So you do spend time in the castle?' she asked him. She was finding it so hard to look at anything that wasn't Matty, yet Rafael's presence was somehow…intriguing? Unable to be ignored.

'I've been there since Kass died.'

'But not before.'

'My mother still lives in the dower house. I didn't see eye to eye with Kass or his father and left the country as soon as I was able, but my mother…well, the memories of her life there with my father are a pretty strong hold. And then there's Matty. She loves him.'

So it seemed that at least her little son had been loved. Her nightmares of the last five years had been impersonal nannies, paid carers, no love at all. But thanks to this man's mother… And now thanks to this man…

'What do I do now?' Kelly whispered, and Rafael looked at her with sympathy.

'Get to know your son.'

'But…why?'

'Kelly, my mother and I have talked this through. Yes, Matty's the Crown Prince of Alp de Ciel, but you're his mother. What happens now is up to you. Even if you insist he stay here until he's of an age to make up his mind…no matter what the lawyers say, we've decided it's your right to make that decision. You're his mother again, Kellyn. Starting now.'

CHAPTER TWO

TO SAY Kelly was stunned would be an understatement. She was blown away. For five years she had dreamed of this moment—of this time when she'd be with her son again. But she'd never imagined it could be like this.

It was ordinary. Domestic. World-shattering.

'Why don't you take a bath and get some dry clothes on?' Rafael suggested, and the move between world-shattering and ordinary seemed almost shocking.

'Excuse me?'

'You're wet through,' he said. 'You've been shivering since we met you, and it's not just shock. You've been ill. You shouldn't stay wet. Matty and I aren't going anywhere. We'll stay here and eat your chocolate cake and wait for you.'

'But…where are you staying?'

'We have a place booked in town,' he said. 'But there are things we need to discuss before we leave. Go take your bath and we'll talk afterwards.'

She had no choice but to agree. Her head wasn't working for her. If he'd told her to walk the plank she might calmly have done it right now.

And she couldn't stop shivering.

So she left them and ran a bath, thinking she'd dip in and out and return to them fast. But when she sank into the hot water her body reacted with a weird lethargy that kept her right where she was.

She had no shower—just this lovely deep bath tub. The water pressure was great, which meant that by the time she'd fumbled through getting her clothes off the bath was filled. The water enveloped her, cocooned her, deepening the trance-like state she'd felt ever since she'd seen Matty.

She could hear them talking through the door.

'She makes very good cake.' That was Matty. As a compliment it was just about the loveliest thing she could imagine. Her grandmother had given her the chocolate cake recipe. Her son was eating her grandma's chocolate cake.

'I think your mama is a very clever lady.' That was Rafael. His compliment didn't give her the same kind of tingle. She thought of the lovely things Kass had said to her when he'd wanted to marry her, and she still cringed that she'd believed him. This man was a de Boutaine. Every sense in her body was screaming *beware*.

'Why is she clever?' Matty asked.

'She's an archaeologist and a historian. Archaeologists need to be clever.'

'Why?'

'They have to figure out…how old things are. Stuff like that.'

'Was that why she was at our castle? Trying to figure out how old it is?'

'I guess.'

'It's five hundred and sixty-three years old,' Matty said. 'Crater told me. It's in a book. Mama could have just read the book.'

'People like your mama would have written the book. She could have worked it out. Maybe you could ask her how.'

'She does make good cake,' Matty said and Kelly slid deeper into the hot water and felt as if she'd died and gone to heaven.

What did they want? Where would she take things from

here? No matter. For this moment nothing mattered but that her son was sitting by her kitchen fire eating her grandma's cake.

She hadn't taken dry clothes into the bathroom. This was a tiny cottage and her bathroom led straight off the kitchen. She hadn't been thinking, and once she was scrubbed dry, pinkly warm, wrapped in her big, fuzzy bathrobe and matching pink slippers she kept in the bathroom permanently and with her hair wrapped in a towel, she felt absurdly self-conscious about facing them again.

There was hardly a back route from bathroom to bedroom unless she dived out of the window. Face them she must, so she opened the door and they both turned and smiled.

They'd been setting the table. There were plates and spoons and knives in three settings. Rafael had cut the bread on the sideboard. The sense of domesticity was almost overwhelming.

'That's much better,' he said approvingly, his dark eyes checking her from the fluffy slippers up.

'You look pretty,' Matty said and then amended his statement. 'Comfy pretty. Not like the ladies my papa brought to the castle.'

She flushed.

'You're pink,' Matty said, and she flushed some more.

'I guess the water was too hot.'

'At least you're warm,' Rafael said. 'Sit down and eat. I know we've done this the wrong way round—cake before soup—but it does seem sensible to eat. That is, if you don't mind sharing.'

'I…no, of course I don't mind. But it's all I've got.'

'Until next pay day?' he asked, teasing, and she flushed even more. Drat her stupid habit of blushing. Though, come to think of it, she hadn't blushed for a very long time.

'I meant soup and toast is all there is.'

'After a hard day down the gold-mines? It's hardly workman's fare.'

'I need to get dressed,' she said.

'You're not hungry?'

She was hungry. She'd fiddled with her cake, not able to pay it any attention. Now she was suddenly aware that she was ravenous.

But to sit in her bathrobe…

'We're jet lagged,' Rafael said, seeing her indecision. 'We need to get some sleep pretty soon, but this soup smells so good we'd love to share. If you don't mind eating now.'

She gave up. Thinking was just too hard. 'Fine.'

'Great,' he said.

'We can't find your toaster,' Matty told her, moving right on to important matters.

'I make my toast with the fire.'

'How?'

Okay. She was dressed in a bathrobe and fluffy slippers and nothing else. She was entertaining the Prince Regent and the Crown Prince of Alp de Ciel in her kitchen. A girl just had to gather her wits and teach them how to make toast.

She tied another knot—firmly—in the front of her bathrobe, flipped open the fire door and produced a toasting fork. She pulled a chair up to the stove, lifted Matty on to it—she couldn't believe she did that—she just lifted him on to the chair as if it were the most natural thing in the world—she arranged a piece of bread on the toasting fork and set him to work.

It was the first time she'd touched him. She felt breathless.

'Wow,' Matty breathed and she smiled, and Matty turned to see if Rafael was smiling too, and so did Kelly and suddenly she didn't feel like breathing.

It was the shock, she told herself. Not the smile. Not.

It was his cousin's smile. The de Boutaine smile.

She remembered almost every detail of Kass's courtship. One moment she'd been part of a team excavating in the palace grounds; the next she'd looked up and Kass had been watching her. He had been on his great, black stallion.

He'd been just what a prince ought to look like—tall and

dark and heart-stoppingly handsome, with a dangerous glint behind his stunning smile. And his horse… She'd spent half her childhood with thoroughbreds but the stallion had made her gasp. The combination, prince and stallion, had been enough to change her world.

'Cinderella,' he murmured. 'Just who I need.'

It was a strange comment, but then he left his horse, stooped beside her in the dust and watched her brush the dust from an ancient pipeline she was uncovering. He seemed truly interested. He spent an hour watching her and then he asked her out to dinner.

'Anywhere your heart desires,' he told her. 'This Principality is yours to command.'

He meant it was his to command. Kass's ego was the size of his country, but it had taken her too long to find that out.

Stunned, she went out to dinner with him. She was mesmerized by his looks, his charm and the fact that he seemed equally fascinated by her. It was heady stuff.

The next morning he met her at the stables. He mounted her on a mare, almost as beautiful as his stallion, Blaze, and they rode together into the foothills of the mountains in the early morning mist. The magic of the morning blew her away. It left her feeling mind-numbingly, blissfully in love, transported to a parallel universe where normal rules of sense and caution no longer applied.

That night, as she finished work, he appeared again, in his dress uniform. Regal and imperious and still utterly charming, he was focusing all his attention on her. He'd just come from a ceremonial function, he told her, but she suspected now that he'd dressed that way to overwhelm her.

And overwhelmed she was. Royalty and stallions. Swords and braid and wealth. He chartered a private plane to take her to Paris. No matter that she had nothing to wear—they'd shop for clothes in Fabourg Saint-Honoré, he told her. He'd take her personally this night, before their weekend started.

For Kelly, the only child of disinterested academic parents, whose only love had been her neighbour's horses, this seemed a fairy-tale.

Instead it was a nightmare. One where she ended up losing everything.

So now Rafael was smiling at her and there was no way she was smiling back. That way led to disaster. Royalty…no and no and no.

'I'm not Kass,' he said and she blinked.

'Pardon?'

'I know there's a family resemblance,' he told her, and there was a note of anger behind his studied gentleness. 'But I'm not Kass and I'm not like him. You have no reason to fear me, Kelly.'

'I…'

'Let's make toast,' he said, and smiled some more and supervised turning the bread on the toasting fork. 'You pour the soup.'

So eat they did, by the fireside. Matty was hungry and Kelly was hungry for him. She could scarcely take her eyes from him.

'He'll still be here tomorrow,' Rafael said and leaned over the table, filled her soup spoon and guided her lifeless hand to her lips. 'You look like you need a feed as much as Matty.'

'You'll still be here tomorrow?'

'Yes.'

There should have been a fuss, she thought, bewildered. She thought of Kass, flying to Paris that first weekend she'd met him. There'd been minions everywhere—pomp and pageantry, recognition of Kass's rank and dignity.

'Why aren't there reporters?' she asked, forcing herself to drink her soup as Rafael had directed, if only to stop him force-feeding her. He had the look of a man who just might.

He was frowning at her. He looked as if he was worried about her. That was crazy.

'Just how sick were you?' he demanded and she flushed and spooned a bit more soup in.

'It was a horrid flu but I'm fine now. You haven't answered my question. Why are there no reporters? If you're indeed Prince Regent…'

'We came incognito.'

'Oh, sure.'

'It can be done,' he said. 'In fact I changed my name to my mother's when I left the country. I have an American passport—I'm Rafael Nadine.'

'And Matty?'

'Trickier,' he said. 'But not impossible when you know people in high places.'

'As you do.'

'As we do,' he said gravely. 'It was important. To sweep in here in a Rolls-Royce or six with a royal entourage behind me…it wouldn't achieve what I hoped to achieve.'

'Which was what?'

'To find out for sure what my investigators have been telling me. That you are indeed a woman of principle. That you are indeed a woman who should have all the access to your son that you want.'

'Oh,' she said faintly.

'Eat your soup.'

'I don't think…'

'We're not talking about anything else until you've eaten your soup and at least three slices of toast,' he said roughly. 'Matty, something tells me your mama needs a little looking after. As a son, that's your duty. Finish your soup and then make us all some more toast.'

Matty crashed. Just like that. One minute he was bright and bubbly and enthused about toast-making, but the next minute, as he ate his third piece of toast, spread thickly with honey, his eyelids drooped. He pushed aside his plate, put his head on his hands and sighed.

'My head feels heavy,' he said. 'Uncle Rafael…'

'We need to go,' Rafael said ruefully. 'We hadn't meant to stay this long.' He smiled at her—that damned smile again. 'It's your fault. The soup smelled so good.'

'Where are you staying?' she asked.

'The Prince Edward.'

'But that's…' She paused, dismayed.

'That's what?' Rafael said. 'We found it on the Internet, Matty and I. It looks splendid. We checked in this afternoon and it seems really comfortable.'

'Yes, but it's over a really popular pub,' she said. 'Thursday night here is most people's pay night. The Prince Edward is the party pub. By two in the morning it'll be moving up and down on its foundations.'

'Oh,' he said, in a voice which said that if Matty hadn't been present he might have said something else.

'I need to go to sleep,' Matty said unnecessarily.

'You can stay here,' Kelly said before she realized she intended to say it.

'We can't…'

'I've just got the one bedroom,' she said quickly. 'But it's a double bed. You and Matty could have it and I can sleep on the settee.'

'This settee?' Rafael asked. There was no separate living area from the kitchen in this cottage. The settee stretched out along one wall, big and piled with cushions and incredibly inviting.

'I could sleep on that,' Matty announced.

'So you could,' Rafael said. 'If that's okay with your mama. I'll go back to the Prince Edward.'

Matty's face fell. 'I want to go with you,' he whispered.

Of course. Kelly was his mother but he'd known her for all of two hours. Rafael was his security.

But now she'd said it, Kelly knew the invitation had come from the heart. She so wanted them to stay. She wanted *Matty* to stay.

Rafael was watching her face. He wouldn't have to be brilliant to see the aching need she had no way of disguising.

The thought of them going to the Prince Edward, where she knew they'd lie awake all night rocked by the vibrations of truly appalling bands was almost unbearable. But in truth the thought of Matty going anywhere was unbearable. She'd put up with Rafael—with a de Boutaine in her house—to know that Matty was under her roof.

'So here's a plan,' Rafael said gently, looking from Matty to Kelly and back again. 'Matty, your mama says the hotel we're planning on staying in is very noisy. She's invited us to stay in this little cottage with her. Would you like to do that?'

'Yes, but only if you stay here too,' Matty said, and his bottom lip trembled.

'Then I will,' Rafael said. 'But you know, you and your mama look as tired as each other. Why don't you pop under the blankets on one side of your mama's bed? Your mama can sleep on the other side and I'll sleep by the fire.'

'Why can't you and mama sleep in the bed while I sleep by the fire?' Matty whispered but he was losing force. He was drooping as they watched.

'It wouldn't be dignified,' Rafael said. 'You know Aunt Laura says you and I need to learn to be dignified.'

'It's not dignified to sleep in the same bed as my mama?'

'For you, yes. For me, no.'

'Okay,' Matty said, caving in with an alacrity born of need. 'Can I go to bed now?'

And an hour later she was in bed with her son.

It felt like a weird and spacey dream. She lay in her big double bed and listened to him. Her son was breathing.

No big deal. To listen to a child breathe…

How could she go to sleep? She'd left the blind open and the moon was shining over her little vegetable garden, into the window, washing over her little son's face.

Normally she blocked the moon out. She had a single woman's need for security—privacy—so the blind went down every night.

There was no way the blind was coming down this night. She lay and watched Matty's chest rise and fall, his small face intent even in sleep, the way his lashes curled, the way his fingers pressed into his cheek…

She could see his father. She could see the de Boutaine side. But she could also see little things about herself. She had funny quirky eyebrows, too thick for beauty. Whenever she had a haircut, the hairdresser tut-tutted and thinned them out.

Here were those same thick brows.

On a guy they'd be gorgeous.

On Matty they were gorgeous.

Her son.

There were vague sounds from outside and she looked out of the window in time to see the security guards wandering past her back fence. Yes, she should get up and close the blind. It wasn't safe.

It was safe, for just through the door Rafael de Boutaine was stretched out on her settee.

Her son was in bed beside her. The Prince Regent of Alp de Ciel was just through the door.

'As if that makes us safe,' she muttered into the night.

But…but…

'He's different from Kass. He's honourable, I know.

'How do you know?' She was whispering into the dark. Her hand was lying on Matty's pillow. She wouldn't touch him. She wouldn't for the world wake him, startle him. But with her hand on his pillow she could feel his breathing. It was enough.

'Rafael brought him home.

'There must be some underlying motive.

'Maybe, but he's brought him home,' she whispered and the thought of Rafael lying in the darkness just through the door remained solid. Good. Comforting in a way she hadn't been comforted for years.

Her little boy was asleep beside her. Rafael had brought him to her.

What more could a woman want?

'I have my son,' she whispered into the dark and thought how could she sleep with such happiness?

But she was still recuperating from the flu. She hadn't slept well for weeks.

She leaned up on her elbows and gazed for one long last moment at her son. She touched her lips with her finger and then transferred the kiss to her son with a feather touch that wouldn't disturb him for the world.

She snuggled down on to her pillows where she could watch her son's breathing.

He breathed. He breathed.

Rafael was just through the door. Prince Regent of Alp de Ciel. A prince who'd brought her son to her.

She felt warm and safe and almost delirious with love.

She slept.

Kelly woke to the smell of coffee. She opened one eye. They were standing at the bedroom door, smiling. Both of them. Identical smiles, where warmth and mischief combined.

Rafael was dressed in the same casual cords and soft sweater he'd been wearing the night before. Last night Matty had been wearing jeans and a soft blue coat. Now he was wearing almost identical cords to Rafael and a sweater of the same colour as well. They looked… They looked…

She blinked fiercely. She'd been awake for seconds and she was close to tears already.

'H…hi.'

'Hi, yourself, sleepyhead,' Rafael said, carrying in a mug of steaming coffee. 'Mathieu. Toast.' Mathieu almost saluted, but his hands were occupied in balancing a plateful of toast.

The toast was spread liberally with marmalade and butter. Yum. But…

She glanced at the bedside clock and sat bolt upright as Matty reached the bed with the toast. It was almost a calamity, but not quite, for Rafael moved like a big cat, pouncing on the plate, lifting it away while spilling not a drop of coffee.

She was stunned, but she was still staring at the clock. 'It's after nine,' she stammered. 'How…'

'We turned off your alarm clock,' Matty said proudly and removed the plate of toast from Rafael's grasp and put it carefully on her knee. 'Uncle Rafael and me woke up really early because it doesn't feel like morning. Uncle Rafael says it's because we're all the way round the other side of the world and the sun hasn't caught us up. Uncle Rafael says if we keep flying we'll catch up with it again but we don't want to keep flying yet 'cos we have to give you toast. And the man outside in the uniform said you've been really, really sick and someone ought to look after you 'cos you sure as hell don't look after yourself.'

He paused, looking up at Rafael with uncertainty. 'Did I say that right? In *Anglais*?'

'You certainly did,' Rafael said. 'I told you my mother's American,' he told Kelly. 'Matty's been brought up bilingual. Isn't he terrific?'

'Terrific,' Kelly said and managed a smile. Terrific? He was more than terrific. He was…he was…

Her son.

But there was still the little matter of the time.

'I'm supposed to be at work.'

'You're not. Rob's back,' Rafael said. 'The two tour guides are back at work today. There's no urgency. The powers that be say you're to take the day off if you need.'

'The powers that be…'

'We've been busy,' he told her. 'We went back to the hotel to get our gear. Then we visited your administration. The lady there—Diane?—she was in at eight. We introduced ourselves.'

'You never told her…'

'We said we were relations,' he said, placating her. 'And we were worried about you. It seems Diane is worried about you too.'

'She's a mother hen,' Kelly said fretfully, wondering what Diane would be thinking. Knowing what Diane would be thinking. 'Look, thank you for the thought but I need to…'

'Take us through the theme park,' Rafael said. 'Matty's aching to go down a gold-mine. We thought we might do that first, if it's okay with you.' He smiled down at her with that heart-stopping smile that sent her brain straight into panic. 'That is, unless you'd like to stay in bed and sleep while Matty and I explore?'

Matty explore without her? The idea had her reaching to toss off her covers but Rafael caught her hands and stopped her.

'No,' he said, gently but firmly. 'You stay in bed until you've had your toast. Matty and I are going to eat more toast until you're ready. You're not to rush. We have all the time in the world.'

'Really?'

The smile faded. 'No,' he admitted. 'Not really. But for today I'm going to pretend that's true, so I'd like you to play along if you will. Let's get ourselves breakfasted and go find some gold.'

She wore her favourite dress. Matty's words stayed with her—*I thought my mother would wear a pretty dress.* So she did.

Most of Kelly's work in the theme park was done in the administration. She researched new displays, she assessed the veracity of potential tenants for the commercial sites—were their wares truly representative of the eighteen-fifties? She worked with the engineers as they combined authentic mining methods with new-age safety. She examined artefacts as they were found, donated or offered for sale.

In the short times she was off site she wore what the park

staff loosely termed civvies, but while she was in the park, like every other employee, she dressed for the times.

She loved her clothes. Yes, she had the hard-wearing moleskins and flannels for when she needed to go underground, but mostly she was a woman wearing clothes that a woman would have worn in the eighteen-fifties—hooped skirts, shawls, bonnets. She loved the way her skirts swished against her, how they turned her into a citizen of a bygone age. She loved disappearing into the world of nearly two hundred years ago.

And this morning Matty was waiting for his mother. So she chose a pale blue muslin gown, beautifully hand-embroidered herself in the long winter nights before the fire. She teamed it with a soft woollen shawl of a deeper blue and cream. She tied her soft chestnut curls into a knot and placed a bonnet on top, a soft straw confection with ribbons of three colours combined. Then she pinched her cheeks to give them colour as girls used to do in times past. She smiled to herself. She was dressing for her son. Surely he wouldn't notice colour in her cheeks.

She was also dressing for Rafael and he might.

Which was a nonsense, she told herself, suddenly angry. She wasn't dressing for Rafael. She'd never dress for a de Boutaine again. She wanted nothing to do with the family.

But her son was a de Boutaine. How could she swear never to have anything to do with a royal family headed by her son?

It was too hard. It made her head spin. She picked up the little cane basket she carried instead of a purse and opened the door to the kitchen.

They were washing dishes. Rafael was washing, Matty was wiping. Rafael had his sleeves rolled up. He'd used too much soap and suds were oozing out of the porcelain bowl and on to the wooden bench. Matty was manfully trying to wipe suds off plates. He had suds on his nose.

There it was again. The combination of de Boutaine sexiness that made her want to gasp.

She swallowed it firmly, but both guys had turned to her and were looking at her in frank admiration.

'Wow,' said Matty.

'Wow,' Rafael repeated and she felt herself blushing.

'I…it's what we all have to wear.'

'My mama's pretty,' Matty said, satisfied. 'Isn't she, Uncle Rafael?'

'She certainly is,' Rafael agreed. 'Modern men don't know what they're missing.'

'It certainly covers me,' she said, struggling for lightness. 'There could be absolutely anything under these hoops.'

'Hoops,' Matty said. He walked forward, fascinated, and gave one of her hoops a tentative poke.

Her skirt swayed out behind her.

'It's like a little tent,' Matty said. 'Mama could have really, really fat legs. Or she could be hiding something. A little dog.'

It was said with a certain amount of hope and for a dumb moment Kelly wished she had a dog.

A dog under her skirt. Right.

'There's nothing your mama needs to hide,' Rafael said, turning his back to the suds, eyeing them with a degree of bewilderment and then sternly turning back to her. 'Let's go play on the goldfields.'

'You haven't finished washing up.'

'My suds seem to be taking over the world,' he said. 'I just shook the little holder with the washing up liquid in and suds went everywhere. I think we should go out and shut the door and lock it after us. And hope like crazy the suds don't follow us down the mineshafts.'

They loved it.

Kelly could do the guide thing on autopilot. She walked them through the little town, down to the creek where tourists were panning for gold. She showed the boys how to use the tin pans and then sat on a log and watched them.

The park was quiet. The flu epidemic had hit the whole state. It was autumn. Nearly all the staff had been laid low early and were now returning to work. With the worst of the sickness past, they'd be almost overmanned for the rest of the season. So she could afford to take this day. To simply watch as Matty and Rafael explored.

They were so alike.

Rafael wasn't even Matty's uncle, she reminded herself. Rafael had been Kass's cousin. That made him—what—second cousin to Matty?

But Matty loved him. He trusted him absolutely. Their two heads were bowed over the pan, searching for specks of gold, and she thought that Rafael could easily be his father.

What sort of man was he? The Prince Regent of Alp de Ciel.

It didn't matter.

It did matter, for there was a burning question hanging over her head. Where did she go from here?

She'd been handed back her son, but Matty was his own little person. He had allegiances. There were people he loved, and those people didn't include her.

Rafael had said it was her decision to make.

She'd keep him here. She watched as he found a tiny speck of gold in his pan and held it on his thumb, admiring. He could live with her here. She'd take care of him. He could have a wonderful life, living on the diggings. Lots of staff had their kids here—he'd be part of the kid-pack who wore period clothes and treated the park as their personal playground. He'd go to school here. She'd keep him…

Hidden?

It was on the tip of her tongue, the edge of her thoughts. That was what she'd been doing, she thought. For the last five years she'd been hiding. She was hiding still, behind her hoops and her bonnet and her period self.

The Kelly who'd looked up to see Prince Kass gazing down at her, the Kelly who'd ridden out with Kass at dawn, who'd launched herself into life six years back, had been locked firmly away.

Yes, she was hiding. She was still in there somewhere, the Kelly who craved excitement and adventure and…romance? But she was very firmly hidden and there was no way the sensible Kelly would ever let her emerge again.

Pete was walking down the hill towards them. Trouble. She knew the security guard well and the expression on his face had Kelly standing up, moving automatically between Pete and the two gold-panners.

Between the outside world and her son.

'What's wrong?' she called before he reached her, and Rafael looked up from gold-panning, handed the pan over to Matty and came to join her.

'There's media at the gate,' Pete said harshly. 'They're asking Diane where to find someone called the Prince Regent of some country or other. Diane told them she's never heard of anyone like that but they described—' he hesitated as Rafael reached them '—they described you, sir.'

'Damn,' Rafael said, but he said it wearily as if he'd expected it.

'We'll go back to the cottage,' Kelly said, uncertain, but he shook his head.

'They'd find us there. We'll be forced to stay inside while they camp and wait for us to come out. It'll just delay the inevitable.'

'I can see them off,' Pete said. 'Begging your pardon, but… are you a prince?'

'For my sins, yes,' Rafael said ruefully. 'And this is a public theme park. They can demand admission. I'll have to head them off. Kelly, can you blend into the tourist scene with Matty?'

'I…sure. Are they looking for me?' She sounded scared. She knew it but there wasn't anything she could do about it. Five years ago she'd been hunted as the press had searched the world for her. She'd been turned into the wicked princess, reviled by all.

To have photographers here now…

'Not yet,' Rafael said. 'At least I hope not. I hope it's just that they've tracked me down. They'll assume Matty's at home in Alp de Ciel.'

'What have you told them? Do they know you're letting me have access to Matty?'

'I've told them nothing,' he said, looking grim. 'But it's not going to last.'

'What's going on?' Pete demanded, bewildered.

'It's private,' Kelly said urgently, but she knew Pete's brain was forming questions more quickly than his mouth could ask them.

'They'll find us soon,' she whispered.

'Yes, but I'll buy time.' Rafael shrugged. 'I'm sorry, Matty,' he said. Matty had straightened from his panning and was looking bewildered. 'It's the press,' he said, as if that explained all, and Kelly could see that the words were meaningful to her little son. He'd been hounded by the media in the past, then. 'I need to go.'

'Will I come with you?' Matty drew himself up and Kelly had a flash of recognition. This was a prince in training. His shoulders came back and he met Rafael's look directly. 'Do they wish to talk to me?'

'They might eventually,' Rafael conceded. 'But your job here is to protect your mother. If it's okay,' he said to Kelly, 'I'll leave—I'll give them some sort of interview and try to deflect them—and come back when the park is closed. Matty, is that okay with you?'

'Y-yes,' Matty said but his bottom lip trembled again. He really was a very little boy.

'We'll have fun,' Kelly said, stooping to look directly into his eyes. 'Matty, we can go down a gold-mine. We can play tenpin bowling with old wooden skittles. Do you know how to bowl?'

'Y-yes.'

'We can learn how to make damper—it's a lovely type of

bread that's really Australian. Then we can go back to my little house and sit by the fire and read books. Before you know it, your Uncle Rafael will be back.'

'I want my Aunt Laura,' Matty quavered, and Kelly couldn't help herself. She gathered him to her and hugged. His little body was stiff and unyielding.

'They're coming this way,' Pete said urgently and Rafael looked up the hill and swore.

'Damn, I...'

'Just go,' Kelly said, holding Matty tight. 'Please.' She wasn't ready to face the media yet and the thought of cameras aimed at Matty was unbearable. 'But you will come back?'

'Of course I'll come back.'

'Thank you,' she said simply and, as Pete moved up the hill to deflect the dozen or so men and women walking purposefully towards them, she crossed the little bridge over the creek and carried Matty away. Hoping the media had been too far away to guess that she and Rafael had been together.

The Chinese camp was just behind them. Yan, the camp guide, was a personal friend.

'Can I take Matty through the Joss house?' she demanded and Yan stepped aside. The inside of the Joss house was a sacred place, out of bounds for anyone but worshippers.

'Go,' he said without asking questions, his eyes flicking to the group of men and women clustering about Rafael. Shouting questions. Lifting cameras high and taking photographs over people's heads.

She went. But before Yan closed the gate behind her she turned with Matty in her arms to take a last glimpse of Rafael.

Royalty.

She wanted no part of it.

She had a part of it. He was in her arms right now, tense and frightened and to be protected at all costs.

Her Matty. Her son.

The only person standing between Matty and the media—between Matty and the world—was Rafael.

A de Boutaine.

Her world was upside down.

'Let's go underground for a while,' she whispered to Matty as she fled out through the back entrance.

'I don't think I want to go underground,' Matty said and Kelly thought, neither do I.

She'd had five years of being underground.

Maybe it was time to emerge.

Maybe she had no choice.

CHAPTER THREE

THEY explored the goldfields until Matty's legs gave out. He was cheerful, interested and polite. They ate their dinner early—a damper they'd made together and a thick Irish stew. Kelly settled him into her big bed and his eyelids drooped.

Fatigue was sapping his courage. He was half a world away from his people.

'I want Uncle Rafael,' he murmured.

'He'll come,' Kelly said. 'But he said he might not be able to return until late. I'll have him come in here and say good-night the minute he arrives.'

'Do you promise?'

'I promise.'

'I miss Aunt Laura,' he said fretfully. 'I miss Ellen and Marguerite. I want to go home.'

Her heart twisted. Home. Home was where the heart was.

Her home was right here. Her home was with this small boy, who was so alone.

The Crown Prince of Alp de Ciel.

'Let me read you a story,' she said, and she found an ancient book she'd loved when she had been his age, a book she'd held on to just in case, just in case…

The Poky Little Puppy.

The book was battered and dog-eared. It had been given

to her by her grandmother when she had been just Matty's age. She'd loved it.

So did Matty. He relaxed, snuggling into his pillows. She so wanted to lift him into her arms, to cuddle him to sleep, but she knew he wasn't ready for that. She was a stranger even if she was his mother.

She had to get to know him slowly.

Could he stay on the diggings with her?

'My Aunt Laura will like this story,' Matty murmured sleepily. 'Can you read it to Uncle Rafael when he comes?'

'I…yes.'

He had his own people. His own family.

Where did she fit in?

She didn't know.

He came at nine p.m., after she'd almost given up on him. She'd expected a call from security at the gate, but instead there was a soft knock on the door.

She opened it and there he was.

But it wasn't the Rafael she'd seen before. This was… This was…

His Royal Highness, Prince Rafael, Prince Regent of Alp de Ciel. He was wearing full dress regalia. A deep blue-black suit, immaculately cut. A slash of gold across his chest. Rows of medals and insignia at his breast and a dress sword at his side.

She took an instinctive step back. Kass…

'Gorgeous, aren't I?' he said and any resemblance to Kass flew out of the window. Kass, laughing at himself? No way.

'I…yes. Very pretty,' she managed and he grinned.

'Can I come in?'

'Where's the rest of the royal entourage?'

'I gave them the slip,' Rafael said. 'You have no idea how much trouble I had getting back here.'

'Maybe jeans and a windcheater might be more appropriate for creeping round after dark.'

'Yes, but I wouldn't have had my sword for coping with bogeymen.' He grimaced down at his gorgeous self. 'Don't worry, Kelly. I hate this as much as you do. Politics demanded that I bring it, however, and politics demand that I talk to you now. Can I come in?'

She stood wordlessly aside as he walked in, hauled his jacket off, unbuttoned the top three buttons of his stiffly starched shirt and set his sword by the door.

Royalty off duty.

'So you thought you might change into dress uniform… why?' she asked faintly as he opened the fire box on the stove and held his hands out for warmth.

'Press conference and hastily organised civil reception,' he said briefly. 'With your mayor. You can't imagine how excited everyone is.'

'Um…why?'

'Alp de Ciel is known for its gold-mining,' he said blandly. 'We've heard that this is the best theme park in the world for showcasing historical events. What could be more natural than the Prince Regent of Alp de Ciel—needing a little breathing-space from the demands of his royal duties—doing a little exploring?'

'They never believed it.'

'They did,' he said. 'The press believe what they want to believe. This makes a fabulous story. Prince found incognito in local theme park. Prince agrees to have dinner with local bigwigs for photographic opportunity. Prince excuses himself towards the end of dinner pleading jet lag but everyone's got their photographs by now. So I slipped away.'

'You had your dress uniform with you just on the off chance of a photographic opportunity?'

His smile faded. 'I did suspect,' he said, 'that this journey might be discovered. Like it or not, I'm now head of state of Alp de Ciel. For me to come to Australia and not give a press conference at least would be an insult. The palace officials told me that in no uncertain terms. So yes, I brought my royal toggery. No, I didn't want to unpack it but here it is, in all its glory.'

She was staring at the medals, fascinated.

'So tonight,' she said. 'You just…slipped away from your royal reception. You called a cab—wearing that?'

'Yes, it was hard giving everyone the slip but the limousine driver's currently miffed because I took a cab and a cab driver's happily pocketed a fare and a half for dropping me in the middle of nowhere and saying nothing. It was only a mile or so down the road and I kept to the shadows.'

'Wearing your dress sword.' She couldn't keep her eyes off his chest. It was some…chest.

'A prince has to be prepared,' he said patiently. 'In case of bogeymen.' His smile deepened. 'Stop looking like that. Pete let me in and he's under instructions to say no one's come. He'll admit no one else.'

She shook her head in disbelief. 'You think you're clever,' she said wonderingly.

'I do,' he said smugly.

'Matty wants you to wake him and say goodnight.'

His face stilled. 'He was okay with you?'

'Yes.'

'But he was asking for me?'

'He loves you. You and your mother.'

'I guess that hurts,' he said cautiously.

'I can't expect anything else.'

'He'll learn…'

'I don't think he can stay here,' she whispered and something in her face had him crossing the room to her in two swift strides and taking her hands in his.

'Kelly, don't look like that.'

'Like…like what?'

'As if you're tearing yourself in two.'

'I'm not. I'm not. Go and say goodnight to Matty.' She pulled away from him roughly. For a moment he stood, looking down at her face, obviously troubled, but she wouldn't look at him.

Finally he wheeled away. He disappeared into the bedroom. She stood, feeling lost, bewildered, distressed, listening to the sound of the two faint voices. Matty must have only been snoozing. He'd been waiting. Waiting for his Uncle Rafael.

He's a good man, she thought. This was no Kass. She could trust him with her son.

Matty's home was in Alp de Ciel. Matty was royal.

But how could she let Matty go again?

And then Rafael was back, returning to warm his hands by the fire. Were they really cold, she wondered, or was it just to give him something to do?

'They'll find Matty here,' she said miserably, going straight to the heart of the matter. 'The press might think Matty's safely at home in Alp de Ciel now, but as soon as they figure he's missing they'll put two and two together. You come out here on a whim. Prince Mathieu disappears at the same time. It'll take them no time at all to figure where Matty might be.'

'And?'

'And I can't protect him here,' she whispered. 'Not from the goldfish bowl that's the royal way of life.'

'So what do you want to do?'

'I don't know.'

'Come back to Alp de Ciel?' he said, and then, at the look on her face, he came to her again. Once again he took her hands in his, his rough, callused hands completely enclosing her smaller ones. 'It's what my mother and I hope for. It's what should happen. That you should come home to the castle.'

'It's not my home.'

'It's your son's home.'

'I hate it.'

'So do I,' he said surprisingly. 'I can't tell you how much I loathe being part of the whole royalty bit. But there's no choice.'

'There must be a choice.'

'If I don't take the Regency on,' he said, 'there are others who would. Others like Kass. You know Kass and his father were lousy rulers. They stripped the country of all they could get their hands on.'

'Of course I know that,' she said angrily. 'But it's nothing to do with me.'

'It is,' he said harshly. 'In as much as it's your son who'll eventually make the decisions about the country's future. If I refuse to take on the Regency, then someone else will take charge until Matty is twenty-five. The next in line is my cousin, Olivier. Olivier is a compulsive gambler. He'd see the Regency as a way to get his hands on the country's coffers. And worse,' he added softly, 'he'd also have absolute say in how Matty is raised. Neither you nor I nor my mother, who until now has been his one constant, would have any influence at all.'

Kelly gasped. 'But…'

'It is unfair,' Rafael said. He was still holding her, using his strength to augment the urgency of what he was saying. 'I know that. But there's not a thing I can do about it. My mother says I don't have a choice and she's right.'

'Your mother…'

'Don't get me wrong. My mother hates the royal bit as much as I do. We're not doing this for personal gain, Kelly.' He hesitated. 'Look, it's too much. I hoped I'd given the press the slip, which would have given you a few days to sort things out. But tomorrow morning the press will be camped outside my accommodation…'

'You're not staying here?'

'How can I?'

'You've gone back to the Prince Edward?'

'I'm being put up in the mayoral residence,' he said ruefully. 'They think I'm home in bed now, getting over jet lag, instead of here, trying to convince you to come with me back to Alp de Ciel.'

'I don't want to.' She sounded like a child—petulant—and she winced but he looked at her with understanding.

'Of course you don't. But this way you'll have your son.'

'There must be another way.'

'There is,' he said reluctantly. 'We could set you up somewhere else, some gated community where you'd be safe. You have all the royal allowance you've never touched, and if it's used to care for Matty even you might swallow your principles and use it. But you'd be even more isolated than you are here.'

'I'm not isolated.'

'I think you are,' he said softly. 'You've been so badly hurt that you've run, not just back to Australia but back in time. Kelly, you're the mother of the Crown Prince of Alp de Ciel. You knew that when you bore Matty. The crown is his birthright, and it's your duty to be his mother.'

'But your mother loves him. His Aunt Laura…'

'Are you saying you don't want to be his mother?'

'No, I…'

'He doesn't know you yet,' Rafael said. 'He will. He's already proud of what you do—fascinated. He already thinks you're beautiful. Trust takes time, and so does love. Kelly, can you give that to him?'

'But to go back…'

To where she'd been stripped of everything that was important to her—her heart, her pride, her son. How could she go back?

'You won't be alone. My mother will be there.' The grip on her hands grew stronger. 'You didn't meet her last time. She comes across to Manhattan in the worst of Alp de Ciel's winter and spends time with me. You were at the castle for only six weeks after the old prince died, in the last stages of your pregnancy and after Mathieu's birth. The fuss was such that my mother stayed longer with me and when she returned your son was there but you were gone. You'll love her.'

'I don't do love,' she snapped and he stilled.

'Are you saying you don't love Matty?'

'Of…of course…'

'Of course you do,' he agreed softly. 'Love isn't something you can turn on and off again at will.'

'And you know this how?'

He winced. A shadow of pain crossed his face and she thought, I know nothing about him. Nothing. A toy-maker from Manhattan. The Prince Regent of Alp de Ciel.

Rafael.

'You need to come,' he said softly but she was replaying the conversation over in her head, trying to sort it out. There was something not right.

You won't be alone. My mother will be there.

'Will you be there?' she asked. She'd hit a nerve. A muscle moved at the side of his mouth. Infinitesimal—but there was something.

'I'll be there when I need to be.'

'You'll be there when you need to be.' She almost gasped. 'Prince Regent of Alp de Ciel…a country that's desperate for reorganization… There when you need to be?'

'Yes.'

'So…once a week? A week a year?'

'I'm not sure.'

'Then I'm not going,' she said flatly, suddenly sure that she was right. 'The minute I step into the goldfish bowl there'll be no going back. I know how hard it was to shake the press off last time. I had to change my name, change my country, change my whole way of life. I can't do it twice. And you… You'll be there when you can. What sort of commitment is that?'

'Do you want me to be there?'

'No. No!' She should pull away from his hands but she didn't. What she was trying to say was too important. She almost needed personal contact to get it through.

'You're asking me to trust,' she said softly, thinking it as she spoke. 'You're asking me to take my place in a role

I hate. Yet you want to be a part-time prince. There's no such thing.'

'Kelly…'

'Your toy workshops could be relocated to Alp de Ciel, couldn't they?'

'Yes, but…'

'And that way the pressure's off Matty,' she said, suddenly more certain of her ground. 'You're Prince Regent. You'll be swanning round the country doing Prince Regent things. Going to movie premières with gorgeous women in tow.'

'Hey!'

'You're not married already, are you?' she demanded and looked down at his ring finger. 'Tell me you're not married.'

'I'm not married.'

'Engaged?'

'No.'

'There you are, then,' she said. 'No celebrity magazine in its right mind will focus on Matty when one of the world's most eligible bachelors is doing his thing in the country.'

'So let me get this straight,' he said faintly. 'You want me to stay permanently in the country and provide fodder for the gossipmongers for the next twenty years to keep the limelight off you and Matty.'

'Yes.'

He blinked. 'I don't…'

But she wasn't to be interrupted. 'If neither of us return,' she said, thinking it through, 'if I don't take Matty back and you return to Manhattan, there'll be no royal permanently in the palace. Which is, I gather, unthinkable. That's why contracts stipulating Matty belonged to the palace were meant to be watertight. Even in my short time with Kass I learned the alternative was chaos. Kass said his father was stuck with him. If he didn't go home the government converted to rule through Council. The Council's been corrupt for generations. Only a prince residing permanently in the country keeps the Principality from turmoil.'

'Which is why we need Matty to stay at the castle.' Rafael tugged his hands back from hers and raked his fingers though his thick black curls. 'Hell, Kelly, I don't want to stay there permanently.'

'Neither do I.'

'It's your…'

'Duty?' Her green eyes flashed anger. 'Don't dare give me that. I wasn't born into royalty like you were. I was lied to, I was married in an attempt to infuriate the old prince and I was kicked out of the country. You said you came here to give me my son. More lies. How dare you say I have a duty now?'

'You have a duty to your son.'

'As you have a duty to the child who will be Crown Prince. Snap.'

'But…'

'There's no but, Rafael,' she said grimly. 'I have no idea what I'm getting into. More than anything in the world, I want to be with Matty, to watch him grow up, to be his mother. I'm willing to sacrifice a lot for that. But not everything. He will not be the total royal focus.'

'You can't ask that of me.'

'I'm not asking. As you're not asking me to be Matty's mother. I'm simply stating facts. You came here to offer me my child back. That's what you said. But you're making no such offer. Not really. You're simply blackmailing me into returning to the castle.'

'I am giving you Matty back.'

'With no strings?'

'He's the Crown Prince of Alp de Ciel. Of course there are strings. Hell, Kelly…I didn't come here to be pressured.'

'No, you came here to pressure me. If you don't like what I'm saying, you can leave. I'll do what I think best with Matty.'

'Which is?'

'It's none of your business.'

'It is my business,' he snapped, exploding. 'Hell, woman, I have total control. According to the contracts you signed, I can take him back tomorrow. I thought I'd give you the choice.'

'No, you didn't. You thought you'd persuade me to come.'

'You're supposed to be *meek*!'

There was a loaded pause. It went on. And on. And on.

'Funny, that,' she said at last, almost cordially. 'I'm not.'

'I can see you're not,' he snapped, goaded.

'You want me to be meek?'

'I want you to be sensible.'

'What's sensible about living as royalty?'

'It's every girl's dream.'

'Hey, I've lived the dream, remember?' she said. 'It's not a dream. It's a nightmare.'

'Which is why I don't want…'

'To be part of it. Neither do I.'

'You have to be.'

'So do you,' she snapped. 'I've been thinking and thinking, all day while I've been waiting for you. I know I can't bring Matty up as I'd want him brought up here. There'll be too much media attention when people realise who he is. I know I can't give him a normal childhood. To haul him away from everything he knows…'

'So you will come?' he demanded, starting to sound relieved.

'Only if you agree to stay permanently in the castle.'

'That's not fair.'

'It is fair,' she snapped. 'It's entirely fair. It's your inheritance—Prince Regent. It's your responsibility to take the pressure off Matty until he's twenty-five. If he stays here, even if we buy into a gated community, he'll be cloistered and not able to have a normal boyhood. And he'll miss you and your mother desperately. But if he goes back to the castle and you head off back to your very important life in the States it'll be much, much worse. So *fair* doesn't come into it. We're both having to do what we do to survive. I won't have Matty in the limelight any more than he has to be.'

'You mean *you* don't want to be in the limelight.'

'Of course I don't. Neither do you, but from where I'm standing you're the one who can take it best.'

'You know nothing about what I can take.'

'Ditto,' she snapped. 'I'm making judgements. But, the way I see it, there are two of us I'm protecting. Me and Matty. You think I'll let you stand aside and leave Matty exposed?'

'No, I…'

'You came here saying I was welcome to keep Matty with me,' she said. 'If I did that you'd be stuck.'

'I never imagined…'

'That I wouldn't jump at the chance to be princess again? I can see that.'

'Kelly…' He reached for her hands again and held them urgently.

'Rafael.'

This was ludicrous. It was like some weird tug of war. But she wasn't giving in. The thought of staying in the castle as the Princess Royal, of having all that media directed at her and her small son… She'd been through that. She never wanted to go there again.

She didn't care about this man's story. She couldn't care that there might be valid reasons for him to wish to avoid the limelight. She had to make a decision now and she could only do that on the information she had.

He was gripping her hands with a strength that almost frightened her. How had that happened? With the linking of their hands he seemed almost an extension of herself—she was arguing with herself instead of him.

But…it was different. The feel of his hands on hers was doing strange things to her. It was feeding her strength, she thought obliquely. If he withdrew his hands she might falter. She might not have the strength to stand up to him.

She held on and his grip tightened still more, as if it were the same for him.

'Kelly, you can do it,' he said urgently and she shook her head.

'Rafael, you can do it.'

'I don't...'

'Neither do I. And my reasons are better than yours,' she said. 'As far as I know. Is there anything you're not telling me?'

'No!'

'There you are, then.'

'It's blackmail,' he snapped and she shook her head.

'It's no such thing. It's sense. You bring your toys and you come home.'

Home. The word drifted between them, strangely poignant.

Rafael stared down into her eyes, seemingly baffled. She met his gaze firmly, unflinching. Did he know he was feeding her strength with his hold? she thought. Why didn't he pull away?

She didn't want him to pull away. She had a feeling that if she did... Well, the world was a huge and scary place. To think about going back...to relive the terror...

She couldn't do it alone. She had to have an ally.

And this man could be an ally. She'd grown up enormously over the last five years. Men like Kass... Well, he'd taught her a hard life lesson but she'd learned it well. Never again would she throw her heart in the ring but, as well as that, she'd also learned to judge. In these last few years she'd learned who her true friends were. And this man...

This man was trustworthy. There were things in his background she didn't understand. There were shadows—real shadows—and they must be linked to his revulsion at taking on the Prince Regent role, but the sensation that he was solid, that he was a man of his word, was growing rather than receding.

His disinclination to take on the Prince Regency did him no disservice in her eyes. How could anyone want such a job?

How could she return to that lifestyle?

'It's an awful thing you're asking me to do,' she whispered. 'To go back and be part of royalty again. But you've brought the only enticement that could ever get me there—my son. I have to be deeply, profoundly grateful, and I am. But not enough to do this on my own, Rafael. I need you there.'

'You don't need me.'

'Well, maybe you're right. Maybe I don't need anyone,' she conceded. 'I've made sure of that over these last five years. But this is different. It's not you personally. I need your presence. I need there to be a sovereign to take the limelight from Matty. Maybe you made a mistake bringing him here, offering what you've offered. But you have offered it. And…and I made a call this afternoon. I phoned immigration.'

'You what?'

'I can keep him right here, whether you say so or not, and under my terms,' she said, jutting her chin forward in a dumb gesture of defiance. 'A contract signed in Alp de Ciel holds no weight here when it comes to child custody rights. I'm Matty's mother and he has no father. Matty is in Australia. You brought him to me—his Australian mother—for which I'm profoundly thankful but now…you can't change your mind and take him back. The laws of this country will support me.'

He stared down at her, baffled. Whatever route he'd planned this conversation to take, it clearly wasn't this one.

'I only wanted you to have your son back,' he said and he sounded so bewildered that she smiled.

'You did. It was lovely of you.'

'I assumed you'd want to come back.'

'That was sweet of you too, but silly.'

'I don't believe,' he said cautiously, 'that silly comes into it. Or sweet either, for that matter.'

'Regardless…sweet or silly…you will stay permanently in Alp de Ciel?'

'Hell, Kelly…'

'I know,' she said. 'That's royalty. I hate it and I want no part in it but maybe I'm prepared to take it on for Matty's sake. He does stand to inherit one day and I realize it'd be very much better if he was brought up in the environment he'll have to face. But for you… Like Matty, you don't have a choice. You're Prince Regent, like it or not. We do this together, Rafael, or not at all.'

'I can't.'

'Then neither can I,' she said implacably, and waited.

He stared down into her eyes. She met his gaze, unflinching. He didn't really look like his cousin, she thought. The resemblance was only superficial. Kass's eyes had been piercing, brutal, cold. Rafael's…They were troubled now. Shadowed.

She knew she was forcing him to go where he had no wish to tread, but she had no choice. All afternoon the alternatives had been slamming at her, one after another.

There wasn't an alternative. She knew it.

Rafael knew it.

'You will take some of the limelight,' he said, sounding desperate, and she smiled.

'They can photograph me if they want, but I'll bet you have women on your arm more glamorous than I'll ever be.'

'I don't do glamour.'

'Says the man who just walked into my cottage wearing a dress sword.'

'Kelly…'

'Rafael.'

'You really are serious.'

'I really am serious.'

'So I get to stay in Alp de Ciel until Matty turns twenty-five?'

'There you go, then,' she said, trying to sound cheerful. 'It's only a twenty-year sentence. Whereas I…'

'You can leave any time.'

'Sure,' she said. 'You let Matty sleep in my bed and then you tell me I can leave any time. My sentence is as long as yours, Rafael, maybe even longer.'

There was a loaded pause. They were still holding hands. It was as if the urgency of their conversation required physical contact as well as verbal.

'Fine,' he said at last. 'Okay, then. But it is blackmail.'

'On both our sides,' she said gently. 'We're forced into this.'

'The palace doesn't need us both.'

'No,' she said wearily. 'But as it's both or neither then we might as well get on with it. And Matty…Matty needs someone. I'm hoping it might be me, but for now he needs you. I'll fight for that too, Rafael. I'll fight for what my son needs.'

It caught him. Something in her voice made him pause. He tugged sharply at her hands, forcing her to look up at him.

'Kelly, it's not really a life sentence,' he said.

'You know it is.'

'It might even be fun.'

'Says the man who wants to flee to Manhattan.'

'We could make it fun.'

'Like how?'

His mouth twisted. 'Don't ask me.' He glanced at his wristwatch and grimaced. 'I need to go. Any minute now the dinner will end and there'll be questions as to why I'm not in the royal bed.'

'Matty will miss you when he wakes.'

'Remind him you're his mother,' he said softly. Then, at the look on her face, he said more urgently, 'It's the truth. You are his mother. You love him already and his love will come.'

'I don't think…'

'No, don't think,' he said urgently. 'That's the way of madness. One day at a time. Starting now. We can do this.' And then, before she knew what he was about, he'd caught her chin with his fingers and forced her face up to meet his. His mouth lowered on hers in a swift, demanding kiss.

It shocked them both. She could feel it, like a stab of white-hot heat coming from nowhere. It lasted seconds, hardly even that, and then it was over but, as he released her, her hands flew to her lips and she gazed up at him in bewilderment.

Where had that come from? Why on earth…?

He was looking as bewildered as she was. As if some force other than his had propelled the kiss. As if he, too, didn't understand what had just happened.

'I guess it's a pact,' he said at last as he stepped back and she gazed at him in stupefaction. 'A kiss to seal a bargain.'

'A handshake would have done,' she whispered.

'Nah,' he said and suddenly he grinned and it was like the sun had come out. He was suddenly like a kid in mischief. 'Where's the fun in a handshake? A kiss is much more satisfactory. Don't look like that, Your Highness. I meant no disrespect.'

'I didn't think…'

'It's just as well you don't think,' he said. 'As the mother of the Crown Prince, you could probably have my head skewered and served on a platter for breakfast for doing what I just did. So let's just forget the kiss. Good though it was.' He lifted his dress sword and slid it into its scabbard. His smile faded.

'So, like it or not, we have a deal. We're in this together, Kellyn Marie. I won't see you now until we leave. Can you be ready to return with me on Tuesday? Yes? Unless you want to be overrun with media before then, I shouldn't return here, and now I'm outed I'll have to do the full diplomatic round. Tell Matty I love him, and tell him he has a mother in a million.'

'Even if she's a blackmailing cow.'

'She's not so bad for a blackmailing cow,' he said and grinned. 'I've seen worse things come out of cheese.'

What the hell had he done?

Rafael walked out through the darkened historical village and thought he must have gone completely mad.

He'd just agreed to stay in Alp de Ciel until Matty was twenty-five.

He didn't have to. He could promise and then leave anyway once Matty was safely back in the country.

He couldn't. He thought back to Kelly's face by the firelight. She trusted him.

He was trustworthy. Hell!

He'd kissed her.

Why had he done that?

It was just that she was so damned kissable. She was such a juxtaposition of sweet, meek and…dragon, he thought ruefully. Life had slapped her around and that was what she looked like, that was how she sounded, but underneath there was a fierce and determined sprite.

What had Kass been thinking to treat her so appallingly?

She'd just blackmailed him into moving his life to Alp de Ciel.

His mother would be delighted.

But Anna…

Whoops.

He needed to talk to Anna before she learned of things via the media, he thought. Kelly might come across as a bit of a dragon but that was nothing to how Anna came across when she was angry.

Would Anna relocate to Alp de Ciel?

Ha.

Too hard. It was all just too hard.

Pete was on the gate, obviously waiting for him to leave. Rafael tugged a note from his wallet to leave him something for his pains, but Pete shook his head at the offering as if he was personally offended.

'I don't want your money.'

'I'm sorry,' Rafael said, surprised.

'I just don't want you mucking our Kelly about,' Pete said strongly. 'She's had a rough trot, our Kell.'

'You could help by not telling anyone I was here tonight. And not telling anyone Kelly has a strange little boy staying with her.'

'You think I'd do that?'

'No,' Rafael said with a faint smile.

'You really are a prince?' the old man demanded, and Rafael nodded.

'Yes.'

'And the wee one…'

'He's Kelly's son,' Rafael said, for there was no use dissembling here. 'The Crown Prince of Alp de Ciel.'

Pete gave a long, low whistle. 'Well, I'll be damned. Our Kelly, royalty. We always knew there was something…' But then he returned to what had obviously been gnawing at him. 'She's upset. Anyone can see she's upset.'

'It's been a harrowing day for her.'

'You'll be taking her back to…where…Alp de Wotsit?'

'She's agreed to go, yes.'

'Then I'll say something to you now, boy,' the old man growled and, dress sword or not, Rafael found himself backed against the wall with the old man's gnarled finger poking him in the midriff. 'You take care of her. She's gone through the mill, that one. Oh, we're not supposed to know, but there's not many of the staff here don't know that she lost her kiddy. We thought maybe he'd died. She's wanted to be anonymous, she hasn't wanted to talk about it, and we've respected that. We'd keep her secret for as long as she wants. But this place is almost family. She might not have a mum and dad but she has all of us and if she's mistreated we'll…we'll…'

'Send the dragoons?' Rafael asked faintly, and the old man relented a little and gave a crooked smile.

'Yeah, well, the troops we have here may only be make-believe but we can surely make a fuss. So watch it. Watch her.'

'She'll be okay.'

'You guarantee it, sir?'

Now there was an ask. What was he letting himself into? As Prince Regent he was responsible for the well-being of the Crown Prince. Now he was being asked to make guarantees about Kelly.

But Pete was waiting, and behind the belligerence was anxiety. He was genuinely fond of her, Rafael thought. He was genuinely anxious.

So once again he promised. 'I guarantee she'll be okay.'

'You'll watch over her.'

And stay permanently in Alp de Ciel? With or without Anna? With or without his business?

Anna would kill him. To make such a decision without talking it through with her… But the decision was made.

'I'll watch over her,' he said weakly, and thought, Anna without Fifth Avenue? Without pastrami on rye? His business without Anna?

'I'll watch over her,' he promised again and he was allowed to leave.

But the pressure of Pete's finger in his chest stayed with him. Pressure… Hell!

He'd kissed her.

How had that happened? Why? Kelly watched Rafael disappear down the main street towards the exit, then started to get ready for bed. She undressed by the fire, thinking that she didn't want to get undressed in her bedroom yet. Matty was too much a stranger. Her little boy…

It was set. She was going back to Alp de Ciel to take her place as mother of the Crown Prince.

Rafael had kissed her.

She raised a finger to her lips. They still felt bruised, which was crazy. He hadn't kissed her hard enough to bruise.

But she could still feel where he'd kissed her.

She tugged her nightgown on, then sank into the rocker by the stove, flipped open the fire door and watched the flames. To leave here…

The thought was terrifying.

She had to leave on Tuesday.

There was no choice. She'd known that the moment she'd

set eyes on Matty. No matter what she had to do, now she'd seen her son again she would move heaven and earth rather than endure further separation.

Rafael had kissed her.

'And that was stupid,' she told herself fiercely. 'That's enough of that. You've let no man touch you since Kass and you'd be crazy to break that rule now. And with a de Boutaine? No and no and no.'

On impulse she crossed to her desk and booted her computer. Her nineteenth-century cottage boasted wireless Internet—hooray. She typed in Rafael's name and waited.

There was too much to take in. It was mostly about his work, his toys, awards he'd won, speeches he'd given. He ran some youth apprentice training scheme—very worthy.

She was becoming cynical in her old age, she thought ruefully, and then decided she'd had enough of reading about him.

She clicked on Google Images.

The first one that appeared was at a gala charity event in New York. There was Rafael, looking impossibly handsome in a magnificently cut, deep black dinner suit and a classy white silk scarf.

And on his arm was a stunner—a woman whose legs almost seemed to reach her armpits. She was a magnificent, classy blonde and she was clinging to Rafael's arm and smiling possessively at him as he smiled at the camera.

The caption read 'Rafael de Boutaine and his partner, Anna Louise St Clair.'

'Well, there you go, then,' she muttered to herself. 'He has a partner.'

He'd said he wasn't married or engaged.

He had a partner.

For someone completely disinterested, there was no way of explaining the sudden lurch of loss she felt in the pit of her stomach.

'It's only that he'd suit my purpose better if he's a real bachelor,' she told herself. 'He'd get more media attention.'

And then she looked again at Anna and thought, Nope, gaining media attention was never going to be a problem for these two. The pair would be the ruling couple of Alp de Ciel.

'Which is what you want,' she said fiercely, slamming down the lid of her computer. 'How dumb are you to ask if he's married or engaged?' she demanded of herself as she headed for bed. 'How quaint. It's just as well I'm a historian because that's what I feel like.' She stopped herself from tossing a pillow at the wall just in time. For Matty was sleeping. Her Matty. Who this was all about.

'So it'll suit our purpose,' she told her sleeping son, lowering her voice to a whisper. 'It's just that he kissed me, Matty. How crazy's that? And I let him. I must be going out of my mind.'

CHAPTER FOUR

WAS there ever any doubt she'd go with him? Whether Rafael had a partner or not was immaterial. Matty belonged in Alp de Ciel. Matty was her son.

She was going.

So over the next few days Kelly packed her gear, said goodbye to the place that had protected her for the last five years and prepared to be a princess again.

She still was the Princess Kellyn, she thought ruefully. Kass had never bothered with divorce. In truth, it had suited Kass to remain married. He had the heir he needed so what purpose marriage? He'd been able to play around with as many women as he'd wanted.

While Kelly hadn't worn a wedding ring for five years, Kass had worn his to the end. He'd married her as a snub to his father. His continuing marriage had been a snub to any eligible woman in the Principality who might have been presumptuous enough to think of joining him on the throne.

So, regardless of Kass's motives, Kelly was now returning as the widow of the old Crown Prince and the mother of the new one. Somehow she had to make a life for herself in a country she loathed. She had no idea how she was going to do it, but she had no choice.

At least her departure was managed without media hype. Whatever the staff of the park knew of her past or of her intentions now, they were saying nothing to the outside world, giving her a few blessed days to come to terms with what she must do.

Rafael couldn't come near them. He rang when he could but the media attention meant that he had to stay well away. So Kelly had a few short days to think about what life might have been if Matty wasn't a prince.

It would have been magic.

For Matty was absorbed into the life of the park as seamlessly as if he'd been born there. For the first twenty-four hours he was homesick for Rafael, but the park kids—the children of the staff here—were friendly and eager to show him everything. There were things going on everywhere and by the time they were ready to leave he was simply part of the park pack.

She so wished he could stay like this. He was mischievous, inquisitive, alert and interested. Once he was reassured that Rafael hadn't deserted him, that there was a definite end to his stay, he was totally relaxed, and Kelly thought, If only he could stay, if only…

But it was impossible. No one had yet twigged that the Crown Prince was missing from Alp de Ciel. As soon as they did, it'd be only a matter of days before he was found and he'd never be let alone again.

So they had to go. She felt sick at the thought and even Matty was crestfallen on Tuesday as they prepared to leave.

'Uncle Rafael will cheer us up,' Matty said, holding her hand as they walked together for the last time from her cottage down to the park entrance. 'Don't be sad, Mama. He'll make you happy again.'

Terrific. Although Kelly was fighting really hard to blink back tears, she had no desire to have Rafael to buoy her spirits. In truth, the fact that she'd be travelling with Rafael was a downside—he made her feel disconcerted and vulnerable.

And she'd miss this place so much… She was so close to breaking it was all she could do to walk those last few steps from the park gates to the waiting limousine. To where Rafael was waiting, holding the door wide for her.

He was watching her with sympathy, she thought as she dashed her hand across her eyes with a fierce anger that was surely irrational. The last thing she needed was sympathy, but it shouldn't make her angry.

'Hey,' he said as Matty reached him. He stooped down and hugged Matty hard and that had Kelly blinking all over again. Then he straightened and looked at Kelly. He was dressed formally—not in his dumb dress uniform but in a smart grey lounge suit. 'Are you okay?' he asked softly.

'I'm fine.' She gulped a couple of times and turned to help Pete, who was putting her luggage into the trunk. 'Where's… where's your retinue?'

'Retinue?'

'Reporters. Cameramen.'

'Thankfully my presence doesn't warrant the type of paparazzi outriders Princess Di was burdened with,' he said, smiling. 'I'd imagine there'll be photographers at the airport but that's okay—we'll be in the door, on the plane and out of here before they realize we have Matty.' He hesitated as she hugged Pete goodbye. 'Kelly, you're sure you're okay?'

'I'm okay,' she said, feeling sick. She dived past him into the car and slid across the vast leather interior of the limousine until she was as far away from his side as it was possible to be. Matty was on the opposite seat, but as Rafael climbed in after her he sidled across to Rafael and sat hard against him.

Rafael tugged him close, which had Kelly unsettled all over again. Her son was being hugged by Rafael. Whatever decisions she'd made about the man, she still couldn't entirely trust him. He was too damned good-looking. He was a prince. He was a de Boutaine!

She crossed her arms and didn't say anything. He was hugging her son. Her son! How could she catch up on five long years?

'So you've decided to go casual,' he said politely as the chauffeur drove the big car out on to the road.

'What...what do you mean?'

'It's the first time I've seen you in civvies.'

'You mean not in historical dress.'

'Mmm.'

'Is something wrong with what I'm wearing?'

'You'll be landing in Alp de Ciel like that?' he asked gently. 'Or do you intend to keep something separate from your luggage to change into?'

'Why should I?'

'I would have thought...'

'Thought what?'

'Maybe a little more formality?'

'I'm fine like I am,' she said, keeping her arms folded defensively across her breasts and glaring straight ahead.

In truth she was making a statement. She'd stared at her wardrobe last night for almost an hour before she'd decided what to wear.

For the last four years Kelly had worn almost exclusively historical costumes. However, there had been times when she'd been out doing research, when she had given presentations about the park, when she had attended awards dinners, when she'd had to wear normal clothes. Then she'd worn a standard business suit. Sensible.

Once upon a time she'd loved clothes. She'd ached for them. When she was a child her parents had frowned on what they called frivolity. She'd been repressed to the point of cruelty, forced to wear her school uniform when it had been entirely inappropriate, given a meagre allowance that had been inadequate to buy anything but the basic necessities.

She remembered the dress she'd bought with her first pay cheque. It was a sliver of scarlet, an almost indecently short crimson cocktail dress. She'd loved it.

She'd worn it to dinner the first night she'd met Kass.

Yeah, well, so much for fancy clothes. Like horses, clothes were something she didn't let herself think about. Now she was wearing ancient jeans, an oversized, shapeless sweater that reached almost to her knees and her leather work boots. She'd tugged her hair into a knot with an elastic band. She was wearing no make-up.

Yes, it was a statement and she didn't care who heard it.

'Mama packed most of her clothes into boxes and sent them to storage,' Matty offered from the other seat.

Rafael frowned. 'I told you to pack them up for shipping.'

'It's no use shipping historical costumes overseas,' Kelly said. 'I'm bringing what I need.'

'So did you send anything to the shipping company I told you about?'

'No.'

'So let me see,' Rafael said faintly. 'You're moving to Alp de Ciel permanently. And you've got…one suitcase?'

'It's summer there right now. If it's cold later on I may have to buy a couple of things. I assume there are still shops.'

'There are shops,' he said, eyeing her sweater with a certain amount of trepidation. 'But there'll be media meeting us off the plane. Do you have…a frock or something?'

'A frock,' she said, and her lips twitched at his obvious discomfort. 'I don't believe I do have a frock.'

'You know what I mean. Something respectable.'

'This is respectable.'

'For bumming round the stables maybe. Not for meeting your people.'

'Whose people?'

'You're a princess.'

'In name only,' she retorted. 'I thought we agreed. You're the centre of media attention. You wear your braid and your dress sword and I'll wear my sweater and jeans.'

'It's not very pretty,' Matty said, disapproving.

'I don't need to be pretty.'

'No, but you are,' Matty said, sounding upset. 'And you're my mama.'

Oh, great. She hadn't thought this one through. It was all very well planning to be plain Jane, speaking when spoken to, staying in the background, keeping herself small.

But Matty was obviously disappointed.

'You can't do that to the kid,' Rafael said and she swallowed her vague guilt and thought, what was she asking? That Matty cope with a mama who didn't dress like...like Rafael's partner.

'You're saying my wearing jeans might damage Matty for life?'

'No, I...'

'Good then. I'm fine,' she muttered. 'This is me. This is who I am. Matty, I'm sorry if you don't like it but I don't want to be a princess. I'm your mama and I hope you like me anyway but I'm not going to wear a tiara. Not for anything.'

'How about a frock?' Rafael growled and she glowered.

'Nope. Matty, you and your Uncle Rafael are royalty,' she said bluntly. 'I get to stay in the background and watch.'

'You'll watch?' Rafael demanded, incredulous.

'Yes.'

'You don't think you might get bored?' Rafael said.

'No.'

'What will you do, then?' Matty asked while Rafael looked on with bemusement. He seemed to be having trouble figuring her out, which was fine as she was having trouble figuring him out. All she knew about him was that, in his own way, he was as dangerous to her peace of mind as Kass had been. He was a de Boutaine and he'd kissed her. That was enough for her to stay in sackcloth and ashes every time she was near him for the next hundred years. To do anything else...that was the crazy route.

'I've thought about it,' she said seriously, having in fact done little over the last three days but think about how she could sustain the life they were asking her to lead. 'I'm intending to write books.'

'Books,' Rafael said blankly.

'That's the plan,' she said happily. 'Matty, I'm a historian and your castle is steeped in history. I can find myself a nice quiet attic and research to my heart's content. But I'll be there for you whenever you need me, Matty—if you need me. Otherwise, I'll be perfectly happy writing my book.'

'You can't,' Rafael said blankly.

'Why not?'

'I was hoping…'

'Don't hope,' she said bluntly. 'Alp de Ciel is your principality, not mine. Stop hoping for anything from me, other than loving Matty. For that's all I'm going to do.'

They let her be.

They travelled first class on the aircraft—of course—which meant the seats were in pairs, cocoons that turned into beds. Rafael and Matty shared one pair. A Japanese businessman shared Kelly's. She was courteously given the window seat, which meant that she was buffered from the pair across the aisle.

She hardly talked to them.

Rafael and Matty slept. She stared straight ahead, feeling sick.

Finally they landed. There were photographers, reporters, politicians, all waiting. They were stunned to see Matty.

Kelly hung back, trying to blend in as part of the luggage. She was afraid that Rafael would haul her forward and introduce her but he did no such thing. At the last minute, as the limousine was about to leave, he motioned for her to join them and she slid into the car before the photographers could register who she might be.

Now she was doing the defensive bit again, huddled in the far corner of the car, staring out at the countryside.

Remembering how she'd fallen in love with this country the first time she'd seen it.

She'd forgotten how breathtaking it was.

She'd forgotten how she'd fallen in love.

The four Alp countries had been severed from their larger neighbours centuries ago to form principalities for warring brothers, and each one of them was a magical place in its own right.

Alp de Ciel…Alps towering to the skies.

Even though it was late spring there was still snow on the highest peaks. The lowlands stretching from the coast to the mountains consisted of magnificent undulating pastures, rich and fertile. There were quaint villages, houses hewn from the local rock hugging the coastline, some of the houses seemingly carved from the cliffs themselves. There were harbours with fishing fleets that looked straight off picture postcards. Too small to involve itself in the world wars, too insignificant to be fought over, Alp de Ciel had remained almost unchanged for centuries.

The first time Kelly had seen it she'd been speechless with delight and it affected her just as deeply now. She stared out of the car window as they left the port city, then followed the river road to the foothills of the mountains, through Zunderfied, the small village which had served the castle for generations and then further to where the palace of Alp de Ciel lay in all its glory.

It was no wonder she'd fallen for Kass, an older and wiser Kelly thought sadly. This place breathed romance. She'd been lonely and awed and in love with this country—Kass must have found her more than ripe for the picking.

She couldn't let herself be swayed by beauty this time. Nor by words.

Nor by a de Boutaine…

'It's not all as beautiful as it looks,' Rafael told her as she sat with her nose squashed against the window, and she cast him a look that was almost scared.

'It *is* beautiful.'

'Surface gorgeous. You know how Kass financed his latest bout of gambling debts? He allowed logging almost to the edge of Zunderfied. The land here gets saturated with the snow melts. We've had two minor landslips there with spring already. That's just one problem among hundreds.'

She turned and gazed upward and saw the scarred hillside, the jarring ugliness of the leavings from clear felling. But…to allow herself to worry about the countryside…the people…

She wasn't royal. She wasn't!

She mustn't care.

'You love it,' Rafael said softly as the car slowed and turned into the palace grounds.

'Not…not any more.'

'There's no need to be defensive,' he said. 'There's no one who wants you to do anything you don't want. I dare say the villagers can worry about their landslips very well themselves without you worrying on their behalf.' He grimaced. 'If you want to cloister yourself in your attic in your remarkable sweater then your wish will be respected.'

'Does that mean Mama is allowed to wear that sweater?' Matty demanded, astounded.

'It's her business.'

'Ellen will say it's not royal.'

'Ellen will say no such thing,' Rafael said firmly. 'Your mother is here as her own person. She can do exactly as she pleases.'

Damn, why was she blinking again? She glanced out of the back window of the car and saw the tiny township of Zunderfied perched below a swathe of freshly cleared mountainside. She'd boarded there when she'd first come here and thought it was delightful—a tiny alpine village that was steeped in history.

But the logging… How could Kass have agreed to such a

thing? Even from here it seemed the little town was in peril. She wanted to get out of the car and start replanting *now*.

No! NMP, she told herself fiercely.

Not My Problem.

There was no hiding in the background when they arrived at the palace. She was expected.

The first time she'd arrived here it had been with the archaeological dig team. They'd worked out of sight of the main castle, sifting through the remains of ancient castle sites. So the only time she'd been in this forecourt had been the time she'd arrived with Kass.

She'd been eight months pregnant. Her pregnancy had been dreadful. She'd been sick all the time, and Kass had hardly been near.

But then his father was dead and he was triumphant. He'd hauled her home, almost as a trophy.

'This is my wife,' he'd said, tugging her out of the limousine and not caring that she almost fell. 'She's carrying my heir. A son. This is now my country. *My country.*'

The domestic staff had all been there to greet him—they'd lined up on either side of the castle entrance. She remembered the silence. The silent, cold disapproval.

Kass had swept inside, leaving her to follow.

'Take care of her,' he'd snapped to a couple of the domestic staff. 'She's to have everything she needs to deliver a perfect child.'

It had stayed with her. The dismay in the eyes of everyone around her. The contempt. Even…pity?

But now…

This was very, very different.

Yes, the staff were assembled. Not as many. It was a pared down staff, maybe only a quarter as big.

Every one of the staff was smiling.

'Ellen,' Matty yelled, launching himself out of the car and

heading straight for a buxom woman at the end of the line. Then, as she scooped him into her arms and hugged, he turned from her shoulder and whooped as he saw more friends, 'Marguerite. Aunt Laura.'

They were all beaming at her little son. Rafael was smiling too. A man she remembered…Crater—the palace Secretary of State, more stooped than she remembered and his hair more silver—was stepping forward to grasp Rafael's hand.

'It's good to have you back, sir.'

'It's good to be back,' Rafael said. He turned to hug a woman near him—a lady around the same age as Crater. She was wearing a flowing skirt, a cardigan that reached almost to her knees and a paint-spattered pinafore over everything. Her abundance of silver hair was tied up in a knot and there was paint there too. She was smiling with everyone else but sniffing into a paint-smudged handkerchief.

'Mama, don't you dare cry.' He picked her up and whirled her round as he might have whirled a child. 'I've been away only a week. Kelly will think you're soppy.'

'Kelly,' the lady whispered and Rafael set her down and turned her to face Kelly.

'Mama, this is Kelly. Everyone, this is our own Princess Kellyn Marie de Boutaine. She's been sorely wronged but she's finally consented to take her place where she ought to be. It gives me huge pleasure to tell you all that our Kelly has finally come home.'

And for a moment—for just a moment—Kelly wished she looked more like a princess. The last thing she wanted was to be thought of as a poor relation. She hadn't thought it through…

But she couldn't think it for long for Laura gave her no chance. With a cry of delight, Laura abandoned Rafael and took swift steps to where she was standing. Kelly could hardly be self-conscious of her clothes in the face of layers of paint. There was even a daub of purple on Laura's left eyebrow.

And there was no disguising the sincerity of her welcome. Smiling warmly, Laura took her by both hands and held her at arm's length, surveying her from head to toe. But Kelly thought she wasn't seeing the clothes. She was looking deeper.

'So you've come home,' Laura whispered. 'Oh, my dear, we are so sorry. This country's done you such a wrong. I don't know how you can ever forgive us, but from now on…we're overjoyed to have you here. Welcome home, Kelly, dear.'

She turned and held Kelly's hand high in hers.

'Our Matty has his mother home,' she said to the assemblage. 'And we have our princess. Thank you, Rafael, for bringing our Kellyn home.'

But of course she wasn't 'our Kellyn'. She'd never been part of this royal family and she had no intention of being slotted neatly into an allocated space now.

The next few hours passed in a haze of shock and confusion and jet lag. Somehow, however, she managed to keep her wits about her enough to insist on her independence from the first.

With the first greetings over, with Matty scampering off to greet his friends, to make sure nothing had changed in his absence and to distribute the myriad of souvenir gifts he'd stocked up on, Laura and Rafael showed her to her rooms. To her horror, she found she was expected to sleep in the same ghastly, opulent suite she'd been confined to while she'd waited for Matty to be born. It had been closed when she left and hadn't been used since. She glanced through to the bathroom and the dressing gown she'd worn when she was pregnant was folded neatly on a side table. Cleaned and pressed. Waiting for her to return?

She backed out in horror. No and no and no.

Rafael raised his eyebrows in bemusement. 'These are the best we have,' he said. 'Rooms fit for a royal bride. Kass never felt any desire to put anyone else in them.'

'Then get yourself a royal bride to put in them,' she said

crisply, staring round at the gilt and chandeliers and rich crimson velvet with loathing. 'I think I get to be described as the royal relic from now on. I don't want anything to do with this stuff.'

'You don't look like a relic.'

'If she doesn't want gilt she doesn't have gilt,' Laura said stoutly. 'There's not a scrap of gilt in the dower house. Not that I'm offering to share. It's a wee bit cosy.'

'My mother paints,' Rafael said unnecessarily, smiling at his mother in affection. 'The dower house has five bedrooms. Or it did have five bedrooms. Now it has five studios, one of which has my mother's bed crammed in the corner.' He hesitated, looking at Kelly's face and registering her real distress. 'Meanwhile this lady wants an attic,' Rafael said softly. 'Mama, which are our most respectable attics?'

The staff seemed flummoxed but she was then given a guided tour of the place.

Matty had almost a wing to himself—the palace nurseries. Right above was an attic wing—two rooms with turret windows, facing south, with sunlight streaming in through the ancient, hand-blown glass.

The furnishings were faded. 'I think someone's maiden aunt might have used these rooms a long time ago,' Laura said, looking about her at the doilies and antimacassars and overstuffed armchairs. And the tiny narrow bed.

'It's fine,' Kelly said.

'Only if we can get you a new bed,' Rafael growled, so she graciously accepted, asked for a desk and a decent reading light and prepared to start being a recluse.

It didn't quite work straight off. For a start she needed to read Matty his bedtime story. 'For surely that's your role now,' Laura said gently.

It was, and she loved that Laura and Rafael—and Marguerite and Ellen and every one of the palace staff—seemed determined to let her be Matty's mother in every sense of the word.

So she read to Matty in a big armchair in front of the nursery fire. Halfway through the story he sidled on to her knee and promptly fell asleep in her arms. The sensation was indescribable. It almost made her forget her vow to be a recluse.

So she'd be a recluse who did the odd cuddle on the side.

Then supper was ready. 'We waited for you,' Ellen told her and Kelly thought tomorrow she'd figure how she could use the kitchen and make herself toasted sandwiches because that was all she felt like, but tonight she was stuck.

She remembered the grand dining room where she'd been served in the past with pomp and rigid silence. She followed Ellen downstairs with a sinking heart but, instead of being ushered into the grand salon she remembered, Ellen led the way through less formal corridors, down worn stone steps and into…a kitchen. A vast kitchen with a range that took half a wall, with a table big enough to feed a football team, ancient wood, worn with scrubbing.

Laura was sitting at the table buttering bread. Rafael was at the range cooking…toasted sandwiches?

'I wanted to make you dinner myself tonight,' Laura said, smiling at her obvious discomposure. 'I have a much less grand kitchen. But we thought Matty would be asleep here and you might want to stick close.'

'Close?' she queried faintly, thinking of the corridors she'd just navigated, and Rafael flipped the sandwich he was toasting and grinned.

'Close in castle terms. Less than half a day's march. Can we interest you in a toasted cheese sandwich?'

'What happened to silver service?' she said faintly and Laura winced.

'Don't say you liked it.'

'No, I…'

'The minute Kass died we locked up the dining room. Matty hates it, you see,' she explained. 'It was the only time Matty ever saw his father. When Kass was in the palace, at the end of every meal he'd send for Matty and grill him on his lessons. Matty used to shake every time he passed the dining room. So we thought we wouldn't use it.'

'My mother's pretty definite,' Rafael said. 'But, of course, it's your call now. If you want to use the dining room…'

'It's not my call. It's you who's Prince Regent.'

'If it's up to me, I like it just fine where I am,' he said. 'Actually, no. I like it better in Manhattan but, since I've been blackmailed…'

'You've been no such thing,' Laura retorted. 'Kelly, I refuse to let you feel guilty. Rafael's known from the moment Kass died that his responsibility was here.'

'You want him to stay?'

'No,' Laura said bluntly. 'Well, no, in terms of no, I don't want him to have to assume the mantle of royalty. But in terms of having someone round who can cook great toasted sandwiches…' She smiled, a smile that matched her son's to a T as he flipped a sandwich on to her plate. 'I taught him his culinary skills,' she said proudly. 'It's my greatest feat. He'll make some woman very happy some day. He'll keep her in toasted sandwiches for ever.'

'Does Anna like toasted sandwiches?' Kelly asked before she could stop herself and the two identical grins faded.

'Probably not,' Laura said cautiously.

'You mean definitely not,' Rafael retorted.

'Have you broken the news to Anna that you're relocating here permanently?' his mother asked.

'Nope.'

'Coward.'

'I am a coward,' he admitted and he turned his attention back to his pan. 'You know Anna. You'd be a coward too. Kelly, two sandwiches or more?'

It was a lovely, laughing informal meal, about as different from what she remembered of castle life as it was possible to be. She ate three rounds of toasted cheese sandwiches and a vast bowl of sun-ripened strawberries picked only hours ago from the palace gardens. Then Rafael made coffee using a mysterious Turkish coffee-maker that he swore made coffee that was a legend in its own time.

It was pretty good coffee. It was pretty good company. Kelly said little, content to listen to Laura and her son catch up on castle gossip, on trivial domestic stuff, on a life she was starting to feel maybe wouldn't be as bad as she'd thought it would be.

'I need to go,' Laura said reluctantly after the coffee was finished and the plates were cleared into the sink. 'Rafael has a deputation to meet at eight and I don't want to be around when they come.'

'A deputation?'

'Just a welcome home committee,' Rafael said and grimaced. 'The mayor and the town's dignitaries welcoming me home. Or, more probably, to make sure I know the deforestation issue is urgent. Plus about a thousand other grievances. They wanted to come in the morning but my gear's coming so they've agreed to come tonight.' He hesitated. 'They won't meet with Crater. They see him as part of the old establishment. Which leaves me. I wouldn't mind some support.'

'You're a big boy,' Laura said, but she suddenly sounded strained. 'You can meet them yourself.'

'Should we wash up?' Kelly asked a bit too fast, not wanting to think about anyone needing support. A royal welcome… It was all very well eating toasted sandwiches but no one in this family would forget for long that they were royal. Including her?

And Rafael was shrugging. Moving on. He had no choice—he might as well move forward with good humour.

'If you think I'm meeting dignitaries plus doing the washing-up you have rocks in your head,' he retorted and managed a grin. 'There has to be some advantage of being royal. We can leave the washing-up to the staff.'

'I'm a failure as a mother,' Laura mourned.

'If you're starting to count my shortcomings then we'll walk you home,' Rafael told her, smiling across at Kelly. 'That is if you feel like a walk before bed. If you're like me, you'll still be thinking it's morning. My entire body clock is upside down.'

Hers, too. She'd slept in the plane. She felt wide awake.

She felt…

'I can walk myself home,' Laura said briskly. 'It's just past the gatehouse.'

'There are bogeymen out there,' Rafael said. 'The ghosts of a thousand royals.'

'And your father's one of them,' Laura retorted. 'You think any bogeyman would get me when your father's around to protect me?' She smiled fondly up at her son and caught his hand, letting him swing her to her feet. 'Rafael's father died here when Rafael was fifteen,' she told Kelly. 'It's why I've never wanted to leave. It still feels as if he's here.'

'You're just a romantic,' her son said.

'And you're not?'

'Absolutely not,' Rafael retorted. 'What about it, Kelly? Will you help escort my mother home, keeping her from bogeymen?'

'Are you staying with your mother?'

'No,' he said brusquely and Kelly thought he and his mother must have talked about this already. It seemed to have touched a nerve. 'My mother believes if I'm to do a decent job as Prince Regent then I live here. In the State Apartments.'

Kass's rooms. She'd never been admitted to them in the time she'd been here, but she'd walked past open doors. She'd never seen so much opulence in her life.

'You'll enjoy that,' she managed and he stared at her as if she'd lost her mind.

'Plenty of room for toys,' she ventured and his mother choked.

'There surely is. See, Rafael, there's a new way of looking

at things.' She was walking towards the door. 'I don't need an escort, thank you, children, but…'

'But you're having an escort,' Rafael growled.

CHAPTER FIVE

SO THEY walked Laura through the magnificent palace grounds, across the manicured lawns and past the extravagant fountains, down through the tiered rose gardens, brushing around the edge of the woodland area, following a path that was worn from years of royal tread. The moon was full. The woodland held night birds Kelly had never heard before, their calls eerie and wondrous in the moonlight. Nightingales? Maybe. She'd never heard a nightingale. She remembered feeling romantic all those years ago, wishing she'd hear one.

Romance was for the past. She was a sensible woman who'd learned her lesson.

She walked silently on the left of Laura. Rafael walked on her right, holding his mother's arm lightly.

He seemed protective, Kelly thought, and wondered why. Was there a reason he needed to protect her? She seemed a totally self-contained lady.

'So who gets to support Matty at the coronation?' Laura asked and there was a deathly silence.

'Coronation?' Kelly said cautiously.

'Uh-oh,' Rafael said.

'You knew it was coming,' his mother said. 'Didn't you?'

'Yes, but…'

'But you intended to be back in Manhattan. Not possible now. Not possible ever. You need to be part of it, Rafael.'

'Dress uniform,' he said with loathing.

'You like your dress sword,' Kelly said and he shook his head.

'I look ridiculous in a dress sword.'

'You look...' She hesitated.

'Magnificent is the word you're looking for,' Laura said fondly. 'His papa looked wonderful in dress regalia too.'

'And it did a lot for Papa,' Rafael said curtly. 'I suppose I have to be there.'

'Of course you do,' Laura told him. 'Crater's been organizing it while you've been away. You need to swear all sorts of things—basically whatever Matty would have to swear if he was old enough.'

'I think Kelly should do it,' Rafael said and Kelly winced.

'Hey, not me. I'm not royal material.'

'Neither of you sound committed,' Laura said cautiously.

Kelly said solidly, 'That's because I'm not.'

'You know, this country does need a royal presence,' Laura said. They'd reached the gate into the dower house and paused. The dower house was a miniature castle—exquisite. The garden here was a mass of wild flowers and shrubbery that seemed almost a wilderness. Kelly could smell jasmine and roses and...gardenia? Honeysuckle? The scene in the moonlight was fantastic.

But Laura wasn't focusing on gardens. She had a wider picture. 'This country's been let go,' Laura said, speaking earnestly to both of them. 'Neither Kass nor his father cared a toss about the country. Rafael, it nearly killed your father...'

'It did kill my father,' he said bitterly.

'A fall from a horse killed your father.'

'And then he wasn't permitted near the old Prince because disability made him nervous. So he couldn't do a thing.'

'Rafael's father tried to manage the economy of the place,' Laura explained to Kelly. 'He did what he could to make things easier for the people of Alp de Ciel. Then, when he was injured, his father, the old Prince, simply took all his royal duties from him.'

'Which pretty much killed him,' Rafael said. 'So why you'd think I'd want to pick up the pieces now…'

'Your father would want you to.'

'My father's dead,' Rafael said. 'I'm a toy-maker, Mama.'

'And a good one,' she said warmly and stood on tiptoe to kiss him. 'But the two aren't mutually exclusive. Prince of the blood and toy-maker on the side.'

'I'm a toy-maker,' he repeated. 'I'll do what I must here, and nothing more.'

'See, that's just the problem,' she said. Instead of opening the garden gate, she hitched herself up to sit on the drystone wall round the garden. She swung her legs against the stone and surveyed Kelly and Rafael with care.

'This country is a responsibility,' she said. 'A huge responsibility. And Matty's too little to take it on.'

'No one's taken it on for the last fifty years,' Rafael said.

'Your father tried to. It wasn't his job but…'

'You're right. It wasn't his job. It isn't mine.'

'It is,' she said forcibly. 'You're Prince Regent. The country needs you.'

'Don't you start,' he snapped. 'Kelly's already blackmailed me into staying.'

'Ah, yes,' Laura said softly. 'Kelly.'

'Hey, don't look at me,' Kelly said, startled. 'I'm not even royal.'

'I'm sorry, my dear, but that's where you're wrong,' Laura said sternly. 'You were royal from the minute you married Kass. You were even more royal the moment you bore him a son. This is your country.'

'It's not my country.'

'Someone has to take responsibility for it,' she said sadly. 'It's impoverished. Everyone knows that. The industries need a complete overhaul—the farming techniques are antiquated.

There's money in the royal coffers to subsidise improvements, reform, but nothing's done. So far there's been little protest by the people. We have an extraordinarily accepting population. But now…'

'Now what?' Rafael said ominously and his mother kicked the stone wall some more and looked from Rafael to Kelly and back again.

'Now there are three countries leading by example,' she said. 'Alp de Montez, Alp d'Estella and Alp d'Azuri. Three of the four principalities created all those centuries ago and almost destroyed by generation after generation of royalty who bled them dry with their own greed. Within the last few years each of these three countries have had their governments transformed. Each royal house has finally taken responsibility for their countries. They're now run as true democracies with an overarching sovereign. Their industries are thriving. Tourists are attracted in droves and the people here are looking at their neighbours and asking why not us?'

'They can do it,' Rafael said nervously.

'No, dear, *they* can't,' his mother said. '*They* being individuals within this country who want change. There's no avenue for change. The only way change is possible is with constitutional reform, and with enormous amounts of energy, commitment and sheer hard work by the incumbent sovereign. And, in case you hadn't noticed, that's you two.'

'Not me,' Kelly said,

'Not me, either,' Rafael said and his mother sighed.

'That's what Kass said.'

'Mama, I'm only here because Kelly forced me to be here,' Rafael growled. 'To take this all on…' He sounded bleak.

But there was a trace of acceptance in his voice, Kelly thought. There was more than a trace of his father in him. Despite his distaste for royalty, he'd agreed to meet this deputation tonight. She watched his face and thought yes, he'd do it. And it wasn't just her blackmail that was making him commit.

He was no Kass.

But was Laura asking her to share?

'I'm only here for my son,' she whispered.

'Do you think you can stay separate?' Laura asked gently.

'I think I don't know anything,' she whispered.

'You're a historian. You do the minimum amount of research on this place and you'll find out what I say is the truth.'

'So what do you want me to do about it?'

'I think you should both be royal,' Laura said gently and then, as Kelly stared at her in dismay, she shook her head, rueful.

'Rafael, you know it's what your father would have wanted. He hated what his father and his brother did to this country.'

'I hated what they did to him,' Rafael retorted.

'It's not the country's fault. Nor is what Kass did to you the country's fault, my dear,' she told Kelly. 'Do the research,' she ordered and swung herself off her wall and opened the gate. 'Make no promises yet. But think, my dears. Think, oh, think, of what the pair of you could achieve. Rafael, you're due to meet the country's representatives in half an hour. Kelly, if you could find it in you to help…'

'I can't.'

'Just think about it,' she demanded flatly, and disappeared into the house before either of them could reply.

Why had she come with Rafael and his mother, Kelly thought frantically as Laura disappeared. It meant she had to walk home alone with Rafael and he was making her nervous. He was big and silent and just…there.

He was as preoccupied as she was. Laura's words were echoing in the night air. So much to take on board…

They walked slowly through the woodland path towards the stables. The castle loomed before them, vast and majestic. The night was warm and filled with scents from the garden—a magic night.

'Is that a nightingale?' she asked before she could help herself and Rafael paused and listened and then shrugged.

'Yep. They're common.'

'Nightingales are common?'

'It's this whole damned fairy tale setting,' he said morosely. 'It does your head in. Like wearing a dress sword. I make toys. I don't want to live in make-believe any more than I have to.'

'I won't live in make-believe.'

'The problem is,' he said, 'it's not make-believe. It's real. Your son has to take over responsibility for this country and he's five years old.'

'My son needs to take over responsibility for this country in twenty years.'

'Meaning you're landing it fair in my corner.'

'Yes,' she said and walked on. Rafael stopped and stared at her.

'You could at least sound guilty,' he called and she turned and kept walking, but backwards so she could watch him in the moonlight.

'Why should I feel guilty?'

'If you hadn't had Matty I wouldn't be in this mess.'

'Yes, you would. Some other woman would have had the heir to the throne. Kass would still have died and you might have got someone who wasn't nicely determined to keep herself out of your way, out of trouble, out of sight.'

'So during the coronation…'

'I'll watch,' she conceded. 'I'll find myself a corner up the back.'

'You look ridiculous in baggy sweaters,' he said and she froze.

'I beg your pardon.'

'You're meant to be royal. You looked fantastic in crinoline and hoops.'

'And you look fantastic in your dress sword,' she said.

'But I was playing dress-ups for a reason that no longer exists. Your reasons keep going for another twenty years.'

'Kelly, help me here.'

'Help you do what?'

'We can do it together,' he said, pleading. 'You can take some of the pressure from me. If you'll play the princess…'

'No.'

'Kelly…'

'No!' She turned and stalked round the corner of the stables. And stopped.

Matty was walking towards them. He was in his pyjamas and bedroom slippers. He had his thumb in his mouth. He was walking determinedly towards the stables and he looked not even his full five years old.

'Matty,' she said and he looked up and saw them and froze.

'It's okay,' she said quickly. Rafael came round the corner of the stables and paused beside her. 'It's okay, Matty. It's only Rafael and me.'

'I want to see Blaze,' Matty whispered. He'd relaxed a little when he'd seen Rafael but he still sounded guilty.

'Blaze?'

'My papa's horse,' he said in a thread of a whisper. Then his voice firmed. 'Blaze is my horse now. I thought about him while I was in Australia. I thought and thought. Papa's dead. I don't think anyone's told Blaze.'

'I'm sure someone's already told him,' Kelly said. 'And we can tell him again in the morning. Sweetheart, you should be in bed.'

'I was in bed for hours and hours,' Matty said. 'I woke up and it feels like morning. So I had to tell Blaze.'

'Matty, Blaze already knows that your papa is dead,' Rafael said. They were standing side by side, looking down at the little prince. Matty was looking young, vulnerable but also determined. His small chin jutted forward in a gesture Kelly was starting to recognize.

'I should have told him myself,' Matty said fretfully. 'He's my horse.'

'I guess we need to come with you then, to make sure he's okay,' Rafael said. 'If it's okay with your mama.'

Horses. She didn't want to go anywhere near horses. Especially not Kass's horse. Blaze was the magnificent animal that had propelled her into trouble in the first place. She cast a despairing glance at Rafael but, to her astonishment, he took her hand and squeezed, almost as if he understood.

'A quick visit and then bed,' he said. 'Better than wasting time arguing. Matty, do you know where Blaze is stabled?'

'Of course I do,' Matty said scornfully.

'Then lead on,' Rafael said gently and the little boy looked uncertainly up at the adults before him, then shrugged and led the way into the stables.

They were just as Kelly remembered.

Six years ago Kass had brought her in here at dawn, introduced her to each of the royal horses and then said, 'Choose your mount.'

For Kelly, who loved horses almost more than life itself, it had been the sexiest thing Kass could possibly have done. She'd walked between each stall while Kass had stood indulgently back, like a genie who'd just oozed from his bottle and snapped his fingers.

Then he'd called the stable-hands to saddle the mare of her choice; he'd mounted the huge black stallion with the blaze of white on its forehead and they'd ridden out into the dawn together.

It had been heady stuff for a kid who'd spent her life lusting after a horse of her own. Heady enough stuff to remove any sense of self-preservation, to make her walk straight into a web that she could never walk out of.

Now she walked into the stables feeling just the same—as

if a door would slam behind her and she'd be stuck. But Matty was walking steadily forward to the first stall.

Kelly peered nervously over the door. A mare stood placidly at the rear of the stall, head down in the manger.

'It's not Blaze.'

'He's here somewhere. I have to find him.'

'He's at the end,' Rafael said and motioned along the doorways. His height gave him the advantage. Kelly turned and saw what Rafael was seeing, the great stallion standing at ease, staring out at them with seeming unconcern.

She flinched and Rafael stepped forward and took her arm.

'It's okay.'

'I know it's okay,' she muttered. 'I…I know horses.'

'Do you know Blaze?' Matty asked.

'I've met him,' she muttered. 'Matty, he's too big for you to go near.'

'He's my horse,' Matty said, sounding rebellious. 'My papa said the Prince has to have the best, and Blaze is the best. I knew when he died I'd have to take care of him. Like the country. Crater says I have to take care of the country.'

It was such an astounding statement coming out of the mouth of a five-year-old that neither Rafael nor Kelly could think of a response.

'But Crater says you'll help,' Matty said, almost indulgently, and walked forward to Blaze's stall. He stood looking uncertainly up at the big horse, as if unsure how to approach him. 'He's very big.'

'I think your father would want you to ride a much smaller horse for a while,' Kelly said but Matty shook his head.

'Someone has to ride Blaze.'

'Maybe Rafael…'

'I don't ride,' Rafael said.

'Me either,' Kelly retorted.

'Crater said my mother rides like the wind,' Matty said,

turning to stare at her as if he'd been given deeply erroneous information—information that was very, very important.

'People change,' Kelly said. 'I…I don't ride any more.'

'Why not?'

'I just don't,' she said helplessly. 'I study instead.'

'Who will help me look after the horses?'

'I…we'll employ people,' Kelly said. 'Maybe…I mean we probably already do. Don't we, Rafael?'

'I guess.' Rafael peered hopefully into the stalls. 'They've all got hay and fresh water. They're obviously being taken care of.'

'But I need to know for sure,' Matty said definitely. 'I'll find out tomorrow. And Ellen says there's a dep…a deputation coming from the village. I need to see them.'

'They're coming tonight and they're coming to see your Uncle Rafael,' Kelly told him.

'I'm the Prince,' Matty said. 'Uncle Rafael doesn't want to be the Prince.'

'Uncle Rafael is the Prince until you're older,' Kelly said.

'He doesn't even want to ride horses.'

'He doesn't have a choice,' Kelly snapped. It was too much. Her tiny prince was looking cold and shaky. She picked him up before he could make a protest and held him close. 'Meanwhile, you need to go back to bed. Stop worrying about tomorrow.'

'I have to worry about it,' Matty said. 'I'm…'

'You're a little boy who needs to be a little boy,' she said solidly. 'And little boys need to do what their mothers tell them. Which is go to bed and not worry. Your Uncle Rafael will take care of everything.'

'Sure,' Rafael said morosely.

'See,' Matty said. 'He doesn't want to.'

'I do want to,' Rafael said. 'I meant to say *sure*. As in happy sure. It's just because I have jet lag that it came out grumpy.'

'You're sure?'

'I'm sure,' he said and beamed. Kelly almost laughed. It

was some crazy beam. It was a Cheshire cat beam, ridiculous in its insincerity.

But it seemed to do the trick. Matty relaxed into her arms and snuggled against her.

'I just thought…I worried about Blaze. And the villagers… They used to come to see Papa when he was alive. Papa called them fools but Ellen said if Papa was a proper prince he'd listen to what they need and do something about it. I want to be a proper prince.'

'You will be,' Kelly said unsteadily. 'Later. Not now. Not until you're almost as high as Blaze.'

'Uncle Rafael will take care of everything?'

'Uncle Rafael will take care of everything,' she said. 'Now, I'm taking you back to bed.'

She tucked him into bed, and stayed with him until he was asleep. She decided she ought to go to bed herself, but when she looked out of the nursery window she saw Rafael.

He was sitting on one of the garden seats, staring out towards the Alps beyond. He was dressed in his royal regalia again. She wasn't sure about the sword, but she could see braid on his shoulders.

A prince waiting to meet the townspeople.

What had he said?

'We can do it together. You can take some of the pressure from me. If you'll play the princess…'

She wasn't about to play the princess. Once she had. Never again.

She should close the curtains.

She couldn't.

Rafael had been asked to take on what she couldn't. She couldn't let him off the hook, but that didn't stop her feeling guilty.

Matty was solidly asleep again. Marguerite was right next door. And Rafael looked…alone.

She glanced down at her clothing—jeans and baggy sweater. It was hardly princess wear.

That was okay.

Not okay if she wanted to help.

Could she help?

Maybe she could, she thought. Just a little. After all, Rafael was in a relationship with his Anna. He was no threat to her. To hide up here like a hermit… Maybe it was even silly.

But what to wear…

She bit her lip.

'Go on, Kelly,' she told herself, whispering into the night. 'You've been playing dress-ups for five years now. Maybe you can play dress-ups a little bit longer.'

Her rooms were just as she'd left them. Kelly turned the handle of the vast oak doors leading into the suite she'd stayed in five years ago and the sight of the dressing gown on the side table made her frown again. Why hadn't it been thrown out?

But then… This suite was one of many and it was as far from Kass's apartments as it was possible to be. If Kass had brought guests—women—here he'd want them a lot closer. For the staff to destroy her possessions would have taken a direct order and Kass must simply never have given the order.

The crib that had stood beside the bed for those few short weeks had gone. Otherwise it was exactly as she'd left it. Cleaned and cared for and ready for her to come home.

She wasn't home. She had no place here.

Not true. She was Matty's mother. And maybe it wouldn't hurt to help.

She was being silly. Dumb. But just on the off chance…

She walked across to the vast bank of wardrobes and slid back the doors. And found what she'd half expected.

Here was her wardrobe. A wardrobe fit for a princess.

The first few weeks with Kass had been dreamlike. A royal fantasy. She'd been whisked to Paris, she'd been showered with every luxury, she'd been wooed with every one of Kass's several charms.

He'd taken her shopping. Not the shopping normal people did, but shopping where he'd take her into the most expensive boutiques he could find, introduced her grandly as Kellyn, Princess of Alp de Ciel, settled himself into a settee, called for a drink and watched as she tried on one outfit after another.

For Kelly, who'd thought the epitome of fashion was her little red dress, it had been an eye-opener. For a while she'd thought it was fantastic.

And these were the legacy, left behind as Kass had forced her to leave. One designer gown after another. Dresses that had been so expensive their price tags had made her eyes water.

Ridiculous dresses.

She was here for a purpose. She had to do it fast or she'd lose courage.

She tugged a dress from the racks—an elegant black cocktail frock, tiny capped sleeves, a sweetheart neckline, a hemline that was too long for Kass's taste but which the boutique owner had gasped over.

'Oh, Your Highness, it makes you look just like Audrey Hepburn.'

Hardly, Kelly thought, but she grinned and held it up in front of her. She was the same size as six years ago. It wouldn't hurt to dress up just a little.

Her shoes were still here. All her shoes. What about her jewellery?

Was she being really, really dumb? she demanded of herself as she pulled out the top drawer of her bureau.

Maybe she was, but Rafael was waiting.

The men were angry and impatient and barely civil. Rafael didn't blame them. Their needs were urgent and they'd been ignored for too long.

'We need to sit down and look at the whole situation,' he said, but that was just what they didn't want to hear.

'You're just like your cousin,' one of the men snapped. 'He didn't care and neither do you. Do you realise the threat to the village…?'

'He doesn't realise it yet, but he will,' a soft voice said from the doorway. 'We both will.'

Rafael turned—and gasped.

He'd brought the men into the first of the salons just by the grand entrance. The room was vast and ornate, with magnificent settees gathered around a fireplace that was truly awesome. But outside in the entrance there were marble columns, a chandelier with so many crystals it must take an army to clean it, a truly magnificent entry.

Kelly was framed against it. A slip of a girl in a dress that was the epitome of elegance. It hugged her figure, showing off every lovely curve. Her hair was swept up into a knot that might be casual—wisps of curls were escaping—but it accentuated the simplicity of her dress. Her legs looked long and elegant, her black sandals made her feet look sooo sexy…

The whole outfit made her look sooo sexy. The eight men in the deputation were rising to their feet as one and Rafael did too.

'I'm so sorry I'm late,' Kelly was murmuring as she crossed to Rafael's side. 'My son is a little unsettled after the flight and I needed to make sure he was asleep before I left.'

'Princess…Kellyn?' someone breathed and Rafael caught his breath and made the introductions.

Her outfit was brilliant, he thought as he watched the men's reactions. She'd been described to the country as a slut. This outfit made her look anything but.

She rested her hand lightly on his arm. It wasn't a proprietorial gesture. It was a gesture of solidarity.

'You do need to give us a little time,' she said softly, glancing up at Rafael and smiling, as if this was something they'd discussed in depth. 'My husband has just died, and

Prince Rafael has only just been able to bring me back here. Yes, there's been major damage done to the country by royal neglect. But injustice has been done to Rafael and to me, as well as to you, his people. Prince Kass forbade me access to my son. He refused to allow Prince Rafael or his father before him to assist you. These great injustices can now be reversed. I understand your anger. Rafael and I share that anger and we intend to do everything we can to redress the situation.'

It was brilliant, Rafael thought, stunned. In one fell swoop she'd deflected the anger, by linking herself to him, by acting as if they were a team. Yes, these people were furious that their country had been neglected, but this slip of a girl had been kicked out of the country and denied her child.

'We thought you…we thought…'

'There have been many lies spread about the Princess Kellyn,' Rafael said strongly. 'Those lies need to be redressed. As many things in this country need to be redressed. You people are from the village. What I want from you is a list of your immediate concerns and your suggestions as to what can be done to address them. Can you get that to me as soon as you can? I need to go further—get things moving throughout the whole country—but of course you people are our neighbours and maybe your concerns have to take priority.'

'When will you be leaving again?' one of the men asked, but the belligerence had gone out of his voice. He was clearly unsure.

'I won't be,' Rafael said, and his voice was clear and calm and sure. He put a hand over Kelly's. If she was to help…

If she was to stand by his side…anything was possible, he thought. The bleakness that had been with him since he'd heard of Kass's death lifted for the first time. These people needed his help. He could do this.

'There will be occasional trips abroad,' he said, and it was a struggle now not to let this strange sense of exultation enter his voice. 'Made out of necessity. I know there was anger that

I left last week, so soon, but my priority was to restore Princess Kellyn to her rightful place. Now that's been done, both of us will be based here. Ready to listen to what you need of us.'

'My role is mother to Prince Mathieu,' Kelly said, suddenly sounding nervous. 'You understand that my brief marriage to Kass hasn't fitted me for any other role. But I'll be supporting Prince Rafael in the background.'

There was a murmur of approval. And sympathy. And… excitement?

'We understand it will take time for you both to find your feet here,' one of the men—the leader—said at last. He moved forward to shake Rafael's hand. 'We've heard enough tonight to content us. We'll make this list and we'll get it to you as soon as possible. And we look forward to working with you.' He glanced across at Kelly. 'With both of you.'

They walked out into the grand entrance, to the huge sweep of carved steps, to see the deputation off. The men climbed into their several cars and departed. Rafael and Kelly stood side by side until they were out of sight.

'Thank you,' Rafael said softly as the sound of the cars faded. 'You saved my hide. They were all ready for a spot of anarchy.' He moved away a little so he could see her. 'Wow,' he said softly. 'Wow and wow and wow. You took their breath away. You took my breath away.' He frowned. 'But I thought you didn't bring a dress.'

'It's part of my past,' she said. 'It seems I still have a wardrobe of dresses here. Mostly chosen by Kass.'

'Kass never chose that.'

'No.' She ran her hands self-consciously along her sides and the luxurious silk felt smooth and lovely under her hands. 'I chose this.'

'You like clothes,' he said on a note of discovery.

'For my pains. I try not to.'

'Don't try,' he said urgently. 'You're beautiful. The people will love you.'

'You're saying I should wear the clothes Kass chose for me?'

'Of course I'm not. You could come to Manhattan with me,' he said. 'When we get this place sorted. Money's not an issue—the royal coffers have an amount set aside that is purely for personal maintenance of the immediate royal family. That's us. It's enough to make you think that maybe buying a lottery ticket might be a waste of time. You and Matty could take a few days and come play on Fifth Avenue.' He grinned and looked her up and down, his smile enough to make her blush—really blush. 'Matty and I would love to watch you enjoy yourself setting yourself up for your new life here.'

'What about Anna?' she asked curiously, trying to get her colour under control. 'Isn't she due here?'

'She should be here tomorrow,' Rafael said. 'I've organized the stuff from my development workshop to be freighted over and she's supervising. But don't worry about Anna. Any shopping we're organising, she'll have her hand up before me.'

'Oh.' She wasn't quite sure what was happening here. The appreciation in his eyes was warm and intimate. Yet he spoke about Anna with matter-of-fact directness.

'Why aren't you in your attic?' he asked, cutting across her train of thought.

'I saw you out here.' She hesitated. 'I felt…I don't know. Maybe if I can help I will. Just occasionally,' she added hastily as she saw the leap of hope in his eyes. 'Not on a regular basis.' She bit her lip. 'I…maybe I've been a bit mean. I am grateful to you. For Matty,' she said softly. 'I do need to thank everyone here. You've all done a lovely job of bringing him up. He's a darling.'

'And so responsible,' Rafael said.

'He doesn't need to be responsible.'

'As long as I'm responsible. Or you're responsible. And look at us. We even look like royals.'

'I'm play-acting,' she said, 'to help out. I'm going back to my attic tomorrow.'

'That's a damned waste.'

'It shouldn't be.'

'You don't need me.'

'No?'

For a long moment he stared at her as if she'd just asked a question that was really dumb. She gazed back at him, bewildered. But then…

But then things started clicking into place.

It had been five years since any man had looked at her like Rafael was looking at her, but she knew the signs. He was staring at her as if he were hungry. As if she were…

Desirable?

'No,' she said and held up her hands as if in defence.

'It's all very well to say no,' Rafael snapped, stepping towards her so fast he was suddenly way too close. 'It's the last thing I want. Or it should be the last thing I want.'

'What?' she said, confused.

'You,' he said and the world stood still again.

'I…don't,' she said at last, somehow taking a step back, and he shook his head as if trying to clear a fog.

'Yeah. Maybe I'm being dumb. Go to bed, Kelly.'

'You're sending me to bed?'

'I'm sending you away,' he said, exasperated. 'I need you to go away.'

'Like Kass.'

'No!' And, before she knew what he was about, he'd seized her hands and tugged her close. 'That's just it. Don't you see—I'm not the least like Kass. Kass represented everything about this place that I hate. Royalty. The perfection of it… Do you know my father was thrown from his horse and maimed? He was crippled but as well as that he had a massive scar running down the side of his face. He lost the sight of one eye. Until then, he'd worked like a navvy in this place—that the Principality hasn't bankrupted itself until now is solely down to my father's economic acumen and the fact that the old prince never bothered to interfere. But as soon as my father was injured he wasn't permitted any part of the running of the place. He was simply struck off. It just killed him—his injuries, but more—the fact that he was useless. My mother and I could do nothing. And here I am, being useful again. Useful. And here you are and you're Kass's bride…'

'Hey…'

'And the last thing I want is to feel sorry for you,' he said. 'And I don't and that's just the trouble. Sympathy is something I could deal with. But you're standing here looking so damned sexy it's melting the soles of my boots, and the way I feel…I just…'

'You just?' She was trying to pull away but he was having none of it.

'I just,' he said and he tugged her tight against him.

And he kissed her.

The shock made her freeze.

For the first couple of seconds—those vital seconds when she should have pulled away, before his mouth even touched hers—shock didn't let her move. His hands were holding hers with a warmth and a strength that locked her to him. She'd been tugging back—sort of—but not with real desperation. But now…

His hands tugged her tight and his mouth lowered on to hers. In shock she looked up at him, and then his lips claimed hers and it was a done deal. She was being kissed, whether she willed it or not.

Rafael…

He felt…He felt…

She stopped trying to figure what he felt. She stopped trying to figure what she felt. She just…was.

She hadn't touched a man for six years. She'd sworn to never…

So much for swearing, for there was no way any mere resolution could get in the way of this.

Her mouth met his, merged, and her body simply went into meltdown. She had no will to do anything but simply be—to let him take her as he willed, to let his hands create their magic, to let the sensations sweeping over her take their course, transform her as they willed, lift her out of her dreary yesterdays and turn her into a woman desired.

For that was what she was. There was no mistaking the urgency of how he felt about her. His hands had her firmly round the waist, tugging her into him so her breasts were flattened against his chest. She could feel his heart beating under hers. She opened her lips and felt his tongue begin a slow, delicious plunder that would have made her moan in pleasure if in doing so she might not have risked breaking the moment.

She was risking nothing. She was doing her own holding, taking what she needed from this man, soaking in the warmth and strength and arrant male desire.

It had been too long. Far too long.

Rafael…

She was kissing him back, as fiercely as he was kissing her, taking as well as giving, quenching her own desperate needs.

Needs she'd told herself didn't exist.

Only, of course, they did. Six long years of nothing. Isolation and loneliness and betrayal.

Rafael…

The kiss went on and on. Neither wanted it to end. Neither could conceive of it ending. The night was still and warm. There was no movement in the forecourt—the castle staff had long gone to bed. There was only this man and this woman, taking what they both desperately needed.

And when the kiss finally ended, as even the best kiss must

inevitably do, Kelly took a step back and put her fingers to her lips and knew that her world had changed.

'N…no,' she whispered and she saw her own shock mirrored in Rafael's eyes.

'No,' he agreed, sounding as if he didn't know what the word meant.

'I didn't want to kiss you,' she whispered.

'You're Kass's woman,' he said blankly and that brought reality crashing back around the pair of them.

Kass's woman…

The feeling of unreality dissipated. Here and now crashed right back.

'How dare you?'

'I don't dare,' he said. 'That was dumb.'

She stared at him, confounded. The kiss had been dumb. Of course it had been dumb. But to say it…

'Don't you touch me,' she stammered and the confusion in his eyes faded.

'You don't want it?'

'Of course not.'

'Of course not. We're birds of a feather, Kelly. We want nothing to do with this.'

'But it's not this we're talking about,' she managed. 'Not royalty. Not now. No, I don't want any more contact than I'm forced to have with royalty to be a good mother to Matty. But as far as kissing you…'

'You looked at me,' he said as if that explained everything and she glared.

'So you're saying I goaded you into it. Like wearing red patent shoes.'

'Pardon?' he said, startled.

'You don't wear red patent shoes,' she said patiently. 'Everyone knows they incite the senses and reflect your knickers.'

'Really?'

'Not that it has anything to do with the here and now,' she said, fighting to get a grip. 'And I should never have worn this dress. When's Anna coming?'

'I told you. Tomorrow.'

'Then starting tomorrow, let's get this on a sensible footing,' she snapped. 'You and me…we see each other in terms of official duties. That's all.'

'That's all I want, too.'

'Because, of course, I'm Kass's woman.'

'I didn't mean to say that.'

'You did say it,' she snapped. 'And it hurt. I was dumb enough to fall for a good royal come-on, and if you think I'd be dumb enough to fall twice…Kass's woman or not…you'd be out of your mind. So you needn't look at me as if I'm trying to jump you or, heaven forbid, put another wedding ring on my finger…'

'I'm not.'

'Because I'm not,' she snapped, refusing to let him interrupt. 'I'm going to bed.'

'Good.'

'And Kass's…the royal suite is round the far side of the castle,' she said. 'As far from my attics as it's possible to get. And I can lock my doors.'

'Kelly, I'm not trying to seduce you.'

'You kissed me and that's enough. More than enough. I don't even want a handshake from a prince of the blood.'

'I'm not…'

'A prince of the blood. Yes, you are.'

'As you're Kass's bride,' Rafael said, sounding goaded. 'Princess Royal. You represent everything I don't want about this place.'

'Well, it's good we have that cleared up,' she snapped. 'Just so we're clear. You dragged me back here and now you tell me I'm part of your problem. Sorry, Rafael, I have problems of my own to sort.'

She should stalk away. She should just turn and leave. Instead, she stood in the moonlight and watched him try to think of something else to say—something that would make sense of this crazy situation they'd landed in.

He couldn't. He didn't. And finally there was no choice. She turned away. 'Goodnight,' she said stiffly.

'Kelly?'

She didn't turn round. She simply stood still and waited for him to say what he needed to say.

'I'm sorry,' he said at last. 'That should never have happened. It won't happen again. I promise.'

'Just as well,' she muttered.

And went to bed.

But not to sleep.

What had she been thinking of—to let him kiss her and to kiss him back?

It was because he was…gorgeous?

Rafael de Boutaine, Prince Regent of Alp de Ciel. He'd kissed her senseless.

As Kass had.

No. He was as different from Kass as it was possible to be. Kelly lay in the lovely double bed Rafael had organized to be delivered into her attic room and watched the moonbeams play on the ceiling. She shouldn't have the new bed, she thought. She wanted to be like a forgotten relation, left to penury while on the other side of the castle, on the royal side, Rafael swanned round in luxury, enjoying his magnificent suite of rooms, being…Prince Regent.

'I'd hate it,' she muttered.

She didn't hate Rafael. She'd loved it tonight, she conceded. She'd loved feeling beautiful. She'd loved standing side by side with Rafael while he'd organized affairs of state. She'd loved the way he'd gasped as she'd walked into the room. And the way the warmth had stayed in his eyes.

In fact, the way she was feeling about Rafael…had to be suppressed. The part of her that had been wounded to the core five years ago clenched into horror.

To fall in love with another prince…

What was she thinking? How could she be falling in love? Just because the man had kissed her…

'The man's seriously fabulous,' she told the ceiling and closed her eyes, as if she could block out the thought of him.

His partner would be here tomorrow—a woman called Anna. They'd get on with the ruling Laura told them was needed and she'd retire to her books. For the next twenty years.

'Which is what I want,' she whispered into the dark, 'isn't it?'

'Yes,' her mind screamed but there was a tiny part of her that was stubbornly refusing to agree.

Why had he kissed her? Did he have no sense at all?

Yes, he'd agreed to take on the Regency, but that was as far as it went. He didn't want to get any more fond of Matty than he already was, and he sure as hell didn't want to get any more fond of Matty's mother.

But he'd kissed her.

The thought shocked him. He hadn't known what he intended to do until it happened and then…then it was too late. It was lucky that Kelly had sense for the pair of them.

It's like quicksand, he thought savagely, the royal quagmire hauling him in.

He thought back to the days after his father's accident. Up until then, Rafael had been cool with being royal. Kass, his older cousin, had been an arrogant, egotistical bore. Worried about the influence Kass might have, his parents had sent Rafael to boarding school. He'd thoroughly enjoyed it, but he'd loved coming back in the holidays. He'd lived on horseback, roaming this beautiful little country with an ever-growing appreciation.

But then his father had been injured, and over the course

of one summer life had changed. Kass and his father had simply cut off the brother and uncle who'd once been useful to them, but whose use-by date had been the moment he'd become uncomfortable to look at.

The last time he'd come outside… It had been just before Rafael was due to go back to school. Laura had convinced her husband to get some sun, so she and Rafael had pushed him into the garden.

Kass had walked past and had stopped dead. 'He's not to stay here,' he'd said harshly, speaking to Laura and not directly to his uncle. 'It upsets the staff. It makes me feel sick. He's not to come within sight of the castle.'

That one vicious order had been enough to make Rafael's father return to the house. He'd died two months later, without having set foot in the garden again.

Rafael had made that vow as well. There was no way he ever intended to be of use to royalty. He wouldn't set foot in the castle. He'd hoped his mother would move. She hadn't and their access to each other had become confined to Laura's visits to the States.

And now, like it or not, here he was—of use to royalty as his father had once been of use to the old Prince and to Kass. It made him feel ill.

And tonight he'd kissed Kass's wife.

Why?

It was a web, he thought, a fine, gossamer web drawing him in tighter and tighter. Conscience and duty had him stuck here.

Like Kelly was stuck.

She wasn't stuck, he thought savagely. She could stay up in her attic and be an academic and not do anything, not be a part of it. Or do as she'd done tonight, emerge from her attic for a moment and then retreat the moment things got intense.

So why had he kissed her?

'Because I'm a fool,' he told the darkness and he rolled over in the royal bed and thought he could roll over six or seven times and not reach the edge.

'It's ludicrous.

'It's life as you'll know it for the next twenty years,' he said grimly. 'So get used to it. And keep your hands off that woman!'

CHAPTER SIX

KELLY woke to the sound of shouting in the forecourt. For a moment she couldn't remember where she was—the strange bed and the thick stone walls and narrow casement windows confused her. Then, as the events of the last few days flooded back, her bedroom door was flung open and Matty launched himself across her bed.

'Uncle Rafael's toys are here,' he said. 'Mama, come and see. Come and see.'

'I don't…'

'You have to come,' he said before she could protest. 'There's pancakes for breakfast and Cook's made heaps and heaps 'cos the truck drivers have come all the way from the border this morning and Anna's here and she's really crabby and I'll sit on your bed and wait for you to get dressed.'

She stared at her little son, helpless in the face of his enthusiasm. How could she tell him she'd been thinking of putting a little kitchenette up here, so that she didn't have to go down to the royal kitchens?

What sort of mother would say that?

He wanted her to come.

She peered through the casement. Men were unloading vast crates, carrying them into the main entrance.

'Where's Rafael?'

'He's in the dungeons,' Matty said with relish, as if the

dungeons were truly gruesome. 'Cook said once upon a time there were ghosts in our dungeons with clanking chains, but Uncle Rafael said that the best way to get rid of ghosts is to bury them with sawdust. He's working already. Anna says he's burying his head in the sand but I think he's burying it in sawdust.'

'Well,' Kelly said cautiously, digesting this with care. She'd spent a lot of time figuring things out before she'd gone to sleep. Rafael had kissed her. Rafael was a de Boutaine. The man was obviously a womaniser, just like Kass.

She could deal with this situation, she thought. Disdain—that was the way to go. And distance.

'Maybe if Rafael's working I can come down to breakfast.'

'And then come to the stables?' Matty pleaded. 'Will you come riding?'

'I don't ride,' she said flatly. She pushed back her bedcovers. The silk dress was draped over the bedside chair. She pushed it back so it fell on to the floor behind, out of sight. 'Sorry, Matty, but that's an absolute.'

It was like a vast family. The huge kitchen was filled with people and noise and food.

For Kelly, whose only experience at the castle was silence, fear and formality, the sight that met her eyes as she walked into the kitchen was almost astonishing.

There was a big, buxom woman flipping pancakes in the world's biggest frying-pan on the vast electric range. There were two younger girls, one stirring what seemed to be a vat of batter, the other peeling a mound of potatoes a foot high. The men Kelly had seen carting the crates were seated at one end of the table, wrapping themselves round mounds of the pancakes, looking as if all their Christmases had come at once. Laura was there, talking to a man Kelly recognized as Crater. Crater. The sight of him made her flinch. She hadn't seen him since she'd arrived yesterday.

There was a younger woman as well—tall, almost statuesque, looking svelte in cream linen trousers and a lovely Aran pullover. Her blonde hair was piled high in an elegantly casual knot, she wore fabulous, dangling silver earrings and she looked amazing.

Kelly recognized her from the photograph she'd seen on the Internet—Anna.

'I've brought Mama down to breakfast,' Matty said in his clear voice, and everyone in the kitchen turned and looked at her. Kelly wanted to run.

But Matty had her hand and was tugging her forward. 'I said we were having pancakes so she came,' he said and Crater rose from his seat next to Laura and came round the table with his hand outstretched in welcome.

'Princess Kellyn. Your Highness.'

'Kelly,' she whispered, and dropped Matty's hand and backed instinctively away. The last time she'd talked to this man he'd been talking through the impossibility of her ever seeing her son again. She couldn't bear it.

'I need to apologise,' the elderly man said softly, but Anna was suddenly there, standing beside Crater, looking belligerent.

'Hell, no,' she said. 'Don't apologise to this woman. She's stuffed my life.'

'Hey,' Rafael said from the doorway behind her. He'd come in behind her without her hearing. 'She's stuffed whose life?'

'Everyone's,' Anna said. 'Every single one of our kids.'

'Whose kids?' Kelly asked blankly.

'Twenty kids thinking he's their hero,' Anna said bitterly. 'Twenty kids…'

'Who now need to swap their allegiance to you,' Rafael told her.

'I don't do kids,' Anna said flatly. 'I run a business. A business, Rafael, not a damned charity. Here you are, hauling the personal stuff over here, and if you think…'

'I absolutely think,' Rafael said and put his arms round her and hugged her.

But Anna hadn't finished with her grievance yet. She swiped his hands away and glowered. 'Don't you try your sweet-talk on me. Richard's having all sorts of fits—he didn't even want me to come now. And how the hell Kelly got you here…'

'I don't think I know what's going on,' Kelly said.

'That's because you haven't had breakfast,' Laura said calmly, rising from the table and handing her a warmed plate. 'Wrap yourself round some pancakes.'

'Then you can come down and see what I have in my dungeons. Meanwhile, we need to stop Anna being mean to you,' Rafael said. 'Come on, Anna, you can handle it. It's not like I had any choice.'

'Because of Kelly.' Anna glowered. 'You said you'd just need to spend a little time here for ceremonial duties, that all you had to do was persuade Kellyn to take over her rightful role and you could fade into the background again. Someone take that woman's pancakes away from her.'

'Not on your life,' Kelly said, concentrating on the only thing she could understand. Cook was ladling a stack of hot pancakes on to her plate and they smelled extraordinary. She didn't have a clue what was happening between Rafael and Anna, but guilt was hovering, ready to pounce.

She didn't have to accept it. She didn't have to find out what Anna was talking about, she told herself. Rafael's life was none of her business. She sat at the far end of the table, one of the truckers handed her a jug of maple syrup and she got down to business.

'I knew you'd like pancakes,' Matty said, pleased, and she smiled at his pleasure. This was her business—making her son smile.

The kitchen felt great, she thought as she ate. It was big and warm and friendly. She didn't feel out of place back in her jeans and baggy sweater. Even Anna's hostility seemed not particularly hostile—more resigned.

It was none of her business but some things seemed impossible. Maybe she could just ask…

'So you two have twenty children?' she ventured cautiously, and Rafael choked.

'Right. You see what you've done?'

'They might as well be your kids,' Anna retorted, unabashed. 'For all the trouble you've put into them.'

'I don't have twenty kids,' Rafael said. 'I have a sheltered workshop which employs twenty disabled young men and women.'

'Who are currently ready to hate the Princess Kellyn of Alp de Ciel,' Anna said. 'Because you've taken away their precious Rafael.'

'Oh,' Kelly said in a small voice.

'He had to come away anyway,' Laura said.

'Not all the time, he didn't,' Anna said. 'When Kass died he said he might have to spend a bit more time here. Not all the time.'

'So it's my fault,' Kelly said.

'Yes,' Anna retorted. Kelly thought about it. Rafael was looking at her as if he was quite happy for her to take the blame. How unfair was that?

'You'd think someone could have told me,' she said bluntly and fixed him with a look that put the blame right back where it belonged.

He didn't look the least bit guilty. He grinned. His grin made her feel warm from the toes up.

Ridiculous!

'You didn't tell her?' Anna demanded, turning back to Rafael.

'What was I supposed to tell her?' Rafael asked.

'How I'm dependent on you.'

'I told Kelly I had a partner.'

'Just not twenty kids.'

'It seemed a bit over-dramatic.'

'Rafael makes toys,' Laura said, taking pity on Kelly's

confusion. 'Rafael has the most wonderful sheltered workshop in the world. He's built it up from one tiny idea, and now they export all over the world.'

'Robo-Craft,' Kelly said. 'He did tell me that.' She frowned. So what hadn't he told her? Her ultimatum had real repercussions, not just for Rafael? She set down her knife and fork, her appetite suddenly gone.

'It's not like I'm closing down,' Rafael told her quickly. 'I'm just moving development here. Production will stay in Manhattan, overseen by Anna.'

'Who keeps trying to run the business like a business,' Anna said, sighing theatrically. 'Only production's dropped already, as everyone loves Rafael.'

'And now they have to learn to love Anna,' Rafael said. 'And they will.'

'So…' Kelly swallowed. There was a lot here to think about and she didn't know whether she had it right yet. 'So when I said you had to stay here…'

'Then I had to reorganize my business,' Rafael said. 'Which I've done.'

'And Anna's your…?'

'Business partner,' Anna said bluntly. 'More fool me. I'm an accountant.'

'Not your…partner-partner?'

'No,' Anna said, astonished. 'Why would you think that? I'd have brained him ten years ago if he was my partner-partner. Any sane woman would. Now my Richard—who is my partner-partner—is threatening to brain him for me.'

'Oh,' Kelly said. She was starting to feel wobbly.

Last night had seemed fraught. Dangerous. But last night she'd thought Rafael was messing around, being a typical de Boutaine, because Rafael had a partner.

This morning she'd discovered that Anna was his business partner. And she'd discovered more. That Rafael had some truly noble motives in there among his de Boutaine blood.

Last night she'd thought Rafael was sexy but a de Boutaine.

Now…now she just thought he was sexy. Clever. Skilled. Kind.

Unattached.

Very, very sexy.

She suddenly felt really, really exposed. The kitchen was too warm. It was almost claustrophobic.

She pushed her pancakes away.

'Is something wrong?' Laura asked, watching her with concern.

'I didn't want to blackmail anyone to come here.'

'If you did, we're very grateful to you,' Crater said, smiling on her with approval. 'We need Rafael to run this principality. Someone has to take on the Crown.'

'But that's me,' Matty piped up. 'You said I'm the Crown Prince. This country is my res…responsibility.'

'Which Rafael will take care of for you until you're of age,' Crater told him gravely.

'You said I have to look after my people. I am the Prince.'

It silenced them all—this wisp of a child calmly accepting a burden that Rafael and Kelly would do anything to avoid.

Kelly stared down at her half-eaten pancakes, gulped and hauled the plate back in front of her. Maybe she couldn't bolt to her garret quite yet. But the pancakes didn't taste as good.

'You've taught Matty his royal duties?' Rafael asked Crater.

Crater nodded unhappily. 'He's had lessons.'

'Not from his father.'

'No. But Kass has hardly been here. I've taken it upon myself…'

'To load Matty with the burden of the Crown.'

'There was hardly a choice,' Crater said. 'I could never have predicted what's happened. This country's desperate for leadership. Thankfully, now it's up to you.'

Oh, help, Kelly thought.

Until now she'd hardly seen Rafael, she thought bleakly. Or she had seen him but she'd seen a de Boutaine.

Now, he stood alone, a big man, loose-limbed, dressed in casual trousers, an open-necked shirt with sleeves rolled up to his elbows, a streak of grease on his forehead.

He looked vulnerable, she thought suddenly. He looked as if he were backed into a corner he hated.

She could retire to her garret when she wished. He couldn't.

'You don't have to worry.' Matty was clearly trying hard to understand what was going on. He came to his big cousin's side and slipped his hand into Rafael's before Rafael could guess what he intended. 'You can make your toys and I'll be the Prince. My mama will help me be the Prince.'

'Your mama intends to stay in her attic and read her books.'

'You might persuade her to come out a bit,' Anna said, enthusiastic again. 'For long enough to let Rafael come back to Manhattan and make his kids happy from time to time.'

'My life's here,' Rafael said, sounding as if it were a life sentence.

'But you will help,' Matty said to Kelly and she swallowed.

'I...of course. When I can.'

But she was suddenly much more unsure than she had been last night. Dressing up last night had seemed...well, even a little bit of fun. But to go any further, and to do it by Rafael's side when...when Anna wasn't his partner...

'I want you to ride with me,' Matty said and her heart closed—snap—like a clam closing on expected pain.

'Matty, I can't.'

'You can't ride?'

'I don't want to.'

'There's lots of that about,' Laura said sadly, standing and starting to clear plates. 'Let's just take each day as it comes. Starting now. We'll get these trucks unpacked and that'll make Rafael happy. He'll have his dungeons to play in.'

'And Mama will stay in her attic,' Matty said. 'Aunt Laura, it's you and me who'll have to be Prince and Princess.'

'Aren't you the lucky ones?' Anna said and smiled, but Laura looked at her son's partner as if she were a sandwich short of a picnic.

'Anna, I'm afraid you don't have a clue what these two are fighting,' she whispered. 'Oh, my dears, I wish I could help. But Matty…yes, until Rafael and your mama work themselves out then I guess we're it.'

In the end, keeping herself to herself was easy. She just had to be ruthless. She just had to say no firmly to Matty and walk away.

The castle libraries were amazing. Distressed and confused on that first morning, while Laura took Matty down to the stables to chat to the horses and to listen to his adventures in Australia, Kelly roamed the shelves and found tomes and documents and charts that could keep a historian happy for a century or more.

She blocked out the sound of Matty's voice drifting up from the courtyard. She blocked out the sound of the men's voices unloading the trucks, Rafael giving orders, Anna arguing…

The gong sounded for lunch but she'd already warned Cook and Matty that she seldom stopped for lunch. She didn't want to be part of that big familiar kitchen again. She worked on, trying to figure where to start. Maybe cataloguing to begin with. Mindless work while she got her bearings.

At about three in the afternoon she decided the castle was silent and she might conceivably have the kitchen to herself. She went down to make herself a sandwich.

She didn't have the kitchen to herself. Rafael was seated alone at the vast table. He had a bottle of beer before him, and the remnants of a sandwich.

She blinked. Prince Regent of Alp de Ciel with a beer and a sandwich?

He looked up as she entered, like a kid who'd been caught in a crime.

'I'm sorry,' she said, suppressing an involuntary smile, and tried to back out.

'I know. I should be eating caviare patties and drinking champagne,' he said mournfully. 'But I kinda like beer. I'm happy to share, though. I'm not sure where the caviare is, but the makings of sandwiches are in the first refrigerator.'

'I don't need…'

'If you're like me, you do need. It's just the whole company bit that worries you.'

She hesitated. Okay, it would be surly to back away now. She might as well eat. 'So why does it worry you?' she asked.

'It's not as bad as it used to be,' he admitted. 'Castle meals used to be a nightmare. A dining table twenty feet long with a damned great epergne set in the middle of it, so you couldn't see who was at the far end. The minute Kass died my mother decreed that everyone—servants and all—would eat in here. Actually, until Kass died Matty would mostly eat at the dower house, but now Kass is dead my mother thinks Matty's place is here.'

'Matty thinks his place is here,' she said cautiously and he nodded.

'Yeah. How to give a man a guilty conscience…' He swigged his beer from the bottle and watched her make a sandwich.

'So where's Anna?' she asked.

'Gone.'

'Already?'

'I'm guessing she thinks she might get stuck if she stays any longer,' he said. 'She came under protest, to make sure the more delicate bits of equipment were treated with respect. She hates that I'm staying. She gave me a blast and a half and then she retreated. She wants me to go back to Manhattan to talk to the kids.'

'And will you?'

'Not until after the coronation,' he said morosely. 'And even then…there's a vast amount to do here. Sure, I don't want to care. I think I'm forced to. I don't have an attic.'

'Don't give me a hard time,' she growled. 'And, by the way, don't try kissing me again.'

'That was a mistake,' he agreed gravely.

'It certainly was.'

He watched her, considering. 'You didn't like it just a little bit?'

'No.'

His eyes creased at the corners, with just the faintest hint of lurking laughter. 'Liar.'

'I fell in love with Kass,' she reminded him. 'One de Boutaine in a lifetime is enough.'

It took the teasing right away from his eyes. The laughter disappeared.

'You kissed me because I look like Kass?'

'Why else would I kiss you?'

'Right,' he said flatly. 'Right.'

'And you kissed me because?' She shouldn't ask, she thought, but the question had just sort of popped out before she could stop it.

'God knows,' he said bluntly. He shrugged. 'God knows why I want to kiss you again now.'

'You want to kiss me again now?' Her voice broke on a squeak.

'I do,' he conceded. 'Maybe it's because I find your sweater almost irresistibly sexy.'

She looked down at her shapeless wool smock and she winced. It really was dreadful. She'd bought it mid-winter at a clearance sale and wore it for comfort. It was almost as old as Matty. Until now, she'd never worn it out of doors.

Once it had been crimson but it had faded with constant washing so now was a dreary pink. There was a moth hole in the bottom hem. She'd worried it a bit and the hole had extended.

'Who knows what would happen if I ever saw you in lingerie,' Rafael said bluntly. 'Though, by the look of that sweater, I can only imagine what your lingerie's like.' He shook his head, set his beer bottle aside and rose. 'A man could go hot and cold just thinking about it. I think I need to go and take a cold shower. If you'll excuse me…'

'So there'll be no more kissing?' she whispered before she could stop herself and thought frantically, Why did I do that? It was as if she was pushing to extend the conversation. Which surely she wasn't.

She hadn't.

'If you're kissing me back because I look like Kass, what do you think?' he said heavily and left her to her sandwich.

It was the pattern of their days. Working on their private projects. Avoiding each other.

In a way it was the ideal method of getting to know her son, Kelly thought as the days progressed. Matty had his own life mapped out in this castle. Up until now he hadn't had a mother and hadn't really seen the need for one. To have her thrust upon him, demanding a part of his life, would be likely to overwhelm him.

But Matty loved the idea that he had a mother. He was disappointed that she didn't seem interested in his passion—which was definitely horses—but the rest… He took to including her rooms as part of his domain. He followed the routine set down before his father had died—rigid meal times, introductory school work, working with Crater—but in between he'd hurry up to his mother's rooms to report the latest news, to make her feel included.

He was a gracious, loving little boy, Kelly thought. She was blessed. And when, at the end of the first week, he announced that Marguerite had sore legs and she couldn't go very far and would Mama like to come with him instead on his afternoon walks, Kelly thought this was as good as it got.

She had her son again. She didn't have to include herself any more than occasionally in the life of the castle.

She could swallow guilt about the load Rafael was carrying. He was still a de Boutaine, and the way he made her feel scared her witless. She was right to stay aloof.

But, 'Why don't you like my Uncle Rafael?' Matty asked as he skipped ahead through the fabulous woodland around the castle and she thought, uh-oh, had it been as obvious as that?

'I don't not like him.'

'You haven't even seen his dungeon.'

'He hasn't asked me.'

'Yes, he did. He asked you to see it on the day all his tools arrived and you didn't say anything. It's really cool down there. You should see the things he's making. He's working on a new base at the moment that will fit spaceships. He says I can have the pro…prot…protype.'

'Prototype?'

'Yes,' Matty said in satisfaction. 'Will you come and see it?'

'I think your Uncle Rafael is too busy for visitors.'

'That's silly,' Matty said and tucked his hand confidingly into hers. 'I want to show you the…prototype. Can you come and see when we get back from the walk?'

There was a cost, she thought. She'd accepted Matty's invitation to walk with him with pleasure. How could she make the boundaries clear when she kept crossing them?

He was looking up at her, anxious, sensing that things weren't right. 'My Uncle Rafael is very kind,' he said, as if he felt the need to reassure her.

'I'm sure he is.'

'He might even make you something.'

'He makes things for children.'

'And for big kids too,' Matty said. 'Aunt Laura and I read about Robo-Craft on the Internet. It says it's for kids from five to a hundred and five. How old are you?'

'Twenty-nine,' she said faintly.

'See,' Matty said. 'It's perfect for you. You will come and see it, won't you? Oh, look, Mama! There's a deer with a baby.'

* * *

He was finding it really hard to concentrate. There were so many intrusions.

Back in Manhattan, the intrusions had all been work-related. They'd been annoying but Anna had protected him from the worst and they hadn't taken him out of his head like the intrusions here.

He was trying to develop a new base. He had it almost right. Manhattan was gearing up for production for the Christmas rush—that meant he had to get it perfect by the end of this month.

But so far today he'd had Matty three times, Crater twice about finances for the treasury and now an alderman from the town with a list a mile long and a need to talk to him about land stabilization above Zunderfied.

He knew nothing about land stabilization.

He had to learn.

At the end of the basement room there was a narrow window almost at ceiling level. It was ground level outside.

He could see Kelly and Matty out on the far side of the forecourt, heading into the woods.

For one daft minute he felt an almost irresistible urge to join them.

Yeah. As if he needed domesticity added to his duties.

He had to focus.

'Maybe we need to get the land surveyed,' the man said. 'There are some who say the need is urgent. What if we contact the university and see if we can get experts to tell us what they think?'

'Who says the need is urgent?' Rafael asked uneasily, still looking out of the window. They looked great, he thought—Kelly and Matty.

She was still wearing that appalling sweater.

'Only a couple of the old men,' the alderman said soothingly, but he still looked anxious. 'There seems no immediate threat. I'll contact the university.'

'Let's do that immediately,' Rafael said, thinking about the raw scar above the town and feeling more uneasy. 'Can you set that in train? If we offer generous funding we should get people here straight away.'

The man's anxious look faded. He left, relieved, and Rafael turned again to his mechanical base.

His mind wasn't on it.

Instead, he stared out of the window again. Kelly and Matty were out there somewhere.

And a little town with erosion above it and waterlogged soil.

There was nothing more he could do. Was there?

Damn.

And then they came. The knock on the door was more tentative than Matty's usual bang, but that was the only unusual part. Before he could respond, Matty had the door open and was dragging his mother inside.

'He's here. You don't have to wait. He always says come in. Uncle Rafael, Mama has come to look at your prototype.'

Matty was tugging his mother by the hand. Kelly looked completely disoriented, embarrassed, confused…

Adorable.

He could so easily slip into this, he thought. He could pick up where his cousin had left off.

Right. As if Kelly would ever want that. And where did that leave him? Right in the middle of the royal mess with no way of walking, even after twenty years.

Maybe he could have a good time for twenty years.

'Hi,' he said and smiled and she looked even more confused. Even more adorable.

'Matty wanted to show me your toys.'

'Would you like a guided tour?'

She gazed round, clearly astonished. 'It's a workshop.'

It was. The big underground cavern had been transformed. Back in Manhattan, he'd had a workshop set apart from the normal production premises, specially set up so he could have time alone to think, to work peaceably on his latest ideas. He'd had the entire contents transported here. Anna had supervised the shift. Nothing had gone wrong, and already he had a workplace he loved.

And he had the work he loved. His father had introduced him to woodwork, and to rudimentary mechanics. The two of them had worked together when Rafael was a kid, in the slivers of time his father had been able to spare from his royal duties.

Those slivers of time had seemed like gold. They'd instilled in Rafael a love of working with his hands, and now it was the place he found peace.

Did Kelly find such peace in her books?

'You know how Robo-Craft works?' he asked her.

'I've seen it in the shops,' Kelly said and that was enough encouragement for Matty to gasp in shock and drag her to the table.

'You mean you don't even know how it works? Look, Mama. It's very, very wonderful. Uncle Rafael invented it all by himself.'

He set a tiny mechanism on the middle of the table, then grabbed a sizeable plank, balanced it on top of the mechanism and flipped the switch.

The plank swung round like a slow ceiling fan.

'Now look,' Matty ordered and fiddled with the controls.

The plank swayed like a drunken ceiling fan.

'And now…'

The mechanism lifted, rolled. Amazingly the plank stayed balanced. The whole thing started moving steadily to the side of the table.

'Will it go up?' Matty demanded.

'I suspect our plank is too heavy for launch,' Rafael said. 'Why not make something that looks like a rocket? Make it a bit lighter than the plank. In fact, make it a lot lighter than the plank.'

Matty was already gazing round the room, looking for materials.

'Can I use that?' he asked, pointing to some plywood.

'Go right ahead. Here's a hacksaw and here's some craft glue. Kelly, are you going to watch?'

But Kelly was gazing at the little mechanism with longing. It looked awesome.

'Can I make a bus?' she asked and he grinned at the wistfulness in her voice. He loved it when he caught a kid's attention, even if that kid was twenty-nine years old.

'Any special reason why you'd like to make a bus?'

'It's just that rolling action. I had to spend hours on a school bus when I was a kid and the thing bucketed just like your plank. I reckon I could make a bus to sit on it and…'

'Go right ahead,' he said and beamed and she was sucked in, hook, line and sinker.

What followed was peace.

It was probably the first time Rafael had felt at peace since he'd heard of Kass's death.

He'd always found solace in his work—it had always been an escape for him—but for the past few weeks he hadn't been able to disappear. Even when he was alone, when the demands of his new role weren't pounding on his door, his conscience was doing its own pounding. So was his worry for the future—for the fact that he had no choice in the role he was expected to play. He worked with his hands down here but even as he worked his thoughts wriggled and twisted and tried to find an escape.

But just here…just for now…there was no need to escape. He had no wish to escape. This was great.

Kelly and Matty were totally entranced. They had the material they needed. They sat on high stools at his biggest work bench, their heads bent over their projects, deep in concentration.

He'd hardly seen the similarity between mother and son, but he saw it now. The way their brows creased together, puckering into a tiny line just above their noses. The way they focused absolutely. When they picked up the hacksaws and made their first tentative notch, then paused and held the plywood out to make sure they were doing the right thing, their actions were identical.

They looked…

Like mother and son.

More. They looked endearing. Enchanting. He was giving them both pleasure and the thought was enough to settle a deep, aching pain in his gut that had been there…maybe ever since his father had died.

A measure of the success of Robo-Craft was that it pulled people in regardless. If you could put a plain, unadorned plank on this tiny mechanism and watch it transform into something that suggested an old school bus or a spaceship—anything—and if you could see that very easily you could make such a thing and watch it work…

'Yeah, it's brilliant,' Kelly said, smiling, and he grinned at her across the table.

'Was it that obvious?'

'That you love this stuff. Yes, it is. I can see why Anna's cross at you being dragged back here.'

'Uncle Rafael wants to be here,' Matty said stoutly. He'd glued four pieces of wood together and was now chopping a nose cone out of Styrofoam with his hacksaw. His tongue was out a little, to the side; he was concentrating fiercely, but he was ready to join in this adult conversation. 'You both want to be here, don't you?'

'Because you're here,' Kelly said warmly. 'Yes, we do.'

Easy for you to say, Rafael thought, but out of deference to Matty he didn't say it.

They returned to work. Rafael concentrated on trying not to watch the pair of them. He had his own work to do and he was free to do it.

He'd rather watch them.

'Mama, Crater says you really can ride horses,' Matty said into the silence and the atmosphere in the workshop changed.

'I can't,' Kelly said shortly.

'He said you rode with my papa.'

'That was a long time ago. I've forgotten.'

'I could help you to remember,' Matty said, considering the shape of his cone and sandpapering a little off one side. 'Crater said he saw you the first morning you met my papa. He said Papa rode Blaze and you rode a horse called Tamsin. Crater said he saw you gallop up the mountain and he said you looked just like a prince and a princess.' He wrinkled his nose over his wobbly cone. 'How can you forget how to ride?'

'What happened to Tamsin?' Kelly asked before she could help herself.

'Papa sold her,' Matty said, disapproving. 'I asked once and he got angry and yelled at me. But there's more horses in the stables you could ride. When Papa had other ladies here they rode with him. You could ride one of their horses.'

'Matty, when I get on a horse,' Kelly said, concentrating on her plywood school bus, 'I forget to be sensible.'

'Me, too,' Matty said cheerfully. 'Papa says when I'm on a horse I'm a true prince. He says I have royal hands.' He looked down at his fingers, covered liberally with craft glue. 'What do you think he means by that?'

'You have blue blood,' Rafael said, trying to deflect attention from Kelly. She'd forgotten she was enjoying herself. She looked as if she wanted to bolt again, back to her books and her attic.

'I don't have blue blood, silly,' Matty reproved. He held up his forefinger for inspection—it had a sticking plaster over its tip. 'Yesterday, I tried to carve a nose cone with Uncle Rafael's big knife,' he told Kelly. 'There was a man in here talking to Uncle Rafael and I borrowed his knife without asking. My finger slipped and my blood was really, really red.'

'You didn't tell me,' Kelly said, startled, and thought that a real mother would have noticed.

'Uncle Rafael says it's our own secret,' he said with a guilty look at Rafael. Then, clearly anxious to change the subject, he turned to Rafael. 'Why don't you ride horses?'

'I just don't,' Rafael said flatly.

'Crater said you used to.'

'Crater says too much for his own good,' Rafael growled.

'He said you rode with your papa. But then your papa was hurt really badly on a horse. Was that when you stopped riding?'

'I stopped riding when I decided that riding royal horses was for royals,' Rafael said.

'You're royal.'

'Yes, but only a little bit royal. Not as royal as you, and I'd rather be a toy-maker.'

'You'll be a more important royal even than me until I'm twenty-five. I thought that and Crater said yes.'

'You're too clever for your own good.'

'Yes,' Matty said, satisfied with Rafael's opinion. 'So you'll be a very important prince for years and years. You could ride lots and lots in that time. We could get Mama another horse called Tamsin…'

'I don't want a horse,' Kelly managed.

'Why not?' Matty demanded, astonished. 'Papa said it's royal to ride horses. Good horses. He said it's in our blood. Real royals learn to ride before they walk.'

'But I'm not royal,' Kelly said flatly and set her bus down so hard the unset craft glue gave up its tenuous hold and it disintegrated into four separate pieces. 'I need to go back to work.'

'You haven't finished your bus,' Rafael said gently.

'No,' she whispered. 'And I'm not going to. I shouldn't be here. Discussing royal blood. Discussing royal horses. For a moment there I almost forgot who I am. Thank you, Matty, for reminding me.'

She should destroy every gown in her old suite, she thought savagely as she made her way back to her rooms. They were too much of a temptation. She should never have put on that little black dress. But there were so many more gowns, hanging there…

Waiting.

CHAPTER SEVEN

AFTERWARDS—after a dinner where Kelly hadn't appeared, pleading lack of appetite, when his mother had returned to the dower house, when Matty was well in bed, the servants had dispersed for the night and there seemed little risk of him being disturbed—Rafael wandered down to the stables. It was almost as if a magnet were pulling him. Matty's conversation had stirred something within him that he'd thought he'd buried long since.

Riding was royal? He'd never thought of it as such. Riding was the thing he'd done with his father, an extension of his legs, a merging of himself and the wonderful animal beneath him.

Until that day…

He remembered it still in his dreams. Kass had been here with a group of his friends, and Rafael, at fifteen, had been home from boarding school. His parents had always been uneasy about him being here when Kass was home. As Rafael had been. He'd loathed his ego-driven cousin and he hadn't needed his parents' encouragement to steer clear of him.

On the last day of his holidays Rafael and his father had risen early, planning to ride up to the lower foothills where they could see the sun rise over the Alps. It was something they'd done every time Rafael left—a small personal ritual that both pretended meant little but in truth they'd both loved.

They'd set out in the pre-dawn dimness, walking their

horses carefully through the woodland, speaking softly, half-awed by the early morning hush.

The shot had come from nowhere, zinging over the horses' heads, terrifying in the stillness. Later, Rafael had found the track of the bullet in the hide of his father's big gelding. The horse had been grazed across the neck. No wonder he'd reared, terrified, lunging backward, hurling his rider back with a savagery and ferocity no rider could cope with unprepared.

Rafael's father had been thrown against the trunk of an oak, an unyielding, implacable barrier. A lower branch had ripped his face. The solid trunk had crushed his spine.

Rafael had him in his arms when Kass and his cronies had burst through the undergrowth. It seemed they'd been drinking all night and had decided bed was boring—they'd do a little pre-dawn hunting before sleeping off the drink. They had been mounted on the royal horses—horseflesh worth millions.

Each and every one of them had been carrying a loaded gun, but only Kass's had been discharged. His friends had seemed appalled, but Kass had either been too drunk or too arrogant to care. He'd stared down at Rafael and his father and he'd sneered, 'You ride in my woods, you expect what you get. Surely he should know how to hold his seat by now. That's the commoner side of the family coming out.'

He'd turned his horse and cantered off, uncaring, leaving his companions, who had more conscience than he did, to cope with an almost fatally injured man and his distraught son.

It was the last time Rafael had been on a horse. The commoner side of him had decided right there that the non-royal part of him was the only side he cared about.

'You hate them as much as I do,' a soft voice said behind him and he whirled.

'Kelly.'

'Matty said he left his sweater here,' she said. She hesitated and then walked forward to where a crimson sweater lay crumpled on the oat bin.

'The servants would have fetched it.'

'I don't do servants.' She lifted the sweater, holding it against her almost as a shield. She walked back towards the door, but then she turned.

'Your mother told me you hate the horses,' she murmured. She was standing in the doorway, a shadow against the moonlight outside. 'She told me why.'

'I don't hate them. I just...don't ride. And you?'

'I don't ride either.'

'Crater said you do.'

'Crater said I did. Past tense.'

'You know why I don't ride,' he said, as a mare behind him nuzzled his hair, pressuring him to pay her attention. 'That's a bit lopsided.'

'I used to love horses,' she whispered. 'That's what got me into trouble.'

'I don't understand.'

'I don't...'

'Tell me, Kelly,' he said urgently. There was a moment's silence while she thought about it, and then she shrugged.

'The morning after I met Kass...' she ventured, not moving from her doorway. 'That first day, he came out of the castle dressed like you were that day back at the gold-diggings. In his dress sword and medals. He looked gorgeous. He seemed angry—but then he seemed to change. He sat by me as I worked and he asked question after question, like he was fascinated. I couldn't believe he was interested in me or my work. But he was and he took me out to dinner that night and I felt so special...you wouldn't believe. He asked me to sleep with him—well, of course—but I had enough sense to hold back on that one. And then he asked me to ride at dawn.'

'I...I see.'

'Maybe you do and maybe you don't,' she said listlessly. 'I was an only kid. My parents were academics—true academics—almost reclusive. My father had inherited enough to keep us financially secure, so they spent their lives studying. We lived in a house chock-full of books, as far from civilisation as it was possible to get while allowing for emergency dashes to get more books. Our cottage was on a hundred acres, near no one. I was an accident. The only reason I made it into the world was that my mother was so preoccupied with her studies she didn't realize she was pregnant until it was too late to do anything about it. They barely tolerated me. Their only pleasure in me was the amount I could learn, and my only pleasure was horses.'

'How did that happen?'

'You can't have a farm without animals,' she said, talking flatly, as if it was a dreary little story that affected someone else—some stranger. 'Or some method of keeping the grass down. My parents wanted the solitude but not the bother. So they rented the land to a local horse stud. There were horses everywhere. I loved them. The farmer's name was Matt Fledgling and it's no accident I agreed to call my son Matty for I'll remember Matt with gratitude for ever. Anyway, when I was about eight and spending hour upon hour talking to horses that were three times as tall as me, Matt took pity on me and taught me to ride. From then on, Matt let me help exercise his stock. He said, rightly or wrongly, that I was doing him a favour. His horses were mostly gallopers, racehorses, thoroughbreds, and I loved them. So when Kass asked me to ride... Oh, I said yes, and he put me on a mare who was the most wonderful horse I'd ever ridden. We went high up into the Alps. I was showing off. I didn't care. It was my skill, and I was with a prince who was taking notice of me, who was looking at me as if he thought I was beautiful. I can't tell you what an aphrodisiac it was.

'And then it all fell in a heap,' she whispered. 'My arrogance. My pride. My delight in showing off. Look where it got me. My parents said the only true friend anyone has is a book. Boring but dependable.'

'Boring's right,' Rafael said and she cast an angry glance at him.

'It's my choice.'

'It doesn't have to keep being your choice.'

'So what would you have me do?' she demanded.

'You might try being a human,' he snapped. 'Being a mother to your son.'

'I am.'

'You're not. Bolting up to your garret whenever things get personal. Staying in the background like the good little girl your parents wanted you to become. They've succeeded, haven't they, Kelly? You're as afraid to come out of your books as they are.'

'You won't get on a horse.'

'And you won't even make a wooden school bus. Hell, Kelly, life's not for fearing.'

'I don't fear…'

'You're terrified. Even your wardrobe full of fabulous gowns. You're terrified of them.'

'I do what I have to do to protect myself.'

'You do what you have to do to make yourself miserable. Kelly, you could be so much.'

'No.'

'It's true,' he said and, before she could react, he'd crossed the gap between them. She looked like a waif, he thought. A lost soul, out of place, wondering where on earth her place was.

'Maybe it's time you tried life,' he said as he reached forward to take her in his arms.

Third time lucky?

Third time true.

For Rafael, at least, this was a measured, certain step. He'd been watching her in the doorway, a fleeting shadow looking as if she might melt away into the night. And suddenly, as he'd watched her, the way he felt about her formed a tangible shape, a vision of what she could be if she could just set her fear aside.

Underneath the hurt and fear there was a woman, a lovely sprite of a woman, who could laugh with her son, who could dress to the nines, who could be a true royal princess and enjoy it. Who could live!

If only she could break through that armour plating she'd built so carefully around herself. A psychologist might have some hope of breaking it down—doing it the right way. Not Rafael. He had no weapons against it, other than the weapon his body was telling him he had—the fact that she was all woman and he was seeing her as she should be. The fact that she'd been Kass's woman, that she was someone he'd sworn never to touch, dissipated in that one moment of insight, and all that was left was warmth and heat and desire.

Quite simply, he wanted her as he'd wanted no other woman. The first time he'd seen her, in her appalling moleskin dungarees, in her mud and grime, he'd felt this strange link that had done nothing but grow and grow.

He reached her now, but he reached for her slowly, giving her room to back off if she would. For even now, even wanting her as much as he did, he'd not coerce her. He'd not frighten her any more than she'd been frightened.

But she was braver than she thought she was. He knew that about her. She was a strong, determined woman and under that cold armour she was as needful as he. Maybe even needful of the same thing. To hold herself aloof for six long years—longer—all her life, if you didn't think of that one appalling encounter with his cousin…

His hands caught her waist and he held. But, instead of kissing her straight away, he simply looked down at her, holding her at arm's length in the moonlight, asking her a wordless question with his eyes.

She gazed up at him, seemingly troubled. But not pulling

away. Asking her own questions—questions it seemed she couldn't answer.

'I very much want to kiss you,' he whispered and she gazed up at him in bewilderment.

'Rafael, why?'

'You're beautiful.'

'Right,' she said, self-mocking, and he looked down at her appalling sweater and smiled.

'We could take that off.'

'In your dreams.'

'You are in my dreams,' he whispered. 'Hell, Kelly, even in that damned disgusting garment you're in my dreams. Imagine where we'd be without it.'

'In diabolical trouble. Rafael, I don't want this.'

She didn't mean it. He could hear it in her voice—the uncertainty, the doubt.

'What is it about me you don't want?' he asked and waited for her to think about it. For his own doubts were dissolving.

He'd always thought of her as Kass's woman. He'd sworn he could never have anything to do with Kass, but he knew now that Kass was a tiny part of her past, a nightmare that maybe he could help vanquish. The more he knew of her, the more he saw her just as Kelly. Kelly in her disgusting dungarees, Kelly in her hoops and crinoline, Kelly in her Audrey Hepburn gown, Kelly with her tongue out to the side as she adjusted the sides of her school bus…

'I glued your bus together,' he told her. 'It works magnificently. Come and see it tomorrow.'

'I can't.'

'Why can't you?'

'I just…don't trust myself.'

'Then trust me.'

'How can I trust you?' she said with sudden asperity. 'I only came here because I thought you were a womanizing toad like all the de Boutaines are, and you'd deflect the media away from me and my son. Then you tell me you have a partner—how deceitful is that? And then she's not even your partner. She's as fed up with you as I am and deservedly so. Tell me how I can trust a man like that?'

'You can.'

'I know I can and it scares me stupid,' she said and her voice was a wail.

He smiled. He pulled her against him and held—simply held her—asking nothing, expecting nothing, just resting his chin on her hair, breathing in the scent of her, waiting for her heart to settle, for her to decide that yes, she could trust, yes, maybe she could lift her face and be kissed.

'It's too soon,' she whispered and he nodded gravely.

'Of course it's too soon.'

'I don't even know you.'

'You married Kass within…'

'See, even you,' she spat and hauled herself away from his grip and glared. He had, it seemed, made a bad tactical error. 'I married Kass fast. I was a fool. You think I'll jump into bed with you…'

'I haven't even asked…'

'You don't have to ask. You want. Don't you?'

'Yes,' he agreed gravely for he could do nothing else. He definitely wanted.

'And just because you're here you expect me to kiss you.'

'I'm just sort of hoping.'

'Well, stop hoping.'

'I can't,' he said honestly. 'Kelly, I can't. Like you, I thought this was crazy. I never thought I'd feel like this about you, but I do.'

'You're just doing it to suck me in.'

'Why would I do that?'

'Because you want someone to share the limelight. Share the throne.'

'You told me I had to pick gorgeous young women. Models and such. Not someone—' he hesitated, aware it behoved him to act cautiously '—in a really, really big sweater.'

She gave a gasp that ended on choked laughter, quickly suppressed. 'I won't share royalty. I won't share the limelight.'

'If you keep wearing that sweater you should be fine,' he reassured her, but her glare intensified.

'If I'm anywhere near you...'

'They'll take photographs of my sword. Not of you.'

'Rafael, I don't want it!'

'You don't want what, my love?'

'You,' she wailed. 'I don't trust myself. You stand there and you look so gorgeous and you smile at me, and I shouldn't have come to the stables—I shouldn't—but I saw you come and it was like I was just pulled. Matty's sweater was just an excuse. See? How stupid is that? And I know I just have to move an inch and you'll kiss me senseless.'

'Less than an inch.'

'And it's taken me years to get away from it,' she continued, refusing to be deflected. 'How can I re-establish a relationship with Matty when the whole royal goldfish bowl is operating around us? How can I make sense of what's happened?'

'Maybe we could kiss in private?' he said, without much hope and she glowered.

'Right. Any minute you'll ask me to get back on a horse.'

'You want to.'

'As you do,' she snapped.

'I don't.'

'Then it's for very sensible reasons. Like mine. Rafael, we're all wrong for each other.'

'We feel right.'

'I'm going to bed,' she snapped. The mare behind them gave a sharp whinny. She glanced past him at the horse and her expression softened.

'You still love them,' he said gently.

'Because I'm pathetic,' she admitted. 'I keep thinking of Tamsin.'

'Not of Kass?' he said, suddenly hopeful, and she shook her head.

'Not of Kass. Never of Kass. I think all this trouble started with a horse. I need my head read to be here now, with you. With the horses.'

'And yet you're here.'

'I...'

'Kelly,' he said and he placed his hands on either side of her face; he stooped and kissed her gently on the mouth. It was over before she could object, a feather kiss of reassurance, nothing more. Demanding nothing. Expecting nothing.

But the beginning of loving.

'Kelly, work it out,' he said softly. 'Take your time. I'll not rush you. For me...I think I'm falling in love. I didn't intend to. In fact, it's the last thing I intended. But hey, it's happening. I know what's before us is hard. But maybe...maybe we could do it together. Maybe we could even give this royalty thing a go. Given time. Given trust.'

'Yeah? Like riding again,' Kelly said and she knew she sounded bitter but she couldn't help it. 'How many years will it take before you get on a horse?'

'We don't have to ride before we trust each other.'

'We don't have to do anything,' Kelly said and then, with a tiny sound between a laugh and a sob, she tugged away. 'Please, Rafael, don't do this. I'm not royal. I never, ever should have learned to ride. I never, ever should have met Kass. And I never, ever should give my heart to anyone but my son. That's all I want. I'm not royal. I'm not part of this household. I'm just me.'

And, before he could say a word in response, she turned and fled.

He let her go. There was nothing else to do. For he even agreed with her.

He didn't want to be royal. How could he persuade Kelly to be something he didn't want himself?

He couldn't.

But things had changed. Or maybe they hadn't changed but he'd suddenly seen them for what they really were.

He'd suddenly seen inside his heart, and what he saw there… It was terrifying, but then again, he wouldn't want it any other way.

Kelly…

Kelly. Princess Kellyn Marie de Boutaine.

Could he persuade her to take on the royal role a second time? He must.

But how?

The Prince Regent of Alp de Ciel stood in the doorway of the stables, looking across the empty palace forecourt for a very long time.

CHAPTER EIGHT

WHERE there was a death and a new Crown Prince, there was also a coronation. Rafael had put it off for as long as possible but it had to be faced. In the days that followed, as Kelly retreated to her study, as the routine of the palace formed some semblance of normality, Crater's insistence that the coronation take place had to be considered.

'Matty's far too young,' Rafael growled when it was first brought up.

'You'll be at his side,' Crater told him. 'You make the vows on his behalf. It will be you who carries them out until he's twenty-five.'

'And what about his mother?'

'Kellyn wishes to be treated as a commoner,' Crater said. 'She'll attend but not in an official capacity.'

'She's still officially Kass's widow. She should have a place in the ceremony.'

'See if you can persuade her,' Crater said. 'I can't.'

And neither could Rafael. In truth, since the night in the stables he hardly saw her. Matty spent time with her, but she'd intensified her planned routine of study and self-containment.

She'd opened herself a little, he thought. In doing so she'd terrified herself and had then retreated.

He hated it. He hated that she hid herself away. Damn her parents, he thought, and wondered if it wasn't too late to find them and horsewhip them. Damn Kass for being dead so he couldn't do the same to him.

He felt like weeping on her behalf—for the stupid waste of it, for the fact that the laughing, happy woman she could be had been repressed in such a brutal manner.

And damn if the weather didn't agree with him. The glorious sunshine that had greeted their arrival had given way to steady dripping rain, making everything grey, dreary and waterlogged.

Not the best time for a coronation.

'There'll never be a perfect time,' Crater told him. 'But I've approached each of the royal houses of Alp d'Azuri, Alp d'Estella and Alp de Montez. The royals are all available at the end of this month. If we leave it much longer, Phillippa, the Princess Royal of Alp d'Estella, risks being confined with their first child. Max won't leave her. We need their presence.'

'Why?'

'If we're to gain any economic strength,' Crater said tentatively, 'we need to get the four countries working together. It was a dream of your father's. Until now I've hardly dared to hope the four Alp countries could become a Federation. But if you brought in reforms to bring Alp de Ciel into line with them politically…'

'Hey…'

'It would take commitment on your part,' Crater said. 'But you've come this far.'

'I don't want…'

'To commit yourself yet,' Crater said hurriedly, clearly not wanting him to veto a dream in an instant. 'But if we have the coronation soon and we have Raoul and Max and Nikolai and Rose here… It seems a wonderful opportunity.'

'You're steamrollering me.'

'No, sir,' Crater said sadly, 'I can't. I'm just saying it's a dream you might wish to pursue. Meanwhile, this coronation has to happen. The country's expecting it. Can I announce that it'll be on the twenty-sixth of this month?'

'Fine,' Rafael growled. 'But there's no way I can sit up in the back in the dark like someone else we could mention?'

'No, sir,' Crater said firmly. 'No chance at all.'

'Come and see.'

Kelly was mid-manuscript. The pages dated from the seventeenth century. They should be locked away in a temperature-controlled vault. Instead, they'd been sitting in the bookshelves here for the last four hundred years, an unnoticed, untouched treasure trove.

It was historian heaven. She should be in heaven.

Instead, she was lonely and bored. If she could pick Matty up and take him back to the goldfields it'd be great, she thought. Other than that, she had to bury herself in the studies her parents had loved, but every time there were voices in the forecourt she'd look down and sometimes it'd be Rafael and she thought her equilibrium had been messed with for ever.

Somehow she had to restore it. She had to forget those dangerous kisses and get on with…her boring life.

But here was Matty, at a time when he was scheduled for a lesson with Crater, bursting into her room and grabbing her hand and tugging her after him.

'Mama, the clothes are here. For the coronation. They're here, they're here, and Ellen says I have to try them on now, and there's a sword just like my Uncle Rafael's. It's splendid. Mama, you have to see.'

Bemused, she let him lead her downstairs, along the corridor to the workrooms behind the kitchen. She could hear the murmur of women's voices as she approached, and she relaxed. Matty's coronation outfit had been a source of interest and enthusiasm for the last week. Needlewomen had come in from Zunderfied and the castle had been humming.

'You should have something royal to wear,' Crater had said, reproving, but there was no way she was going down that road. She'd married in simple clothes in Paris. She'd never been a royal bride.

She wasn't royal now.

Matty was tugging her forward, hurrying her on. He reached the big oak doors of the workrooms and threw them open.

Rafael was there.

She stopped breathing.

He was gorgeous. Stunning. Breathtakingly amazing.

A real prince.

His clothes fitted like a second skin. Deep black leggings—skintight. Glossy Hessian boots, jet-black with tassels. What looked to be a morning jacket, but inset with red, black and gold panels, intricately embroidered. The royal crest was emblazoned on the jacket breast. A deep gold sash lay across his breast. There were rows of medallions, epaulettes, gold tassels…

A sword lay at his side, longer than the one she'd seen in Australia, its grip a cunningly wrought gold three-dimensional symbol of the royal house of de Boutaine.

His black curls were flicked back as they always were, raked back by fingers that worried. He'd been gazing in the mirror, his cool grey eyes smiling, half mocking. As the door opened and he turned to see who entered, his smile still lingered.

He was laughing at himself, she thought, but there was no way she was laughing.

Rafael…

It was as much as she could do not to sink into a curtsey. As it was, she gripped the door handle and held.

'It's a bit much,' he said, smiling across at her, and she thought wildly, Don't do that—don't smile, don't!

'Mine's just like it,' Matty said with deep satisfaction. 'Aren't we gorgeous?'

'Gorgeous,' she agreed faintly.

'What will you be wearing, Mama?' Matty asked. He crossed to where Ellen was waiting to help him into his costume. 'It'll have to be something very beautiful to match my Uncle Rafael and me.'

'I couldn't come near matching you,' she whispered.

'But you will wear a pretty dress.'

'Maybe,' she said. Thinking of those gowns. Thinking of what had happened the one night she'd worn one.

'One of the pretty ones you wore on the goldfields?' Matty said hopefully. He was in leggings now, turning to the mirror and sticking his small chest out with manly pride. 'Are they pretty enough for the coronation, Uncle Rafael?'

'No,' Rafael said.

'Then it's just as well I didn't bring them,' she retorted.

'If you please, ma'am…'

There were four women in the room. One had been adjusting the base of Rafael's coat. Two were sitting at the table sewing, and Ellen was helping Matty on with his vest. But now she interjected. She rose stiffly to her feet and stood, unsure. 'I…we have a suggestion.'

'A suggestion?' Kelly frowned and glanced suspiciously at Rafael, but he was looking as in the dark as she was.

'The clothes Prince Rafael and Prince Mathieu will wear are traditional. We wondered…seeing you're a historian…' Ellen gave a nervous gasp, looked to her friends for support and crossed to the corner of the room. There was a mannequin there, shrouded with dust-sheets.

Ellen cast Kelly another nervous glance and then she tugged off the dust-sheet.

The dress was breathtaking. It looked almost Elizabethan, a creation of the most exquisitely cut gold and ivory silk, skilfully set over a rich crimson underskirt. The neckline was almost square, cut low to reveal the swell of breasts. Filigree sleeves were gathered into elegant lace wristbands in the finest of gold. The waist cinched into a deep V, designed to make any woman's waist look tiny.

And the embroidery. Such embroidery—all fire, swirls

and curves. The gown shimmered and glistened as Ellen pulled the dust-sheet free, almost assuming a life of its own. There were hoops underneath, spreading the dress almost as wide at the hem as the gown was high. There was a train—Ellen was setting it out now. It was embroidered to represent a golden dragon, running from waist to maybe ten metres behind.

Kelly gasped with shock. She couldn't help herself. She stepped forward, almost reverently, hardly brave enough to touch it.

'It's…'

'Over two hundred years old,' Ellen breathed. 'When the old Prince was pressuring Kass to be married, he ordered it to be restored. But then…then Kass married you.'

'Not a princess,' she whispered.

'But you are a princess,' Ellen said stubbornly. 'You should have had the right to wear it. You have the right to wear it now. We've measured it against your gowns here. It'll take very little alteration.'

'Wow,' Rafael breathed. 'Kelly, you have to wear it.'

'I don't,' she said, feeling so out of her depth she was close to tears. 'I'm not royal.'

'No, but you are,' Matty repeated. 'You were married to my father. You're a real princess.'

'I'm a commoner.'

'You're Australian,' Ellen said with satisfaction.

'So what?' She was bewildered. Maybe she even sounded angry, but she couldn't help it. The sight of the dress was so awesome it took her breath away. And the way Rafael was looking at her didn't help. Plus the way Rafael looked…She had a sudden vision of the two of them. Rafael in his dress uniform and she in this dress.

No and no and no.

But Ellen was speaking. She had to listen. What did being an Australian have to do with anything?

'The palace gossip was that was why Kass chose you,' Ellen said, answering her question before she'd framed it. 'When Kass's father heard of Prince Raoul's marriage to Jessica in Alp d'Azuri to a commoner—to an Australian—he laughed about it. He said Raoul was a fool and the country would never accept such a marriage. And then you and your team were working so close to here…'

'So he just picked me,' Kelly whispered.

'And we were so excited,' Ellen said stoutly. 'The people of Alp d'Azuri have had nothing but prosperity since their prince's marriage. We had such hopes…'

'Of me?'

'You were our princess from the time Prince Kass married you,' Ellen retorted. 'We hated that you went away. We've always wanted you to come home. And we hated that the old Prince made us put this gown away.' She faltered and bent her head over the train, pretending to straighten a crease. 'We… we need a royal family.'

'You have Rafael and Matty,' Kelly whispered.

'It's not a family.'

'Leave her,' Rafael said, sounding suddenly angry. 'Ellen, this isn't fair.'

'No, sir.'

'You don't need to defend me,' Kelly told him.

'Don't I?'

'No,' she flashed, and he grinned that heart-stopping grin and lifted his sword from its scabbard.

'I guess it's not me alone. You have two men to do it now,' he said, seemingly determined to turn what had been too serious a moment into a joke. 'The decision about the dress can be made later. Matty, we need you to have some fencing lessons. *En garde, petit…*'

'Not here,' Ellen shrieked as Matty picked up his sword and giggled. 'Not near the dress.'

But Rafael was changing the subject away from the dress,

away from her, distracting them all from a topic she found too hard. She could merge into the background, she thought thankfully.

He was protecting her.

But…but…

We had such hopes.

She'd never thought of it from the people's point of view. She'd always believed they'd thought her a tramp. Someone they were lucky to be rid of.

She swallowed. Ellen had caught Matty's sword which, mercifully, had a blunt end. She'd put it firmly aside. Now she was manoeuvring him into a jacket that matched Rafael's.

Her two royal princes.

A family?

No. No, they weren't. Matty was her family, but he also belonged to another.

She was on the outside of that other, not even wanting to look in.

The dress was there. A dare. A challenge.

A role that was already hers.

'Come on in, the water's fine,' Rafael said softly and she blinked at him in astonishment.

'I don't…'

'I know.'

'I can't.'

'You can.'

'Rafael…'

And then the earth moved.

It was a mere tremor—a shift that made the light above Ellen's head sway slightly on its long lead from the high ceiling. A vase sitting on the edge of the mantelpiece slipped sideways and crashed on to the hearth. It left Kelly feeling just slightly off balance, as if she'd stood up too fast and felt a little dizzy, but then balance was restored and things were okay.

But the light was still swinging, casting weird shadows over the half dressed Matty. Ellen was staring upward, mesmerized by the swinging light, but Kelly was over the far side of the room in an instant, grabbing Matty to her, holding him close.

The light was still swaying. The vase was still smashed on the hearth.

'Outside,' Rafael said harshly into the stunned silence. 'Get outside, everyone—into the forecourt and away from the building.'

He didn't have to say it twice. Kelly was already moving, carrying Matty as she ran. Rafael moved to intercept her but she shook her head and kept running.

'We're fine. Get everyone out.'

She'd experienced this before—an earth tremor. It had been a small quake, measuring three on the Richter scale, and it had shaken some of her parents' beloved books from the shelves. That had been all the damage.

That was all this would be, she told herself as she ran.

'Mama…' Matty quavered.

'It's just an earth tremor,' she said, not pausing. She could put him down but he was in bare feet and she had him in her arms and that was where it felt like he belonged. She was running down the vast stone steps that led out to the forecourt. Behind her, she could hear Rafael shouting orders.

'Assemble outside, everyone, and I mean everyone. Ellen, take a roll call. Crater, go over to the dower house and see if my mother's okay. Get her outside too. Marsha, the dogs are already outside, you go back inside and I'll come after you with a whip…'

It was just an earth tremor. A minor one. Kelly sank to the ground on the lawns beside the forecourt and looked up at the towering castle walls. This castle had stood intact for centuries. It was clearly intending to stay intact for longer. There was no movement.

'We wait outside,' Rafael commanded into the morning stillness. 'We wait.'

So they waited. Fifteen minutes. Twenty. Luckily, the constant rain of the past few days had given way to warm sunshine so waiting wasn't a hardship. Rafael had them all gathered together. He was still dressed in his royal finery.

Laura ducked back into the dower house—against her son's orders—and fetched shoes for Matty. He accepted them with gratitude, left the safety of his mother's arms—he'd clung really close while the tremors had been happening—and started to be a little prince again.

'We've had an earthquake,' he said importantly. 'An earthquake's very dangerous.'

'An earth tremor,' Kelly corrected. 'Not so bad.'

'What's the difference between an earthquake and an earth tremor?'

'A tremor happens a lot,' Kelly said. 'When a little bit of the earth moves way, way down deep and everything on the top settles a bit. In an earthquake a whole lot of the earth settles. Your Uncle Rafael says we should stay outside until we're sure it won't get any worse but I think it's okay.'

Everyone else obviously did too. After half an hour standing in the sun Rafael decided it seemed safe to return to normal.

'The phone lines are down.' Crater was fretting. 'There must be damage somewhere.'

'I'll have someone check in the village,' Rafael said, but as he did there was a shout from outside the castle gates.

There was a boy running. Shouting. Rafael stepped forward to meet him.

Rafael looked like a man in charge, Kelly thought, in his full royal regalia, his dress sword still in its scabbard, his whole bearing royal. The boy ran naturally to him. He was a teenager, sixteen maybe, wide-eyed with shock and breathless with worry.

'Sir,' he gasped in his own language. 'Sir, we're in trouble.

The landslip… There's been a huge landslip above the village. The houses… There are people buried. The road's blocked. Sir, you have to come. Please.'

Rafael gripped the boy's shoulder while he told his story. The boy looked to Rafael to take charge but Rafael's wonderful uniform didn't give him the local knowledge he needed now.

He'd hardly been home since he was fifteen. Crater knew the land, the people, the emergency drills. He was in his seventies but he stepped forward now and started giving orders.

The road was cut. They needed to get an assessment of what the damage was. He'd send a team to climb high above the castle to where a man could see right across the valley.

'I'll go,' Rafael said. 'I have radio gear in the workshop. I can use that to contact the outside world if the telephones stay cut. Crater, I'll give you a handset as well so I can get back to you.'

'You won't get up there.'

'I'll take a horse,' Rafael said and Kelly gasped. For him to ride again…

'The villagers might need you,' Crater said, not hearing the implications of what Rafael had said, thinking only of what was before them.

'I'll get back down and help dig, whatever you want, as soon as I can.'

'You're our prince,' Crater said obliquely. 'We'll want you in the village.'

'I'll be there as soon as I can,' Rafael said. 'Kelly, love, make sure things stay safe here. Any more tremors, you're in charge.'

She was in charge but there was nothing to do. Everyone else left. Even Laura disappeared, donning stout walking boots and going with Ellen and Marguerite down to the little village hospital to see if they could be of help.

Kelly stayed with Matty.

'We should be down in the village too,' Matty said, more and more insistently as the afternoon wore on.

'We'd just get in the way,' she told him. 'Crater's taken everyone who can dig with him. Your Uncle Rafael will be down there by now. We need to look after the castle.'

'It's cowardly to stay in the castle when our people need us.'

It did feel wrong. But every able-bodied man and woman had joined the team to go to the village, so Kelly needed to stay here with her son. Even though it killed her not to know what was happening. Where Rafael was. What had happened in the village.

'I'm the Prince and you're the Princess,' Matty told her, deeply disapproving of her decision to stay where they were. 'Crater says it's the job of a prince to lead his people.'

'You're five years old and I'm not a princess,' she said helplessly. 'Maybe we could play Scrabble.'

He looked at her calmly, figuring out whether she meant it or not and intelligent enough to see that she did.

'Okay,' he said at last. 'Will we play in your room?'

'I…yes.' Retire to her attic. 'Why not?'

'The Scrabble set's in the nursery,' he told her. 'I'll fetch it.'

Only he didn't. Kelly checked on the dogs in the kitchen—the dog Marsha had been worried about was a bitch about to whelp and Kelly had promised to check on her every half hour. The bitch was lying peaceably in her basket, with three pups already at teat.

'See, you have your priorities right,' Kelly said, bending to fondle the big dog's ears. 'Home and hearth. It'd be good if we could be of help down in the village but a mother's place is with her kids.'

The dog gave her a long lick, which cheered Kelly immeasurably. She walked up the stairs to her attic, but when she reached it Matty wasn't there yet.

She wanted to tell him about the pups.

Maybe he'd had trouble finding the Scrabble set, she thought. She walked downstairs, along to the nursery.

She was worried, and not just about Matty. She hadn't heard anything about what was happening out in the village. No one had come back. Rafael was out there somewhere in his magnificent uniform doing heroic stuff. Laura and Crater were down in the village helping. She was stuck here minding Matty.

Only where was Matty?

He wasn't in the nursery.

Suddenly she felt sick.

'Matty?' she yelled, but her voice echoed ominously around the empty halls.

'Matty…'

A clatter of horse hooves on the cobbles below drew her to the window.

'Matty!'

If he heard her scream he didn't acknowledge it. He was on a horse. Somehow he'd managed to saddle one of the smaller mares. He was firm in the saddle, his hands keeping good control, turning the mare's head towards the gate and digging his small heels into her flanks.

'Matty,' she screamed again but he was gone.

Out of the gate towards the village.

For a long moment she simply stared at the gate as if she couldn't believe what she'd seen. But she'd seen all right. Through the open window she could hear the faint clip-clop of the mare's hooves as she disappeared from sight.

Matty was gone. Into a situation of which she knew nothing.

Her son.

Since Kass had kicked her out, Kelly had had her escape in a century past, a time warp that had held her close, protecting her from outside forces. Here she'd done her best to create a sanctuary again, where the outside world belonged to those who wanted it.

She didn't want the outside world. But her son was riding into it, with the heart of a prince.

Something played back in her mind, some crazy lesson he'd repeated to her when she'd said it didn't make much difference that he was a prince. When she'd talked to him of the possibility of staying in Australia.

'They're my people. I should be with them,' he'd said sternly. 'Crater says when there's peril that's when the people need their prince. He said in World War Two the English King and his Queen and their two little princesses should have gone to America to be safe. Only they didn't. They stayed, and every time there was bombing the King would be there, just to say to everyone be brave.'

He was right. King George's commitment to his people had possibly been the difference between submission or victory.

But Matty was too young to make such a call. He was her son. He was five years old.

He was her prince.

And so was Rafael. Somewhere out there was Rafael. With…his people? While she stayed here like some Cinderella, hiding in her attic. Being no one.

Not even brave enough to put on a dress.

All these thoughts took no more than seconds—seconds while her frightened mind came to terms with what had happened and what now must happen.

She wheeled away, taking the stairs at a run, across the forecourt to the stables. Tamsin would no longer be here but other horses would. The road would be impassable for cars. She had to ride.

She might be a nuisance in the village. She couldn't see how her presence and Matty's presence could make a difference. Her reasons for staying separate from the royal household might still hold true.

But Matty…Prince Mathieu…and Prince Rafael, Crown Prince and Prince Regent of Alp de Ciel, had decided otherwise.

What was their royal princess to do but support them?

She hit mud at the first bend after the castle and her mare reacted with alarm, seeing the damage before she did. She'd been looking ahead, not at the road, and the horse edged sideways, rearing in fright.

She looked to where the horse was looking and looked again.

There was seeping, oozing mud in the woodlands on the higher side of the road. The road was still clear but it looked as if a flood of mud-laden water had slopped down the mountainside.

The horse—a mare whose name above her stable door decreed she was Gigi—must have come this way often. She knew it was different now. She whinnied in nervousness as Kelly settled her and forced her to keep on.

They slowed. Matty was somewhere ahead but the road now had patches of silt, with small stones and bigger rocks in their path.

How fast would Matty have come? Where would he go?

And where was Rafael?

There was no other road than this. She had to follow it.

Where was everyone?

'Come on, Gigi. Come on, girl. You can do it.'

The horse flattened her ears, but responded to her reassurance and picked her way on.

And then they were at the outskirts of the village and fear was starting to wash over in waves that made her tremble. She was frantically trying to suppress it. Horses sense fear and she had to keep Gigi calm. But… But…

The road ran through the foothills of the mountains. Above and beyond, she could see rough, jagged and newly formed scarring, a mass of ripped earth as if a great chunk of the hillside had slipped from its moorings.

There was silence as they approached the township. The mare was whinnying in fear and it took all Kelly's skill to keep her from turning home.

She couldn't go home. Somewhere ahead was Matty. He'd be moving faster than she was. He wouldn't have an adult's fear that the horse might slip on loose rocks; that he might be thrown.

He was heading for the village. Heading to his people. Was Rafael before him?

And then she rounded the final curve in the hills before the village, and as she did she drew in her breath in horror.

The full extent of the slip could now be seen. It was a great gash on the hillside, starting as a thin wedge maybe a mile above, reaching down to a slash of tossed earth maybe half a mile wide. It was as if a great chunk of the earth had simply slid out from where it should have been and lurched its way towards the village.

The village… Dear God, the village.

She could see massive destruction. Huge trees uprooted, cast aside by the power of the earth.

Houses…

What had been houses.

She put her hand to her mouth, feeling ill. She wanted to stop. She wanted to block it out.

She forced herself to look.

There were people. From here they were in the distance, like ants over an anthill, looking insignificant, moving aimlessly, or simply standing on the great mounds of tumbled earth.

She saw a red coat—a sliver of crimson on a horse…

Matty.

Sick at heart, she motioned her mare forward. 'It's okay, Gigi. It's okay.'

Only of course it wasn't. She could see from here…

Houses crushed. Roads impassable…

She pressed on. The ants became people, tearing at their

houses, working furiously. The mud was everywhere. They didn't notice her as she passed—tragedy was everywhere.

Matty…

She reached him. He hadn't seen her approach. He'd stopped in the middle of the road. He was still on his horse, staring before him, his eyes wide with terror.

There was another horse beside his. He was holding the reins in his hand. He looked crazily small so near such a great creature.

The horse was Blaze. Kass's stallion.

How had Blaze reached here?

Rafael?

'Matty,' she whispered and the child turned to her, his face devoid of all colour. She had him, reaching across to take him from his horse, hauling him into her arms whether he willed it or not. He came but he was still enough of a horseman—enough of a prince—to keep the reins of both the other horses in his hand.

Before them were people, men and women, attacking a vast mound of debris with their hands. The silence was broken by sobbing.

A sign on a flattened gate told her what horror they were facing.

A school. Crushed.

'Matty,' she whispered into his hair and he crumpled against her, his face soaked with tears.

'My Uncle Rafael,' he whispered against her breast. 'He's gone in there. He's gone in there and the stuff moved on top of him and no one can get him out.'

CHAPTER NINE

KELLY had spent the last five years on the goldfields. She'd panned for gold and she'd dug. Sure she'd been a research historian, she'd spent hours at her desk, but she could handle a spade with the best of the men.

She also knew the basics of mining. She'd researched every shaft dug back at the theme park and they were authentic. She knew what the miners had done to make themselves safe a hundred and fifty years ago, and she knew what they'd had to do to make the tourist mines even safer now.

She handed Matty to the care of the women. She took a deep, steadying breath, looked at the heap of sludge they were facing and decided they risked more people being buried alive the way they were going.

The school house was built against a cliff face. The sludge had washed down the mountain from the other direction. In most places it had swept over and onward, but here the cliff face had stopped it, so it had mounded up in a vast heap, completely obscuring the school buildings.

It was one vast, unstable mass. To dig in without shoring it up as they went was the way of disaster. She rolled up her sleeves and started issuing orders.

Amazingly, the men listened. Amazingly, they did what she said.

Matty couldn't dig but he wouldn't shift from where he

was. The older people in the town would have taken him into one of the undamaged homes but Matty refused. He stayed, taking care of the horses. Wanting desperately to dig himself if only his elders would let him.

The damage in the town was awful, Kelly learned as she worked, but not as catastrophic as she'd first thought. Yes, houses were crushed, but the landslip had started high up. The tremors had been felt before it had hit, and most people had been outside. The mass had moved slowly, giving people time to run to higher ground.

Two elderly couples had been killed instantly when their houses had crashed around them. There were injuries—people had been hit by the sliding mud—but the worst of the rush of earth had been over before it had hit the town.

But the school… It was on the outskirts, which meant it had been one of the first buildings to be hit. To have the children run to higher ground would have been impossible.

'There's a basement underneath,' Kelly was told by the grim-faced mayor. 'We're thinking the teacher panicked and had everyone head for the basement. Then the mud hit the front, blocking the exit. When we got here, we could hear screaming. Prince Rafael…he took a torch in. He could just make it in through a gap in the debris and we thought we could get everyone out that way. Only then the whole lot shifted and the roof came down. And now…'

'You can't hear?'

'Muffled stuff when everything's still,' the mayor told her. 'We're hoping against hope they're all down there. Twenty kids and their teacher and our Prince. And all we can do is dig.'

'Is help coming?' she asked, trying not to sound terrified.

'The roads are all blocked,' the mayor told her. 'The tremors have been felt all the way to the border so outside help isn't going to happen. We can't get equipment in.'

So they dug. It sounded simple. Moving a small mountain

of mud from over a basement. Trying not to do any more damage. Working from the outside in, so no more weight would go on to the basement roof—if indeed it had held.

There were people alive in there. When the mayor held up his hand for silence they could hear faint cries but the mass of mud stifled everything.

'If Rafael's down there...he has a radio,' Kelly said as she dug and the men around her looked at each other and didn't respond.

If he had a radio then he'd be able to communicate. He wasn't communicating. He wasn't...he couldn't be...

She dug.

It was mind-numbing work, with nothing to alleviate the fact that tons of mud had to be shifted by hand. No one thought of bringing in machinery—to cause vibrations on top of the basement would be crazy. Care was taken to distribute diggers so no further pressure was on the mass, making the risk of further falls as small as possible.

Fatalities elsewhere had been accounted for—the injured were being cared for. This was the only area where people had yet to be found.

There were twenty children missing, one schoolteacher—and Rafael.

The workers who'd been here when Rafael had gone in were grim-faced. They'd cleared an area around the stairway into the basement. What they thought had happened was that the front of the building had collapsed. The rear of the building was set hard against the cliff face, leaving no form of exit. So the children must have fled for safety downstairs.

They'd heard them calling clearly when they'd first arrived. They were safe, they were okay. So they'd hauled the mass of timber blocking the path away. As it had cleared, the teacher below had wanted to send children up, but Rafael had stopped them.

'Let me try it first,' he'd growled. 'I don't want a child halfway up if that mass above decides it's unstable.'

Which was pretty much what had happened. Armed with a torch, Rafael had disappeared into the gloom. And then another tremor had struck and the entire building and some of the cliff face behind had subsided, leaving a mountain of debris with no one knew what underneath.

Had Rafael reached the safety of the basement? Was the basement still safe? They could hear muffled cries through the rubble but it was too thick to decipher words.

Please…

Please.

Kelly dug as she'd never dug in her life before. But all around…

People were deferring to her.

'What should we do?'

'Should we send for bulldozers?'

'It doesn't seem safe but if you think we should…'

It didn't seem safe and no, she didn't think they should but that they deferred to her was astonishing. She was a historian.

A historian who knew about mine management, she conceded, but they didn't know that. She found herself snapping orders—sending people to find shoring timbers, assessing load strengths, standing back from digging every few moments to see the whole picture…

She did know what to do. The history of gold-mining was littered with tragedy and she knew enough now to prevent mindless tunnelling from parents desperate to reach their children at any cost.

But it wasn't her role as historian that these people were reaching out to, though, she thought as she dug. It was her role as royal.

Like Matty, standing white-faced and grim just out of reach of the diggings. Every other small child had been hauled away, well out of danger. Matty had a right to be here.

Matty's duty was to be here. He knew it. It'd been instilled from birth by those around him. Today he'd acted with a gut instinct that seemed almost inbred.

'My people need me.'

Royalty might be anachronistic, totally outdated, unfair. But right now it was what these people needed.

She dug on, and the picture came to her again of the young King during the Second World War, touring the diggings. Winston Churchill with his cigar, standing on a heap of bomb site rubble with King George beside him. The King and the Prime Minister, with the people they represented.

If she left now…if she took Matty, as was her right, and left this place, left the digging to others…

It could be done. She could give orders as to how to shore up the tunnel they were working on. She could take Matty home, cuddle him until the colour came back into his face, maybe play with Rafael's toys until he forgot…

She could never do such a thing. Because Rafael was under there? Because Rafael had kissed her?

Yes, but more than that.

Because there were twenty children and their teacher trapped?

Yes, but more than that too.

Matty was right. What he had was an age-old heritage—the leadership of his people. And, by marrying Kass, she'd inherited it as well.

Sure, she could walk away. Royals had done that since time immemorial—had walked away from their royal duties, had elected to live a normal life.

But… But…

But the good ones stayed.

'The sounds are getting clearer,' someone yelled. 'There's more'n one alive.'

'That's great. So slow down,' she yelled. 'And let's increase the rate of supports. No unnecessary risks.'

'No, ma'am.'

The good ones stayed. Queen Elizabeth, taking on the throne as a young mother, a young bride. Overseeing change in the monarchy so the people had a say in the government, so monarchy wasn't an absolute.

Doing what she saw as her duty, no matter what. And in times of crisis…

Giving a focus. A sense of leadership. A sense of continuity, regardless of personal grief.

Kelly's hands had blisters on blisters. She could stop. Men were taking turns. But the fact that she was beside them was driving them forward with renewed energy. She didn't understand it, but the fact was that monarchies had endured for century after century and here she was, a princess…fighting for her two princes. One behind her, staring at his mother as if he'd like to be part of her. He'd be digging in a heartbeat, she knew, if she let him. Matty. Mathieu. Her own little prince.

And below ground…

Rafael.

They weren't digging indiscriminately. As every layer was worked through they probed cautiously before they dug, just in case…just in case…

In case Rafael hadn't made it. In case he was trapped before the entrance to the basement. In case his body was caught up in this mass of mud and sludge and mess.

The thought had her choking and fiercely hauling her arm across eyes that welled with tears before she could stop them. She paused, fighting for breath.

'Are you okay, Your Highness?' a man asked beside her and she turned and saw his eyes were red and swollen.

'You have a child down there?' she whispered.

'Two,' he muttered. 'Heidi. She's eight. And Sophie, who's six.'

'Then we have no time for tears,' Kelly managed and wiped her face again, this time with a savage determination she knew would stay with her to the end. 'We only have time to dig.'

* * *

And in the end…

In the end it happened so fast she could scarcely believe it. One minute they were digging, the next they'd reached what seemed a vast, solid door. Six feet across, eight feet long. Mounded with debris.

They'd dug across and down, but not tunnelling. They were open cut mining, completely removing the mass of dirt above and shoring the sides. It made things slower but surely safer. To tunnel in these unstable conditions would be madness, Kelly had decreed, and the red-eyed men and women around her had agreed.

So now they had a trench thirty feet long, starting at the edge of the mass of debris and working in, dropping fast, so the sides were twelve, fourteen feet high. The trench was big enough for two men to work side by side, while those behind cleared and passed the rubble back.

And now…The last few spadefuls had exposed the slab. The men in front edged shovels sideways, exploring.

Hitting wood.

'It's holding the whole mess off us,' a man's voice called weakly from below, and Kelly's heart seemed to almost stop. The voice was muffled but finally they could make out words. And the voice…the voice was surely Rafael's.

'Your Highness…' someone called.

'We're okay. Take your time. Get it right,' he called.

'Madame Henry?' The man beside Kelly—Heidi and Sophie's dad—could barely speak through tears as he called down to the schoolteacher they hoped was still safe.

'The children are all here.' The teacher must be elderly, Kelly thought. She sounded little and acerbic and frightened—and also just a wee bit bossy. 'Prince Rafael got down here just in time before the mess came down. When it started moving he blocked the door so it couldn't crash through but then the stuff moved again and he was caught…'

'Rafael was caught?' Kelly demanded, tugging loose debris free with her hands. They were so close…

'I'm fine,' Rafael called from through the rubble but she knew from his muffled voice that he wasn't.

'We have to get this free.'

'We take our time.' It was Sophie and Heidi's dad, pulling her back, putting both hands on her shoulders and setting her aside. 'We don't undo Prince Rafael's work—your work—by moving that slab until we're sure the land will hold.'

'Y-yes.'

'You've done enough,' he said gently and then looked at the seemingly impenetrable slab and sighed. 'And so have I. Everyone behind us is willing. We let those whose hearts aren't behind the slab make the decisions from now on.'

He was right. It nearly killed her but he was right. She was ushered out of the trench. Matty was waiting, staring at the entrance to the trench as if by will alone he could bring them out alive. She hugged him close. She was soaked to the skin, coated in thick, oozing mud. Women came forward carrying blankets. They would have ushered her away but she'd have none of it.

Rafael…Rafael…

But finally her prayers were answered. Finally the slab was moved. They inched it from its resting place with almost ludicrous caution, moving with so much care that it took them three long hours—hours when Matty and Kelly seemed to turn to stone.

But finally it was done. There was a growl of satisfaction as the trench stayed intact, that the shoring timbers held. And then the first child—a tiny girl, coated with thick, oozing clay, was handed up through the gap. She was grabbed by willing hands. A faint scream sounded behind them as the child was handed back, hand over hand, until she reached the end of the trench.

The last hands to reach her were her parents.

'Evaline,' a woman's voice said brokenly, and there was the sound of a man's hoarse sobs.

But those in the trench weren't hearing. Already more children were being handed out. Speed was of the essence here. This mass of mud and debris was unstable to say the least. It only needed one more earth tremor…

They had a chain operating. The children were being lifted out. There was no talking—just solid effort.

They seemed okay, Kelly thought, dazed. She'd left Matty with the women again and was at the neck of the trench where it narrowed down into the cavity under the slab. But she wasn't strong enough to be part of the chain handing back the children, so she slipped back to lean against the shoring timber and simply watched. Every face appearing at the hole under the slab she watched with terror. She'd forgotten to breathe. She'd forgotten to do anything.

So few injuries… There were cuts and bruises, but most of the children could put their arms up to be lifted. Most could cling to their rescuers. Most could reach out to their parents and sob and hold and sink into their parents' embrace as if they'd never let go.

One or two were hurt. There was one small boy with what looked like a broken arm. He whimpered as he was pulled out, but he still managed a smile when his mother whispered his name. There was an older boy with a nasty laceration to his cheek. 'I had to help Prince Rafael move the door,' he said with weak bravado, and it looked doubtful that he'd let such a wound be stitched. His parents were clasping him with pride and there was a shining pride in his own eyes. This was clearly a hero's wound. He'd helped his prince save the children.

Rafael…

Her heart was whispering the word, over and over. She glanced back along the line and saw Matty. His face was as white as hers. He was seeing all these happy endings but, like Kelly, he wanted his own.

She should ask. She should say to the boy with the cut face, What of Rafael?

She couldn't.

'That's twenty,' someone said in a gruff voice that wasn't quite concealing tears. 'Just the schoolteacher and the Prince to go.'

'You,' said a fierce woman's voice from under the slab, and the weary voice came in reply.

'When you're all out I'll be out but not before. Stop wasting time.'

'You're hurt.'

'Go!'

He was hurt. She'd known it. Dear God…

Hands were reaching up, small woman's hands. The schoolteacher was grasped and tugged free and hugged fiercely by the man who'd pulled her up.

'Romain, I have my dignity,' the little lady managed in between hugs and the men laughed and ignored her dignity and handed her back along the line as if she was also a child. As if she were made of the most precious porcelain…

And then… And then…

One hand came through the gap under the slab. A man's hand with a signet ring she recognized.

'Both hands,' the man at the front said, in a voice that was none too steady. 'We need a grip.'

'One hand.' Rafael's voice was muffled and pain-filled.

'You want us to come under and help?'

'No one comes under this slab. Get me out of here.'

'Rafael,' Kelly cried before she could help herself.

'Kelly,' Rafael muttered. 'What the hell are you doing here?'

'Come out and find out,' she whispered.

'Will we hurt you pulling you out?' someone asked him.

'A lot less than if this whole thing collapses.' His one hand was the only thing in sight and he pushed it higher. 'Pull.'

Each of the children and the schoolteacher too, had been lifted. But there was no one to lift Rafael. They were tugging him up by his one arm, holding his entire weight as they pulled.

He was hurt—badly hurt, Kelly thought, listening to his voice. But unless he'd let someone in to him…And he wouldn't. Their torches showed little—his mud-slicked face and blackness.

'Pull,' he ordered again and there was nothing to do but obey. And he came. He emerged into daylight with a savage groan, sliding out on to the floor of the trench and lying there, gasping for breath.

Kelly was in there, scrambling through the mud, on her knees, touching his face, scarcely able to breathe.

'Rafael.'

'Kell…' he gasped as she wiped mud from his eyes with her shirt, as she wept. 'Our magnificent Princess Kellyn. Of course. A mine manager. I knew you'd make a magnificent princess.'

And then he passed out.

CHAPTER TEN

RAFAEL'S shoulder was dislocated. His leg was badly gashed. He'd be okay.

Officialdom took over. The little village had a very competent doctor and two efficient nurses. They carried him into the nearest intact house, put his shoulder back into place, stitched his leg, cleaned him up as much as they could and then ordered bedrest.

'When I'm back at the castle,' Rafael growled.

Kelly and Matty had been relegated to the background. They'd sat at the kitchen table while the women of the house plied them with soup and towels and as much comfort as they could. But Kelly's hands didn't stop shaking. She was holding Matty and she was aware that he was trembling as well.

He needed his nursery, she thought. He needed Marguerite and Ellen and Laura. He was clinging to her; she was his mama, but he needed the familiarity of home to ground him.

Home. The castle. The royal palace of Alp de Ciel.

They couldn't get a car there. 'But I'm thinking a horse and cart,' the doctor said.

'I'll ride,' Rafael countered, but the doctor looked at him as if he were crazy.

'A horse and cart it is,' Kelly said, and thus half an hour later the royal family made its way in somewhat less than royal state—a sturdy carthorse leading the way, tugging a small haycart. The haycart was filled with mattresses and pillows. Rafael complained every inch of the way but he had a nurse who looked like Brunhilda the Great by his side, there were two burly farmers leading the horse and clearing rocks from their path as they went, and he had no choice but to submit.

Kelly brought up the rear, riding her lovely mare. Matty, whose bravado had disappeared about the time Rafael had been declared safe, had crumpled into a little boy again. He was cradled before her, almost a part of her, clinging as close as he could get. His own horse and Rafael's stallion were being led behind.

It was like a scene from hundreds of years ago, Kelly thought, dazed. A wounded prince returning from battle, his lady following behind.

Rafael's lady…

For that was what she was, she thought wearily as she followed the steady hoof-beats before her. Rafael's lady. Some time in the last few dreadful hours that was what she'd become.

Princess to Rafael's Prince.

Princess to this country.

'I thought you couldn't ride,' Matty whispered. Some time this dreadful day his allegiance had shifted as well. She was suddenly his mother. Yes, she'd always been that, but in his eyes she'd also been one of many people who'd flitted through his five years. Laura and Crater had been caught up at the hospital. Without his aunt, he'd needed someone to hold him, and that someone was his mother.

'I can ride,' she whispered into his hair. 'I chose not to because I was fearful of taking risks. But today…I think risks are something to be faced with courage. Not stupid risks, but those risks that need to be faced. Like being a part of this royal family.'

'You want to be royal?' He twisted a little, trying to see her face. 'But you can't be royal if you live in an attic.'

'Maybe it's time I came out of my attic,' she whispered. 'Maybe it's time I started to live. Maybe…maybe I need to think about putting on that dress.'

The nurse and the housekeeper whisked Rafael away as soon as they arrived at the castle. Ellen and Marguerite clucked over Kelly and Matty in concern. They were washed. Their bruises and scratches were anointed with care. Kelly tucked a cleaned and fed Matty into bed and watched him close his eyes before he even reached the pillows.

She was exhausted but there was no way she was heading for her bed. She made her way though the vast passages to the north tower—the tower where the ruling prince had his suite of private apartments.

When Rafael had arrived here after Kass's death he'd been horrified to find he was expected to use them. Crater had told her that, but he'd also told her, 'Prince Rafael has accepted he'll do what needs to be done. He can't be a part-time prince.'

So he was ensconced in state. She, however, was dressed in her jeans again, clean but faded. She needed to do something about her clothes, she thought.

Tomorrow. It was hardly the time for royal gowns tonight.

But for now…

Rafael.

She stood at the vast oak doors leading into his suite and felt almost shy. She'd never been in these rooms. By the time Kass had brought her to the castle he'd long since stopped wanting her.

Such memories… They were of a different person, she thought. A child bride. A girl who'd fallen in love with royalty before she knew what it was.

She knew what it was now. She also knew that as soon as she opened this door there'd be no going back.

She'd turned her back on royalty once before. Yes, it had

been Kass who'd shunned her, but if there'd been a choice... Yes, she would have fled. She would have taken her small son with her but still she would have fled.

Rafael was right through this door. Rafael, who had almost as much call as she to hate royalty but who'd accepted his responsibilities; his duty.

Anna would go on with the merchandising of his toys, Kelly thought. Rafael would still be able to develop them, but his life had changed. The wealthy Manhattan bachelor had accepted his heritage.

This wasn't her heritage, but she loved Matty and because she loved Matty she'd come back to the castle.

And because she loved Rafael, she'd stay.

All she had to do was tell him.

Such a little thing.

It was so hard to open the door.

'Open the door or go back to your attics,' she told herself sternly. 'Go on, Kelly. You can do it.'

'Princess Kelly,' she whispered back to herself. 'Princess Kellyn Marie de Boutaine. Open the door, stupid.'

His bed was enormous—the size of a small room! The four-poster bed was hung with acres of rich velvet curtains tied back with vast gold ropes and tassels. The eiderdowns were in matching crimson and purple and gold, as were the mountains of pillows at the end of the bed.

For a moment she couldn't see that anyone was in the bed.

'Kelly?' a loved voice said and she stilled.

'H-Hi. If you want to sleep I can come back later.'

'You're here,' he said in sleepy satisfaction. 'They've given me painkillers. They're making me woozy. Tell me I'm not dreaming. Tell me we got all those kids out and you're here.'

She crossed to the bed in a little run, and then stopped short—absurdly self-conscious.

'We got every single kid out,' she said unsteadily. 'And the schoolteacher. And you. Rafael, you might have been killed.'

'We got 'em out,' he said in sleepy satisfaction and his hand came out and caught her wrist and held. Hard. 'What's the final toll?'

'Six,' she whispered. 'All elderly people who couldn't get out of the way fast enough—the slip made a huge noise on the way down and most people were outside anyway.'

'Injuries?'

'None life-threatening. We've been lucky.'

'And elsewhere?' His voice was hoarse with worry. Kelly sank into the chair beside the bed, put her hand up to his face and traced his cheekbone with her finger.

'It was a minor earth tremor,' she whispered. 'There's little damage apart from in the village. There's been some road damage near the border but nothing major. It was only the recent deforestation of the hillside that caused the slip.'

'Kass should never have allowed…'

'You will never allow,' she said strongly. 'It's your call now, Rafael.'

'We will never allow,' he said, his voice strengthening.

'You'll turn the country into a democracy?' she asked, wondering. It was what the other three Alp countries had done—altered the constitution so the monarchy was a titular head only.

'Of course, but that's not what I meant when I said *we*,' he said, and his hold on her wrist tightened.

Her heart stilled.

'Rafael…'

'Kelly,' he said and he smiled.

She gazed down at him. Her battered hero. His face was a mass of scratches and bruises. A long, thin scratch ran from ear to chin. The doctor had put a couple of stitches in the lower reaches. They'd cleaned him as much as they could but he wasn't fit yet for a full shower so his hair was still spiked with mud.

She loved him with all her heart.

'I love you,' he said and her heart restarted. If it was possible for a heart to sing, it sang now. She could hear it. A heart full of nightingales.

'I guess I love you too,' she said unsteadily. 'All the time you were under that slab…'

'You love me?'

'Maybe it's fear. Maybe.'

'Maybe nothing,' he growled. 'The guys tell me it was your skill that had them tunnelling in so professionally. We were lucky the whole thing didn't come down on us.'

It had. She didn't tell him that but he'd learn it anyway. Just after they'd pulled Rafael out, a final tremor had come through. The mass of mud had settled again, and their basement refuge had turned into what would have been a mass grave.

She shivered.

'Damn,' he said and struggled to sit up.

'Rafael, no.'

'Then lie down beside me,' he said, his voice gaining strength. 'A man's got to say what a man's got to say. Dammit, I should go down on bended knee.'

On bended knee…

'I don't think any of us are capable of bending for quite a while,' she whispered, and amazingly she heard herself chuckle. His tug was insistent. Well, what the heck. She hauled back the covers, wiggled in and lay down beside him.

He pulled her as close as he could, he turned his face to hers and he kissed her.

Fourth kiss? It was the best, she decided. It was the best by a country mile. It was a kiss of release of terror. It was a kiss of love. It was a kiss of promise.

'You know we can't go further,' he said, his voice laced with passion as finally he let her go. Only an inch, mind, but release her he did. 'I'm so full of drugs…'

'And you need to sleep.'

'Sleep be damned,' he said. 'Kelly, will you marry me?'

'Yes.'

'Just like that?'

'Just like that.'

'It's putting you in the royal goldfish bowl again,' he said, holding her close.

'But I'll be in it with you,' she whispered. 'And with Matty. If it's a goldfish bowl with you guys or a big wide world without, it's a no-brainer.'

'I'm your second prince.'

'Kass was no prince,' she said scornfully. 'He might have been born royal but he never earned the title. You, however… You're prince through and through.'

'I'm a toy-maker.'

'And an equestrian,' she said, snuggling against him. He was wearing pyjamas. Self striped, flannel pyjamas. They'd have to go, she thought. Maybe not right now, though. A girl should show some restraint in the face of an injured hero.

He'd asked her to marry him!

'I guess riding again wasn't so bad,' he admitted.

'Your father loved it.'

'My father would have loved you.'

'My son loves you already.'

'Kelly,' he murmured and the strength had left his voice again. He had been heavily sedated to put his shoulder back in, she knew. He should be asleep.

'Yes, my love?'

'We can be a family?'

'Yes.'

'A royal family?'

'I'll even wear a tiara,' she teased and the hand around her waist tightened.

'Kelly?'

'Mmm.'

'I'm probably not capable of anything at all…'

'No, but…'

'No, but I can try,' he said. 'You know I asked you to marry me?'

'Yes.'

'And if a thing's promised then it's as good as done—right?'

'I guess,' she said dubiously, not sure where this was going.

'Then I have a wife,' he said in sleepy satisfaction. 'I have a princess. And, as a princess, as a wife, there are certain duties you'll be expected to face.'

'I…I guess.'

'Then we might as well start now,' he said, resigned.

'Um…right.' She thought about it. She twisted and pushed herself up so she was looking down into his beloved face. He was smiling. He was even laughing! And the look in his eyes…

It was a very royal look. It was a look of complete seduction.

'I only have one good arm,' he whispered as he tugged her down to him. 'Kelly, my love, my princess, my wife, I need help right now.'

'To do…to do what?'

'To take off these pyjamas!'

As coronations went it was magnificent.

Crater, as Secretary of State of Alp de Ciel, had been to the coronations in each of the Alp countries. He'd watched with wonder and with outright envy as the new generation of royals had taken their places as leaders in their countries, leading the way to prosperity for all.

They were here now. Prince Raoul of Alp d'Azuri was here, with the Princess Jessica, with their little son Edouard and with their twin daughters, Nicky and Lisle. Prince Maxsim of Alp d'Estella was in the next pew, with his Pippa and Marc and Sophie and Claire and bump. Prince Nikolai of Alp de Montez, with his beloved Princess Rose, with no bump as yet, were free to be best man and matron of honour.

There might be no bump, but by the way they were looking at each other Crater knew the succession of Alp d'Estella was assured.

As it was assured here in Alp de Ciel. For this coronation was also a wedding.

'I'm damned if we're dragging all these dignitaries here twice,' Rafael had decreed. 'You say the coronation has to take place almost immediately. That's how Kelly and I feel about our wedding. Besides, Anna will kill me if I drag her away from New York twice in a month, and I'm tired of her yelling at us. So we combine.'

So combine they did. The vast and ancient cathedral in Alp de Ciel's capital was full to bursting. Every dignitary worthy of the name was crammed in, plus representatives of all walks of life in Alp de Ciel. The staff from the diggings in Australia sent representatives, beaming with approval at this happy ending for a loved staff member. Pete, as senior representative, was giving the bride away. Even Rafael's work team from Manhattan was here—his disabled staff—as many as could fly over. Rafael was planning a local workforce with the same background. It was an outward sign of the changes that were already sweeping the country.

'For this government is *of the people, for the people, by the people,* starting now,' Rafael and Kelly had decreed, and Crater agreed entirely. Their attitude meant a motley guest list, but so what? Royalty was changing for the better, in ways Crater could only wonder at.

Everywhere Crater looked there was approval—and no more so than at the end of the aisle where one small page-boy was holding a ring, waiting impatiently for Kelly and Rafael to need it.

Matty had reacted with joy to the news of Rafael and Kelly's engagement, whooping and bouncing with an excitement that made him seem less of a Crown Prince and more of a little boy with the world at his feet. From the time of the landslip the castle seemed to be tumbling with new life and new puppies and a kid who'd been released from his royal imperatives.

His lessons from Crater had been quartered. 'For there's all the time in the world for Matty to learn his royal obligations,' Kelly had decreed. 'For the next twenty years, those obligations are the responsibility of his parents.'

His parents…

For Matty had parents now and he approved entirely. Rafael would be his father as well as Prince Regent. Matty thought that was the neatest thing in the whole world. In the mornings he bounced into bed with Kelly, hugging her tight, claiming to the world that he had a mother he loved.

His Aunt Laura was in the front pew, weeping into a still inevitably paint-spattered handkerchief. Matty couldn't figure that one out. Why was she crying? He was watching this wedding with joy and love and anticipation of a very good party.

If they'd just get on with it.

And so they did.

'With this ring I thee wed…'

Rafael took the ring from Matty and he placed it on his bride's finger. His bride…Kelly, who'd embraced the royal wedding with enthusiasm and love. Her dress was truly wondrous. She looked like an Elizabethan bride, a true royal princess. Her dragon train swept out behind her, the golden embroidery shimmering in the sunlight streaming through the ancient stained glass windows. She looked truly regal.

But she also looked like a woman in love. She smiled mistily up at her bridegroom and the whole cathedral seemed to dissolve.

There wasn't a dry eye in the house, Crater thought, wiping away a surreptitious tear himself. And then, as he thought of what approached—the formal joining of these four nations to become one mighty Federation, he abandoned trying and let his tears flow freely.

These four Princes with their brides…Who said love

couldn't conquer all? he thought. Love was making a damned fine fist of conquering all, right here, right now.

And the next morning—the first morning of their married life—they started as they meant to go on. Prince Rafael and Princess Kellyn rode together at dawn.

For their wedding gifts to each other were horses. Blaze would be ridden and loved and cared for, as would the other horses in the stables, but Blaze had been a part of Kass's life. He belonged to Matty now.

Kelly and Rafael needed to find their own future.

So they'd stolen two days from the mad preparation for the wedding and they'd spent those days looking at horses. They'd found Kelly's mare first. She was a silky-coated two-year-old, a soft grey with white markings, fearless and gentle in equal measure. She'd been bred for sale, but the farmer who'd bred her couldn't bear to part with her. Until now.

When the word had gone out that the Princess Kellyn needed a horse, she'd been quietly proffered. Her name was Cher, meaning beloved, and she already was.

And for Rafael…Nero had taken longer to find, and in the end they'd had to travel to Italy. But he was worth every moment of travelling time. Nero was all black. When they'd first seen him, he'd seemed too big, too powerful, too breathtaking. But Rafael had mounted him and looked down at Kelly, his eyes gleaming with excitement and pleasure.

They'd bought him. Of course they'd bought him. For this was what the future held for them. Excitement and pleasure and challenge.

Hard work and commitment.

Love.

They rode side by side now, silent, each overwhelmed with the enormity of the step they'd taken, the pleasure—no, the bliss—of the night before and the knowledge that this was the beginning of their life together.

They emerged from the woodlands to the open pastures. Here the horses could have their heads, taking the gentle rise at a gallop. Finally they reached the summit, where the land swept down again deep into a valley before rising to the Alps beyond.

They reined in their horses and turned to look back the way they'd come.

From here they could see the castle, vast and regal in the soft, dawn light. They could see the village, and the scar of raw earth above it. But from here they could also see the mass of green, the blanket planting of trees that was the first of many such undertakings.

This country would grow now, and flourish.

As would their marriage.

Rafael leaned across and took Kelly's hand. The horses edged together, as if sensing they were part of this partnership, part of this loving.

'We've done it,' Rafael said softly as the first rays of the sun appeared over the distant Alps, casting a golden hue over the entire landscape. 'We can't go back now, my love.'

'No,' she whispered and she trusted Cher enough to put both her arms around her husband, hold him close and raise her face to be kissed. 'Why would we want to?' she asked unsteadily when he finally, reluctantly, released her. 'We have a country to rebuild. We have a family to love. We have each other.'

'Do you think that's enough?' he asked, his eyes wicked with laughter and desire and happiness.

'Not quite,' she said, leaning against him and soaking in the first rays of the golden sun. 'I believe I have a bus to build as well.'

'What about a gold-mine or two to dig?'

'Maybe that too,' she said serenely. 'And a library to catalogue.'

'Just as well we have a lifetime,' Rafael said with satisfaction and kissed her again, so deeply she felt herself melt in a pool of white-hot desire. 'So much to do, my love, and so much loving to fit in along the way.' He released her again with reluctance, and twisted on Nero to tug blankets free from his saddle-bags. He smiled across at her as he tossed them down on the lush pasture, his smile wicked and wanton and filled with pure, unadulterated lust.

'Maybe we should start now,' he said softly. 'For I doubt if a lifetime is long enough.'

CINDERELLA: HIRED BY THE PRINCE

BY
MARION LENNOX

PROLOGUE

'RAMÓN spends his life in jeans and ancient T-shirts. He has money and he has freedom. Why would he want the Crown?'

Señor Rodriguez, legal advisor to the Crown of Cepheus, regarded the woman before him with some sympathy. The Princess Sofía had been evicted from the palace of Cepheus sixty years ago, and she didn't wish to be back here now. Her face was tear-stained and her plump hands were wringing.

'I had two brothers, Señor Rodriguez,' she told him, as if explaining her story could somehow alter the inevitable. 'But I was only permitted to know one. My younger brother and I were exiled with my mother when I was ten years old, and my father's cruelty didn't end there. And now… I haven't seen a tiara in sixty years and, as far as I know, Ramón's never seen one. The only time he's been in the palace is the night his father died. I've returned to the palace because my mother raised me with a sense of duty, but how can we demand that from Ramón? To return to the place that killed his father…'

'The Prince Ramón has no choice,' the lawyer said flatly. 'And of course he'll want the Crown.'

'There's no "of course" about it,' Sofía snapped. 'Ramón spends half of every year building houses for some charity in Bangladesh, and the rest of his life on his beautiful yacht. Why should he give that up?'

'He'll be Crown Prince.'

'You think royalty's everything?' Sofía gave up hand

wringing and stabbed at her knitting as if she'd like it to be the late, unlamented Crown Prince. 'My nephew's a lovely young man and he wants nothing to do with the throne. The palace gives him nightmares, as it gives us all.'

'He must come,' Señor Rodriguez said stiffly.

'So how will you find him?' Sofía muttered. 'When he's working in Bangladesh Ramón checks his mail, but for the rest of his life he's around the world in that yacht of his, who knows where? Since his mother and sister died he lets the wind take him where it will. And, even if you do find him, how do you think he'll react to being told he has to fix this mess?'

'There won't be a mess if he comes home. He'll come, as you have come. He must see there's no choice.'

'And what of the little boy?'

'Philippe will go into foster care. There's no choice there, either. The child is nothing to do with Prince Ramón.'

'Another child of no use to the Crown,' Sofía whispered, and she dropped two stiches without noticing. 'But Ramón has a heart. Oh, Ramón, if I were you I'd keep on sailing.'

CHAPTER ONE

'JENNY, lose your muffins. Get a life!'

Gianetta Bertin, known to the Seaport locals as Jenny, gave her best friend a withering look and kept right on spooning double choc chip muffin mixture into pans. Seaport Coffee 'n' Cakes had been crowded all morning, and her muffin tray was almost bare.

'I don't have time for lectures,' she told her friend severely. 'I'm busy.'

'You need to have time for lectures. Honest, Jen.' Cathy hitched herself up onto Jenny's prep bench and grew earnest. 'You can't stay stuck in this hole for ever.'

'There's worse holes to be stuck in, and get off my bench. If Charlie comes in he'll sack me, and I won't have a hole at all.'

'He won't,' Cathy declared. 'You're the best cook in Seaport. You hold this place up. Charlie's treating you like dirt, Jen, just because you don't have the energy to do anything about it. I know you owe him, but you could get a job and repay him some other way.'

'Like how?' Jenny shoved the tray into the oven, straightened and tucked an unruly curl behind her ear. Her cap was supposed to hold back her mass of dark curls, but they kept escaping. She knew she'd now have a streak of flour across her ear but did it matter what she looked like?

And, as if in echo, Cathy continued. 'Look at you,' she

declared. 'You're gorgeous. Twenty-nine, figure to die for, cute as a button, a woman ripe and ready for the world, and here you are, hidden in a shapeless white pinafore with flour on your nose—yes, flour on your nose, Jen—no don't wipe it, you've made it worse.'

'It doesn't matter,' Jenny said. 'Who's looking? Can I get on? There's customers out there.'

'There are,' Cathy said warmly, peering out through the hatch but refusing to let go of her theme. 'You have twenty people out there, all coming here for one of your yummy muffins and then heading off again for life. You should be out there with them. Look at that guy out there, for instance. Gorgeous or what? That's what you're missing out on, Jen, stuck in here every day.'

Jenny peered out the hatch as well, and it didn't take more than a glance to see who Cathy was referring to.

The guy looked to be in his mid-thirties. He was a yachtie—she could tell that by his gear—and he was seriously good-looking. It had been raining this morning. He was wearing battered jeans, salt-stained boating shoes and a faded black T-shirt, stretched tight over a chest that looked truly impressive. He'd shrugged a battered sou'wester onto the back of his chair.

Professional, she thought.

After years of working in Coffee 'n' Cakes she could pick the classes of boaty. Holding the place up were the hard-core fishermen. Then there were the battered old salts who ran small boats on the smell of an oily rag, often living on them. Next there was the cool set, arriving at weekends, wearing gear that came out of the designer section of the *Nautical Monthly* catalogue, and leaving when they realized Coffee 'n' Cakes didn't sell Chardonnay.

And finally there were the serious yachties. Seaport was a deep water harbour just south of Sydney, and it attracted yachts doing amazing journeys. Seaport had a great dry dock where repairs could be carried out expertly and fast, so there were often one or two of these classy yachts in port.

This guy looked as if he was from one of these. His coat looked battered but she knew the brand, even from this distance. It was the best. Like the man. The guy himself also looked a bit battered, but in a good way. Worn by the sea. His tan was deep and real, his eyes were crinkled as if he spent his life in the sun, and his black hair was only really black at the roots. The tips were sun-bleached to almost fair.

He was definitely a professional sailor, she thought, giving herself a full minute to assess him. And why not? He was well worth assessing.

She knew the yachting hierarchy. The owners of the big sea-going yachts tended to be middle-aged or older. They spent short bursts of time on their boats but left serious seafaring to paid staff. This guy looked younger, tougher, leaner than a boat-owner. He looked seriously competent. He'd be being paid to take a yacht to where its owner wanted it to be.

And for a moment—just for a moment—Jenny let herself be consumed by a wave of envy. Just to go where the wind took you… To walk away from Seaport…

No. That'd take effort and planning and hope—all the things she no longer cared about. And there was also debt, an obligation like a huge anchor chained around her waist, hauling her down.

But her friend was thinking none of these things. Cathy was prodding her, grinning, rolling her eyes at the sheer good looks of this guy, and Jenny smiled and gazed a little bit more. Cathy was right—this guy was definite eye-candy. What was more, he was munching on one of her muffins—lemon and pistachio. Her favourite, she thought in approval.

And then he looked up and saw her watching. He grinned and raised his muffin in silent toast, then chuckled as she blushed deep crimson and pushed the hatch closed.

Cathy laughed her delight. 'There,' she said in satisfaction. 'You see what's out there? He's gorgeous, Jen. Why don't you head on out and ask him if he'd like another muffin?'

'As if,' she muttered, thoroughly disconcerted. She shoved

her mixing bowl into the sink. 'Serving's Susie's job. I'm just the cook. Go away, Cathy. You're messing with my serenity.'

'Stuff your serenity,' Cathy said crudely. 'Come on, Jen. It's been two years…' Then, as she saw the pain wash across Jenny's face, she swung herself off the bench and came and hugged her. 'I know. Moving on can't ever happen completely, but you can't keep hiding.'

'Dr Matheson says I'm doing well,' Jenny said stubbornly.

'Yeah, he's prescribing serenity,' Cathy said dourly. 'Honey, you've had enough peace. You want life. Even sailing… You love the water, but now you don't go near the sea. There's so many people who'd like a weekend crew. Like the guy out there, for instance. If he offered me a sail I'd be off for more than a weekend.'

'I don't want…'

'Anything but to be left alone,' Cathy finished for her. 'Oh, enough. I won't let you keep on saying it.' And, before Jenny could stop her, she opened the hatch again. She lifted the bell Jenny used to tell Susie an order was ready and rang it like there was a shipwreck in the harbour. Jenny made a grab for it but Cathy swung away so her body protected the bell. Then, when everyone was watching…

'Attention, please,' she called to the room in general, in the booming voice she used for running the Seaport Ladies' Yoga Sessions. 'Ladies and gentlemen, I know this is unusual but I'd like to announce a fantastic offer. Back here in the kitchen is the world's best cook and the world's best sailor. Jenny's available as crew for anyone offering her excitement, adventure and a way out of this town. All she needs is a fantastic wage and a boss who appreciates her. Anyone interested, apply right here, right now.'

'Cathy!' Jenny stared at her friend in horror. She made a grab for the hatch doors and tugged them shut as Cathy collapsed into laughter. 'Are you out of your mind?'

'I love you, sweetheart,' Cathy said, still chuckling. 'I'm just trying to help.'

'Getting me sacked won't help.'

'Susie won't tell Charlie,' Cathy said. 'She agrees with me. Don't you, Susie?' she demanded as the middle-aged waitress pushed her way through the doors. 'Do we have a queue out there, Suse, all wanting to employ our Jen?'

'You shouldn't have done it,' Susie said severely, looking at Jenny in concern. 'You've embarrassed her to death.'

'There's no harm done,' Cathy said. 'They're all too busy eating muffins to care. But honest, Jen, put an ad in the paper, or at least start reading the Situations Vacant. Susie has a husband, four kids, two dogs and a farm. This place is a tiny part of her life. But for you… This place has become your life. You can't let it stay that way.'

'It's all I want,' Jenny said stubbornly. 'Serenity.'

'That's nonsense,' Susie declared.

'Of course it's nonsense,' Cathy said, jumping off the bench and heading for the door. 'Okay, Stage One of my quest is completed. If it doesn't have an effect then I'll move to Stage Two, and that could be really scary.'

Coffee 'n' Cakes was a daytime café. Charlie was supposed to lock up at five, but Charlie's life was increasingly spent in the pub, so at five Jenny locked up, as she was starting to do most nights.

At least Charlie hadn't heard of what had happened that morning. Just as well, Jenny thought as she turned towards home. For all Cathy's assurances that she wouldn't be sacked, she wasn't so sure. Charlie's temper was unpredictable and she had debts to pay. Big debts.

Once upon a time Charlie had been a decent boss. Then his wife died, and now…

Loss did ghastly things to people. It had to her. Was living in a grey fog of depression worse than spending life in an alcoholic haze? How could she blame Charlie when she wasn't much better herself?

She sighed and dug her hands deep into her jacket pockets. The rain from this morning had disappeared. It was warm enough, but she wanted the comfort of her coat. Cathy's behaviour had unsettled her.

She would've liked to take a walk along the harbour before she went home, only in this mood it might unsettle her even more.

All those boats, going somewhere.

She had debts to pay. She was going nowhere.

'Excuse me?'

The voice came from behind her. She swung around and it was him. The guy with the body, and with the smile.

Okay, that was a dumb thing to think, but she couldn't help herself. The combination of ridiculously good-looking body and a smile to die for meant it was taking everything she had not to drop her jaw.

It had been too long, she thought. No one since…

No. Don't even think about going there.

'Can I talk to you? Are you Jenny?'

He had an accent—Spanish maybe, she thought, and seriously sexy. Uh oh. Body of a god, killer smile and a voice that was deep and lilting and gorgeous. Her knees felt wobbly. Any minute now he'd have her clutching the nearest fence for support.

Hey! She was a grown woman, she reminded herself sharply. Where was a bucket of ice when she needed one? Making do as best she could, she tilted her chin, met his gaze square on and fought for composure.

'I'm Jenny.' Infuriatingly, her words came out a squeak. She turned them into a cough and tried again. 'I…sure.'

'The lady in the café said you were interested in a job,' he said. 'I'm looking for help. Can we talk about it?'

He was here to offer her a job?

His eyes were doing this assessing thing while he talked. She was wearing old jeans and an ancient duffel, built for service rather than style. Was he working out where she fitted in the social scale? Was he working out whether she cared what she wore?

Suddenly she found herself wishing she had something else on. Something with a bit of…glamour?

Now that was crazy. She was heading home to put her feet up, watch the telly and go to bed. What would she do with glamour?

He was asking her about a job. Yeah, they all needed deck-hands, she thought, trying to ground herself. Lots of big yachts came into harbour here. There'd be one guy in charge—someone like this. There'd also be a couple of deckies, but the guy in charge would be the only one paid reasonable wages by the owners. Deckies were to be found in most ports—kids looking for adventure, willing to work for cheap travel. They'd get to their destination and disappear to more adventure, to be replaced by others.

Did this man seriously think she might be interested in such a job?

'My friend was having fun at my expense,' she said, settling now she knew what he wanted. Still trying to firm up her knees, though. 'Sorry, but I'm a bit old to drop everything and head off into the unknown.'

'Are you ever too old to do that?'

'Yes,' she snapped before she could stop herself—and then caught herself. 'Sorry. Look, I need to get on.'

'So you're not interested.'

'There's a noticeboard down at the yacht club,' she told him. 'There's always a list of kids looking for work. I already have a job.'

'You do have a job.' His smile had faded. He'd ditched his coat, leaving only his jeans and T-shirt. They were faded and old and…nice. He was tall and broad-shouldered. He looked loose-limbed, casually at ease with himself and quietly confident. His eyes were blue as the sea, though they seemed to darken when he smiled, and the crinkles round his eyes said smiling was what he normally did. But suddenly he was serious.

'If you made the muffins I ate this morning you're very,

very good at your job,' he told her. 'If you're available as crew, a man'd be crazy not to take you on.'

'Well, I'm not.' He had her rattled and she'd snapped again. Why? He was a nice guy offering her a job. 'Sorry,' she said. 'But no.'

'Do you have a passport?'

'Yes, but…'

'I'm sailing for Europe just as soon as I can find some company. It's not safe to do a solo where I'm going.'

'Round the Horn?' Despite herself, she was interested.

'Round the Horn,' he agreed. 'It's fastest.'

That'd be right. The boaties in charge of the expensive yachts were usually at the call of owners. She'd met enough of them to know that. An owner fancied a sailing holiday in Australia? He'd pay a guy like this to bring his boat here and have it ready for him. Maybe he'd join the boat on the interesting bits, flying in and out at will. Now the owner would be back in Europe and it'd be up to the employed skipper—this guy?—to get the boat back there as soon as he could.

With crew. But not with her.

'Well, good luck,' she said, and started to walk away, but he wasn't letting her leave. He walked with her.

'It's a serious offer.'

'It's a serious rejection.'

'I don't take rejection kindly.'

'That's too bad,' she told him. 'The days of carting your crew on board drugged to the eyeballs is over. Press gangs are illegal.'

'They'd make my life easier,' he said morosely.

'You know I'm very sure they wouldn't.' His presence as he fell into step beside her was making her thoroughly disconcerted. 'Having a press-ganged crew waking up with hangovers a day out to sea surely wouldn't make for serene sailing.'

'I don't look for serenity,' he said, and it was so much an echo of her day's thoughts that she stopped dead.

But this was ridiculous. The idea was ridiculous. 'Serenity's important,' she managed, forcing her feet into moving again. 'So thank you, but I've said no. Is there anything else you want?'

'I pay well.'

'I know what deckies earn.'

'You don't know what I pay. Why don't you ask?'

'I'm not interested.'

'Do you really sail?' he asked curiously.

He wasn't going away. She was quickening her steps but he was keeping up with ease. She had the feeling if she broke into a run he'd keep striding beside her, effortlessly. 'Once upon a time, I sailed,' she said. 'Before life got serious.'

'Your life got serious? How?' Suddenly his eyes were creasing in concern. He paused and, before she could stop him, he lifted her left hand. She knew what he was looking for.

No ring.

'You have a partner?' he demanded.

'It's none of your business.'

'Yes, but I want to know,' he said in that gorgeous accent, excellent English but with that fabulous lilt—and there was that smile again, the smile she knew could get him anything he wanted if he tried hard enough. With these looks and that smile and that voice… Whew.

No. He couldn't get anything from her. She was impervious.

She had to be impervious.

But he was waiting for an answer. Maybe it wouldn't hurt to tell him enough to get him off her back. 'I'm happily single,' she said.

'Ah, but if you're saying life's serious then you're not so happily single. Maybe sailing away on the next tide could be just what you want.'

'Look,' she said, tugging her hand away, exasperated. 'I'm not a teenager looking for adventure. I have obligations here. So you're offering me a trip to Europe? Where would that leave me? I'd get on your boat, I'd work my butt off for passage—I know you guys get your money's worth from the kids you employ—and then I'd end up wherever it is you're going. That's it. I know how it works. I wouldn't even have the fare home. I'm not a backpacker, Mr Whoever-You-Are, and I live here. I don't know you, I don't trust you and I'm not interested in your job.'

'My name's Ramón Cavellero,' he said, sounding not in the least perturbed by her outburst. 'I'm very trustworthy.' And he smiled in a way that told her he wasn't trustworthy in the least. 'I'm sailing on the *Marquita*. You've seen her?'

Had she seen her? Every person in Seaport had seen the *Marquita*. The big yacht's photograph had been on the front of their local paper when she'd come into port four days ago. With good reason. Quite simply she was the most beautiful boat Jenny had ever seen.

And probably the most expensive.

If this guy was captaining the *Marquita* then maybe he had the funds to pay a reasonable wage. That was an insidious little whisper in her head, but she stomped on it before it had a chance to grow. There was no way she could walk away from this place. Not for years.

She had to be sensible.

'Look, Mr Cavellero, this has gone far enough,' she said, and she turned back to face him directly. 'You have the most beautiful boat in the harbour. You can have your pick of any deckie in the market—I know a dozen kids at least who would kill to be on that boat. But, as for me… My friend was making a joke but that's all it was. Thank you and goodbye.'

She reached out and took his hand, to give it a good firm handshake, as if she was a woman who knew how to transact business, as if she should be taken seriously. He took it, she shook, but, instead of pulling away after one brief shake, she found he was holding on.

Or maybe it was that she hadn't pulled back as she'd intended.

His hand was strong and warm and his grip as decisive

as hers. Or more. Two strong wills, she thought fleetingly, but more…

But then, before she could think any further, she was aware of a car sliding to a halt beside them. She glanced sideways and almost groaned.

Charlie.

She could sense his drunkenness from here. One of these days he'd be caught for drink-driving, she thought, and half of her hoped it'd be soon, but the other half knew that'd put her boss into an even more foul mood than he normally was. Once upon a time he'd been a nice guy—but that was when he was sober, and she could barely remember when he'd been sober. So she winced and braced herself for an explosion as Charlie emerged from the car and headed towards them.

Ramón kept on holding her hand. She tugged it back and he released her but he shifted in closer. Charlie's body language was aggressive. He was a big man; he'd become an alcoholic bully, and it showed.

But, whatever else Ramón might be, it was clear he knew how to protect his own. His own? That was a dumb thing to think. Even so, she was suddenly glad that he was here right now.

'Hey, I want to speak to you, you stupid cow. Lose your friend,' Charlie spat at her.

Jenny flinched. Uh oh. This could mean only one thing—that one of the patrons of the café had told Charlie of Cathy's outburst. This was too small a town for such a joke to go unreported. Charlie had become universally disliked and the idea that one of his staff was advertising for another job would be used against him.

At her expense.

And Ramón's presence here would make it worse. Protective or not, Charlie was right; she needed to lose him.

'See you later,' she said to Ramón, stepping deliberately away and turning her back on him. Expecting him to leave. 'Hello, Charlie.'

But Charlie wasn't into greetings. 'What the hell do you

think you're doing, making personal announcements in my café, in my time?' He was close to yelling, shoving right into her personal space so she was forced to step backward. 'And getting another job? You walk away from me and I foreclose before the day's end. You know what you owe me, girl. You work for me for the next three years or I'll have you bankrupt and your friend with you. I could toss you out now. Your friend'll lose her house. Great mess that'd leave her in. You'll work the next four weekends with no pay to make up for this or you're out on your ear. What do you say to that?'

She closed her eyes. Charlie was quite capable of carrying out his threats. This man was capable of anything.

Why had she ever borrowed money from him?

Because she'd been desperate, that was why. It had been right at the end of Matty's illness. She'd sold everything, but there was this treatment… There'd been a chance. It was slim, she'd known, but she'd do anything.

She'd been sobbing, late at night, in the back room of the café. She'd been working four hours a day to pay her rent. The rest of the time she'd spent with Matty. Cathy had found her there, and Charlie came in and found them both.

He'd loan her the money, he said, and the offer was so extraordinary both women had been rendered almost speechless.

Jenny could repay it over five years, he'd told them, by working for half wages at the café. Only he needed security. 'In case you decide to do a runner.'

'She'd never do a runner,' Cathy had said, incensed. 'When Matty's well she'll settle down and live happily ever after.'

'I don't believe in happy ever after,' Charlie had said. 'I need security.'

'I'll pledge my apartment that she'll repay you,' Cathy had said hotly. 'I trust her, even if you don't.'

What a disaster. They'd been so emotional they hadn't thought it through. All Jenny had wanted was to get back to the hospital, to get back to Matty, and she didn't care how. Cathy's generosity was all she could see.

So she'd hugged her and accepted and didn't see the ties.

Only ties there were. Matty died a month later and she was faced with five years bonded servitude.

Cathy's apartment had been left to her by her mother. It was pretty and neat and looked out over the harbour. Cathy was an artist. She lived hand to mouth and her apartment was all she had.

Even Cathy hadn't realised how real the danger of foreclosure was, Jenny thought dully. Cathy had barely glanced at the loan documents. She had total faith in her friend to repay her loan. Of course she had.

So now there was no choice. Jenny dug her hands deep into her pockets, she bit back angry words, as she'd bitten them back many times before, and she nodded.

'Okay. I'm sorry, Charlie. Of course I'll do the weekends.'

'Hey!' From behind them came Ramón's voice, laced with surprise and the beginnings of anger. 'What is this? Four weekends to pay for two minutes of amusement?'

'It's none of your business,' Charlie said shortly. 'Get lost.'

'If you're talking about what happened at the café, I was there. It was a joke.'

'I don't do jokes. Butt out. And she'll do the weekends. She has no choice.'

And then he smiled, a drunken smile that made her shiver. 'So there's the joke,' he jeered. 'On you, woman, not me.'

And that was that. He stared defiance at Ramón, but Ramón, it seemed, was not interested in a fight. He gazed blankly back at him, and then watched wordlessly as Charlie swung himself unsteadily back into his car and weaved off into the distance.

Leaving silence.

How to explain what had just happened? Jenny thought, and decided she couldn't. She took a few tentative steps away, hoping Ramón would leave her to her misery.

He didn't. Instead, he looked thoughtfully at the receding car, then flipped open his cellphone and spoke a few sharp words. He snapped it shut and walked after Jenny, catching up and once again falling into step beside her.

'How much do you owe him?' he asked bluntly.

She looked across at him, startled. 'Sorry?'

'You heard. How much?'

'I don't believe that it's…'

'Any of my business,' he finished for her. 'Your boss just told me that. But, as your future employer, I can make it my business.'

'You're not my future employer.'

'Just tell me, Jenny,' he said, and his voice was suddenly so concerned, so warm, so laced with caring that, to her astonishment, she found herself telling him. Just blurting out the figure, almost as if it didn't matter.

He thought about it for a moment as they kept walking. 'That's not so much,' he said cautiously.

'To you, maybe,' she retorted. 'But to me… My best friend signed over her apartment as security. If I don't pay, then she loses her home.'

'You could get another job. You don't have to be beholden to this swine-bag. You could transfer the whole loan to the bank.'

'I don't think you realise just how broke I am,' she snapped and then she shook her head, still astounded at how she was reacting to him. 'Sorry. There's no need for me to be angry with you when you're being nice. I'm tired and I'm upset and I've got myself into a financial mess. The truth is that I don't even have enough funds to miss a week's work while I look for something else, and no bank will take me on. Or Cathy either, for that matter—she's a struggling painter and has nothing but her apartment. So there you go. That's why I work for Charlie. It's also why I can't drop everything and sail away with you. If you knew how much I'd love to…'

'Would you love to?' He was studying her intently. The concern was still there but there was something more. It was as if he was trying to make her out. His brow was furrowed in concentration. 'Would you really? How good a sailor are you?'

That was a weird question but it was better than talking

about her debts. So she told him that, too. Why not? 'I was born and bred on the water,' she told him. 'My dad built a yacht and we sailed it together until he died. In the last few years of his life we lived on board. My legs are more at home at sea than on land.'

'Yet you're a cook.'

'There's nothing like spending your life in a cramped galley to make you lust after proper cooking.' She gave a wry smile, temporarily distracted from her bleakness. 'My mum died early so she couldn't teach me, but I longed to cook. When I was seventeen I got an apprenticeship with the local baker. I had to force Dad to keep the boat in port during my shifts.'

'And your boat? What was she?'

'A twenty-five footer, fibreglass, called *Wind Trader*. Flamingo, if you know that class. She wasn't anything special but we loved her.'

'Sold now to pay debts?' he asked bluntly.

'How did you know?' she said, crashing back to earth. 'And, before you ask, I have a gambling problem.'

'Now why don't I believe that?'

'Why would you believe anything I tell you?' She took a deep breath. 'Look, this is dumb. I'm wrecked and I need to go home. Can we forget we had this conversation? It was crazy to tell you my troubles and I surely don't expect you to do anything about them. But thank you for letting me talk.'

She hesitated then. For some reason, it was really hard to walk away from this man, but she had no choice. 'Goodbye, Mr Cavellero,' she managed. 'Thank you for thinking of me as a potential deckhand. It was very nice of you, and you know what? If I didn't have this debt I'd be half tempted to take it on.'

Once more she turned away. She walked about ten steps, but then his voice called her back.

'Jenny?'

She should have just kept on walking, but there was something in his voice that stopped her. It was the concern again. He sounded as if he really cared.

That was crazy, but the sensation was insidious, like a siren song forcing her to turn around.

'Yes?'

He was standing where she'd left him. Just standing. Behind him, down the end of the street, she could see the harbour. That was where he belonged, she thought. He was a man of the sea. He looked a man from the sea. Whereas she…

'Jenny, I'll pay your debts,' he said.

She didn't move. She didn't say anything.

She didn't know what to say.

'This isn't charity,' he said quickly as she felt her colour rise. 'It's a proposition.'

'I don't understand.'

'It's a very sketchy proposition,' he told her. 'I've not had time to work out the details so we may have to smooth it off round the edges. But, essentially, I'll pay your boss out if you promise to come and work with me for a year. You'll be two deckies instead of one—crew when I need it and cook for the rest of the time. Sometimes you'll be run off your feet but mostly not. I'll also add a living allowance,' he said and he mentioned a sum that made her feel winded.

'You'll be living on the boat so that should be sufficient,' he told her, seemingly ignoring her amazement. 'Then, at the end of the year, I'll organise you a flight home, from wherever *Marquita* ends up. So how about it, Jenny?' And there was that smile again, flashing out to warm parts of her she hadn't known had been cold. 'Will you stay here as Charlie's unpaid slave, or will you come with me, cook your cakes on my boat and see the world? What do you say? *Marquita*'s waiting, Jenny. Come sail away.'

'It's three years' debt,' she gasped finally. Was he mad?

'Not to me. It's one year's salary for a competent cook and sailor, and it's what I'm offering.'

'Your owner could never give the authority to pay those kind of wages.'

He hesitated for a moment—for just a moment—but then he smiled. 'My owner doesn't interfere with how I run my boat,' he told her. 'My owner knows if I…if he pays peanuts, he gets monkeys. I want good and loyal crew and with you I believe I'd be getting it.'

'You don't even know me. And you're out of your mind. Do you know how many deckies you could get with that money?'

'I don't want deckies. I want you.' And then, as she kept right on staring, he amended what had been a really forceful statement. 'If you can cook the muffins I had this morning you'll make my life—and everyone else who comes onto the boat—a lot more pleasant.'

'Who does the cooking now?' She was still fighting for breath. What an offer!

'Me or a deckie,' he said ruefully. 'Not a lot of class.'

'I'd…I'd be expected to cook for the owner?'

'Yes.'

'Dinner parties?'

'There's not a lot of dinner parties on board the *Marquita*,' he said, sounding a bit more rueful. 'The owner's pretty much like me. A retiring soul.'

'You don't look like a retiring soul,' she retorted, caught by the sudden flash of laughter in those blue eyes.

'Retiring or not, I still need a cook.'

Whoa… To be a cook on a boat… With this man…

Then she caught herself. For a moment she'd allowed herself to be sucked in. To think *what if.*

What if she sailed away?

Only she'd jumped like this once before, and where had it got her? Matty, and all the heartbreak that went with him.

Her thoughts must have shown on her face. 'What is it?' Ramón asked, and his smile suddenly faded. 'Hey, Jenny, don't look like that. There's no strings attached to this offer. I swear you won't find yourself the seventeenth member of my harem, chained up for my convenience in the hold. I can even give you character references if you want. I'm extremely honourable.'

He was trying to make her smile. She did smile, but it was a wavery smile. 'I'm sure you're honourable,' she said—despite the laughter lurking behind his amazing eyes suggesting he was nothing of the kind—'but, references or not, I still don't know you.' Deep breath. *Be sensible.* 'Sorry,' she managed. 'It's an amazing offer, but I took a loan from Charlie when I wasn't thinking straight, and look where that got me. And there have been…other times…when I haven't thought straight either, and trouble's followed. So I don't act on impulse any more. I've learned to be sensible. Thank you for your offer, Mr Cavellero…'

'Ramón.'

'Mr Cavellero,' she said stubbornly. 'With the wages you're offering, I know you'll find just the crew you're looking for, no problem at all. So thank you again and goodnight.'

Then, before she could let her treacherous heart do any more impulse urging—before she could be as stupid as she'd been in the past—she turned resolutely away.

She walked straight ahead and she didn't look back.

CHAPTER TWO

HER heart told her she was stupid all the way home. Her head told her she was right.

Her head addressed her heart with severity. This was a totally ridiculous proposition. She didn't know this man.

She'd be jumping from the frying pan into the fire, she told herself. To be indebted to a stranger, then sail away into the unknown… He *could* be a white slave trader!

She knew he wasn't. Take a risk, her heart was commanding her, but then her heart had let her down before. She wasn't going down that road again.

So, somehow, she summoned the dignity to keep on walking.

'Think about it,' Ramón called after her and she almost hesitated, she almost turned back, only she was a sensible woman now, not some dumb teenager who'd jump on the nearest boat and head off to sea.

So she walked on. Round the next corner, and the next, past where Charlie lived.

A police car was pulled up beside Charlie's front door, and Charlie hadn't made it inside. Her boss was being breathalysed. He'd be way over the alcohol limit. He'd lose his licence for sure.

She thought back and remembered Ramón lifting his cellphone. Had he…

Whoa. She scuttled past, feeling like a guilty rabbit.

Ramón had done it, not her.

Charlie would guess. Charlie would never forgive her.

Uh oh, uh oh, uh oh.

By the time she got home she felt as if she'd forgotten to breathe. She raced up the steps into her little rented apartment and she slammed the door behind her.

What had Ramón done? Charlie, without his driving licence? Charlie, thinking it was her fault?

But suddenly she wasn't thinking about Charlie. She was thinking about Ramón. Numbly, she crossed to the curtains and drew them aside. Just checking. Just in case he'd followed. He hadn't and she was aware of a weird stab of disappointment.

Well, what did you expect? she told herself. I told him press gangs don't work.

What if they did? What if he came up here in the dead of night, drugged her and carted her off to sea? What if she woke on his beautiful yacht, far away from this place?

I'd be chained to the sink down in the galley, she told herself with an attempt at humour. Nursing a hangover from the drugs he used to get me there.

But oh, to be on that boat…

He'd offered to pay all her bills. Get her away from Charlie…

What was she about, even beginning to think about such a crazy offer? If he was giving her so much money, then he'd be expecting something other than the work a deckie did.

But a man like Ramón wouldn't have to pay, she thought, her mind flashing to the nubile young backpackers she knew would jump at the chance to be crew to Ramón. They'd probably jump at the chance to be anything else. So why did he want her?

Did he have a thing for older women?

She stared into the mirror and what she saw there almost made her smile. It'd be a kinky man who'd desire her like she was. Her hair was still flour-streaked from the day. She'd been working in a hot kitchen and she'd been washing up over steaming sinks. She didn't have a spot of make-up on, and her nose was shiny. *Very* shiny.

Her clothes were ancient and nondescript and her eyes were shadowed from lack of sleep. Oh, she had plenty of time for sleep, but where was sleep when you needed it? She'd stopped taking the pills her doctor prescribed. She was trying desperately to move on, but how?

'What better way than to take a chance?' she whispered to her image. 'Charlie's going to be unbearable to work with now. And Ramón's gorgeous and he seems really nice. His boat's fabulous. He's not going to chain me to the galley, I'm sure of it.' She even managed a smile at that. 'If he does, I won't be able to help him with the sails. He'd have to unchain me a couple of times a day at least. And I'd be at sea. At sea!'

So maybe…maybe…

Her heart and head were doing battle but her heart was suddenly in the ascendancy. It was trying to convince her it could be sensible as well.

Wait, she told herself severely. She ran a bath and wallowed and let her mind drift. Pros and cons. Pros and cons.

If it didn't work, she could get off the boat at New Zealand.

He'd demand his money back.

So? She'd then owe money to Ramón instead of to Charlie, and there'd be no threat to Cathy's apartment. The debt would be hers and hers alone.

That felt okay. Sensible, even. She felt a prickle of pure excitement as she closed her eyes and sank as deep as she could into the warm water. To sail away with Ramón…

Her eyes flew open. She'd been stupid once. One gorgeous sailor, and…Matty.

So I'm not that stupid, she told herself. I can take precautions before I go.

Before she went? This wasn't turning out to be a relaxing bath. She sat bolt upright in the bath and thought, *what am I thinking*?

She was definitely thinking of going.

'You told him where to go to find deckies,' she said out loud. 'He'll have asked someone else by now.'

No!

'So get up, get dressed and go down to that boat. Right now, before you chicken out and change your mind.

'You're nuts.

'So what can happen that's worse than being stuck here?' she told herself and got out of the bath and saw her very pink body in the mirror. Pink? The sight was somehow a surprise.

For the last two years she'd been feeling grey. She'd been concentrating on simply putting one foot after another, and sometimes even that was an effort.

And now…suddenly she felt pink.

'So go down to the docks, knock on the hatch of Ramón's wonderful boat and say—yes, please, I want to come with you, even if you are a white slave trader, even if I may be doing the stupidest thing of my life. Jumping from the frying pan into the fire? Maybe, but, crazy or not, I want to jump,' she told the mirror.

And she would.

'You're a fool,' she told her reflection, and her reflection agreed.

'Yes, but you're not a grey fool. Just do it.'

What crazy impulse had him offering a woman passage on his boat? A needy woman. A woman who looked as if she might cling.

She was right, he needed a couple of deckies, kids who'd enjoy the voyage and head off into the unknown as soon as he reached the next port. Then he could find more.

But he was tired of kids. He'd been starting to think he'd prefer to sail alone, only *Marquita* wasn't a yacht to sail by himself. She was big and old-fashioned and her sails were heavy and complicated. In good weather one man might manage her, but Ramón didn't head into good weather. He didn't look for storms but he didn't shy away from them either.

The trip back around the Horn would be long and tough, and he'd hardly make it before he was due to return to Bangladesh. He'd been looking forward to the challenge, but at the same time not looking forward to the complications crew could bring.

The episode in the café this morning had made him act on impulse. The woman—Jenny—looked light years from the kids he generally employed. She looked warm and homely and mature. She also looked as if she might have a sense of humour and, what was more, she could cook.

He could make a rather stodgy form of paella. He could cook a steak. Often the kids he employed couldn't even do that.

He was ever so slightly over paella.

Which was why the taste of Jenny's muffins, the cosiness of her café, the look of her with a smudge of flour over her left ear, had him throwing caution to the winds and offering her a job. And then, when he'd realised just where that bully of a boss had her, he'd thrown in paying off her loan for good measure.

Sensible? No. She'd looked at him as if she suspected him of buying her for his harem, and he didn't blame her.

It was just as well she hadn't accepted, he told himself. Move on.

It was time to eat. Maybe he could go out to one of the dockside hotels.

He didn't feel like it. His encounter with Jenny had left him feeling strangely flat—as if he'd seen something he wanted but he couldn't have it.

That made him sound like his Uncle Iván, he thought ruefully. Iván, Crown Prince of Cepheus, arrogance personified.

Why was he thinking of Iván now? He was really off balance.

He gave himself a fast mental shake and forced himself to go back to considering dinner. Even if he didn't go out to eat he should eat fresh food while in port. He retrieved steak, a tomato and lettuce from the refrigerator. A representation of the height of his culinary skill.

Dinner. Then bed?

Or he could wander up to the yacht club and check the noticeboard for deckies. The sooner he found a crew, the sooner he could leave, and suddenly he was eager to leave.

Why had the woman disturbed him? She had nothing to do with him. He didn't need to regard Jenny's refusal as a loss.

'Hello?'

For a moment he thought he was imagining things, but his black mood lifted, just like that, as he abandoned his steak and made his way swiftly up to the deck.

He wasn't imagining things. Jenny was on the jetty, looking almost as he'd last seen her but cleaner. She was still in her battered coat and jeans, but the flour was gone and her curls were damp from washing.

She looked nervous.

'Jenny,' he said and he couldn't disguise the pleasure in his voice. Nor did he want to. Something inside him was very pleased to see her again. *Extremely* pleased.

'I just… I just came out for a walk,' she said.

'Great,' he said.

'Charlie was arrested for drink-driving.'

'Really?'

'That wouldn't have anything to do with you?'

'Who, me?' he demanded, innocence personified. 'Would you like to come on board?'

'I…yes,' she said, and stepped quickly onto the deck as if she was afraid he might rescind his invitation. And suddenly her nerves seemed to be gone. She gazed around in unmistakable awe. 'Wow!'

'Wow' was right. Ramón had no trouble agreeing with Jenny there. *Marquita* was a gracious old lady of the sea, built sixty years ago, a wooden schooner crafted by boat builders who knew their trade and loved what they were doing.

Her hull and cabins were painted white but the timbers of her deck and her trimmings were left unpainted, oiled to a warm honey sheen. Brass fittings glittered in the evening light and, above their heads, *Marquita*'s vast oak masts swayed majestically, matching the faint swell of the incoming tide.

Marquita was a hundred feet of tradition and pure unashamed luxury. Ramón had fallen in love with her the moment he'd seen her, and he watched Jenny's face now and saw exactly the same response.

'What a restoration,' she breathed. 'She's exquisite.'

Now that was different. Almost everyone who saw this boat looked at Ramón and said: 'She must have cost a fortune.'

Jenny wasn't thinking money. She was thinking beauty.

Beauty… There was a word worth lingering on. He watched the delight in Jenny's eyes as she gazed around the deck, taking in every detail, and he thought it wasn't only his boat that was beautiful.

Jenny was almost as golden-skinned as he was; indeed, she could be mistaken for having the same Mediterranean heritage. She was small and compact. Neat, he thought and then thought, no, make that cute. Exceedingly cute. And smart. Her green eyes were bright with intelligence and interest. He thought he was right about the humour as well. She looked like a woman who could smile.

But she wasn't smiling now. She was too awed.

'Can I see below?' she breathed.

'Of course,' he said, and he'd hardly got the words out before she was heading down. He smiled and followed. A man could get jealous. This was one beautiful woman, taking not the slightest interest in him. She was totally entranced by his boat.

He followed her down into the main salon, but was brought up short. She'd stopped on the bottom step, drawing breath, seemingly awed into silence.

He didn't say anything; just waited.

This was the moment for people to gush. In truth, there was much to gush about. The rich oak wainscoting, the burnished timber, the soft worn leather of the deep settees. The wonderful colours and fabrics of the furnishing, the silks and velvets of the cushions and curtains, deep crimsons and dark blues, splashed with touches of bright sunlit gold.

When Ramón had bought this boat, just after the accident that had claimed his mother and sister, she'd been little more than a hull. He'd spent time, care and love on her renovation and his Aunt Sofía had helped as well. In truth, maybe Sofía's additions were a little over the top, but he loved Sofía and he wasn't about to reject her offerings. The result was pure comfort, pure luxury. He loved the *Marquita*—and right now he loved Jenny's reaction.

She was totally entranced, moving slowly around the salon, taking in every detail. This was the main room. The bedrooms were beyond. If she was interested, he'd show her those too, but she wasn't finished here yet.

She prowled, like a small cat inspecting each tiny part of a new territory. Her fingers brushed the burnished timber, lightly, almost reverently. She crossed to the galley and examined the taps, the sink, the stove, the attachments used to hold things steady in a storm. She bent to examine the additional safety features on the stove. Gas stoves on boats could be lethal. Not his. She opened the cupboard below the sink and proceeded to check out the plumbing.

He found he was smiling, enjoying her awe. Enjoying her eye for detail. She glanced up from where she was inspecting the valves below the sink and caught him smiling. And flushed.

'I'm sorry, but it's just so interesting. Is it okay to look?'

'It's more than okay,' he assured her. 'I've never had someone gasp at my plumbing before.'

She didn't return his smile. 'This pump,' she breathed. 'I've seen one in a catalogue. You've got them all through the boat?'

'There are three bathrooms,' he told her, trying not to sound smug. 'All pumped on the same system.'

'You have three bathrooms?' She almost choked. 'My

father didn't hold with plumbing. He said real sailors used buckets. I gather your owner isn't a bucket man.'

'No,' he agreed gravely. 'My owner definitely isn't a bucket man.'

She did smile then, but she was still on the prowl. She crossed to the navigation desk, examining charts, checking the navigation instruments, looking at the radio. Still seeming awed.

Then… 'You leave your radio off?'

'I only use it for outgoing calls.'

'Your owner doesn't mind? With a boat like this, I'd imagine he'd be checking on you daily.'

Your owner…

Now was the time to say he was the owner; this was his boat. But Jenny was starting to relax, becoming companionable, friendly. Ramón had seen enough of other women's reactions when they realised the level of his wealth. For some reason, he didn't want that reaction from Jenny.

Not yet. Not now.

'My owner and I are in accord,' he said gravely. 'We keep in contact when we need to.'

'How lucky,' she said softly. 'To have a boss who doesn't spend his life breathing down your neck.' And then she went right on prowling.

He watched, growing more fascinated by the moment. He'd had boat fanatics on board before—of course he had—and most of them had checked out his equipment with care. Others had commented with envy on the luxury of his fittings and furnishings. But Jenny was seeing the whole thing. She was assessing the boat, and he knew a part of her was also assessing him. In her role as possible hired hand? *Yes*, he thought, starting to feel optimistic. She was now under the impression that his owner trusted him absolutely, and such a reference was obviously doing him no harm.

If he wanted her trust, such a reference was a great way to start.

Finally, she turned back to him, and her awe had been

replaced by a level of satisfaction. As if she'd seen a work of art that had touched a chord deep within. 'I guess now's the time to say, *Isn't she gorgeous*?' she said, and she smiled again. 'Only it's not a question. She just is.'

'I know she is,' he said. He liked her smile. It was just what it should be, lighting her face from within.

She didn't smile enough, he thought.

He thought suddenly of the women he worked with in Bangladesh. Jenny was light years away from their desperate situations, but there was still that shadow behind her smile. As if she'd learned the hard way that she couldn't trust the world.

'Would you like to see the rest of her?' he asked, suddenly unsure where to take this. A tiny niggle was starting in the back of his head. Take this further and there would be trouble…

It was too late. He'd asked. 'Yes, please. Though…it seems an intrusion.'

'It's a pleasure,' he said and he meant it. Then he thought, hey, he'd made his bed this morning. There was a bonus. His cabin practically looked neat.

He took her to the second bedroom first. The cabin where Sofía had really had her way. He'd restored *Marquita* in the months after his mother's and sister's death, and Sofía had poured all her concern into furnishings. 'You spend half your life living on the floor in mud huts in the middle of nowhere,' she'd scolded. 'Your grandmother's money means we're both rich beyond our dreams so there's no reason why you should sleep on the floor here.'

There was certainly no need now for him, or anyone else on this boat, to sleep on the floor. He'd kept a rein on his own room but in this, the second cabin, he'd let Sofía have her way. He opened the door and Jenny stared in stunned amazement—and then burst out laughing.

'It's a boudoir,' she stammered. 'It's harem country.'

'Hey,' he said, struggling to sound serious, even offended, but he found he was smiling as well. Sofía had indeed gone over the top. She'd made a special trip to Marrakesh, and she'd furnished the cabin like a sheikh's boudoir. Boudoir? Who knew? Whatever it was that sheikhs had.

The bed was massive, eight feet round, curtained with burgundy drapes and piled with quilts and pillows of purple and gold. The carpet was thick as grass, a muted pink that fitted beautifully with the furnishings of the bed. Sofía had tied in crisp, pure white linen, and matched the whites with silk hangings of sea scenes on the walls. The glass windows were open while the *Marquita* was in port and the curtains blew softly in the breeze. The room was luxurious, yet totally inviting and utterly, utterly gorgeous.

'This is where you'd sleep,' Ramón told Jenny and she turned and stared at him as if he had two heads.

'Me. The deckie!'

'There are bunkrooms below,' he said. 'But I don't see why we shouldn't be comfortable.'

'This *is* harem country.'

'You don't like it?'

'I love it,' she confessed, eyes huge. 'What's not to love? But, as for sleeping in it… The owner doesn't mind?'

'No.'

'Where do you sleep?' she demanded. 'You can't give me the best cabin.'

'This isn't the best cabin.'

'You're kidding me, right?'

He smiled and led the way back down the companionway. Opened another door. Ushered her in.

He'd decorated this room. Sofía had added a couple of touches—actually, Sofía had spoken to his plumber so the bathroom was a touch…well, a touch embarrassing—but the rest was his.

It was bigger than the stateroom he'd offered Jenny. The bed here was huge but he didn't have hangings. It was more masculine, done in muted tones of the colours through the rest of the boat. The sunlit yellows and golds of the salon had been extended here, with only faint touches of the crimson and blues. The carpet here was blue as well, but short and functional.

There were two amazing paintings on the wall. Recognizable paintings. Jenny gasped with shock. 'Please tell me they're not real.'

Okay. 'They're not real.' They were. 'You want to see the bathroom?' he asked, unable to resist, and he led her through. Then he stood back and grinned as her jaw almost hit the carpet.

While the *Marquita* was being refitted, he'd had to return to Bangladesh before the plumbing was done, and Sofía had decided to put her oar in here as well. And Sofía's oar was not known as sparse and clinical. Plus she had this vision of him in sackcloth and ashes in Bangladesh and she was determined to make the rest of his life what she termed 'comfortable'.

Plus she read romance novels.

He therefore had a massive golden bath in the shape of a Botticelli shell. It stood like a great marble carving in the middle of the room, with carved steps up on either side. Sofía had made concessions to the unsteadiness of bathing at sea by putting what appeared to be vines all around. In reality, they were hand rails but the end result looked like a tableau from the Amazon rainforest. There were gold taps, gold hand rails, splashes of crimson and blue again. *There was trompe l'oeil*—a massive painting that looked like reality—on the wall, making it appear as if the sea came right inside. She'd even added towels with the monogram of the royal family his grandmother had belonged to.

When he'd returned from Bangladesh he'd come in here and nearly had a stroke. His first reaction had been horror, but Sofía had been beside him, so anxious she was quivering.

'I so wanted to give you something special,' she'd said, and Sofía was all the family he had and there was no way he'd hurt her.

He'd hugged her and told her he loved it—and that night he'd even had a bath in the thing. She wasn't to know he usually used the shower down the way.

'You…you sleep in here?' Jenny said, her bottom lip quivering.

'Not in the bath,' he said and grinned.

'But where does the owner sleep?' she demanded, ignoring his attempt at levity. She was gazing around in stupefaction. 'There's not room on his boat for another cabin like this.'

'I… At need I use the bunkroom.' And that was a lie, but suddenly he was starting to really, really want to employ this woman. Okay, he was on morally dubious ground, but did it matter if she thought he was a hired hand? He watched as the strain eased from her face and turned to laughter, and he thought surely this woman deserved a chance at a different life. If one small lie could give it to her…

Would it make a difference if she knew the truth? If he told her he was so rich the offer to pay her debts meant nothing to him… How would she react?

With fear. He'd seen her face when he'd offered her the job. There'd been an intuitive fear that he wanted her for more than her sailing and her cooking. How much worse would it be if she knew he could buy and sell her a thousand times over?

'The owner doesn't mind?' she demanded.

He gave up and went along with it. 'The owner likes his boat to be used and enjoyed.'

'Wow,' she breathed and looked again at the bath. 'Wow!'

'I use the shower in the shared bathroom,' he confessed and she chuckled.

'What a waste.'

'You'd be welcome to use this.'

'In your dreams,' she muttered. 'This place is Harems-R-Us.'

'It's great,' he said. 'But it's still a working boat. I promise you, Jenny, there's not a hint of harem about her.'

'You swear?' she demanded and she fixed him with a look that said she was asking for a guarantee. And he knew what that guarantee was.

'I swear,' he said softly. 'I skipper this boat and she's workmanlike.'

She looked at him for a long, long moment and what she saw finally seemed to satisfy her. She gave a tiny satisfied nod and moved on. 'You have to get her back to Europe fast?'

'Three months, at the latest.' That, at least, was true. His team started work in Bangladesh then and he intended to travel with them. 'So do you want to come?'

'You're still offering?'

'I am.' He ushered her back out of the cabin and closed the door. The sight of that bath didn't make for businesslike discussions on any level.

'You're not employing anyone else?'

'Not if I have you.'

'You don't even know if I can sail,' she said, astounded all over again.

He looked at her appraisingly. The corridor here was narrow and they were too close. He'd like to be able to step back a bit, to see her face. He couldn't.

She was still nervous, he thought, like a deer caught in headlights. But caught she was. His offer seemed to have touched something in her that longed to respond, and even the sight of that crazy bath hadn't made her back off. She was just like he was, he thought, raised with a love of the sea. Aching to be out there.

So…she was caught. All he had to do was reel her in.

'So show me that you can sail,' he said. 'Show me now. The wind's getting up enough to make it interesting. Let's take her out.'

'What, tonight?'

'Tonight. Now. Dare you.'

'I can't,' she said, sounding panicked.

'Why not?'

She stared up at him as if he were a species she'd never seen.

'You just go. Whenever you feel like it.'

'The only thing holding us back is a couple of lines tied to bollards on the wharf,' he said and then, as her look of panic deepened, he grinned. 'But we will bring her back tonight, if that's what's worrying you. It's seven now. We can be back in harbour by midnight.'

'You seriously expect me to sail with you? Now?'

'There's a great moon,' he said. 'The night is ours. Why not?'

So, half an hour later, they were sailing out through the heads, heading for Europe.

Or that was what it felt like to Jenny. Ramón was at the wheel. She'd gone up to the bow to tighten a stay, to see if they could get a bit more tension in the jib. The wind was behind them, the moon was rising from the east, moonlight was shimmering on the water and she was free.

The night was warm enough for her to take off her coat, to put her bare arms out to catch a moonbeam. She could let her hair stream behind her and become a bow-sprite, she thought. An omen of good luck to sailors.

An omen of good luck to Ramón?

She turned and looked back at him. He was a dark shadow in the rear of the boat but she knew he was watching her from behind the wheel. She was being judged?

So what? The boat was as tightly tuned as she could make her. Ramón had asked her to set the sails herself. She'd needed help in this unfamiliar environment but he'd followed her instructions rather than the other way round.

This boat was far bigger than anything she'd sailed on, but she'd spent her life in a sea port, talking to sailors, watching the boats come in. She'd seen yachts like this; she'd watched them and she'd ached to be on one.

She'd brought Matty down to the harbour and she'd promised him his own boat.

'When you're big. When you're strong.'

And suddenly she was blinking back tears. That was stupid. She didn't cry for Matty any more. It was no use; he was never coming back.

'Are you okay?'

Had he seen? The moonlight wasn't that strong. She

swiped her fist angrily across her cheeks, ridding herself of the evidence of her distress, and made her way slowly aft. She had a lifeline clipped to her and she had to clip it and unclip it along the way. She was as sure-footed as a cat at sea, but it didn't hurt to show him she was safety conscious—and, besides, it gave her time to get her face in order.

'I'm fine,' she told him as she reached him.

'Take over the wheel, then,' he told her. 'I need to cook dinner.'

Was this a test, too? she wondered. Did she really have sea legs? Cooking below deck on a heavy swell was something no one with a weak stomach could do.

'I'll do it.' She could.

'You really don't get seasick?'

'I really don't get seasick.'

'A woman in a million,' he murmured and then he grinned. 'But no, it's not fair to ask you to cook. This is your night at sea and, after the day you've had, you deserve it. Take the wheel. Have you eaten?'

'Hours ago.'

'There's steak to spare.' He smiled at her and wham, there it was again, his smile that had her heart saying, *Beware, Beware, Beware*.

'I really am fine,' she said and sat and reached for the wheel and when her hand brushed his—she could swear it was accidental—the *Beware* grew so loud it was a positive roar.

But, seemingly unaware of any roaring on deck, he left her and dropped down into the galley. In minutes the smell of steak wafted up. Nothing else. Just steak.

Not my choice for a lovely night at sea, she thought, but she wasn't complaining. The rolling swell was coming in from the east. She nosed the boat into the swell and the boat steadied on course.

She was the most beautiful boat.

Could she really be crew? She was starting to feel as if, when Ramón had made the offer, she should have signed a contract on the spot. Then, as he emerged from the galley bearing two plates and smiling, she knew why she hadn't. That smile gave her so many misgivings.

'I cooked some for you, too,' he said, looking dubiously down at his plates. 'If you really aren't seasick…'

'I have to eat something to prove it?'

'It's a true test of grit,' he said. 'You eat my cooking, then I know you have a cast iron stomach.' He sat down beside her and handed her a plate.

She looked down at it. Supermarket steak, she thought, and not a good cut.

She poked it with a fork and it didn't give.

'You have to be polite,' he said. 'Otherwise my feelings will be hurt.'

'Get ready for your feelings to be hurt.'

'Taste it at least.'

She released the wheel, fought the steak for a bit and then said, 'Can we put her on automatic pilot? This is going to take some work.'

'Hey, I'm your host,' he said, sounding offended.

'And I'm a cook. How long did you fry this?'

'I don't know. Twenty minutes, maybe? I needed to check the charts to remind myself of the lights for harbour re-entry.'

'So your steak cooked away on its own while you concentrated on other things.'

'What's wrong with that?'

'I'd tell you,' she said darkly, stabbing at her steak and finally managing to saw off a piece. Manfully chewing and then swallowing. 'Only you're right; you're my host.'

'I'd like to be your employer. Will you be cook on the *Marquita*?'

Whoa. So much for concentrating on steak. This, then, was when she had to commit. To craziness or not.

To life—or not.

'You mean…you really were serious with your offer?'

'I'm always serious. It was a serious offer. It *is* a serious offer.'

'You'd only have to pay me a year's salary. I could maybe

organise something…' But she knew she couldn't, and he knew it, too. His response was immediate.

'The offer is to settle your debts and sail away with you, debt free. That or nothing.'

'That sounds like something out of a romance novel. Hero on white charger, rescuing heroine from villain. I'm no wimpy heroine.'

He grinned. 'You sound just like my Aunt Sofía. She reads them, too. But no, I never said you were wimpy. I never thought you were wimpy.'

'I'd repay…'

'No,' he said strongly and took her plate away from her and set it down. He took her hands then, strong hands gripping hers so she felt the strength of him, the sureness and the authority. Authority? This was a man used to getting his own way, she thought, suddenly breathless, and once more came the fleeting thought, *I should run*.

There was nowhere to run. If she said yes there'd be nowhere to run for a year.

'You will not repay,' he growled. 'A deal's a deal, Jenny. You will be my crew. You will be my cook. I'll ask nothing more.'

This was serious. Too serious. She didn't want to think about the implications behind those words.

And maybe she didn't want that promise. *I'll ask nothing more…*

He'd said her debt was insignificant. Maybe it was to him. To her it was an insurmountable burden. She had her pride, but maybe it was time to swallow it, stand aside and let him play hero.

'Thank you,' she said, trying to sound meek.

'Jenny?'

'Yes.'

'I'm captain,' he said. 'But I will not tolerate subordination.'

'Subordination?'

'It's my English,' he apologised, sounding suddenly very Spanish. 'As in captains say to their crew, "*I will not tolerate insubordination!*" just before they give them a hundred lashes and toss them in the brink.'

'What's the brink?'

'I have no idea,' he confessed. 'I'm sure the *Marquita* doesn't have one, which is what I'm telling you. Whereas most captains won't tolerate insubordination, I am the opposite. If you'd like to argue all the way around the Horn, it's fine by me.'

'You want me to argue?' She was too close to him, she thought, and he was still holding her hands. The sensation was worrying.

Worryingly good, though. Not worryingly bad. Arguing with this guy all the way round the Horn…

'Yes. I will also expect muffins,' he said and she almost groaned.

'Really?'

'Take it or leave it,' he said. 'Muffins and insubordination. Yes or no?'

She stared up at him in the moonlight. He stared straight back at her and she felt her heart do this strange surge, as if her fuel-lines had just been doubled.

What am I getting into, she demanded of herself, but suddenly she didn't care. The night was warm, the boat was lovely and this man was holding her hands, looking down at her in the moonlight and his hands were imparting strength and sureness and promise.

Promise? What was he promising? She was being fanciful.

But she had to be careful, she told herself fiercely. She must.

It was too late.

'Yes,' she said before she could change her mind—and she was committed.

She was heading to the other side of the world with a man she'd met less than a day ago.

Was she out of her mind?

* * *

What had he done? What was he getting himself into?

He'd be spending three months at sea with a woman called Jenny.

Jenny what? Jenny who? He knew nothing about her other than she sailed and she cooked.

He spent more time on background checks for the deckies he employed. He always ran a fast check on the kids he employed, to ensure there weren't skeletons in the closet that would come bursting out the minute he was out of sight of land.

And he didn't employ them for a year. The deal was always that they'd work for him until the next port and then make a mutual decision as to whether they wanted to go on.

He'd employed Jenny for a year.

He wasn't going to be on the boat for a year. Had he thought that through? No, so he'd better think it through now.

Be honest? Should he say, *Jenny, I made the offer because I felt sorry for you, and there was no way you'd have accepted my offer of a loan if you knew I'm only offering three months' work?*

He wasn't going to say that, because it wasn't true. He'd made the offer for far more complicated reasons than sympathy, and that was what was messing with his head now.

In three months he'd be in Bangladesh.

Did he need to go to Bangladesh?

In truth, he didn't need to go anywhere. His family inheritance had been massive, he'd invested it with care and if he wished he could spend the rest of his life in idle luxury.

Only…his family had never been like that. Excluded from the royal family, Ramón's grandmother had set about making herself useful. The royal family of Cepheus was known for indolence, mindless indulgence, even cruelty. His grandmother had left the royal palace in fear, for good reason. But then she'd started making herself a life—giving life to others.

So she and her children, Ramón's father and aunt, had set up a charity in Bangladesh. They built homes in the low lying delta regions, houses that could be raised as flood levels rose, homes that could keep a community safe and dry. Ramón had been introduced to it early and found the concept fascinating.

His father's death had made him even more determined to stay away from royalty; to make a useful life for himself, so at seventeen he'd apprenticed himself to one of Cepheus's top builders. He'd learned skills from the ground up. Now it wasn't just money he was throwing at this project—it was his hands as well as his heart.

During the wet season he couldn't build. During these months he used to stay on the island he still called home, spending time with his mother and sister. He'd also spent it planning investments so the work they were doing could go on for ever.

But then his mother and his sister died. One drunken driver and his family was wiped out. Suddenly he couldn't bear to go home. He employed a team of top people to take over his family's financial empire, and he'd bought the *Marquita*.

He still worked in Bangladesh—hands-on was great, hard manual work which drove away the demons. But for the rest of the year he pitted himself against the sea and felt better for it.

But there was a gaping hole where his family had been; a hole he could never fill. Nor did he want to, he decided after a year or so. If it hurt so much to lose…to get close to someone again seemed stupid.

So why ask Jenny onto his boat? He knew instinctively that closeness was a very real risk with this woman. But it was as if another part of him, a part he didn't know existed, had emerged and done the asking.

He'd have to explain Bangladesh to her. Or would he? When he got to Cepheus he could simply say there was no need for the boat, the owner wanted her in dry dock for six months. Jenny was free to fly back to Australia—he'd pay her fare—and she could fill the rest of her contract six months later.

That'd mean he had crew not only for now but for the future as well.

A crew of one woman.

This was danger territory. The Ramón he knew well, the Ramón he trusted, was screaming a warning.

No. He could be sensible. This was a big enough boat for him to keep his own counsel. He'd learned to do that from years of sailing with deckies. The kids found him aloof, he knew, but aloof was good. Aloof meant you didn't open yourself to gut-wrenching pain.

Aloof meant you didn't invite a woman like Jenny to sail around the world with you.

A shame that he just had.

'The *Marquita*'s reported as having left Fiji two weeks ago. We think Ramón's in Australia.'

'For heaven's sake!' Sofía pushed herself up on her cushions and stared at the lawyer, perplexed. 'What's he doing in Australia?'

'Who would know?' the lawyer said with asperity. 'He's left no travel plans.'

'He could hardly expect this awfulness,' Sofía retorted. 'There's never been a thought that Ramón could inherit.'

'Well, it makes life difficult for us,' the lawyer snapped. 'He doesn't even answer incoming radio calls.'

'Ramón's been a loner since his mother and sister died,' Sofía said, and she sighed. 'It affected me deeply, so who knows how it affected him? If he wants to be alone, who are we to stop him?'

'He can't be alone any longer,' the lawyer said. 'I'm flying out.'

'To Australia?'

'Yes.'

'Isn't Australia rather big?' Sofía said cautiously. 'I mean… I don't want to discourage you, but if you flew to Perth and he ended up at Darwin… I've read about Australia and it does sound a little larger than Cepheus.'

'I believe the smallest of its states is bigger than Cepheus,' the lawyer agreed. 'But if he's coming from Fiji he'll be heading for the east coast. We have people looking out for him at every major port. If I wait in Sydney I can be with him in hours rather than days.'

'You don't think we could wait until he makes contact?' Sofía said. 'He does email me. Eventually.'

'He needs to take the throne by the end of the month or Carlos inherits.'

'Carlos?' Sofía said, and her face crumpled in distress. 'Oh, dear.'

'So you see the hurry,' the lawyer said. 'If I'm in Australia, as soon as we locate his boat I can be there. He has to come home. Now.'

'I wish we could find him before I make a decision about Philippe,' she said. 'Oh, dear.'

'I thought you'd found foster parents for him.'

'Yes, but…it seems wrong to send him away from the palace. What would Ramón do, do you think?'

'I hardly think Prince Ramón will wish to be bothered with a child.'

'No,' Sofía said sadly. 'Maybe you're right. There are so many things Ramón will be bothered with now—how can he want a say in the future of a child he doesn't know?'

'He won't. Send the child to foster parents.'

'Yes,' Sofía said sadly. 'I don't know how to raise a child myself. He's had enough of hired nannies. I think it's best for everyone.'

CHAPTER THREE

THIS was really, really foolish. She was allowing an unknown Spaniard to pay her debts and sweep her off in his fabulous yacht to the other side of the world. She was so appalled at herself she couldn't stop grinning.

Watching Cathy's face had been a highlight. 'I can't let you do it,' she'd said in horror. 'I know I joked about it but I never dreamed you'd take me seriously. You know nothing about him. This is awful.'

And Jenny had nodded solemn agreement.

'It is awful. If I turn up in some Arabic harem on the other side of the world it's all your fault,' she told her friend. 'You pointed him out to me.'

'No. Jenny, I never would have… No!'

She'd chuckled and relented. 'Okay, I won't make you come and rescue me. I know this is a risk, my love, but honestly, he seems nice. I don't think there's a harem but even if there is…I'm a big girl and I take responsibility for my own decision. I know it's playing with fire, but honestly, Cathy, you were right. I'm out of here any way I can.'

And what a way! Sailing out of the harbour on board the *Marquita* with Ramón at the helm was like something out of a fairy tale.

Fairy tales didn't include scrubbing decks, though, she conceded ruefully. There was enough of reality to keep her grounded—or as grounded as one could be at sea. Six days later, Jenny was on her knees swishing a scrubbing brush like a true deck-hand. They'd been visited by a flock of terns at dawn—possibly the last they'd see until they neared land again. She certainly hoped so. The deck was a mess.

But making her feel a whole lot better about scrubbing was the fact that Ramón was on his knees scrubbing as well. That didn't fit the fairy tale either. Knight on white charger scrubbing bird droppings? She glanced over and found he was watching her. He caught her grin and he grinned back.

'Not exactly the romantic ideal of sailing into the sunset,' he said, and it was so much what she'd been thinking that she laughed. She sat back on her heels, put her face up to the sun and soaked it in. The *Marquita* was on autopilot, safe enough in weather like this. There was a light breeze—enough to make *Marquita* slip gracefully through the water like a skier on a downhill run. On land it would be hot, but out here on the ocean it was just plain fabulous. Jenny was wearing shorts and T-shirt and nothing else. Her feet were bare, her hair was scrunched up in a ponytail to keep it out of her eyes, her nose was white with sunscreen—and she was perfectly, gloriously happy.

'You're supposed to complain,' Ramón said, watching her. 'Any deckie I've ever employed would be complaining by now.'

'What on earth would I be complaining about?'

'Scrubbing, maybe?'

'I'd scrub from here to China if I could stay on this boat,' she said happily and then saw his expression and hastily changed her mind. 'No. I didn't mean that. You keep right on thinking I'm working hard for my money. But, honestly, you have the best job in the world, Ramón Cavellero, and I have the second best.'

'I do, don't I?' he said, but his smile faded, and something about him said he had shadows too. Did she want to ask?

Maybe not.

She'd known Ramón for over a week now, and she'd learned a lot in that time. She'd learned he was a wonderful sailor, intuitive, clever and careful. He took no unnecessary risks, yet on the second night out there'd been a storm. A nervous sailor might have reefed in everything and sat it out. Ramón, however, had looked at the charts, altered his course and let the jib stay at full stretch. The *Marquita* had flown across the water with a speed Jenny found unbelievable, and when the dawn came and the storm abated they were maybe three hundred miles further towards New Zealand than they'd otherwise have been.

She'd taken a turn at the wheel that night but she knew Ramón hadn't slept. She'd been conscious of his shadowy presence below, aware of what the boat was doing, aware of how she was handling her. It wasn't that he didn't trust her, but she was new crew and to sleep in such a storm while she had such responsibility might have been dangerous.

His competence pleased her, as did the fact that he hadn't told her he was checking on her. Lots of things about him pleased her, she admitted—but Ramón kept himself to himself. Any thoughts she may have had of being an addition to his harem were quickly squashed. Once they were at sea, he was reserved to the point of being aloof.

'How long have you skippered this boat?' she asked suddenly, getting back to scrubbing, not looking up. She was learning that he responded better that way, talking easily as they worked together. Once work stopped he retreated again into silence.

'Ten years,' he said.

'Wow. You must have been at kindergarten when you were first employed.'

'I got lucky,' he said brusquely, and she thought, *don't go there*. She'd asked a couple of things about the owner, and she'd learned quickly that was the way to stop a conversation dead.

'So how many crews would you have employed in that time?' she asked. And then she frowned down at what she was scrubbing. How on earth had the birds managed to soil under the rim of the forward hatch? She tried to imagine, and couldn't.

'How long's a piece of string?' Ramón said. 'I get new people at every port.'

'But you have me for a year.'

'That's right, I have,' he said and she glanced up and caught a flash of something that might be satisfaction. She smiled and went back to scrubbing, unaccountably pleased.

'That sounds like you liked my lunch time paella.'

'I loved your lunch time paella. Where did you learn to cook something so magnificently Spanish?'

'I'm part Spanish,' she said and he stopped scrubbing and stared.

'Spanish?'

'Well, truthfully, I'm all Australian,' she said, 'but my father was Spanish. He moved to Australia when he met my mother. My mother's mother was Spanish as well. Papà came as an adventuring young man. He contacted my grandmother as a family friend and the rest is history.

'So,' Ramón said slowly, sounding dazed. '*Habla usted español?* Can you speak Spanish?'

'*Sí*,' she said, and tried not to sound smug.

'I don't believe it.'

'There's no end to my talents,' she agreed and grinned, and then peered under the hatch. 'Speaking of talent... How did these birds do this? They must have lain on their sides and aimed.'

'It's a competition between them and me,' Ramón said darkly. 'They don't like my boat looking beautiful. All I can do is sail so far out to sea they can't reach me. But...you have a Spanish background? Why didn't you tell me?'

'You never asked,' she said, and then she hesitated. 'There's lots you didn't ask, and your offer seemed so amazing I saw no reason to mess it with detail. I could have told you I play a mean game of netball, I can climb trees, I have my bronze surf lifesaving certificate and I can play *Waltzing Matilda* on a gum leaf. You didn't ask and how could I tell you? You might have thought I was skiting.'

'Skiting?'

'Making myself out to be Miss Wonderful.'

'I seem to have employed Miss Wonderful regardless,' he said. And then… 'Jenny?'

'Mmm?'

'No, I mean, what sort of Spanish parents call their daughter Jenny?'

'It's Gianetta.'

'Gianetta.' He said it with slow, lilting pleasure, and he said it the way it was supposed to sound. The way her parents had said it. She blinked and then she thought no. Actually, the way Ramón said it wasn't the way her parents had said it. He had the pronunciation right but it was much, much better. He rolled it, he almost growled it, and it sounded so sexy her toes started to curl.

'I would have found out when you signed your contract,' Ramón was saying while she attempted a bit of toe uncurling. Then he smiled. 'Speaking of which, maybe it's time you did sign up. I don't want to let anyone who can play *Waltzing Matilda* on a gum leaf get away.'

'It's a dying art,' she said, relieved to be on safer ground. In fact she'd been astounded that he hadn't yet got round to making her sign any agreement.

The day before they'd sailed he'd handed Charlie a cheque. 'How do you know you can trust me to fill my part of the bargain?' she'd asked him, stunned by what he was doing, and Ramón had looked down at her for a long moment, his face impassive, and he'd given a small decisive nod.

'I can,' he'd said, and that was that.

'Playing a gum leaf's a dying art?' he asked now, cautiously.

'It's something I need to teach my grandchildren,' she told him. And then she heard what she'd said. *Grandchildren.* The void, always threatening, was suddenly right under her. She hauled herself back with an effort.

'What is it?' Ramón said and he was looking at her with concern. The void disappeared. There went her toes again, curling, curling. Did he have any idea of what those eyes did to her? They helped, though. She was back again now, safe. She could move on. If she could focus on something other than those eyes.

'So I'm assuming you're Spanish, too?' she managed.

'No!'

'You're not Spanish?'

'Absolutely not.'

'You sound Spanish.' Then she hesitated. Here was another reason she hadn't told him about her heritage—she wasn't sure. There was something else in his accent besides Spain. France? It was a sexy mix that she couldn't quite place.

'I come from Cepheus,' he said, and all was explained.

Cepheus. She knew it. A tiny principality on the Mediterranean, fiercely independent and fiercely proud.

'My father told me about Cepheus,' she said, awed that here was an echo from her childhood. 'Papà was born not so far away from the border and he went there as a boy. He said it's the most beautiful country in the world—but he also said it belonged to Spain.'

'If he's Spanish then he would say that,' Ramón growled. 'If he was French he'd say the same thing. They've been fighting over my country for generations, like eagles over a small bird. What they've come to realize, however, is that the small bird has claws and knows how to protect itself. For now they've dropped us—they've let us be. We are Cepheus. Nothing more.'

'But you speak Spanish?'

'The French and the Spanish have both taken part of our language and made it theirs,' he said, and she couldn't help herself. She chuckled.

'What's funny?' He was suddenly practically glowering.

'Your patriotism,' she said, refusing to be deflected. 'Like Australians saying the English speak Australian with a plum in their mouths.'

'It's not the same,' he said but then he was smiling again. She smiled back—and wham.

What was it with this man?

She knew exactly what it was. Quite simply he was the most gorgeous guy she'd ever met. Tall, dark and fabulous, a voice like a god, rugged, clever…and smiling. She took a deep breath and went back to really focused scrubbing. It was imperative that she scrub.

She was alone on a boat in the middle of the ocean with a man she was so attracted to her toes were practically ringlets. And she was crew. Nothing more. She was cook and deckhand. Remember it!

'So why the debt?' he asked gently, and she forgot about being cook and deckhand. He was asking as if he cared.

Should she tell him to mind his own business? Should she back away?

Why? He'd been extraordinarily kind and if he wanted to ask… He didn't feel like her boss, and at this moment she didn't feel like a deckie.

Maybe he even had the right to know.

'I lost my baby,' she said flatly, trying to make it sound as if it was history. Only of course she couldn't. Two years on, it still pierced something inside her to say it. 'Matty was born with a congenital heart condition. He had a series of operations, each riskier than the last. Finally, there was only one procedure left to try—a procedure so new it cost the earth. It was his last chance and I had to take it, but of course I'd run out of what money I had. I was working for Charlie for four hours a day over the lunch time rush—Matty was in hospital and I hated leaving him but I had to pay the rent, so when things hit rock bottom Charlie knew. So Charlie loaned me what I needed on the basis that I keep working on for him.'

She scrubbed fiercely at a piece of deck that had already been scrubbed. Ramón didn't say anything. She scrubbed a bit more. Thought about not saying more and then decided—why not say it all?

'You need to understand…I'd been cooking on the docks

since I was seventeen and people knew my food. Charlie's café was struggling and he needed my help to keep it afloat. But the operation didn't work. Matty died when he was two years, three months and five days old. I buried him and I went back to Charlie's café and I've been there ever since.'

'I am so sorry.' Ramón was sitting back on his heels and watching her. She didn't look up—she couldn't. She kept right on scrubbing.

The boat rocked gently on the swell. The sun shone down on the back of her neck and she was acutely aware of his gaze. So aware of his silence.

'Charlie demanded that you leave your baby, for those hours in the last days of his life?' he said at last, and she swallowed at that, fighting back regret that could never fade.

'It was our deal.' She hesitated. 'You've seen the worst of Charlie. Time was when he was a decent human being. Before the drink took over. When he offered me a way out—I only saw the money. I guess I just trusted. And after I borrowed the money there was no way out.'

'So where,' he asked, in his soft, lilting accent that seemed to have warmth and sincerity built into it, 'was Matty's father?'

'On the other side of the world, as far as I know,' she said, and she blinked back self-pity and found herself smiling. 'My Kieran. Or, rather, no one's Kieran.'

'You're smiling?' He sounded incredulous, as well he might.

'Yes, that's stupid. And yes, I was really stupid.' Enough with the scrubbing—any more and she'd start taking off wood. She tossed her brush into the bucket and stood up, leaning against the rail and letting the sun comfort her. How to explain Kieran? 'My father had just died, and I was bleak and miserable. Kieran came into port and he was just…alive. I met him on the wharf one night, we went dancing and I fell in love. Only even then I knew I wasn't in love with Kieran. Not with the person. I was in love with what he represented. Happiness. Laughter. Life. At the end of a wonderful week he sailed away and two weeks later I discovered our precautions hadn't worked. I emailed him to tell him. He sent me a dozen roses and a cheque for a termination. The next time I emailed, to tell him I was keeping our baby, there was no reply. There's been no reply since.'

'Do you mind?' he said gently.

'I mind that Kieran didn't have a chance to meet his son,' she said. 'It was his loss. Matty was wonderful.' She pulled herself together and managed to smile again. 'But I'd imagine all mothers say that about their babies. Any minute now I'll be tugging photographs out of my purse.'

'It would be my privilege to see them.'

'You don't mean that.'

'Why would I not?'

Her smile faded. She searched his face and saw only truth.

'It's okay,' she said, disconcerted. She was struggling to understand this man. She'd accepted this job suspecting he was another similar to Kieran, sailing the world to escape responsibility, only the more she saw of him the more she realized there were depths she couldn't fathom.

She had armour now to protect herself against the likes of Kieran. She knew she did—that was why she'd taken the job. But this man's gentle sympathy and practical help were something new. She tried to imagine Kieran scrubbing a deck when he didn't have to, and she couldn't.

'So where's your family?' she asked, too abruptly, and she watched his face close. Which was what she was coming to expect. He'd done this before to her, simply shutting himself off from her questions. She thought it was a method he'd learned from years of employing casual labour, setting boundaries and staying firmly behind them.

Maybe that was reasonable, she conceded. Just because she'd stepped outside her personal boundaries, it didn't mean he must.

'Sorry. I'll put the buckets away,' she said, but he didn't move and neither did she.

'I don't like talking of my family.'

'That's okay. That's your right.'

'You didn't have to tell me about your son.'

'Yes, but I like talking about Matty,' she said. She thought about it. It wasn't absolutely true. Or was it?

She only talked about Matty to Cathy, to Susie, to those few people who'd known him. But still…

'Talking about him keeps him real,' she said, trying to figure it out as she spoke. 'Keeping silent locks him in my heart and I'm scared he'll shrivel. I want to be able to have him out there, to share him.' She shrugged. 'It makes no sense but there it is. Your family…you keep them where you need to have them. I'm sorry I intruded.'

'I don't believe you could ever intrude,' he said, so softly she could hardly hear him. 'But my story's not so peaceful. My father died when I was seven. He and my grandfather… well, let's just say they didn't get on. My grandfather was what might fairly be described as a wealthy thug. He mistreated my grandmother appallingly, and finally my father thought to put things right by instigating legal proceedings. Only when it looked like my father and grandmother might win, my grandfather's thugs bashed him—so badly he died.'

'Oh, Ramón,' she whispered, appalled.

'It's old history,' he said in a voice that told her it wasn't. It still had the power to hurt. 'Nothing could ever be proved, so we had to move on as best we could. But my grandmother never got over it. She died when I was ten, and then my mother and my sister were killed in a car accident when I was little more than a teenager. So that's my family. Or, rather, that was my family. I have an aunt I love, but that's all.'

'So you don't have a home,' she said softly.

'The sea makes a wonderful mistress.'

'She's not exactly cuddly,' Jenny retorted before she thought it through, and then she heard what she'd said and she could have kicked herself. But it seemed her tongue was determined to keep her in trouble. 'I mean… Well, the sea. A *mistress*? Wouldn't you rather have a real one?'

His lips twitched. 'You're asking why don't I have a woman?'

'I didn't mean that at all,' she said, astounded at herself. 'If you don't choose to…'

But she stopped herself there. She was getting into deeper water at every word and she was floundering.

'Would you rate yourself as cuddly?' he asked, a slight smile still playing round his mouth, and she felt herself colouring from the toes up. She'd walked straight into that one.

He thoroughly disconcerted her. It was as if there was some sort of connection between them, like an electric current that buzzed back and forth, no matter how she tried to subdue it.

She had to subdue it. Ramón was her boss. She had to maintain a working relationship with him for a year.

'No. No!' She shook her head so hard the tie came loose and her curls went flying every which way. 'Of course I'm not cuddly. I got myself in one horrible mess with Kieran, and I'm not going down that path again, thank you very much.'

'So maybe the sea is to be your partner in life, too?'

'I don't want a partner,' she said with asperity. 'I don't need one, thank you very much. You're very welcome to your sea, Mr Cavellero, but I'll stick to cooking, sailing and occasional scrubbing. What more could a woman want? It sounds like relationships, for both of us, are a thing of the past.' And then she paused. She stared out over Ramón's shoulder. 'Oh!' She put her hand up to shade her eyes. 'Oh, Ramón, look!'

Ramón wheeled to see what she was seeing, and he echoed her gasp.

They'd been too intent on each other to notice their surroundings—the sea was clear to the horizon so there was no threat, but suddenly there was a great black mound, floating closer and closer to the *Marquita*. On the far side of the mound was another, much smaller.

The smaller mound was gliding through the water, surfacing and diving, surfacing and diving. The big mound lay still, like a massive log, three-quarters submerged.

'Oh,' Jenny gasped, trying to take in what she was seeing. 'It's a whale and its calf. But why…'

Why was the larger whale so still?

They were both staring out to starboard now. Ramón narrowed his eyes, then swore and made his way swiftly aft. He retrieved a pair of field glasses, focused and swore again.

'She's wrapped in a net.' He flicked off the autopilot. 'Jenny, we're coming about.'

The boat was already swinging. Jenny dropped her buckets and moved like lightning, reefing in the main with desperate haste so the boom wouldn't slam across with the wind shift.

Even her father wouldn't have trusted her to move so fast, she thought, as she winched in the stays with a speed even she hadn't known was possible. Ramón expected the best of her and she gave it.

But Ramón wasn't focused on her. All his attention was on the whale. With the sails in place she could look again at what was in front of her. And what she saw… She drew in her breath in distress.

The massive whale—maybe fifty feet long or more—was almost completely wrapped in a damaged shark net. Jenny had seen these nets. They were set up across popular beaches to keep swimmers safe, but occasionally whales swam in too close to shore and became entangled, or swam into a net that had already been dislodged.

The net was enfolding her almost completely, with a rope as thick as Jenny's wrist tying her from head to tail, forcing her to bend. As the *Marquita* glided past, Jenny saw her massive pectoral fins were fastened uselessly to her sides. She was rolling helplessly in the swell.

Dead?

No. Just as she thought it, the creature gave a massive shudder. She was totally helpless, and by her side her calf swam free, but helpless as well in the shadow of her mother's entrapment.

'*Dios*,' she whispered. It was the age-old plea she'd learned from her mother, and she heard the echo of it from Ramón's lips.

'It's a humpback,' she said in distress. 'The net's wrapped so tight it's killing her. What can we do?'

But Ramón was already moving. 'We get the sails down and start the motor,' he said. 'The sails won't give us room to manoeuvre. Gianetta, I need your help. Fast.'

He had it. The sails were being reefed in almost before he finished speaking, as the motor hummed seamlessly into life.

He pushed it into low gear so the sound was a low hum. The last thing either of them wanted was to panic the whale. As it was, the calf was moving nervously away from them, so the mother was between it and the boat.

'If she panics there's nothing we can do,' Jenny said grimly. 'Can we get near enough to cut?'

They couldn't. Ramón edged the *Marquita* close, the big whale rolled a little, the swell separated them and Jenny knew they could never simply reach out and cut.

'Can we call someone?' she said helplessly. 'There's whale rescue organisations. Maybe they could come out.'

'We're too far from land,' Ramón said. 'It's us or no one.'

No one, Jenny thought as they tried one more pass. It was hopeless. For them to cut the net the whale had to be right beside the boat. With the lurching of the swell there was no way they could steer the boat alongside and keep her there.

How else to help? To get into the water and swim, then cling and cut was far, far too risky. Jenny was a good swimmer but…

'It's open water, the job's too big, there's no way I could count on getting back into the boat,' Ramón said, and she knew he was thinking the same.

'You would do it if you could?' she asked, incredulous.

'If I knew it'd be effective. But do you think she's going to stay still while I cut? If she rolled, if I was pushed under and caught…'

As if on cue, the whale rolled again. Her massive pectoral fins were fastened hard against her, so a sideways roll was all she could do. She blew—a spray of water misted over Jenny's face, but Jenny's face was wet anyway.

'We can't leave her like this,' she whispered. 'We have to try.'

'We do,' Ramón said. 'Jenny, are you prepared to take a risk?'

There was no question. 'Of course.'

'Okay,' he said, reaching under the seat near the wheel and hauling out life jackets. 'Here's the plan. We put these on. We unfasten the life raft in case worst comes to worst and we let the authorities know what's happening. We radio in our position, we tell them what we intend to do and if they don't hear back from us then they'll know we're sitting in a life raft in the middle of the Pacific. We're wearing positional locators anyway. We should be fine.'

'What…what are we intending to do?' Jenny asked faintly.

'Pull the boat up beside the whale,' he said. 'If you're brave enough.'

She stared at him, almost speechless. How could he get so close? And, even if he did, if the whale rolled… 'You'd risk the boat?' she gasped.

'Yes.' Unequivocal.

'Could we be sure of rescue?'

'I'll set it up so we would be,' he said. 'I'm not risking our lives here. Only our boat and the cost of marine rescue.'

'Marine rescue… It'd cost a fortune.'

'Jenny, we're wasting time. Yes or no?'

She looked out at the whale. Left alone, she'd die, dreadfully, agonisingly and, without her, her calf would slowly starve to death as well.

Ramón was asking her to risk all. She looked at him and he met her gaze, levelly and calmly.

'Gianetta, she's helpless,' he said. 'I believe at some subliminal level she'll understand we're trying to help and she won't roll towards us. But you know I can't guarantee that. There's a small chance we may end up sitting in a lifeboat for the next few hours waiting to be winched to safety. But I won't do it unless I have your agreement. It's not my risk, Gianetta. It's our risk.'

Our risk.

She thought about what he was asking—what he was doing. He'd have to explain to his owner that he'd lost his boat to save a whale. He'd lose his job at the very least. Maybe he'd be up for massive costs, for the boat and for rescue.

She looked at him and she saw it meant nothing.

He was free, she thought, with a sudden stab of something that could almost be jealousy. There was the whale to be saved. He'd do what needed to be done without thinking of the future.

Life… That was all that mattered, she thought suddenly, and with it came an unexpected lifting of the dreariness of the last couple of years. She'd fought long and hard for Matty. She'd lost but she'd had him and she'd loved him and she'd worried about the cost later.

She looked out at the whale and she knew there was only one answer to give.

'Of course,' she said. 'Just give me a couple of minutes to stick a ration pack in the life raft. If I'm going to float around for a day or so waiting for rescue flights then I want at least two bottles of champagne and some really good cheeses while I'm waiting.'

Jenny didn't have a clue what Ramón intended, but when she saw she was awed. With his safeguards in place, he stood on the highest point of the boat with a small anchor—one he presumably used in shallow waters when lowering the massive main anchor would potentially damage the sea bed.

This anchor was light enough for a man to hold. Or, rather, for Ramón to hold, Jenny corrected herself. It still looked heavy. But Ramón stood with the anchor attached by a long line and he held it as if it was no weight at all, while Jenny nosed the boat as close to the whale as she dared. Ramón swung the anchor round and round, in wider and wider circles, and then he heaved with every ounce of strength he had.

The whale was maybe fifteen feet from the boat. The anchor flew over the far side of her and slid down. As it slid,

Ramón was already striding aft, a far more secure place to manoeuvre, and he was starting to tug the rope back in.

'Cut the motor,' he snapped. She did, and finally she realized what he was doing.

The anchor had fallen on the far side of the whale. As Ramón tugged, the anchor was being hauled up the whale's far side. Its hooks caught the ropes of the net and held, and suddenly Ramón was reeling in the anchor with whale attached. Or, rather, the *Marquita* was being reeled in against the whale, and the massive creature was simply submitting.

Jenny was by Ramón's side in an instant, pulling with him. Boat and whale moved closer. Closer still.

'Okay, hold her as close as you can,' Ramón said curtly as the whale's vast body came finally within an arm's length. 'If she pulls, you let go. No heroics, Gianetta, just do it. But keep tension on the rope so I'll know as soon as I have it free.'

Ramón had a lifeline clipped on. He was leaning over the side, with a massive gutting knife in his hand. Reaching so far Jenny was sure he'd fall.

The whale could roll this way, she thought wildly, and if she did he could be crushed. He was supporting himself on the whale itself, his legs still on the boat, but leaning so far over he was holding onto the netting. Slicing. Slicing. As if the danger was nothing.

She tugged on. If the whale pulled away, she'd have to release her. They'd lose the anchor. They had this one chance. Please…

But the whale didn't move, except for the steady rise and fall of the swell, where Jenny had to let out, reel in, let out, reel in, to try and keep Ramón's base steady against her.

He was slicing and slicing and slicing, swearing and slicing some more, until suddenly the tension on Jenny's rope was no longer there. The anchor lifted free, the net around the whale's midriff dislodged. Jenny, still pulling, was suddenly reeling in a mass of netting and an anchor.

And Ramón was back in the boat, pulling with her.

One of the whale's fins was free. The whale moved it a

little, stretching, and she floated away. Not far. Twenty feet, no more.

The whale stilled again. One fin was not enough. She was still trapped.

On the far side of her, her calf nudged closer.

'Again,' Ramón said grimly as Jenny gunned the motor back into action and nosed close. He was already on top of the cabin, swinging the anchor rope once more. 'If she'll let us.'

'You'll hit the calf,' she said, almost to herself, and then bit her tongue. Of all the stupid objections. She knew what his answer must be.

'It's risk the calf having a headache, or both of them dying. No choice.'

But he didn't need to risk. As the arcs of the swinging anchor grew longer, the calf moved away again.

As if it knew.

And, once again, Ramón caught the net.

It took an hour, maybe longer, the times to catch the net getting longer as the amount of net left to cut off grew smaller. But they worked on, reeling her in, slicing, reeling her in, slicing, until the netting was a massive pile of rubbish on the deck.

Ramón was saving her, Jenny thought dazedly as she worked on. Every time he leaned out he was risking his life. She watched him work—and she fell in love.

She was magnificent. Ramón was working feverishly, slashing at the net while holding on to the rails and stretching as far as he could, but every moment he did he was aware of Jenny.

Gianetta.

She had total control of the anchor rope, somehow holding the massive whale against the side of the boat. But they both knew that to hold the boat in a fixed hold would almost certainly mean capsizing. What Jenny had to do was to work with the swells, holding the rope fast, then loosening it as the whale rose and the boat swayed, or the whale sank and the boat rose. Ramón had no room for anything but holding on to the boat and slashing but, thanks to Jenny, he had an almost stable platform to work with.

Tied together, boat and whale represented tonnage he didn't want to think about, especially as he was risking slipping between the two.

He wouldn't slip. Jenny was playing her part, reading the sea, watching the swell, focused on the whale in case she suddenly decided to roll or pull away…

She didn't. Ramón could slash at will at the rope entrapment, knowing Jenny was keeping him safe.

He slipped once and he heard her gasp. He felt her hand grip his ankle.

He righted himself—it was okay—but the memory of her touch stayed.

Gianetta was watching out for him.

Gianetta. Where had she come from, this magical Gianetta?

It was working. Jenny was scarcely breathing. Please, please…

But somehow her prayers were being answered. Piece by piece the net was being cut away. Ramón was winning. They were both winning.

The last section to be removed was the netting and the ropes trapping and tying the massive tail, but catching this section was the hardest. Ramón threw and threw, but each time the anchor slipped uselessly behind the whale and into the sea.

To have come so far and not save her… Jenny felt sick.

But Ramón would not give up. His arm must be dropping off, she thought, but just as she reached the point where despair took over, the whale rolled. She stretched and lifted her tail as far as she could within the confines of the net, and in doing so she made a channel to trap the anchor line as Ramón threw. And her massive body edged closer to the boat.

Ramón threw again, and this time the anchor held.

Once more Jenny reeled her in and once more Ramón sliced. Again. Again. One last slash—and the last piece of rope came loose into his hands.

Ramón staggered back onto the deck and Jenny was hauling the anchor in one last time. He helped her reel it in, then they stood together in the mass of tangled netting on the deck, silent, awed, stunned, as the whale finally floated free. Totally free. The net was gone.

But there were still questions. Were they too late? Had she been trapped too long?

Ramón's arm came round Jenny's waist and held, but Jenny was hardly aware of it. Or maybe she was, but it was all part of this moment. She was breathing a plea and she knew the plea was echoing in Ramón's heart as well as her own.

Please…

The whale was wallowing in the swell, rolling up and down, up and down. Her massive pectoral fins were free now. They moved stiffly outward, upward, over and over, while Jenny and Ramón held their breath and prayed.

The big tail swung lazily back and forth; she seemed to be stretching, feeling her freedom. Making sure the ropes were no longer there.

'She can't have been caught all that long,' Jenny whispered, breathless with wonder. 'Look at her tail. That rope was tied so tightly but there's hardly a cut.'

'She might have only just swum into it,' Ramón said and Jenny was aware that her awe was echoed in his voice. His arm had tightened around her and it seemed entirely natural. This was a prayer shared. 'If it was loosened from the shore by a storm it might have only hit her a day or so ago. The calf looks healthy enough.'

The calf was back at its mother's side now, nudging against her flank. Then it dived, straight down into the deep, and Jenny managed a faltering smile.

'He'll be feeding. She must still have milk. Oh, Ramón…'

'Gianetta,' Ramón murmured back, and she knew he was feeling exactly what she was feeling. Awe, hope, wonder. They might, they just might, have been incredibly, wondrously lucky.

And then the big whale moved. Her body seemed to ripple. Everything flexed at once, her tail, her fins... She rolled away, almost onto her back, as if to say to her calf: *No feeding, not yet, I need to figure if I'm okay.*

And figure she did. She swam forward in front of the boat, speeding up, speeding up. Faster, faster she swam, with her calf speeding after her.

And then, just as they thought they'd lost sight of her, she came sweeping back, a vast majestic mass of glossy black muscle and strength and bulk. Then, not a hundred yards from the boat, she rolled again, only higher, so her body was half out of the water, stretching, arching back, her pectoral fins outstretched, then falling backward with a massive splash that reached them on the boat and soaked them to the skin.

Neither of them noticed. Neither of them cared.

The whale was sinking now, deep, so deep that only a mass of still water on the surface showed her presence. Then she burst up one more time, arched back once more—and she dived once more and they saw her print on the water above as she adjusted course and headed for the horizon, her calf tearing after her.

Two wild creatures returned to the deep.

Tears were sliding uselessly down Jenny's face. She couldn't stop them, any more than she could stop smiling. And she looked up at Ramón and saw his smile echo hers.

'We did it,' she breathed. 'Ramón, we did it.'

'We did,' he said, and he tugged her hard against him, then swung her round so he was looking into her tear-stained face. 'We did it, Gianetta, we saved our whale. And you were magnificent. Gianetta, you may be a Spanish-Australian woman in name but I believe you have your nationality wrong. A woman like you… I believe you're worthy of being a woman of Cepheus.'

And then, before she knew what he intended, before she could guess anything at all, he lifted her into his arms and he kissed her.

CHAPTER FOUR

ONE moment she was gazing out at the horizon, catching the last shimmer of the whale's wake on the translucence of the sea. The next she was being kissed as she'd never been kissed in her life.

His hands were lifting her, pulling her hard in against him so her feet barely touched the deck. His body felt rock-hard, the muscled strength he'd just displayed still at work, only now directed straight at her. Straight with her.

The emotions of the rescue were all around her. He was wet and wild and wonderful. She was soaking as well, and the dripping fabric of his shirt and hers meant their bodies seemed to cling and melt.

It felt right. It felt meant. It felt as if there was no room or sense to argue.

His mouth met hers again, his arms tightening around her so she was locked hard against him. He was so close she could feel the rapid beat of his heart. Her breasts were crushed against his chest, her face had tilted instinctively, her mouth was caught…

Caught? Merged, more like. Two parts of a whole finding their home.

He tugged her tighter, tighter still against him, moulding her lips against his. She was hard against him, closer, closer, feeling him, tasting him, wanting him…

To be a part of him seemed suddenly as natural, as right,

as breathing. To be kissed by this man was an extension of what had just happened.

Or maybe it was more than that. Maybe it was an extension of the whole of the last week.

Maybe she'd wanted this from the moment she'd seen him.

Either way, she certainly wasn't objecting now. She heard herself give a tiny moan, almost a whimper, which was stupid because she didn't feel the least like whimpering. She felt like shouting, *Yes!*

His mouth was demanding, his tongue was searching for an entry, his arms holding her so tightly now he must surely bruise. But he couldn't hold her tight enough. She was holding him right back, desperate that she not be lowered, desperate that this miraculous contact not be lost.

He felt so good. He felt as if he was meant to be right here in her arms. That she'd been destined for this moment for ever and it had taken this long to find him.

He hadn't shaved this morning. She could feel the stubble on his jaw, she could almost taste it. There was salt on his face—of course there was, he'd been practically submerged, over and over. He smelled of salt and sea, and of pure testosterone.

He tasted of Ramón.

'Ramón.' She heard herself whisper his name, or maybe it was in her heart, for how could she possibly whisper when he was kissing as if he was a man starved for a woman, starved of *this* woman? She knew so clearly what was happening, and she accepted it with elation. This woman was who he wanted and he'd take her, he wanted her, she was his and he was claiming his own.

Like the whale rolling joyously in the sea, she thought, dazed and almost delirious, this was nature; it was right, it was meant.

She was in his arms and she wasn't letting go.

Ramón.

'Gianetta…' His voice was ragged with heat and desire.

Somehow he dragged himself back from her and held her at arm's length. 'Gianetta, *mia*…'

'If you're asking if I want you, then the answer's yes,' she said huskily, and almost laughed at the look of blazing heat that came straight back at her. His eyes were almost black, gleaming with tenderness and want and passion. But something else. He wouldn't take her yet. His eyes were searching.

'I'll take no woman against her will,' he growled.

'You think…you think this is against my will?' she whispered, as the blaze of desire became almost white-hot and she pressed herself against him, forcing him to see how much this was not the case.

'Gianetta,' he sighed, and there was laughter now as well as wonder and desire. Before she could respond he had her in his arms, held high, cradled against him, almost triumphant.

'You don't think maybe we should set the automatic pilot or something?' she murmured. 'We'll drift.'

'The radar will tell us if we're about to hit something big,' he said, his dark eyes gleaming. 'But it can't pick up things like jellyfish, so there's a risk. You want to risk death by jellyfish and come to my bed while we wait, my Gianetta?'

And what was a girl to say to an invitation like that?

'Yes, please,' she said simply and he kissed her and he held her tight and carried her down below.

To his bed. To his arms. To his pleasure.

'She left port six days ago, heading for New Zealand.'

The lawyer stared at the boat builder in consternation. 'You're sure? The *Marquita*?'

'That's the one. The guy skippering her—Ramón, I think he said his name was—had her in dry dock here for a couple of days, checking the hull, but she sailed out on the morning tide on Monday. Took the best cook in the bay with him, too. Half the locals are after his blood. He'd better look after our Jenny.'

But the lawyer wasn't interested in Ramón's staff. He stood

on the dock and stared out towards the harbour entrance as if he could see the *Marquita* sailing away.

'You're sure he was heading for Auckland?'

'I am. You're Spanish, right?'

'Cepheus country,' the lawyer said sharply. 'Not Spain. But no matter. How long would it take the *Marquita* to get to Auckland?'

'Coupla weeks,' the boat builder told him. 'Can't see him hurrying. I wouldn't hurry if I had a boat like the *Marquita* and Jenny aboard.'

'So if I go to Auckland…'

'I guess you'd meet him. If it's urgent.'

'It's urgent,' the lawyer said grimly. 'You have no idea how urgent.'

There was no urgency about the *Marquita*. If she took a year to reach Auckland it was too soon for Jenny.

Happiness was right now.

They could travel faster, but that would mean sitting by the wheel hour after hour, setting the sails to catch the slightest wind shift, being sailors.

Instead of being lovers.

She'd never felt like this. She'd melted against Ramón's body the morning of the whales and she felt as if she'd melted permanently. She'd shape shifted, from the Jenny she once knew to the Gianetta Ramón loved.

For that was what it felt like. Loved. For the first time in her life she felt truly beautiful, truly desirable—and it wasn't just for her body.

Yes, he made love to her, over and over, wonderful love-making that made her cry out in delight.

But more.

He wanted to know all about her.

He tugged blankets up on the deck. They lay in the sun and they solved the problems of the world. They watched dolphins surf in their wake. They fished. They compared toes to see whose little toe bent the most.

That might be ridiculous but there was serious stuff, too. Ramón now knew all about her parents, her life, her baby. She told him everything about Matty, she showed him pictures and he examined each of them with the air of a man being granted a privilege.

When Matty was smiling, Ramón smiled. She watched this big man respond to her baby's smile and she felt her heart twist in a way she'd never thought possible.

He let the boom net down off the rear deck, and they surfed behind the boat, and when the wind came up it felt as if they were flying. They worked the sails as a team, setting them so finely that they caught up on time lost when they were below, lost in each other's bodies.

He touched her and her body reacted with fire.

Don't fall in love. Don't fall in love. It was a mantra she said over and over in her head, but she knew it was hopeless. She was hopelessly lost.

It wouldn't last. Like Kieran, this man was a nomad, a sailor of no fixed address, going where the wind took him.

He talked little about himself. She knew there'd been tragedy, the sister he'd loved, parents he'd lost, pain to make him shy from emotional entanglement.

Well, maybe she'd learned that lesson, too. So savour the moment, she told herself. For now it was wonderful. Each morning she woke in Ramón's arms and she thought: Ramón had employed her for a year! When they got back to Europe conceivably the owner would join them. She could go back to being crew. But Ramón would be crew as well, and the nights were long, and owners never stayed aboard their boats for ever.

'Tell me about the guy who owns this boat,' she said, two days out of Auckland and she watched a shadow cross Ramón's face. She was starting to know him so well—she watched him when he didn't know it—his strongly boned, aquiline face, his hooded eyes, the smile lines, the weather lines from years at sea.

What had suddenly caused the shadow?

'He's rich,' he said shortly. 'He trusts me. What else do you need to know?'

'Well, whether he likes muffins, for a start,' she said, with something approaching asperity, which was a bit difficult as she happened to be entwined in Ramón's arms as she spoke and asperity was a bit hard to manage. Breathless was more like it.

'He loves muffins,' Ramón said.

'He'll be used to richer food than I can cook. Do you usually employ someone with special training?'

'He eats my cooking.'

'Really?' She frowned and sat up in bed, tugging the sheet after her. She'd seen enough of Ramón's culinary skills to know what an extraordinary statement this was. 'He's rich and he eats your cooking?'

'As I said, he'll love your muffins.'

'So when will you next see him?'

'Back in Europe,' Ramón said, and sighed. 'He'll have to surface then, but not now. Not yet. There's three months before we have to face the world. Do you think we can be happy for three months, *cariño*?' And he tugged her back down to him.

'If you keep calling me *cariño*,' she whispered. 'Are we really being paid for this?'

He chuckled but then his smile faded once more. 'You know it can't last, my love. I will need to move on.'

'Of course you will,' she whispered, but she only said it because it was the sensible, dignified thing to say. A girl had some pride.

Move on?

She never wanted to move on. If her world could stay on this boat, with this man, for ever, she wasn't arguing at all.

She slept and Ramón held her in his arms and tried to think of the future.

He didn't have to think. Not yet. It was three months before he was due to leave the boat and return to Bangladesh.

Three months before he needed to tell Jenny the truth.

She could stay with the boat, he thought, if she wanted to. He always employed someone to stay on board while he was away. She could take that role.

Only that meant Jenny would be in Cepheus while he was in Bangladesh.

He'd told her he needed to move on. It was the truth.

Maybe she could come with him.

The idea hit and stayed. His team always had volunteers to act as manual labour. Would Jenny enjoy the physical demands of construction, of helping make life bearable for those who had nothing?

Maybe she would.

What was he thinking? He'd never considered taking a woman to Bangladesh. He'd never considered that leaving a woman behind seemed unthinkable.

Gianetta…

His arms tightened their hold and she curved closer in sleep. He smiled and kissed the top of her head. Her curls were so soft.

Maybe he could sound her out about Bangladesh.

Give it time, he told himself, startled by the direction his thoughts were taking him. You've known her for less than two weeks.

Was it long enough?

There was plenty of time after Auckland. It was pretty much perfect right now, he thought. Let's not mess with perfection. He'd just hold this woman and hope that somehow the love he'd always told himself was an illusion might miraculously become real.

Anything was possible.

'How do you know he'll sail straight to Auckland?'

In the royal palace of Cepheus, Sofía was holding the telephone and staring into the middle distance, seeing not the magnificent suits of armour in the grand entrance but a vision of an elderly lawyer pacing anxiously on an unknown dock half a world away. She could understand his anxiety. Things in the palace were reaching crisis point.

The little boy had gone into foster care yesterday. Philippe needed love, Sofía thought bleakly. His neglect here—all his physical needs met, but no love, little affection, just a series of disinterested nannies—seemed tantamount to child abuse, and the country knew of it. She'd found him lovely foster parents, but his leaving the palace was sending the wrong message to the population—as if Ramón himself didn't care for the child.

Did Ramón even know about him?

'I don't know for sure where the Prince will sail,' the lawyer snapped. 'But I can hope. He'll want to restock fast to get around the Horn. It makes sense for him to come here.'

'So you'll wait.'

'Of course I'll wait. What else can I do?'

'But there's less than two weeks to go,' Sofía wailed. 'What if he's delayed?'

'Then we have catastrophe,' the lawyer said heavily. 'He has to get here. Then he has to get back to Cepheus and accept his new life.'

'And the child?'

'It doesn't matter about the child.'

Yes, it does, Sofía thought. Oh, Ramón, what are you facing?

They sailed into Auckland Harbour just after dawn. Jenny stood in the bow, ready to jump across to shore with the lines, ready to help in any way she could with berthing the *Marquita*. Ramón was at the wheel. She glanced back at him and had a pang of misgivings.

They hadn't been near land for two weeks. Why did it feel as if the world was waiting to crowd in?

How could it? Their plan was to restock and be gone again. Their idyll could continue.

But they'd booked a berth with the harbour master. Ramón

had spoken to the authorities an hour ago, and after that he'd looked worried.

'Problem?' she'd asked.

'Someone's looking for me.'

'Debt collectors?' she'd teased, but he hadn't smiled.

'I don't have debts.'

'Then who…?'

'I don't know,' he said, and his worry sounded as if it was increasing. 'No one knows where I am.'

'Conceivably the owner knows.'

'What…?' He caught himself. 'I…yes. But he won't be here. I can't think…'

That was all he'd said but she could see worry building.

She turned and looked towards the dock. She'd looked at the plan the harbour master had faxed through and from here she could see the berth that had been allocated to them.

There was someone standing on the dock, at the berth, as if waiting. A man in a suit.

It must be the owner, she thought.

She glanced back at Ramón and saw him flinch.

'Rodriguez,' he muttered, and in the calm of the early morning she heard him swear. 'Trouble.'

'Is he the boat's owner?'

'No,' he said shortly. 'He's legal counsel to the Crown of Cepheus. I've met him once or twice when he had business with my grandmother. If he's here… I hate to imagine what he wants of me.'

Señor Rodriguez was beside himself. He had ten days to save a country. He glanced at his watch as the *Marquita* sailed slowly towards her berth, fretting as if every second left was vital.

What useless display of skill was this, to sail into harbour when motoring would be faster? And why was the woman in the bow, rather than Ramón himself? He needed to talk to Ramón, now!

The boat edged nearer. 'Can you catch my line?' the

woman called, and he flinched and moved backward. He knew nothing about boats.

But it seemed she could manage without him. She jumped lightly over a gap he thought was far too wide, landing neatly on the dock, then hauled the boat into position and made her fast as Ramón tugged down the last sail.

'Good morning,' the woman said politely, casting him a curious glance. And maybe she was justified in her curiosity. He was in his customary suit, which he acknowledged looked out of place here. The woman was in the uniform of the sea—faded shorts, a T-shirt and nothing else. She looked windblown and free. Momentarily, he was caught by how good she looked, but only for an instant. His attention returned to Ramón.

'Señor Rodriguez,' Ramón called to him, cautious and wary.

'You remember me?'

'Yes,' Ramón said shortly. 'What's wrong?'

'Nothing's wrong,' the lawyer said, speaking in the mix of French and Spanish that formed the Cepheus language. 'As long as you come home.'

'My home's on the *Marquita*. You know that.'

'Not any more it's not,' the lawyer said. 'Your uncle and your cousin are dead. As of four weeks ago, you're the Crown Prince of Cepheus.'

There was silence. Jenny went on making all secure while Ramón stared at the man on the dock as if he'd spoken a foreign language.

Which he had, but Jenny had been raised speaking Spanish like a native, and she'd picked up French at school. There were so many similarities in form she'd slipped into it effortlessly. Now… She'd missed the odd word but she understood what the lawyer had said.

Or she thought she understood what he'd said.

Crown Prince of Cepheus. Ramón.

It might make linguistic sense. It didn't make any other sort of sense.

'My uncle's dead?' Ramón said at last, his voice without inflexion.

'In a light plane crash four weeks ago. Your uncle, your cousin and your cousin's wife, all killed. Only there's worse. It seems your cousin wasn't really married—he brought the woman he called his wife home and shocked his father and the country by declaring he was married, but now we've searched for proof, we've found none. So the child, Philippe, who stood to be heir, is illegitimate. You stand next in line. But if you're not home in ten days then Carlos inherits.'

'Carlos!' The look of flat shock left Ramón's face, replaced by anger, pure and savage. 'You're saying Carlos will inherit the throne?'

'Not if you come home. You must see that's the only way.'

'No!'

'Think about it.'

'I've thought.'

'Leave the woman to tend the boat and come with me,' Señor Rodriguez said urgently. 'We need to speak privately.'

'The woman's name is Gianetta.' Ramón's anger seemed to be building. 'I won't leave her.'

The man cast an uninterested glance at Jenny, as if she was of no import. Which, obviously, was the case. 'Regardless, you must come.'

'I can look after the boat,' Jenny said, trying really hard to keep up. *I won't leave her.* There was a declaration. But he obviously meant it for right now. Certainly not for tomorrow.

Crown Prince of Cepheus?

'There's immigration...' Ramón said.

'I can sort my papers out,' she said. 'The harbour master's office is just over there. You do what you have to do on the way to wherever you're going. Have your discussion and then come back and tell me what's happening.'

'Jenny...'

But she was starting to add things together in her head and she wasn't liking them. *Crown Prince of Cepheus.*

'I guess the *Marquita* would be *your* boat, then?' she asked flatly, and she saw him flinch.

'Yes, but…'

She felt sick. 'There you go,' she managed, fighting for dignity. 'The owner's needs always come first. I'll stow the sails and make all neat. Then I might go for a nice long walk and let off a little steam. I'll see you later.'

And Ramón cast her a glance where frustration, anger—and maybe even a touch of envy—were combined.

'If you can…'

'Of course I can,' she said, almost cordially. 'We're on land again. I can stand on my own two feet.'

There were complications everywhere, and all he could think of was Jenny. Gianetta. His woman.

The flash of anger he'd seen when he'd confessed that he did indeed own the *Marquita*; the look of betrayal…

She'd think he'd lied to her. She wouldn't understand what else was going on, but the lie would be there, as if in flashing neon.

Yes, he'd lied.

He needed to concentrate on the lawyer.

The throne of Cepheus was his.

Up until now there'd never been a thought of him inheriting. Neither his uncle nor his cousin, Cristián, had ever invited Ramón near the palace. He knew the country had been in dread of Cristián becoming Crown Prince but there was nothing anyone could do about it. Cristián had solidified his inheritance by marrying and having a child. The boy must be what, five?

For him to be proved illegitimate…

'I can't even remember the child's name,' he said across the lawyer's stream of explanations, and the lawyer cast him a reproachful glance.

'Philippe.'

'How old?'

'Five,' he confirmed.

'So what happens to Philippe?'

'Nothing,' the lawyer said. 'He has no rights. With his parents dead, your aunt has organized foster care, and if you wish to make a financial settlement on him I imagine the country will be relieved. There's a certain amount of anger…'

'You mean my cousin didn't make provision for his own son?'

'Your cousin and your uncle spent every drop of their personal incomes on themselves, on gambling, on…on whatever they wished. The Crown itself, however, is very wealthy. You, with the fortune your grandmother left you and the Crown to take care of your every need, will be almost indecently rich. But the child has nothing.'

He felt sick. A five-year-old child. To lose everything…

He'd been not much older than Philippe when he'd lost his own father.

It couldn't matter. It shouldn't be his problem. He didn't even know the little boy…

'I'll take financial care of the child,' Ramón said shortly. 'But I can't drop everything. I have twelve more weeks at sea and then I'm due in Bangladesh.'

'Your team already knows you won't be accompanying them this year,' the lawyer told him flatly, leaving no room for argument. 'And I've found an experienced yachtsman who's prepared to sail the *Marquita* back to Cepheus for you. We can be on a flight tonight, and even that's not soon enough.' Then, as the lawyer noticed Ramón's face—and Ramón was making no effort to disguise his fury—he added quickly, 'There's mounting hysteria over the mess your uncle and cousin left, and there's massive disquiet about Carlos inheriting.'

'As well there might be,' Ramón growled, trying hard to stay calm. Ramón's distant cousin was an indolent gamester, rotund, corrupt and inept. He'd faced the court more than once, but charges had been dropped, because of bribery? He wasn't close enough to the throne to know.

'He's making noises that the throne should be his. Blustering threats against you and your aunt.'

'Threats?' And there it was again, the terror he'd been raised with. *'Don't go near the throne. Ever!'*

'If the people rise against the throne…' the lawyer was saying.

'Maybe that would be a good thing.'

'Maybe it'd be a disaster,' the man said, and proceeded to tell him why. At every word Ramón felt his world disintegrate. There was no getting around it—the country was in desperate need of a leader, of some sort of stability…of a Crown Prince.

'So you see,' the lawyer said at last, 'you have to come. Go back to the boat, tell the woman—she's your only crew?—what's happening, pack your bags and we'll head straight to the airport.'

And there was nothing left for him but to agree. To take his place in a palace that had cost his family everything.

'Tomorrow,' he said, feeling ill.

'Tonight.'

'I will spend tonight with Gianetta,' Ramón growled, and the lawyer raised his brows.

'Like that?'

'Like nothing,' Ramón snapped. 'She deserves an explanation.'

'It's not as if you're sacking her,' the lawyer said. 'I've only hired one man to replace you. She'll still be needed. She can help bring the *Marquita* home and then you can pay her off.'

'I've already paid her.'

'Then there's no problem.' The lawyer rose and so did Ramón. 'Tonight.'

'Tomorrow,' Ramón snapped and looked at the man's face and managed a grim smile. 'Consider it my first royal decree. Book the tickets for tomorrow's flights.'

'But…'

'I will not argue,' Ramón said. 'I've a mind to wash my hands of the whole business and take *Marquita* straight back out to sea.' Then, at the wash of undisguised distress on the lawyer's face, he sighed and relented. 'But, of course, I won't,' he said. 'You know I won't. I will return with you to Cepheus. I'll do what I must to resolve this mess, I'll face Carlos down, but you will give me one more night.'

CHAPTER FIVE

SHE walked for four long hours, and then she found an Internet café and did some research. By the time she returned to the boat she was tired and hungry and her anger hadn't abated one bit.

Ramón was the Crown Prince of Cepheus. What sort of dangerous mess had she walked into?

She'd slept with a prince?

Logically, it shouldn't make one whit of difference that he was royal, but it did, and she felt used and stupid and very much like a star-struck teenager. All that was needed was the paparazzi. Images of headlines flashed through her head—*Crown Prince of Cepheus Takes Stupid, Naive Australian Lover*—and as she neared the boat she couldn't help casting a furtive glance over her shoulder to check the thought had no foundation.

It didn't—of course it didn't. There was only Ramón, kneeling on the deck, calmly sealing the ends of new ropes.

He glanced up and saw her coming. He smiled a welcome, but she was too sick at heart to smile back.

For a few wonderful days she'd let herself believe this smile could be for her.

She felt besmirched.

'I've just come back to get my things,' she said flatly before he had a chance to speak.

'You're leaving?' His eyes were calmly appraising.

'Of course I'm leaving.'

'To go where?'

'I'll see if I can get a temporary job here. As soon as I can get back to Australia I'll organize some way of repaying the loan.'

'There's no need for you to repay…'

'There's every need,' she flashed, wanting to stamp her foot; wanting, quite badly, to cry. 'You think I want to be in your debt for one minute more than I must? I've read about you on the Internet now. It doesn't matter whether anyone died or not. You were a prince already.'

'Does that make a difference?' he asked, still watchful, and his very calmness added to her distress.

'Of course it does. I've been going to bed with a *prince*,' she wailed, and the couple on board their cruiser in the next berth choked on their lunch time Martinis.

But Ramón didn't notice. He had eyes only for her. 'You went to bed with me,' he said softly. 'Not with a prince.'

'You are a prince.'

'I'm just Ramón, Gianetta.'

'Don't Gianetta me,' she snapped. 'That's your bedroom we slept in. Not the owner's. Here I was thinking we were doing something illicit…'

'Weren't we?' he demanded and a glint of humour returned to his dark eyes.

'It was your bed all along,' she wailed and then, finally, she made a grab at composure. The couple on the next boat were likely to lose their eyes; they were out on stalks. Dignity, she told herself desperately. Please.

'So I own the boat,' he said. 'Yes, I'm a prince. What more do you know of me?'

'Apparently very little,' she said bitterly. 'I seem to have told you my whole life story. It appears you've only told me about two minutes of yours. Apparently you're wealthy, fabulously wealthy, and you're royal. The Internet bio was sketchy, but you spend your time either on this boat or fronting some charity organisation.'

'I do more than that.'

But she was past hearing. She was past wanting to hear. She felt humiliated to her socks, and one fact stood out above all the rest. *She'd never really known him.*

'So when you saw me you thought here's a little more charity,' she threw at him, anger making her almost incoherent. 'I'll take this poverty-stricken, flour-streaked muffin-maker and show her a nice time.'

'A flour-streaked muffin-maker?' he said and, infuriatingly, the laughter was back. 'I guess if you want to describe yourself as that… Okay, fine, I rescued the muffin-maker. And we did have a nice time. No?'

But she wasn't going there. She was not being sucked into that smile ever again. 'I'm leaving,' she said, and she swung herself down onto the deck. She was heading below, but Ramón was before her, blocking her path.

'Jenny, you're still contracted to take my boat to Cepheus.'

'You don't need me…'

'You signed a contract. Yesterday, as I remember—and it was you who wanted it signed before we came into port.' His hands were on her shoulders, forcing her to meet his gaze, and her anger was suddenly matched with his. 'So you've been on the Internet. Do you understand why I have to return?'

And she did understand. Sort of. She'd read and read and read. 'It seems your uncle and cousin are dead,' she said flatly. 'There's a huge scandal because it seems your cousin wasn't married after all, so his little son can't inherit. So you get to be Crown Prince.' Even now, she couldn't believe she was saying it. *Crown Prince.* It was like some appalling twisted fairy tale. Kiss a frog, have him turn into a prince.

She wanted her frog back.

'I don't have a choice in this,' he said harshly. 'You need to believe that.' Before she could stop him, he put the back of his hand against her cheek and ran it down to her lips, a touch so sensuous that it made a shiver run right down to her toes. But there was anger behind the touch—and there was also… Regret? 'Gianetta, for you to go…'

'Of course I'm going,' she managed.

'And I need to let you go,' he said, and there was a depth of sadness behind his words that she couldn't begin to understand. 'But still I want you to take my boat home. Selfish or not, I want to see you again.'

Where was dignity when she needed it? His touch had sucked all the anger out of her. She wanted to hold on to this man and cling.

What was she thinking? No. This man was royalty, and he'd lied to her.

She had to find sense.

'I'm grabbing my things,' she said shortly, fighting for some semblance of calm. 'I'll be in touch about the money. I swear I won't owe you for any longer than absolutely necessary.'

'There's no need to repay…'

'There is,' she snapped. 'I pay my debts, even if they're to princes.'

'Can you stop calling me…'

'A prince? It's what you are and it's not new. It's not like this title's a shock to you. Yes, you seem to have inherited the Crown, and that's surprised you, but you were born a prince and you didn't tell me.'

'You didn't ask.'

'Right,' she said, fury building again. She shoved his hands away and headed below, whether he liked it or not. Ramón followed her and stood watching as she flung her gear into her carry-all.

Dignity was nowhere. The only thing she could cling to was her anger.

'So, Jenny, you think I should have introduced myself as Prince Ramón?' he asked at last, and the anger was still there. He was angry? What did that make her? Nothing, she thought bleakly. How could he be angry at her? She felt like shrivelling into a small ball and sobbing, but she had to get away from here first.

'You know what matters most?' she demanded, trying desperately to sort her thoughts into some sort of sense. 'That you didn't tell me you owned the boat. Maybe you didn't lie outright, but you had plenty of opportunities to tell me and you didn't. That's a lie in my books.'

'Would you have got on my boat if you thought I was the owner?'

There was only one answer to that. If he'd asked her and she'd known he was wealthy enough to afford such a boat—his wealth would have terrified her. 'No,' she admitted.

'So I wanted you to come with me.'

'Bully for you. And I did.' Cling to the anger, she told herself. It was all there was. If he was angry, she should be more so. She headed into the bathroom to grab her toiletries. 'I came on board and we made love and it was all very nice,' she threw over her shoulder. 'Now you've had your fun and you can go back to your life.'

'Being a prince isn't my life.'

'No?'

'Gianetta…'

'Jenny!'

'Jenny, then,' he conceded and the underlying anger in his voice intensified. 'I want you to listen.'

'I'm listening,' she said, shoving toiletries together with venom.

'Jenny, my grandfather was the Crown Prince of Cepheus.'

'I know that.'

'What you don't know,' he snapped, 'is that he was an arrogant, cruel womanizer. Jenny, I need you to understand this. My grandfather's marriage to my grandmother was an arranged one and he treated her dreadfully. When my father was ten my grandmother fell in love with a servant, and who can blame her? But my grandfather banished her and the younger children to a tiny island off the coast of Cepheus. He kept his oldest son, my uncle, at the palace, but my grandmother, my father and my aunt were never allowed back. My grandmother was royal in her own right. She had money of her own and all her life she ached to undo some of the appalling things my grandfather did, but when she tried…well, that's when my father died. And now, to be forced to go back…'

'I'm sorry you don't like it,' she said stiffly. What was he explaining this for? It had nothing to do with her. 'But your country needs you. At least now you'll be doing something useful.'

'Is that what you think?' he demanded, sounding stunned. 'That I spend my life doing nothing?'

'Isn't that the best job in the world?' She could feel the vibrations of his anger and it fed hers. *He'd known he was a prince.* 'The Internet bio says you're aligned to some sort of charity in Bangladesh,' she said shortly. 'I guess you can't be all bad.'

'Thanks.'

'Think nothing of it,' she said, and she thought, where did she go from here?

Away, her head told her, harshly and coldly. She needed to leave right now, and she would, but there were obligations. This man had got her out of a hole. He'd paid her debts. She owed him, deception or not.

'Okay, I'll be the first to admit I know nothing of your life,' she said stiffly. 'I felt like I knew you and now I realize I don't. That hurts. But I do need to thank you for paying my debt; for getting me away from Charlie. But now I'm just…scared. So I'll just get out of your life and let you get on with it.'

'You're scared?'

'What do you think?'

'There's no threat. There'd only be a threat if you were my woman.'

That was enough to take her breath away. *If you were my woman…*

'Which…which I'm not,' she managed.

'No,' he said, and there was bleakness as well as anger there now.

She closed her eyes. So what else had she expected? These two weeks had been a fairy tale. Nothing more.

Move on.

'Jenny, I have to do this,' he said harshly. 'Understand it or not, this is what I'm faced with. If I don't take the throne, then it goes to my father's cousin's son, Carlos. Carlos is as bad as my grandfather. He'd bring the country to ruin. And then there's the child. He's five. God knows…' He raked his hair with quiet despair. 'I will accept this responsibility. I must, even if it means walking away from what I most care about.'

And then there was silence, stretching towards infinity, where only emptiness beckoned.

What he most cared about? His boat? His charity work? What?

She couldn't think of what. She couldn't think what she wanted *what* to be.

'I'm sorry, Ramón,' she whispered at last.

'I'm sorry, too,' he said. He sighed and dug his hands deep into his pockets. Seemingly moving on. 'For what's between us needs to be put aside, for the sanity of both of us. But Gianetta…Jenny… What will you do in New Zealand?'

'Make muffins.' Her fury from his perceived betrayal was oozing away now, but there was nothing in its place except an aching void. Yesterday had seemed so wonderful. Today her sailor had turned into a prince and her bubble of euphoria was gone.

'Make muffins until you can afford to go back to Australia?'

'I don't have a lot of choice.'

'There is. Señor Rodriguez, the lawyer you met this morning, has already found someone prepared to skipper the *Marquita*—to bring her to Cepheus. I've already met him. He's a Scottish Australian, Gordon, ex-merchant navy. He's competent, solid and I know I can trust him with…with my boat. But he will need crew. So I'm asking you to stay on. I'm asking you if you'll sail round the Horn with him and bring the *Marquita* home. If you do that, I'll fly you back to Australia. Debt discharged.'

'It wouldn't be discharged.'

'I believe it would,' he said heavily. 'I'm asking you to sail round the Horn with someone you don't know, and I'm asking you to trust that I'll keep my word. That's enough of a request to make paying out your debt more than reasonable.'

'I don't want to.'

'Do you want to go back to cooking muffins?' He spread his hands and he managed a smile then, his wonderful, sexy, insinuating smile that had the power to warm every last part of her. 'And at least this way you'll get to see Cepheus, even if it's only for a couple of days before you fly home. And you'll have sailed around the Horn. You wanted to see the world. Give yourself a chance to see a little of it.' He hesitated. 'And, Jenny, maybe…we can have tonight?'

That made her gasp. After all that stood between them… What was he suggesting, that she spend one more night as the royal mistress? 'Are you crazy?'

'So not tonight?' His eyes grew bleak. 'No. I'm sorry, Gianetta. You and me… I concede it's impossible. But what is possible is that you remain on board the *Marquita* as crew. You allow me to continue employing you so you'll walk away at the end of three months beholden to nobody.'

No.

The word should have been shouted at him. She should walk away right now.

But to walk away for ever? How could she do that? And if she stayed on board….maybe a sliver of hope remained.

Hope for what? A Cinderella happy ending? What a joke. Ramón himself had said it was impossible.

But to walk away, from this boat as well as from this man… Cinders had fled at midnight. Maybe Cinders had more resolution than she did.

'I'll come back to the boat in the morning,' she whispered. 'If the new skipper wants to employ me and I think he's a man I can be at sea with for three months…'

'He's nothing like me,' Ramón said gently, almost bleakly. 'He's reliable and steady.'

'And not a prince?'

He gave a wintry smile. 'No, Gianetta, he's not a prince.'

'Then it might be possible.'

'I hope it will be possible.'

'No guarantees,' she said.

'You feel betrayed?'

'Of course I do,' she whispered. 'I need to go now.'

The bleakness intensified. He nodded. 'As you say. Go, my Gianetta, before I forget myself. I've learned this day that my life's not my own. But first… '

And, before she could guess what he was about, he made two swift strides across the room, took her shoulders in a grip of iron and kissed her. And such a kiss… It was fierce, it was possessive, it held anger and passion and desire. It was no kiss of farewell. It was a kiss that was all about his need, his desire, his ache to hold her to him for this night, and for longer still.

He was hungry for her, she thought, bewildered. She didn't know how real that hunger was, but when he finally put her away from him, when she finally broke free, she thought he was hurting as much as she was.

But hunger changed nothing, she thought bleakly. There was nothing left to say.

He stood silently by as she grabbed her carry-all and walked away, her eyes shimmering with unshed tears. He didn't try to stop her.

He was her Ramón, she thought bleakly. But he wasn't her prince.

He watched her go, walking along the docks carrying her holdall, her shoulders slumped, her body language that of someone weary beyond belief.

He felt as if he'd betrayed her.

So what to do? Go after her, lift her bodily into his arms? Take her to Cepheus?

How could he?

There were threats from Carlos. The lawyer was talking of

the possibility of armed insurrection against the throne. Had it truly become so bad?

His father had died because he hadn't realized the power of royalty. How could he drag a woman into this mess? It would be hard enough keeping himself afloat, let alone supporting anyone else.

How could he be a part of it himself—a royal family that had destroyed his family?

Jenny's figure was growing smaller in the distance. She wasn't pausing—she wasn't looking back.

He felt ill.

'So can we leave tonight?' He looked back and the lawyer was standing about twenty feet from the boat, calmly watching. 'I asked them to hold seats on tonight's flight as well as tomorrow.'

'You have some nerve.'

'The country's desperate,' the lawyer said simply. 'Nothing's been heard from you. Carlos is starting to act as if he's the new Crown Prince and his actions are provocative. Delay on your part may well mean bloodshed.'

'I don't want to leave her,' he said simply and turned back—but she'd turned a corner and was gone.

'I think the lady has left you,' the lawyer said gently. 'Which leaves you free to begin to govern your country. So, the flight tonight, Your Highness?'

'Fine,' Ramón said heavily and went to pack.

But fine was the last thing he was feeling.

His flight left that evening. He looked down from the plane and saw the boats in Auckland Harbour. The *Marquita* was down there with her new skipper on board. He couldn't make her out among so many. She was already dwindling to nothing as the plane rose and turned away from land.

Would Jenny join her tomorrow, he thought bleakly. Would she come to Cepheus?

He turned from the window with a silent oath. It shouldn't

matter. What was between them was finished. Whether she broke her contract or not—there was nothing he could offer her.

Jenny was on her own, as was he.

His throne was waiting for him.

And two days later the *Marquita* slipped its moorings and sailed out of Auckland Harbour—with Jenny still on board. As she watched the harbour fade into the distance she felt all the doubts reassemble themselves. Gordon, her new skipper, seemed respectful of her silence and he let her be.

She was about to sail around the Horn. Once upon a time that prospect would have filled her with adrenalin-loaded excitement.

Now… She was simply fulfilling a contract, before she went home.

CHAPTER SIX

RAMÓN'S introduction to royal life was overwhelming. He walked into chaos. He walked into a life he knew nothing about. There were problems everywhere, but he'd been back in Cepheus for less than a day before the plight of Philippe caught him and held.

On his first meeting, the lawyer's introduction to the little boy was brief. 'This is Philippe.'

Philippe. His cousin's son. The little boy who should be Crown Prince, but for the trifling matter of a lack of wedding vows. Philippe, who'd had the royal surname until a month ago and was now not entitled to use it.

The little boy looked like the child Ramón remembered being. Philippe's pale face and huge eyes hinted that he was suffering as Ramón had suffered when his own father died, and as he met him for the first time he felt his gut wrench with remembered pain.

He'd come to see for himself what he'd been told—that the little boy was in the best care possible. Señor Rodriguez performed the introductions. Consuela and Ernesto were Philippe's foster parents, farmers who lived fifteen minutes' drive from the palace. The three were clearly nervous of what this meeting meant, but Philippe had been well trained.

'I am pleased to meet you,' the little boy said in a stilted little voice that spoke of rote learning and little else. He held out a thin little arm so his hand could be shaken, and Ramón felt him flinch as he took it in his.

Philippe's foster mother, a buxom farmer's wife exuding good-hearted friendliness, didn't seem intimidated by Ramón's title, or maybe she was, but her concern for Philippe came first. 'We've been hearing good things about you,' she told Ramón, scooping her charge into her arms so he could be on eye level with Ramón, ending the formality with this decisive gesture. 'This dumpling's been fearful of meeting you,' she told him. 'But Ernesto and I are telling him he should think of you as his big cousin. A friend. Isn't that right, Your Highness?'

She met Ramón's gaze almost defiantly, and Ramón could see immediately why Sofía had chosen Consuela as Philippe's foster mother. The image of a mother hen, prepared to battle any odds for her chick, was unmistakable. 'Philippe's homesick for the palace,' she said now, almost aggressively. 'And he misses his cat.'

'You have a cat?' Ramón asked.

'Yes,' Philippe whispered.

'There are many cats at the palace,' Señor Rodriguez said repressively from beside them, and Ramón sighed. What was it with adults? Hang on, he was an adult. Surely he could do something about this.

He must.

But he wasn't taking him back to the palace.

Memories were flooding back as he watched Philippe, memories of himself as a child. He vaguely remembered someone explaining that his grandmother wanted to return to the palace and his father would organize it—or maybe that explanation had come later. What he did remember was his father leading him into the vast grand entrance of the palace, Ramón clutching his father's hand as the splendour threatened to overwhelm him. 'There's nothing to be afraid of. It's time you met your grandfather and your uncle,' his father had told him.

His mother had said later that the decision to take him had been made, 'Because surely the Prince can't refuse his grandchild, a little boy who looks just like him.' But his mother had been wrong.

Not only had he been refused, some time in the night while Ramón lay in scared solitude, in a room far too grand for a child, somehow, some time, his father had died. He remembered not sleeping all night, and the next morning he remembered his grandfather, his icy voice laced with indifference to both his son's death and his grandson's solitary grief, snarling at the servants. 'Pack him up and get him out of here,' he'd ordered.

Pack him up and get him out of here… It was a dreadful decree, but how much worse would it have been if the Crown Prince had ordered him to stay? As he was being ordered to stay now.

Not Philippe, though. Philippe was free, if he could just be made happy with that freedom.

'Tell me about your cat,' he asked, trying a smile, and Philippe swallowed and swallowed again and made a manful effort to respond.

'He's little,' he whispered. 'The other cats fight him and he's not very strong. Something bit his ear. Papà doesn't permit me to take him inside, so he lives in the stables, but he comes when I call him. He's orange with a white nose.'

'Are there many orange cats with white noses at the palace?' Ramón asked, and for some reason the image of Jenny was with him strongly, urging him on. The little boy shook his head.

'Bebe's the only one. He's my friend.' He tilted his chin, obviously searching for courage for a confession. 'Sometimes I take a little fish from the kitchen when no one's looking. Bebe likes fish.'

'So he shouldn't be hard to find.' Ramón glanced at Consuela and Ernesto, questioningly. This place was a farm. Surely one cat…

'We like cats,' Consuela said, guessing where he was going. 'But Señor Rodriguez tells us the palace cats are wild.

They're used to keep the vermin down and he says no one can catch one, much less tame one.'

'I'm sure we could tame him.' Ernesto, a wiry, weathered farmer, spoke almost as defiantly as his wife. 'If you, sir, or your staff, could try to catch him for us…'

'I'll try,' Ramón said. 'He's called Bebe, you say? My aunt has her cat at the palace now. She understands them. Let's see what we can do.'

Jenny would approve, he thought, as he returned to the palace, but he pushed the idea away. This was *his* challenge, as was every challenge in this place. It was nothing to do with Jenny.

As soon as he returned to the palace he raided the kitchens. Then he set off to the stables with a platter of smoked salmon. He set down the saucer and waited for a little ginger cat with a torn ear to appear. It took a whole three minutes.

Bebe wasn't wild at all. He stroked his ears and Bebe purred. He then shed ginger fur everywhere while he wrapped himself around Ramón's legs and the chair legs in the palace entrance and the legs of the footman on duty. Jenny would laugh, Ramón thought, but he shoved that thought away as well. Just do what comes next. *Do not think of Jenny.*

Bebe objected—loudly—to the ride in a crate on the passenger seat of Ramón's Boxster, but he settled into life with Philippe—'as if Philippe's been sneaking him into his bed for the last couple of years,' Consuela told him, and maybe he had.

After that, Philippe regained a little colour, but he still looked haunted. He missed the palace, he confided, as Ramón tried to draw him out. In a world of adults who hadn't cared, the palace itself had become his stability.

Pack him up and get him out of here…

It made sense, Ramón thought. If the servants' reaction to Philippe was anything to go by, he'd be treated like illegitimate dirt in the palace. And then there was his main worry, or maybe it wasn't so much a worry but a cold, hard certainty.

There was so much to be done in this country that his role

as Crown Prince overwhelmed him. He had to take it on; he had no choice, but in order to do it he must be clear-headed, disciplined, focused.

There was no link between love and duty in this job. He'd seen that spelled out with bleak cruelty. His grandmother had entered the palace through love, and had left it with her dreams and her family destroyed. His father had tried again to enter the palace, for the love of his mother, and he'd lost his life because of it. There were threats around him now, veiled threats, and who knew what else besides?

And the knowledge settled on his heart like grey fog. To stay focused on what he must do, he could put no other person at risk. Sofia was staying until after the coronation. After that she'd leave and no one would be at risk but him. He'd have no distractions and without them maybe, just maybe, he could bring this country back to the prosperity it deserved.

But Philippe… And Jenny?

They'd get over it, he told himself roughly. Or Philippe would get over his grief and move on. Jenny must never be allowed to know that grief.

And once again he told himself harshly, this was nothing to do with Jenny. There'd never been a suggestion that they take things further. Nor could there be. This was his life and his life only, even if it was stifling.

This place was stifling. Nothing seemed to have changed since his grandfather's reign, or maybe since long before.

Lack of change didn't mean the palace had been allowed to fall into disrepair, though. Even though his grandfather and uncle had overspent their personal fortunes, the Crown itself was still wealthy, so pomp and splendour had been maintained. Furnishings were still opulent, rich paintings still covered the walls, the woodwork gleamed and the paintwork shone. The staff looked magnificent, even if their uniforms had been designed in the nineteenth century.

But the magnificence couldn't disguise the fact that every one of the people working in this palace went about their duties with impassive faces. Any attempt by Ramón to penetrate their rigid facades was met with stony silence and, as the weeks turned into a month and then two, he couldn't make inroads into that rigidity.

The servants—and the country—seemed to accept him with passive indifference. He might be better than what had gone before, the newspapers declared, but he was still royal. Soon, the press implied, he'd become just like the others.

When he officially took his place as Crown Prince, he could make things better for the people of this county. He knew that, so he'd bear the opulence of the palace, the lack of freedom. He'd bear the formality and the media attention. He'd cope also with the blustering threats of a still furious Carlos; along with the insidious sense that threats like this had killed his father. He'd face them down.

Alone.

Once Philippe had recovered from his first grief, surely he'd be happy on the farm with Consuela and Ernesto.

And also… Jenny would be happy as a muffin-maker?

Why did he even think of her? Why had he ever insisted that she come here? It would have been easier for both of them if he'd simply let her go.

For she was Jenny, he reminded himself harshly, a dozen times a day. She was not Gianetta. She was free to go wherever she willed. She was Jenny, with the world at her feet.

Yet he watched the *Marquita*'s progress with an anxiety that bordered on obsession, and he knew that when Jenny arrived he would see her one last time. He must.

Was that wise?

He knew it wasn't. There was no place for Jenny here, as there was no place for Philippe.

He'd been alone for much of his adult life. He could go on being alone.

But he'd see Jenny once again first. Sensible or not.

Please…

Eleven weeks and two days after setting sail from Auckland, the *Marquita* sailed into Cepheus harbour and found a party.

As they approached land, every boat they passed, from tiny pleasure craft to workmanlike fishing vessels, was adorned in red, gold and deep, deep blue. The flag of Cepheus hung from every mast. The harbour was ringed with flags. There were people crowded onto the docks, spilling out of harbourside restaurants. Every restaurant looked crammed to bursting. It looked like Sydney Harbour on a sunny Sunday, multiplied by about a hundred, Jenny thought, dazed, as she made the lines ready to dock.

'You reckon they're here to welcome us?' Gordon called to her, and she smiled.

She'd become very fond of Gordon. When she'd first met him, the morning after Ramón had left, she'd been ready to walk away. Only his shy smile, his assumption that she was coming with him and his pleasure that she was, had kept her on board. He reminded her of her father. Which helped.

She'd been sailing with him now for almost three months. He'd kept his own counsel and she'd kept hers, and it had taken almost all those months for her emotions to settle.

Now…approaching the dock she was so tense she could hardly speak. Normally she welcomed Gordon's reserve but his silence was only adding to her tension.

There was no need for her to be tense, she told herself. She'd had a couple of surreal weeks with royalty. In true princely fashion he'd rescued her from a life of making muffins, and now she could get on with her life.

With this experience of sailing round the Horn behind her, and with Gordon's references, maybe she could get another job on board a boat. She could keep right on sailing. While Ramón…

See, that was what she couldn't let herself think. The future and Ramón.

It had been a two-week affair. Nothing more.

'What's the occasion?' Gordon was behind the wheel, calling to people on the boat passing them. But they didn't understand English, or Gordon's broad mixed accent.

'Why the flags and decorations?' she called in Spanish and was rewarded by comprehension.

'Are you from another planet?' they called, incredulous. 'Everyone knows what's happening today.'

Their language was the mix of Spanish and French Ramón had used with the lawyer. She felt almost at home.

No. This was Ramón's home. Not hers.

'We're from Australia,' she called. 'We know nothing.'

'Well, welcome.' The people raised glasses in salutation. 'You're here just in time.'

'For what?'

'For the coronation,' they called. 'It's a public holiday. Crown Prince Ramón Cavellero of Cepheus accepts his Crown today.'

Right. She stood in the bow and let her hands automatically organize lines. Or not. She didn't know what her hands were doing.

First thought? Stupidly, it was that Ramón wouldn't be meeting her.

Had she ever believed he would? Ramón was a Prince of the Blood. He'd have moved on.

'Is that our berth?' Gordon called, and she caught herself, glanced at the sheet the harbour master had faxed through and then looked ahead to where their designated berth should be.

And drew in her breath.

Ramón wasn't there. Of course he wasn't. But there was a welcoming committee. There were four officials, three men and a woman, all in some sort of official uniform. The colours of their uniform matched the colours of the flags.

This yacht belonged to royalty, and representatives of royalty were there to meet them.

'Reckon any of them can catch a line?' Gordon called and she tried to smile.

'We're about to find out.'

Not only could they catch a line, they were efficient, courteous and they took smoothly over from the time the *Marquita* touched the dock.

'Welcome,' the senior official said gravely, in English. 'You are exactly on time.'

'You've been waiting for us?'

'His Highness has had you tracked from the moment you left Auckland. He's delighted you could be here today. He asks that you attend the ceremony this afternoon, and the official ball this evening.'

Jenny swung around to stare at Gordon—who was staring back at her. They matched. They both had their mouths wide open.

'Reckon we won't fit in,' Gordon drawled at last, sounding flabbergasted. 'Reckon there won't be a lot of folk wearing salt-crusted oilskins on your guest list.'

'That's why we're here,' the official said smoothly. 'Jorge here will complete the care of the *Marquita*, while Dalila and Rudi are instructed to care for you. If you agree, we'll escort you to the palace, you'll be fitted with clothing suitable for the occasion and you'll be His Highness's honoured guests at the ceremonies this afternoon and this evening.'

Jenny gasped. Her head was starting to explode. To see Ramón as a prince…

'We can't,' Gordon muttered.

But Jenny looked at the elderly seaman and saw her mixture of emotions reflected on his face. They'd been at sea for three months now, and she knew enough of Gordon to realize he stacked up life's events and used them to fill the long stretches at sea that he lived for.

He was staring at the officials with a mixture of awe and dread. And desire.

If she didn't go, Gordon wouldn't go.

And, a little voice inside her breathed, she'd get to see Ramón one last time.

Once upon a time Ramón had been her skipper. Once upon a time he'd been her lover. He'd moved on now. He was a Crown Prince.

She'd see him today and then she'd leave.

* * *

For the *Marquita* to berth on the same day as his coronation was a coincidence he couldn't ignore, making his resolution waver.

He'd made the decision to send his apologies when the boat berthed, for Jenny to be treated with all honour, paid handsomely and then escorted to the airport and given a first-class ticket back to Australia. That was the sensible decision. He couldn't allow himself to be diverted from his chosen path. But when he'd learned the *Marquita*'s date of arrival was today he'd given orders before he thought it through. Sensible or not, he would see Jenny this one last time.

Maybe he should see it as an omen, he decided as he dressed. Maybe he was meant to have her nearby, giving him strength to take this final step.

Servants were fussing over his uniform, making sure he looked every inch the Ruler of Cepheus, and outside there was sufficient security to defend him against a small army. Carlos's blustering threats of support from the military seemed to have no foundation. On his own he had nothing to fear, and on his own he must rule.

The last three months had cemented his determination to change this country. If he must accept the Crown then he'd do it as it was meant to be done. He could change this country for the better. He could make life easier for the population. The Crown, this ultimate position of authority, had been abused for generations. If anyone was to change it, it must be him.

Duty and desire had no place together. He knew that, and the last months' assessment of the state of the country told him that his duty was here. He had to stay focused. *He didn't need Jenny.*

But, need her or not, he wanted Jenny at the ceremony. To have her come all this way and not see her—on this of all days—*that* was more unthinkable than anything.

He would dance with her this night, he thought. Just this once, he'd touch her and then he'd move forward. Alone.

The doors were swinging open. The Master of State was waiting. Cepheus was waiting.

He'd set steps in place to bring this country into the twenty-first century, he thought with grim satisfaction. His coronation would cement those steps. Fulfilling the plans he'd set in place over the last few weeks would mean this country would thrive.

But maybe the population would never forget the family he came from, he thought as he was led in stately grandeur to the royal carriage. There were no cheers, no personal applause. Today the country was celebrating a public holiday and a continuum of history, but the populace wasn't impressed by what he personally represented. His grandfather's reputation came before him, smirching everything. Royalty was something to be endured.

The country had celebrated the birth of a new Crown Prince five years ago. That deception still rankled, souring all.

Philippe should be here, he thought. The little boy should play some part in this ceremony.

But, out at the farm, Philippe was finally starting to relax with him, learning again to be a little boy. He still missed the palace, but to bring him back seemed just as impossible as it had been three months ago.

Philippe was now an outsider. As he was himself, he thought grimly, glancing down at his uniform that made him seem almost ludicrously regal. And the threats were there, real or not.

He could protect Philippe. He *would* protect Philippe, but from a distance. Jenny was here for this day only. Sofía would be gone. He could rule as he needed to rule.

'It's time, Your Highness,' the Head of State said in stentorian tones, and Ramón knew that it was.

It was time to accept that he was a Prince of the Blood, with all the responsibility—and loss—that the title implied.

The great chorus of trumpets sounded, heralding the beginning of ceremonies and Jenny was sitting in a pew in the vast cathedral of Cepheus feeling bewildered. Feeling transformed. Feeling like Cinderella must have felt after the fairy godmother waved her wand.

For she wasn't at the back with the hired help. She and Gordon were being treated like royalty themselves.

The palace itself had been enough to take her breath away, all spirals and turrets and battlements, a medieval fantasy clinging to white stone cliffs above a sea so blue it seemed to almost merge with the sky.

The apartment she'd been taken to within the palace had taken even more of her breath away. It was as big as a small house, and Gordon had been shown into a similar one on the other side of the corridor. Corridor? It was more like a great hall. You could play a football match in the vast areas—decorated in gold, all carvings, columns and ancestral paintings—that joined the rooms. Dalila had ushered her in, put her holdall on a side table and instructed a maid to unpack.

'I'm not staying here,' Jenny had gasped.

'For tonight at least,' Dalila had said, formally polite in stilted English. 'The ball will be late. The Prince requires you to stay.'

How to fight a decree like that? How indeed to fight, when clothes were being produced that made her gasp all over again.

'I can't wear these.'

'You can,' the woman decreed. 'If you'll just stay still. Dolores is a dressmaker. It will take her only moments to adjust these for size.'

And Jenny had simply been too overwhelmed to refuse. So here she was, in a pew ten seats from the front, right on the aisle, dressed in a crimson silk ball-gown that looked as if it had been made for her. It was cut low across her breasts, with tiny capped sleeves, the bodice clinging like a second skin, curving to her hips and then flaring out to an almost full circle skirt. The fabric was so beautiful it made her feel as if she was floating.

There was a pendant round her neck that she hoped was paste but she suspected was a diamond so big she couldn't comprehend it. Her hair was pinned up in a deceptively simple knot and her make-up had been applied with a skill so great that when she looked in the mirror she saw someone she didn't recognize.

She felt like…Gianetta. For the first time in her life, her father's name seemed right for her.

'I'm just glad they can't see me back at the Sailor's Arms in Auckland,' Gordon muttered, and she glanced at the weathered seaman who looked as classy as she did, in a deep black suit that fitted him like a glove. He, too, had been transformed, like it or not. She almost chuckled, but then the music rose to a crescendo and she stopped thinking about chuckling. She stopped thinking about anything at all—anything but Ramón.

Crown Prince Ramón Cavellero of Cepheus.

For so he was.

The great doors of the cathedral had swung open. The Archbishop of Cepheus led the way in stately procession down the aisle, and Ramón trod behind, intent, his face set in lines that said this was an occasion of such great moment that lives would change because of it.

He truly was a prince, she thought, dazed beyond belief. If she'd walked past him in the street—no, if she'd seen his picture on the cover of a magazine, for this wasn't a man one passed in the street, she would never have recognized him. His uniform was black as night, skilfully cut to mould to his tall, lean frame. The leggings, the boots, the slashes of gold, the tassels, the fierce sword at his side, they only accentuated his aura of power and strength and purpose.

Or then again…maybe she would have recognized him. His eyes seemed to have lost their colour—they were dark as night. His mouth was set and grim, and it was the expression she'd seen when he'd known she was leaving.

He looked like…an eagle, she thought, a fierce bird of prey, ready to take on the world. But he was still Ramón.

He was so near her now. If she put out her hand…

He was passing her row. He was right here. And as he passed… His gaze shifted just a little from looking steadily ahead. Somehow it met hers and held, for a nano-second, for a fraction that might well be imagined. And then he was gone, swept past in the procession and the world crowded back in.

He hadn't smiled, but had his grimness lifted, just a little?

'He was looking for you,' Gordon muttered, awed. 'The guy who helped me dress said he told the aides where we were to sit. It's like we're important. Are you important to him then, lass?'

'Not in a million years,' she breathed.

She'd come.

It was the only thing holding him steady.

Gianetta. Jenny.

Her name was in his mind, like a mantra, said over and over.

'By the power vested in me…'

He was kneeling before the archbishop and the crown was being placed on his head. The weight was enormous.

She was here.

He could take this nowhere. He knew that. But still, for now, she was here on this day when he needed her most.

She was here, and his crown was the lighter for it.

The night seemed to be organized for her. As the throng emerged from the great cathedral, an aide appeared and took her arm.

'You're to come this way, miss. And you, too, sir,' he said to Gordon. 'You're official guests at the Coronation Dinner.'

'I reckon I'll slope back down to the boat,' Gordon muttered, shrinking, but Jenny clutched him as if she were drowning.

'We went round the Horn together,' she muttered. 'We face risk together.'

'This is worse than the Horn.'

'You're telling me,' Jenny said, and the aide was ushering them forward and it was too late to escape.

They sat, midway down a vast banquet table, where it

seemed half the world's dignitaries were assembled. Gordon, a seaman capable of facing down the world's worst storms, was practically shrinking under the table. Jenny was a bit braver, but not much. She was recognizing faces and names and her eyes grew rounder and rounder as she realized just who was here. There were speeches—of course—and she translated for Gordon and was glad of the task. It took her mind off what was happening.

It never took her mind off Ramón.

He was seated at the great formal table at the head of the room, gravely surveying all. He looked born to the role, she thought. He listened with gravitas and with courtesy. He paid attention to the two women on either side of him—grand dames, both of them, queens of their own countries.

'I have friends back in Australia who are never going to believe what I've done tonight,' she whispered to Gordon and her skipper nodded agreement.

Then once more the aide was beside them, bending to whisper to Jenny.

'Ma'am, I've been instructed to ask if you can waltz.'

'If I can…?'

'His Royal Highness wishes to dance with you. He doesn't wish to embarrass you, however, so if there's a problem…'

No. She wanted to scream, *no*.

But she glanced up at the head table and Ramón was watching her. Those eagle eyes were steady. 'I dare you,' his gaze was saying, and more.

'I can waltz,' she heard herself say, her eyes not leaving Ramón's.

'Excellent,' the aide said. 'I'll come to fetch you when we're ready.'

'You do that,' she said faintly.

What have I done?

The entrance to the grand ballroom was made in state. Ramón led the procession, and it was done in order of rank, which meant Jenny came in somewhere near the rear. Even that was intimidating—all the guests who hadn't been at the dinner were assembled in line to usher the dining party in.

If the ground opened up and swallowed her she'd be truly grateful. Too many people were looking at her.

Why had she agreed to dance?

Ramón was so far ahead she couldn't see him. Ramón. Prince Ramón.

She wasn't into fairy tales. Bring on midnight.

And Gordon had deserted her. As she took the aide's arm, as she joined the procession, he suddenly wasn't there. She looked wildly around and he was smiling apologetically but backing firmly away. But she was being ushered forward and there was no way she could run without causing a spectacle.

Cinderella ran, she thought wildly. At midnight.

But midnight was still a long time away.

Courage. If Cinders could face them all down, so could she. She took a deep breath and allowed herself to be led forward. The aide was ushering her into the ballroom, then into an alcove near the entrance. Before them, Ramón was making a grand sweep of the room, greeting everyone. The heads of the royal houses of Europe were his entourage, nodding, smiling, doing what royalty did best.

And suddenly she realized what was happening. Why she'd been directed to stand here. She was close to the door, where Ramón must end his circuit.

She felt frozen to the spot.

Ramón. Prince Ramón.

Ramón.

The wait was interminable. She tried to focus on anything but what was happening. A spot on the wax of the polished floor. The hem of her gown. Anything.

But finally, inevitably, the aide was beside her, ushering her forward and Ramón was right in front of her. Every eye in the room was on him. Every eye in the room was on her.

She was Jenny. She made muffins. She wanted to have hysterics, or faint.

Ramón was before her, his eyes grave and questioning.

'Gianetta,' he said softly, and every ear in the room was straining to hear. 'You've arrived for my coronation, and I thank you. You've brought my boat home and thus you've linked my old life with my new. Can I therefore ask for the honour of this dance?'

There was an audible gasp throughout the room. It wasn't said out loud but she could hear the thought regardless. *Who?*

But Ramón was holding out his hand, waiting for her to put hers in his. Smiling. It was the smile she loved with all her heart.

Was this how Cinders felt?

And then Cinders was forgotten. Everything was forgotten. She put her hand in his, she tried hard to smile back and she allowed the Crown Prince of Cepheus to lead her onto the ballroom floor.

Where had she learned to dance?

Ramón had been coached almost before he could walk. His grandmother had thought dancing at least as important as any other form of movement. He could thus waltz without thinking. He'd expected to slow his steps to Jenny's, to take care she wasn't embarrassed, but he'd been on the dance floor less than ten seconds before he realized such precautions weren't necessary. He took her into his arms in the waltz hold, and she melted into him as if she belonged.

The music swelled in an age-old, well-loved waltz and she was one with the music, one with him.

He'd almost forgotten how wonderful she felt.

He had to be formal, he told himself harshly. He needed to hold her at arm's length—which was difficult when he was not holding her at arm's length at all. He needed to be courteously friendly and he needed to thank her and say goodbye.

Only not yet. Not goodbye yet.

'Where did you learn to dance?' he managed, and it was a dumb thing to say to a woman after a three-month separation, but the tension eased a little and she almost smiled.

'Dancing's not reserved for royalty. My Papà was the best.'

This was better. There was small talk in this. 'He should have met my grandmother.'

'Yes,' she said, and seemed to decide to let herself enjoy the music, the dance, the sensation of being held for a couple more circuits of the floor while the world watched. And then… 'Ramón, why are you doing this?'

'I'm sorry?'

'Why did you ask me to dance…first?'

'I wanted to thank you.'

'You paid me, remember? It's me who should be thanking. And the world is watching. For you to ask me for the first dance…'

'I believe it's the last dance,' he said, and the leaden feeling settled back around his heart as the truth flooded back. Holding her was an illusion, a fleeting taste of what could have been, and all at once the pain was unbearable. 'I've wanted to hold you for three months,' he said simply, and it was as if the words were there and had to be said, whether he willed them or not. 'Jenny, maybe even saying it is unwise but, wise or not, I've missed you every single night.' He hesitated, then somehow struggled back to lightness, forcing the leaden ache to stay clear of his voice. He couldn't pass his regret onto her. He had to say goodbye—as friends. 'Do you realize how much work there is in being a Crown Prince?'

'I have no idea,' she said faintly. 'I guess…there's speeches to make. Ribbons to cut. That sort of thing.'

'Not so much of that sort of thing.' His hand tightened on her waist, tugging her closer. Wanting her closer. Sense decreed he had to let her go, but still not yet. 'I haven't even been official Crown Prince until today,' he said, fighting to make his voice sound normal. 'I've not even been qualified as a ribbon-cutter until now. I've been a prince in training. Nothing more. Nothing less. But I have been practising my waltzing. My Aunt Sofía's seen to that. So let's see if we can make the ghosts of your Papà and my Grand-mère proud.'

She smiled. He whirled her around in his arms and she felt like thistledown, he thought. She felt like Jenny.

He had to let her go.

He didn't feel like a prince, she thought as he held her close and their bodies moved as one. If she closed her eyes he felt like Ramón. Just Ramón, pure and simple. The man who'd stolen her heart.

It was impossible, he'd said. Of course it was. She'd known it for three months and nothing had changed.

The world was watching. She had to keep it light.

'So it's been practising speeches and waltzing,' she ventured at last. 'While we've been braving the Horn.'

'That and getting leggings to fit,' he murmured into her ear. 'Bloody things, leggings. I'd almost prefer the Horn.'

'But leggings are so sexy.'

'Sexy isn't leggings,' he said. His eyes were on her and she could see exactly what he was thinking.

'Don't,' she whispered, feeling her colour rising. Every eye in the room was on them.

'I've missed you for three long months,' he said, lightness disappearing. He sounded goaded almost past breaking point.

'Ramón, we had two weeks,' she managed. 'It didn't mean anything.'

He stopped dancing. Others had taken to the floor now, but they were on the edge of the dance floor. Ramón and Jenny had central position and they were still being watched.

'Are you saying what we had didn't mean anything to you?' he asked, his voice sounding suddenly calm, almost distant.

'Of course it did,' she said, blushing furiously. 'At the time. Ramón, please, can we keep dancing? I don't belong here.'

'Neither do I,' he said grimly, and he took her in his arms again and slipped back into the waltz. 'I should be leaving for Bangladesh right now. My team's left without me for the first time in years.'

'Speeches are important,' she said cautiously.

'They are.' The laughter and passion had completely disappeared now, leaving his voice sounding flat and defeated. 'Believe it or not, this country needs me. It's been bled dry by my grandfather and my uncle. If I walk away it'll continue to be bled dry by a government that's as corrupt as it is inept. It's not all ribbon-cutting.'

'It's your life,' she said simply. 'You're bred to it and you shouldn't be dancing with me.'

'I shouldn't be doing lots of things, and I'll not be told who I should be dancing with tonight. I know. This can only be for now *but I will dance with you tonight*.'

The music was coming to an end. The outside edge of the dance floor was crowded, but the dancers were keeping clear of the Crown Prince and his partner. A space was left so that, as soon as the dance ended, Ramón could return to his royal table.

Waiting for him were the crowned heads of Europe. Men and women who were watching Jenny as if they knew instinctively she had no place among them.

'You have danced with me,' Jenny said softly, disengaging her hands before he realized what she intended. 'I thank you for the honour.'

'There's no need to thank me.'

'Oh, but there is,' she said, breathless. 'The clothes, this moment, you. I'll remember it all my life.'

She looked up into his eyes and felt an almost overwhelming urge to reach up and kiss him, just a kiss, just a moment, to take a tiny taste of him to keep for ever. But the eyes of the world were on her. Ramón was a prince and his world was waiting.

'I believe there are women waiting to dance with the Crown Prince of Cepheus,' she murmured. 'We both need to move on, so thank you, Ramón. Thank you for the fantasy.'

'Thank you, Gianetta,' he murmured, and he raised his hand and touched her cheek, a feather touch that seemed a gesture of regret and loss and farewell. 'It's been my honour. I will see you before you leave.'

'Do you think…?'

'It's unwise? Of course it's unwise,' he finished for her. 'But it's tonight only. Tomorrow I need to be wise for the rest of my life.'

'Then maybe tomorrow needs to start now,' she said unsteadily and she managed a smile, her very best peasant to royalty smile, and turned and walked away. Leaving the Crown Prince of Cepheus looking after her.

What had he said? *'We can't take it further…'*

Of course they couldn't. What was she thinking of? But still she felt like sobbing. What was she doing here? Why had she ever come? She'd slip away like Gordon, she thought, just as soon as the next dance started, just as soon as everyone stopped watching her.

But someone was stepping into her path. Another prince? The man was dark and bold and so good-looking that if she hadn't met Ramón first she would have been stunned. As it was, she hardly saw him.

'May I request the honour of this dance?' he said, and it wasn't a question. His hand took hers before she could argue, autocratic as Ramón. Where did they learn this? Autocracy school?

It seemed no wasn't a word in these men's vocabularies. She was being led back onto the dance floor, like it or not.

'What's needed is a bit of spine,' she told herself and somehow she tilted her chin, fixed her smile and accepted partner after partner.

Most of these men were seriously good dancers. Many of these men were seriously good-looking men. She thought briefly of Cathy back in Seaport—*'Jenny, get a life!'* If Cathy could see her now…

The thought was almost enough to make her smile real. If only she wasn't so aware of the eyes watching her. If only she wasn't so aware of Ramón's presence. He was dancing with beautiful woman after beautiful woman, and a couple of truly impressive royal matriarchs as well.

He was smiling into each of his partner's eyes, and each one of them was responding exactly the same.

They melted.

Why would they not? Anyone would melt in Ramón's arms.

And suddenly, inexplicably, she was thinking of Matty, of her little son, and she wondered what she was doing here. This strange creature in fancy clothes had nothing to do with who she really was, and all at once what she was doing seemed a betrayal.

'It's okay,' she told herself, feeling suddenly desperate. 'This is simply an unbelievable moment out of my life. After tonight I'll return to being who I truly am. This is for one night only,' she promised Matty. 'One night and then I'm back where I belong.'

Her partner was holding her closer than was appropriate. Sadly for him, she was so caught up in her thoughts she hardly noticed.

Ramón was dancing so close that she could almost reach out and touch him. He whirled his partner round, his gaze caught hers and he smiled, and her partner had no chance at all.

That smile was so dangerous. That smile sucked you in.

'So who are your parents?' her partner asked, and she had to blink a few times to try and get her world moving again.

'My parents are dead,' she managed. 'And yours?'

'I beg your pardon?'

'Who are your parents?'

'My father is the King of Morotatia,' her partner said in stilted English. 'My mother was a princess in her own right before she married. And I am Prince Marcelo Pietros Cornelieus Maximus, heir to the throne of Morotatia.'

'That's wonderful,' she murmured. 'I guess you don't need to work for a living then?'

'Work?'

'I didn't think so,' she said sadly. 'But you guys must need muffins. I wonder if there's an opening around here for a kitchen maid.'

But, even as she said it, she knew even that wasn't possible. She had no place here. This was the fairy tale and she had to go home.

CHAPTER SEVEN

THE night was becoming oppressive. She was passed on to her next partner, who gently grilled her again, and then another who grilled her not so gently until she almost snapped at him. Finally supper was announced. She could escape now, she thought, but then a dumpy little lady with a truly magnificent tiara made a beeline for her, grasped her hands and introduced herself.

'I'm Ramón's Aunt Sofía. I'm so pleased to meet you.' She tucked her arm into Jenny's as if she was laying claim to her—as indeed she was, as there were those around them who were clearly waiting to start the inquisitions again.

'Aunt…'

Sofía turned to see Ramón approaching. He had one of the formidable matrons on his arm. Queen of somewhere? But Sofía was not impressed.

'Go away, Ramón,' Sofía commanded. 'I'm taking Jenny into supper. You look after Her Highness.'

'Sofía was always bossy,' the Queen of somewhere said, but she smiled, and Ramón gave his aunt a smile and gave Jenny a quick, fierce glance—one that was enough to make her toes curl—and led his queen away.

Sofía must rank pretty highly, Jenny thought, so dazed she simply allowed herself to be led. The crowd parted before them. Sofía led them to a small alcove set with a table and truly impressive tableware. She smiled at a passing servant and in two minutes there were so many delicacies before them Jenny could only gasp.

Sofía ate two bite-sized cream éclairs, then paused to demand why Jenny wasn't doing likewise.

'I'm rather in shock,' Jenny confessed.

'Me too,' Sofía confessed. 'And Ramón too, though we're making the best of it.'

'But Ramón's the Crown Prince,' Jenny managed. 'How can he be intimidated?' She could see him through the crowd. He drew every eye in the room. He looked truly magnificent—Crown Prince to the manor born.

'Because he wasn't meant to be royal,' Sofía said darkly, but then her darkness disappeared and she smiled encouragingly at Jenny. 'Just like you're not. I'm not sure what Ramón's told you so I thought maybe there's things you ought to know.'

'I know the succession was a shock,' Jenny ventured, and Sofía nodded vigorously and ate another éclair.

'Yes,' she said definitely. 'We were never expected to inherit. Ramón's grandfather—my father—sent my mother, my younger brother and I out of the palace when my brother and I were tiny. We were exiled, and kept virtual prisoners on an island just off the coast. My mother was never permitted to step back onto the mainland.'

Jenny frowned. Why was she being told this? But she could do nothing but listen as Sofía examined a meringue from all angles and decided not.

'That sounds dreadful,' Sofía continued, moving on to a delicate chocolate praline, popping it in and choosing another. 'But, in truth, the island is beautiful. It was only my mother's pain at what was happening to her country, and at losing her elder son that hurt. As we grew older my younger brother married an islander—a lovely girl. Ramón is their son. So Ramón's technically a prince, but until three months ago the only time he was at the palace was the night his father died.'

There were places here she didn't want to go. There were

places she had no right to go to. 'He...he spends his life on his yacht,' she ventured.

'No, dear, only part of it, and that's only since his mother and sister died. He trained as a builder. I think he started building things almost as soon as he could put one wooden block on top of another. He spends every dry season in Bangladesh, building houses with floating floors. Apparently they're brilliant—villagers can adjust their floor levels as flood water rises. He's passionate about it, but now, here he is, stuck as Crown Prince for ever.'

'I imagine he was trained for it,' Jenny said stiffly, still not sure where this was going.

'Only in that my mother insisted on teaching us court manners,' Sofía retorted. 'It was as if she knew that one day we'd be propelled back here. We humoured her, though none of us ever expected that we would. Finally, my brother tried to reinstate my mother's rights, to allow her to leave the island, and that's when the real tragedy started.'

'That was when Ramón's father was killed?'

'Yes, dear. By my father's thugs,' Sofía said, her plump face creasing into distress. The noise and bustle of the ballroom was nothing, ignored in her apparent need to tell Jenny this story. 'My mother ached to leave, and we couldn't believe my father's vindictiveness could last for years. But last it did, and when my brother was old enough he mounted a legal challenge. It was met with violence and with death. My father invited my brother here, to reason with him, so he came and brought Ramón with him because he thought he'd introduce his little son to his grandfather. So Ramón was here when it happened, a child, sleeping alone in this dreadful place while his father was killed. Just...alone.'

She stared down at her chocolate, but she wasn't seeing it. She was obviously still stunned at the enormity of what had happened. 'That's what royalty does,' she whispered. 'What is it they say? Absolute power corrupts absolutely. So my father had his own son killed, simply because he dared to defy him. We assume...we want to believe that it was simply his thugs going too far, meant to frighten but taking their orders past the point of reason. But still, my father must have employed them, and he must have known the consequences. This place…the whole of royalty is tainted by that murder. And now Carlos…the man who would have been Crown Prince if Ramón hadn't agreed to come home…is in the wings, threatening. He's here tonight.'

She gestured towards the supper table where a big man with more medals than Ramón was shovelling food into his mouth.

'He makes threats but so quietly we can't prove anything. He's here always, with his unfortunate wife towed in his wake, and he's just waiting for something to happen to Ramón. I can walk away—Ramón insists that I will walk away—but Ramón can't.'

Jenny was struggling to take everything in. She couldn't focus on shadows of death. She couldn't even begin to think of Carlos and his threats. She was still, in fact, struggling with genealogy. And Ramón as a little boy, alone as his father died…

'So…so the Crown Prince who's just been killed was your older brother?' she managed.

'Yes,' Sofía told her, becoming calm once more. 'Not that I ever saw him after we left the palace. And he had a son, who also had a son.' She shrugged. 'A little boy called Philippe. There's another tragedy. But it's not your tragedy, dear,' she said as she saw Jenny's face. 'Nor Ramón's. Ramón worries, but then Ramón worries about everything.' She hesitated, and then forged ahead as if this was something she'd rehearsed.

'But, my dear, Ramón's been talking about you,' she confessed. 'He says…he says you're special. Well, I can see that. I watched Ramón's face as he danced with you and it's exactly the same expression I saw on his father's face when he danced with his mother. If Ramón's found that with you…'

'He can't possibly…' Jenny started, startled, but Sofía was allowing no interruptions.

'You can't say it's impossible if it's already happened. All

I'm saying is that you don't have to be royal to be with Ramón. What I'm saying is give love a chance.'

'How could I…?' She stopped, bewildered.

'By not staying in this palace,' Sofía said, suddenly deadly serious. 'By not even thinking about it. Ramón's right when he tells me such a union is impossible, dangerous, unsuitable, and he can't be distracted from what he must do. You don't fit in and neither should you. Our real home, our lovely island, is less than fifteen minutes' helicopter ride from here. If Ramón could settle you there as his mistress, he'd have an escape.'

'An escape?' she whispered, stunned.

'From royalty,' Sofía said bluntly. 'Ramón needs to do his duty but if he could have you on the side…' She laid a hand over Jenny's. 'It could make all the difference. And he'd look after you so well. I know he would. You'd want for nothing. So, my dear, will you listen to Ramón?'

'If he asks…to have me as his some-time mistress?' she managed.

'I'm just letting you know his family would think it was a good thing,' Sofía said, refusing to be deterred by Jenny's obvious shock. 'You're not to take offence, but it's nothing less than my duty to tell you that you're totally unsuitable for this place, even if he'd have you here, which he won't. You're not who Ramón needs as a wife. He needs someone who knows what royalty is and how to handle it. That's what royal pedigree is—there's a reason for it. But, as for a partner he loves…that's a different thing. If Ramón could have you now and then…'

She paused, finally beginning to flounder. The expression on Jenny's face wasn't exactly encouraging. She was finding it impossible to contain her anger, and her humiliation.

'So you'd have him marry someone else and have me on the side,' she said dangerously.

'It's been done for generation upon generation,' Sofía said with asperity. Then she glanced up with some relief as a stranger approached, a youngish man wearing more medals than Ramón. 'But here's Lord Anthony, wanting an introduction. He's frightfully British, my dear, but he's a wonderful dancer. Ramón won't have any more time for you tonight. He'll have so little time… But I'm sure he could fit you in every now and then, if you'll agree to the island. So you go and dance with Lord Anthony, and remember what I said when you need to remember it.'

Jenny danced almost on automatic pilot. She desperately wanted to leave, but slipping away when the world was watching was impossible. As Sofía had warned her, she barely saw Ramón again. He was doing his duty, dancing with one society dame after another.

She'd been lucky to be squeezed in at all, she thought dully. What *was* she doing here?

It wasn't made better with her second 'girls' talk' of the night. Another woman grabbed her attention almost straight after Sofía. This lady was of a similar age to Sofía, but she was small and thin, she had fewer jewels and she had the air of a frightened rabbit. But she was a determined frightened rabbit. She intercepted Jenny between partners. When the next man approached she hissed, 'Go away,' and stood her ground until they were left alone.

'I'm Perpetua,' she said, and then, as Jenny looked blank, she explained. 'I'm Carlos's wife.'

Carlos. The threat.

'He's not dangerous,' Perpetua said, obviously reading her expression, and she steered her into the shadows with an air of quiet but desperate determination. 'My husband's all talk. All stupidity. It's this place. It's being royal. I just wanted to say…to say…'

She took a deep breath and out it came, as if it had been welled up for years. 'They say you're common,' she said. 'I mean…ordinary. Not royal. Like me. I was a schoolteacher, and I loved my work and then I met Carlos. For a while we were happy, but then the old Prince decided he liked my husband. He used to take him gambling. Carlos got sucked into the lifestyle, and that's where he stays. In some sort of fantasy world, where he's more royal than Ramón. He's done some really stupid things, most of them at the Prince's goading. In these last months when he thought he would inherit the throne, he's been…a little bit crazy. There's nothing I can do, but it's so painful to see the way he is, the way he's acting. And then I watched you tonight. The way you looked at Ramón when you were dancing.'

'I don't understand,' Jenny managed.

'Just get away from it,' she whispered. 'Whatever Ramón says, don't believe it. Just run. Oh, I shouldn't say anything. I'm a royal wife and a royal wife just shuts up. Do you want that? To be an appendage who just shuts up? My dear, don't do it. Just run.' And then, as yet another potential partner came to claim Jenny's hand, she gave a gasping sob, shot Jenny one last despairing glance and disappeared into the crowd.

Just run. That was truly excellent advice, Jenny thought, as she danced on, on autopilot. It was the best advice she'd had all night. If she knew where she was, if she knew how to get back to the boat in the dark in the middle of a strange city, that was just what she'd do.

She'd never felt so alone. She was Cinderella without her coach and it wasn't even midnight.

But finally the clock struck twelve. Right on cue, a cluster of officials gathered round Ramón as a formal guard of honour. Trumpets blared with a final farewell salute, and the Crown Prince Ramón of Cepheus was escorted away.

He'd be led to his harem of nubile young virgins, Jenny decided, fighting back an almost hysterical desire to laugh. Or cry. Or both. She was so weary she wanted to sink and, as if the thought had been said aloud, a footman was at her side, courteously solicitous.

'Ma'am, I'm to ask if you'd like to stay on to continue dancing, or would you like to be escorted back to your chambers?'

'I'd like to be escorted back to the yacht.'

'That's not possible, ma'am,' he said. 'The Prince's orders are that you stay in the palace.' And then, as she opened her mouth to argue, he added flatly, 'There's no transport to the docks tonight. I'm sorry, ma'am, but you'll have to stay.'

So that, it seemed, was that. She was escorted back to the palace. She lay in her ridiculously ostentatious bedchamber, in her ridiculously ostentatious bed, and she tried for sleep.

How was a girl to sleep after a night like this?

She couldn't. Her crimson ball-gown was draped on a hanger in the massive walk-in wardrobe. The diamond necklet still lay on her dresser. Her Cinderella slippers were on the floor beside her bed.

At least she'd kept both of them on, she thought ruefully. It hadn't quite been a fairy tale.

Only it had been a fairy tale. Gianetta Bertin—Jenny to her friends—had attended a royal ball. She'd been led out onto the dance floor with a prince so handsome he made her knees turn to jelly. For those few wonderful moments she'd let herself be swept away into a magic future where practicalities disappeared and there was only Ramón; only her love.

And then his aunt had told her that she was totally unsuitable to be a royal wife but she could possibly be his mistress. Only not here. How romantic.

And then someone called Perpetua had warned her against royalty, like the voice of doom in some Gothic novel. *Do not trust him, gentle maiden.*

How ridiculous.

And, as if in response to her unanswerable question, someone knocked on the door.

Who'd knock on her bedroom door at three in the morning?

'Who is it?' she quavered, and her heart seemed to stop until there was a response.

'I can't get my boots off,' a beloved voice complained from the other side of the door. 'I was hoping someone might hang on while I pull.'

'I... I believe my contract was all about muffins and sails,' she managed, trying to make her voice not squeak, trying to kick-start her heart again while warnings and sensible decisions went right out of the window. *Ramón.*

'I know I have no right to ask.' There was suddenly seriousness behind Ramón's words. 'I know this isn't sensible, I know I shouldn't be here, but Jenny, if tonight is all there is then I'm sure, if we read the contract carefully, there might be something about boots. Something that'd give us an excuse for…well, something about helping me for this night only.'

'Don't you have a valet?' she whispered and then wondered how he'd hear her through the door. But it was as if he was already in the room with her.

'Valets scare the daylights out of me,' he said. 'They're better dressed than I am. Please, Jenny love, will you help me off with my boots?'

'I don't think I'm brave enough.'

'You helped a trapped whale. Surely you can help a trapped prince. For this night only.'

'Ramón…'

'Open the door, Gianetta,' he said in a different voice, a voice that had her flinging back her bedcovers and flying to the door and tugging it open. Despite what Sofía had said, despite Perpetua's grim warnings, this was Ramón. Her Ramón.

And there he was. He wasn't smiling. He was just…him.

He opened his arms and she walked right in.

For a long moment she simply stood, held against him, feeling the strength of his heartbeat, feeling his arms around her. He was still in his princely uniform. There were medals digging into her cheek but she wasn't complaining. His heart was beating right under those medals, and who cared about a bit of metal anyway?

Who cared what two royal women had said to her? Who cared that this was impossible?

They had this night.

He kissed the top of her head and he held her tight and she felt protected and loved—and desperate to haul him into the room right there and then.

But there was a footman at the top of the stairs. Just standing, staring woodenly ahead. He was wigged, powdered, almost a dummy. But he was real.

It was hard to seize a prince and haul him into her lair when a footman was on guard.

'Um…we have an audience,' she whispered at last.

He kissed her hair again and said gravely, 'Do you care?'

'If we walk into my room and shut the door we won't have an audience,' she tried.

'Ah, but the story will out,' he said gravely.

'So it should if you go creeping into strange women's bedrooms in the small hours. I should yell the house down.'

She was trying to sound indignant. She was trying to pull back so she could be at arm's length, so she could see his face. She wasn't trying hard enough. She sounded happy—and there was no way she was pulling back from this man.

'You could if you wanted and you'd have help,' he said gravely. 'The footman's on guard duty. In case the Huns invade—or strange women don't want strange men doing this creeping thing you describe. But if the woman was to welcome this strange man, then we don't need an audience. Gianetta, are you hungry?'

Hungry. The thought was so out of left field that she blinked.

'Hungry?'

'I'm starving. I was hoping you might come down to the kitchen with me.'

'After I've pulled your boots off?'

'Yup.'

'You want me to be your servant?'

'No,' he said, lightness giving way instantly to a gravity she found disconcerting. 'For this night, I want you to be my friend.'

Her friend, the prince?

Her friend, her lover?

Ramón.

Part-time mistress?

Forget Sofía, she told herself fiercely. Forget Perpetua. Tonight she'd hold on to the fairy tale.

'So…so there's no royal cook?' she managed.

'There are three, but they scare me more than my valet. They wear white hats and speak with Italian accents and say béchamel a lot.'

'Oh, Ramón…'

'And there's no security camera in the smaller kitchen,' he told her, and she looked up into his face and it was all she could do not to burst into spontaneous combustion.

'So will you come?' His eyes dared her.

'I'm coming.' Mistress or not, dangerous or not, right now she'd take whatever he wanted to give. Stupid? Who knew? She only knew that there was no way she could walk away from this man this night.

'Slippers and robe first,' he suggested and she blinked.

'Pardon?'

'Let's keep it nice past the footman.' He grinned. 'And do your belt up really tight. I like a challenge.'

'Ramón…'

'Second kitchen, no security camera,' he said and gave her a gentle push back into her bedroom. 'Slippers and gown. Respectability's the thing, my love. All the way down the stairs.'

They were respectable all the way down the stairs. The footman watched them go, his face impassive. When they reached the second kitchen another footman appeared and opened the door for them. He ushered them inside.

'Would you like the door closed?' he said deferentially and Ramón nodded.

'Absolutely. And make sure the Huns stay on that side.'

'The Huns?' the man said blankly.

'You never know what they're planning,' Ramón said darkly. 'If I were you, I'd take a walk around the perimeter of the palace. Warn the troops.'

'Your Highness…'

'Just give us a bit of privacy,' Ramón said, relenting at the look of confusion on the man's face. 'Fifty paces from the kitchen door, agreed?'

Finally there was a smile—sort of—pulled back instantly with a gasp as if the man had realized what he was doing and maybe smiling was a hanging offence. Impassive again, he snapped his heels and moved away and Ramón closed the door and leaned on it.

'This servant thing's got knobs on it. Three months and they still treat me like a prince.'

'You are a prince.'

'Not here,' he said. 'Not now. I'm me and you're you and the kitchen door is closed. And so…'

And so he took her into his arms and he held her so tight the breath was crushed from her body. He held her like a man drowning holding on to a lifeline. He held her and held her and held her, as if there was no way he could ever let her go.

He didn't kiss her. His head rested on her hair. He held her until her heart beat in synchronisation with his. Until she felt as if her body was merging with his, becoming one. Until she felt as if she was truly loved—that she'd come home.

How long they stayed there she could never afterwards tell—time disappeared. This was their moment. The world was somewhere outside that kitchen door, the servants, Sofía's words, Perpetua's warnings, tomorrow, but for now all that mattered was this, her Ramón. Her love.

The kitchen was warm. An old fire-stove sent out a gentle heat. A small grey cat slept in a basket by the hearth. All Jenny had seen of this palace was grandeur, but here in this second kitchen the palace almost seemed a home.

It did feel like home. Ramón was holding her against his heart and she was where she truly belonged.

She knew it was an illusion, and so must he. Maybe that was why he held her for so long, allowing nothing, no words, no movement, to intrude. As if, by holding her, the world could be kept at bay. As if she was something that he must lose, but he'd hold on while he still could.

Finally he kissed her as she needed to be kissed, as she ached to be kissed, and she kissed him back as if he was truly her Ramón and the royal title was nothing but a crazy fantasy locked securely on the other side of the door.

With the Huns, she thought, somewhat deliriously. Reality and the Huns were being kept at bay by powdered, wigged footmen, giving her this time of peace and love and bliss.

She loved this man with all her heart. Maybe what Sofía had said was wrong. Maybe the Perpetua thing was crazy.

The cat stirred, coiling out of her basket, stretching, then stepping daintily out to inspect her food dish. The tiny movement was enough to make them stir, to let a sliver of reality in. But only a sliver.

'She's only interested in her food,' Jenny whispered. 'Not us.'

'I don't blame her. I'm hungry, too.' Ramón's voice was husky with passion, but his words were so prosaic that she chuckled. It made it real. Her Prince of the Blood, dressed in medals and tassels and boots that shone like mirrors, was smiling down at her with a smile that spoke of devilry and pure latent sex—and he was hungry.

'For…for what?' she managed, and the devilry in his eyes darkened, gleamed, sprang into laughter.

'I'd take you on the kitchen table, my love,' he said simply. 'But I just don't trust the servants that much.'

'And we'd shock the cat,' she whispered and he chuckled.

'Absolutely.'

He was trying to make his voice normal, Jenny thought. He was trying to make their world somehow normal. In truth, if Ramón carried out his earlier threat to untie the cord of her dressing gown, if he took that to its inevitable conclusion, there was no way she'd deny him. Only sense was prevailing. Sort of.

Where he led, she'd follow, but if he was trying to be prosaic…maybe she could be, too.

'I could cook in this kitchen,' she said, eyeing the old range appraisingly, the rows of pots and pans hanging from overhead rails, the massive wooden table, worn and pitted from years of scrubbing.

'The pantry adjoins both kitchens,' Ramón said hopefully. 'I'm sure there's eggs and bacon in there.'

'Are you really hungry?'

'At dinner I had two queens, one duke and three prime ministers within talking range,' he said. 'They took turns to address me. It's very rude for a Crown Prince to eat while being addressed by a Head of State. My Aunt Sofía was watching. If I'd eaten I would have had my knuckles rapped.'

'She's a terrifying lady,' Jenny said and he grinned.

'I love her to bits,' he said simply. 'Like I love you.'

'Ramón…'

'Gianetta.'

'This is…'

'Just for tonight,' he said softly and his voice grew bleak. 'I know this is impossible. After tonight I'll ask nothing of you, but Gianetta…just for tonight can we be…us?'

His face was grim. There were vast problems here, she knew, and she saw those problems reflected in his eyes. Sofía had said the ghost of his father made this palace hateful, yet Ramón was stuck here.

Can we be us?

Maybe they could go back to where they' started.

'Do you want bacon and eggs, or do you want muffins?' she asked and tried to make her voice prosaic.

'You could cook muffins here?' Astonishment lessened the grimness.

'You have an oven warmed for a cat,' she said. 'It seems silly to waste it. It'll mean you need to wait twenty minutes instead of five minutes for eggs and bacon.'

'And the smell will go all through the palace,' he said in satisfaction. 'There's an alibi if ever I heard one. We could give a couple to Manuel and Luis.'

'Manuel and Luis?'

'Our Hun protectors. They think I'm taunting them if I use their real names, but surely a muffin couldn't be seen as a taunt.' His eyes were not leaving hers. He wanted her. He ached for her. His eyes said it all, but he was keeping himself rigidly under control.

'You think we might find the ingredients?' he asked, but she was already opening the panty door, doing a visual sweep of the shelves, then checking out the first of three massive refrigerators. As anxious as he to find some way of keeping the sizzle between them under control, and to keep the tension on his face at bay.

'There's more ingredients than you can shake a stick at.'

'Pardon?'

'Lots of ingredients,' she said in satisfaction. 'It seems a shame to abandon bacon entirely. You want bacon and cheese muffins, or double chocolate chip?'

'Both,' he said promptly. 'Especially if I get to lick the chocolate chip bowl.'

'Done,' she said and smiled at him and his smile met hers and she thought, whoa I am in such trouble. And then she thought, whatever Sofía said, or Perpetua said, no matter how impossible this is, I'm so deeply in love, there's no way I'll ever be able to climb out.

CHAPTER EIGHT

THEY made muffins. Not just half a dozen muffins because: 'If I'm helping, it's not such a huge ask to make heaps,' Ramón declared. 'We can put them on for breakfast and show the world what my Gianetta can do.'

'You'll upset the chefs,' Jenny warned.

'If there's a turf war, you win hands down.'

'A turf war…' She was pouring choc chips into her mixture but she hesitated at that. 'I'm not interested in any turf war. Frankly, this set-up leaves me terrified.'

'It leaves me terrified.'

'Yes, but…'

'But I have no choice,' he said flatly, finishing the sentence for her. 'I know that. In the good old days, as Crown Prince I could have simply had my soldiers go out with clubs and drag you to my lair.'

'And now you give me choices,' she retorted, trying desperately to keep things light, whisking her muffin mix more briskly than she needed. 'Just as well. I believe clubbing might create an International Incident.'

'I miss the good old days,' he said morosely. He was sitting on the edge of the table, swinging his gorgeous boots, taking taste tests of her mixture. So sexy the kitchen seemed to sizzle. 'What use is being a prince if I can't get my woman?'

My woman. She was dreaming, Jenny thought dreamily. She was cooking muffins for her prince.

My woman?

She started spooning her mixture into the pans and Ramón reached over and took the trays and the bowl from her. 'I can do this,' he said. 'If you do something for me.'

'What?'

'Pull my boots off. I asked you ages ago.'

'I thought you were kidding.'

'They're killing me,' he confessed. 'I've spent my life in either boat shoes, bare feet or steel-toed construction boots. These make me feel like my feet are in corsets and I can't get them off. Please, dear, kind Jenny, will you pull my boots off?'

He was sitting on the table. He was spooning muffin mixture into pans. He was holding his boots out for her to pull.

This was so ridiculous she couldn't help giggling.

She wiped her hands—it'd be a pity to get chocolate on leather like this—took position, took a boot in both hands—and pulled.

The boot didn't budge. It was like a second skin.

'See what I mean,' Ramón said morosely. 'And I really don't want to wake a valet. You think I should cut them off?'

'You can't cut them,' Jenny said, shocked, and tried again. The boot budged, just a little.

'Hey,' Ramón said, continuing to spoon. 'It's coming.'

'I'll pull you off the table if I tug any harder,' Jenny warned.

'I'm strong,' he said, too smugly, keeping on spooning. 'My balance is assured.'

'Right,' she said and glowered, reacting to his smugness. She wiped both her hands on her dressing gown, took the boot in both hands, took a deep breath—and pulled like she'd never pulled.

The boot held, gripped for a nano-second and then gave. Jenny lurched backward, boot in hand, lost her balance and fell backwards.

Ramón slid off the table, staggered—and ended up on the floor.

The half-full bowl slid off after him, tipped sideways and mixture oozed out over the floor.

Jenny stared across at him in shock. Ramón stared back at her—her lovely prince, half bootless, sprawled on the floor, surrounded by choc chip muffin mixture.

Her Ramón.

She couldn't help it. She laughed out loud, and it was a magical release of tension, a declaration of love and happiness if ever there was one, and she couldn't help what happened next either. It was as if restraint had been thrown to the wind and she could do what she liked—and there was no doubting what she'd like. She slid over the floor, she took Ramón's face in both her hands—and she kissed him.

And Ramón kissed her back—a thoroughly befuddled, laughing, wonderful kiss. He tasted of choc chip muffin. He tasted of love.

He tugged her close, hauling her backward with him so she was in his arms, and they were so close she thought she must…they must…

And then the door burst open and Sofía was standing in the doorway staring at them both as if they'd lost their minds.

Maybe they had.

The little cat was delicately licking muffin mixture from the floor. Sofía darted across and retrieved the cat as if she were saving her from poison.

'Hi, Sofía,' Ramón said innocently from somewhere underneath his woman. Jenny would have pulled away but he was having none of it. He tugged her close and held, so they were lying on the floor like two children caught out in mischief. Or more.

Sofía stared down at them as if she couldn't believe her eyes. 'What do you think you're doing?' she hissed.

'Making muffins, Ramón said, and he would have pulled Jenny closer but the mixture of confusion and distress on Sofía's face was enough to have her pulling away. The timer was buzzing. Somehow she struggled to her feet. She opened the oven and retrieved her now cooked bacon muffins. Then she thought what the heck, she might as well finish what she'd started, so she put the almost full tray of choc chip muffins in to replace them.

'Gianetta's a professional,' Ramón said proudly to his aunt, struggling up as well. 'I told you she was fabulous.'

'Are you out of your minds?'

'No, I…'

'You're just like the rest,' she hissed at him. 'They're all womanisers, all the men who've ever held power here. You have her trapped. Ramón, what on earth is it that you're planning?'

'I'm not planning anything.'

'If it's marriage… You can't. I know Philippe needs a mother but this is…'

'It's nothing to do with Philippe,' Ramón snapped. 'Why are you here?'

'Why do you think?' Sofía's anger was becoming almost apoplectic. 'Did you think the two of you were invisible? Everyone knows where you are. Ramón, think about what you're doing. You're no longer just responsible for yourself. You represent a country now! She's a nice girl, I won't let you ruin her, or trap her into this life.'

'I won't do either,' Ramón said, coldly furious. 'We're not talking marriage. We're not talking anything past this night. Jenny will be leaving…'

'Ramón, if she goes to the island now… There'll be such talk. To take her in the palace kitchen…'

'He didn't *take* me…' It was Jenny's turn to be angry now. 'My dressing gown cord's still done up.'

'No one can tell that from outside,' Sofía snapped and walked across and tugged the door wide. 'See? The harm's done,' she said, as two footmen stepped smartly away from the door.

'You can't be happy here,' she whispered. 'No one knows anyone. No one trusts.'

'I know that,' Ramón told her. 'Sofía, stop this.'

'I told her you should take her to the island. I told her. You should have waited.'

'Excuse me?' Jenny said. 'Can you include me in this?'

'It's nothing to do with you,' Sofía said and then seemed to think about it. Her anger faded and she suddenly sounded weary and defeated. 'No. I mean…even if you were suitable as a royal bride—which you aren't—you aren't tough enough. To do it with no training…'

'Sofía, don't do this,' Ramón said. Sofía's distress was clear and real. 'We aren't talking about marriage.'

'Then you're ruining her for nothing. And here's your valet, come to see what all the fuss is about.'

'I don't want my valet,' Ramón snapped. 'I don't want any valet.'

'You don't have a choice,' Sofía said with exasperation. 'None of us do. Ramón, go away. I'll stay here with Jenny until these…whatever you're making…muffins?…are cooked. We'll make the best of a bad situation but there's no way we can keep this quiet. This, with your stupid insistence on dancing with her first tonight… She'll have paparazzi in her face tomorrow, whether she leaves or not.'

'Paparazzi…' Jenny said faintly.

'Leave now, Ramón, and don't go near her again. She needs space to see what a mess this situation is.'

'She doesn't want space.'

'Yes, I do,' Jenny said. Philippe? Paparazzi? There were so many unknowns. What was she getting into?

She felt dizzy.

She felt bereft.

'Jenny,' Ramón said urgently but Sofía was before him, pushing herself between them.

'Leave it,' she told them both harshly. 'Like it or not, Ramón is Crown Prince. He needs to fit his new role. He might think he wants you but he doesn't have a choice. *You* don't belong in our world and you both know it.' She glanced along the corridor where there were now four servants waiting. 'So… There's to be no seduction tonight. We're all calmly eating muffins and going to bed. Yes?'

'Yes,' Jenny said before Ramón could reply. She didn't

want to look at him. She couldn't. Because the laughter in his eyes had gone.

The servants were waiting to take over. The palace was waiting to take over.

She lay in her opulent bed and her head spun so much she felt dizzy.

She was lying on silk sheets. When she moved, she felt as if she was being caressed.

She wasn't being caressed. She was lying in a royal bed, in a royal boudoir. Alone. Because why?

Because Ramón was a Crown Prince.

Even when she'd lain with him in his wonderful yacht, believing he was simply the skipper and not the owner, she'd felt a sense of inequality, as if this couldn't be happening to her.

But it had happened, and now it was over.

What else had she expected?

Since she'd met Ramón her ache of grief had lifted. Life had become…unreal. But here it was again, reality, hard and cold as ice, slamming her back to earth. Grief was real. Loss was real. Emptiness and heartache had been her world for years, and here they were again.

Her time with Ramón, her time tonight, had been some sort of crazy soap bubble. Even before Sofía had spelled it out, she'd known it was impossible.

Sofía said she was totally unsuitable. Of course she was.

But…but…

As the night wore on something strange was happening. Her grief for Matty had been in abeyance during the two weeks with Ramón, and again tonight. It was back with her now, but things had changed. Things were changing.

Ever since Matty was born, things had happened to Jenny. Just happened. It was as if his birth, his medical problems, his desperate need, had put her on a roller coaster of emotions that she couldn't get off. Her life was simply doing what came next.

But the chain of events today had somehow changed

things. What Sofía and then Perpetua had said had stirred something deep within. Or maybe it was how Ramón had made her feel tonight that was making her feel different.

She'd seen the defeat on Ramón's face and she recognized that defeat. It was a defeat born of bleak acceptance.

Once upon a time she'd shared it. Maybe she still should. But…but…

'Why should I run?' she whispered and she wondered if she'd really said it.

It didn't make any sense. Sofía and Perpetua were right. So was Ramón. What was between them was clearly impossible, and there'd be a million more complications she hadn't thought of yet.

Philippe? The child Sofía had talked of?

She didn't go near children. Not after Matty.

And royalty? She had no concept of what Ramón was facing. Threats? The unknown Carlos?

There were questions everywhere, unspoken shadows looming from all sides, but overriding everything was the fact that she wanted Ramón so much she could almost cry out loud for him. What she wanted right now was to pad out into the palace corridor, yell at the top of her lungs for Ramón and then sit down and demand answers.

She'd had her chance. She'd used it making muffins. And kissing her prince.

He'd kissed her back.

The memory made her smile. Ramón made her smile.

Maybe the shadows weren't so long, she thought, but she knew they were.

'I'd be happy as his lover,' she whispered to the night. 'For as long as he wanted me. Just as his lover. Just in private. Back on his boat, sailing round the world, Ramón and me.'

It wasn't going to happen. And would she be happy on his island, being paid occasional visits as Sofía had suggested?

No!

She lay back on her mound of feather pillows and she stared up at the ceiling some more.

She stared at nothing.

Jenny and Ramón, the Crown Prince of Cepheus? No and no and no.

But still there was this niggle. It wasn't anger, exactly. Not exactly.

It was more that she'd found her centre again.

She'd found something worth fighting for.

Gianetta and the Crown Prince of Cepheus? No and no and no.

The thing was, though, sense had gone out of the window.

The car crash that had killed his mother and his sister had left him with an aching void where family used to be. For years he'd carried the grief as a burden, thinking he could bear no more, and the way to avoid that was to not let people close.

He loved his work in Bangladesh—it changed people's lives—yet individual lives were not permitted to touch him.

But there was something about Jenny…Gianetta…that broke the barriers he'd built. She'd touched a chord, and the resonance was so deep and so real that to walk away from her seemed unthinkable.

For the last three months he'd tried to tell himself what he'd felt was an illusion, but the moment he'd seen her again he'd known it was real. She was his woman. He knew it with a certainty so deep it felt primeval.

But to drag her into the royal limelight, into a place where the servants greeted you with blank faces…into a place where his father had died and barely a ripple had been created…where Carlos threatened and he didn't know which servants might be loyal and which might be in Carlos's pay… here his duty lay to his people and to have his worry centred on one slip of a girl…

On Jenny.

No.

Could he love her enough to let her go?

He must.

He had a deputation from neighbouring countries meeting

him first thing in the morning to discuss border issues. Refugees. The thought did his head in.

Royalty seemed simple on the outside—what had Jenny said?—cutting ribbons and making speeches. But Cepheus was governed by royalty. He'd set moves afoot to turn it into a democracy but it would take years, and meanwhile what he did would change people's lives.

Could he do it alone? He must.

He had no right to ask Jenny to share a load he found insupportable. To put her into the royal limelight… To ask her to share the risks that had killed his father… To distract himself from a task that had to be faced alone…

There was no choice at all.

CHAPTER NINE

JENNY didn't see Ramón all the next day. She couldn't. 'Affairs of State,' Sofía told her darkly, deeply disapproving when Jenny told her she had no intention of leaving until she'd spoken to Ramón. 'There's so much business that's been waiting for Ramón to officially take charge. Señor Rodriguez tells me he's booked for weeks. Poor baby.'

Poor baby? Jenny thought of the man whose boot she'd pulled off, she thought of the power of his touch, and she thought 'poor baby' was a description just a wee bit wide of the mark.

So what was she to do? By nine she'd breakfasted, inspected the palace gardens—breathtakingly beautiful but *so* empty—got lost twice in the palace corridors, and she was starting to feel as if she was climbing walls.

She headed out to the gardens again and found Gordon, pacing by one of the lagoon-sized swimming pools. It seemed the darkness and the strange city last night had defeated even him.

'All this opulence gives me the creeps,' he said, greeting her with relief. 'I've been waiting for you. How about if we slope off down to the docks? It's not so far. A mile or so as the crow flies. We could get out the back way, avoid the paparazzi.'

'I do need to come back,' she whispered, looking at the cluster of cameramen around the main gate with dismay, and Gordon surveyed her with care.

'Are you sure? There's talk, lass, about last night.'

And there it was again, that surge of anger.

'Then maybe I need to give them something to talk about,' she snapped.

The meetings were interminable—men and women in serious suits, with serious briefcases filled with papers covered with serious concerns, not one of which he could walk away from.

This country had been in trouble for decades—was still in trouble. It would take skill and commitment to bring it back from the brink, to stop the exodus of youth leaving the country, to take advantage of the country's natural resources to bring prosperity for citizens who'd been ignored for far too long.

The last three months he'd spent researching, researching, researching. He had the knowledge now to make a difference, but so much work was before him it felt overwhelming.

He should be gearing up right now to spend the next six months supervising the construction of houses in Bangladesh, simple work but deeply satisfying. He'd had to abandon that to commit to this, a more direct and personal need.

And this morning he'd had to abandon Jenny.

Gianetta.

The two words kept interplaying in his head. Jenny. Gianetta.

Jenny was the woman who made muffins, the woman who saved whales, the woman who made him laugh.

Gianetta was the woman he took to his bed. Gianetta was the woman he would make his Princess—*if* he didn't care so much, for her and for his country.

Where was she now?

He'd been wrong last night. Sofía had spelled out their situation clearly and he could do nothing but agree.

He should be with her now, explaining why he couldn't take things further. She'd be confused and distressed. But there was simply no option for him to spend time with her today.

So… He'd left orders for her to be left to enjoy a day of leisure. The *Marquita* was a big boat; it was hard work to crew her and she'd been sailing for three months. Last night had been…stressful. She deserved to rest.

He had meetings all day and a formal dinner tonight. Tomorrow, though, he'd make time early to say goodbye. If she stayed that long.

And tomorrow he'd promised to visit Philippe.

He glanced at his watch. Tomorrow. It was twenty-two hours and thirty minutes before a scheduled visit with his woman. Wedging it in between affairs of state and his concern for a child he didn't know what to do with.

Jenny. How could he ever make sense of what he felt for her?

He knew, in his heart, that he couldn't.

The *Marquita* meant work, and in work there was respite.

The day was windless so they could unfurl the sails and let them dry. The boat was clean, but by common consensus they decided it wasn't clean enough. They scrubbed the decks, they polished brass, they gave the interior such a clean that Martha Gardener would be proud of them.

Jenny remade the bed in the great stateroom, plumped the mass of pillows, looked down at the sumptuous quilts and wondered again, what had she been thinking?

She'd slept in this bed with the man she loved. She loved him still, with all her heart, but in the distance she could see the spires of the palace, glistening white in the Mediterranean sunshine.

The Crown Prince of Cepheus. For a tiny time their two disparate worlds had collided, and they'd seemed almost equal. Now, all that was left was to find the courage to walk away.

Perhaps.

Eighteen hours and twenty-two minutes. How many suits could he talk to in that time? How many documents must he read?

He had to sign them all and there was no way he could sign without reading.

His eyes were starting to cross.

Eighteen hours and seven minutes.

Would she still be here?

Surely she wouldn't leave without a farewell.

He deserved it, he thought, but please…no.

They worked solidly until mid-afternoon. Gordon was checking the storerooms, taking inventory, making lists of what needed to be replaced. Jenny was still obsessively cleaning.

Taking away every trace of her.

But, as the afternoon wore on, even she ran out of things to do. 'Time to get back to the palace,' Gordon decreed.

'We could stay on board.'

'She's being pulled out of the water tonight so engineers can check her hull in the morning. We hardly have a choice tonight.'

'Will you stay on as Ramón's skipper?'

'I love this boat,' he said simply. 'For as long as I'm asked, I'll stay. If that means staying at the palace from time to time, I'll find the courage.'

'I don't have very much courage,' she whispered.

'Or maybe you have sense instead,' Gordon said stoutly. He stood back for her to precede him up to the deck. She stepped up—and suddenly the world was waiting for her.

Paparazzi were everywhere. Flashlights went off in her face, practically blinding her. She put her hand over her eyes in an instinctive gesture of defence, and retreated straight back down again.

Gordon slammed the hatch after her.

'Tell us about yourself,' someone called from the dock. 'You speak Spanish, right?'

'We're happy to pay for your story,' someone else called.

'You and Prince Ramón were on the boat together for two weeks, alone, right?' That was bad enough. But then…

'Is it true you had a baby out of wedlock?' someone else called while Jenny froze. 'And the baby died?'

They knew about her Matty? They knew....

She wanted to go home right now. She wanted to creep into a bunk and stay hidden while Gordon sailed her out of the harbour and away.

Serenity. Peace. That was what she'd been striving for since Matty died. Where was serenity and peace now?

How could she find it in this?

'I'll talk to them,' Gordon said, looking stunned and sick, and she looked at this big shy man and she thought why should he fight her battles? Why should anyone fight her battles?

Maybe she had to fight to achieve this so-called serenity, she thought. Maybe that was what her problem had been all along. She'd been waiting for serenity to find her, when all along it was something she needed to fight for.

Or maybe it wasn't even serenity that she wanted.

Then, before she had time to decide she'd lost her mind entirely—for maybe she had; she certainly wasn't making sense to herself and Gordon was looking really worried—she flung open the hatch again and stepped out onto the deck.

His cellphone was on mute in his pocket. He felt it vibrate, checked it and saw it was Gordon calling. Gordon wouldn't call him except in an emergency.

The documents had just been signed and the Heads of State were lining up for a photo call. These men had come for the coronation and had stayed on.

Cepheus was a small nation. These men represented far more powerful nations than his, and Cepheus had need of powerful allies. Nevertheless, he excused himself and answered.

'Paparazzi know about Jenny's baby,' Gordon barked, so loud he almost burst Ramón's eardrum. 'They're on the jetty. We're surrounded. You need to get her out of here.'

He felt sick. 'I'll have a security contingent there in two

minutes,' he said, motioning to Señor Rodriguez, who, no doubt, had heard every word. 'I need to get to the docks,' he told him. 'How long?'

'It would take us fifteen minutes, Your Highness, but we can't leave here,' Rodriguez said. The man was seriously good. He already had security on his second phone. 'Security will have dealt with it before we get there. There's no need…'

There was a need, but as he glanced back at the Heads of State he knew his lawyer was right. To leave for such a reason could cause insupportable offence. It could cause powerful allies to turn to indifference.

His sense of helplessness was increasing almost to breaking point. *He couldn't protect his woman.*

'You can see, though,' Señor Rodriguez said, obviously realising just how he was torn. He turned back to the men and women behind him. 'If you'll excuse us for a moment,' he said smoothly. 'An urgent matter of security has come up. We'll be five minutes, no more.'

'I will go,' Ramón said through gritted teeth.

'It will be dealt with before you arrive,' Señor Rodriguez said again. 'But we have security monitors on the royal berth. I can switch our cameras there to reassure you until you see our security people take over. If you'll come aside…'

So Ramón followed the lawyer into an anteroom. He stared at the monitor in the corner, and he watched in grim desperation as his woman faced the press.

They'd pull her apart, he thought grimly—and there was nothing he could do to help her.

The cameras went wild. Questions were being shouted at her from all directions.

Courage, she told herself grimly. Come on, girl, you've hidden for long enough. Now's the time to stand and fight.

She ignored the shouts. She stood still and silent, knowing she looked appalling, knowing the shots would be of her at her worst. She'd just scrubbed out a boat. She didn't look like anyone famous. She was simply Jenny the deckhand, standing waiting for the shouting to stop.

And finally it did. The journalists fell silent at last, thinking she didn't intend to respond.

'Finished?' she asked, quirking an eyebrow in what she hoped looked like sardonic amusement, and the shouting started again.

Serenity, she told herself. She tapped a bare toe on the deck and waited again for silence.

'I've called His Highness,' Gordon called up from below. 'Security's on its way. Ramón'll send them.'

It didn't matter. This wasn't Ramón's fight, she thought. Finally, silence fell again; baffled silence. The cameras were still in use but the journalists were clearly wondering what they had here. She waited and they watched. Impasse.

'You do speak English?' one asked at last, a lone question, and she nodded. A lone question, not shouted, could be attended to.

And why not all the others, in serene order? Starting now.

'Yes,' she said, speaking softly so they had to stay silent or they couldn't hear her. 'I speak English as well as Spanish and French. My parents have Spanish blood. And I did indeed act as crew for His Highness, Prince Ramón, as we sailed between Sydney and Auckland.' She thought back through the questions that had been hurled at her, mentally ticking them off. 'Yes, I'm a cook. I'm… I *was* also a single mother. My son died of a heart condition two years ago, but I don't wish to answer any more questions about Matty. His death broke my heart. As for the rest… Thank you, I enjoyed last night, and yes, rumours that I cooked for His Highness early this morning are true. I'm employed as his cook and crew. That's what I've been doing for the last three months and no, I'm not sure if I'll continue. It depends if he needs me. What else? Oh, the personal questions. I'm twenty-nine years old. I had my appendix out when I was nine, my second toes are longer than my big toes and I don't eat cabbage. I think your country is lovely and the *Marquita* is the prettiest boat in the world.

However, scrubbing the *Marquita* is what I'm paid to do and that's what I'm doing. If you have any more questions, can you direct them to my secretary?'

She grinned then, a wide, cheeky grin which only she knew how much effort it cost to produce. 'Oh, whoops, I forgot I don't have a secretary. Can one of you volunteer? I'll pay you in muffins. If one of you is willing, then the rest can siphon your questions through him. That's so much more dignified than shouting, don't you think?'

Then she gave them all a breezy wave, observed their shocked silence and then slipped below, leaving them dumfounded.

She stood against the closed hatch, feeling winded. Gordon was staring at her in amazement. As well he might.

What was she doing?

Short answer? She didn't know.

Long answer? She didn't know either. Retiring from this situation with dignity was her best guess, though suddenly Jenny had no intention of retiring.

Not just yet.

This was a state-of-the-art security system, and sound was included. Not only did Ramón see everything, he heard every word Jenny spoke.

'It seems the lady doesn't need protecting,' Señor Rodriguez said, smiling his relief as Jenny disappeared below deck and Ramón's security guards appeared on the docks.

Ramón shook his head. 'I should have been there for her.'

'She's protected herself. She's done very well.'

'She shouldn't have been put in that position.'

'I believe the lady could have stayed below,' the lawyer said dryly. 'The lady chose to take them on. She has some courage.'

'She shouldn't…'

'She did,' the lawyer said, and then hesitated.

Señor Rodriguez had been watching on the sidelines for many years now. His father had been legal advisor to Ramón's grandmother, and Sofía had kept him on after Ramón's father died, simply to stay aware of what royalty was doing. Now he was doing the job of three men and he was thoroughly enjoying himself. 'Your Highness, if I may make so bold…'

'You've never asked permission before,' Ramón growled, and the lawyer permitted himself another small smile.

'It's just…the role you're taking on…to do it alone could well break you. You're allowing me to assist but no one else. This woman has courage and honour. If you were to…'

'I won't,' Ramón snapped harshly, guessing where the lawyer was going and cutting him off before he went any further. He flicked the screen off. There was nothing to see but the press, now being dispersed by his security guards. 'I do this alone or not at all.'

'Is that wise?'

'I don't know what's wise or not,' Ramón said and tried to sort his thoughts into some sort of sense. What was happening here? The lawyer was suggesting sharing the throne? With Jenny?

Jenny as his woman? Yes. But Jenny in the castle?

The thought left him cold. The night of his father's death was still with him, still haunting him.

Enough. 'We have work to do,' he growled and headed back to the room where the Heads of State were waiting.

'But…' the lawyer started, but Ramón was already gone.

CHAPTER TEN

HE MANAGED a few short words with her that night as he passed the supper room. It was all he had, as he moved from the evening's meetings to his briefing for tomorrow. To his surprise, Jenny seemed relaxed, even happy.

'I'm sorry about today,' he said. 'It seemed you handled things very well.'

'I talked too much,' she said, smiling. 'I need to work on my serenity.'

'Your serenity?'

'I'm not very good at it.' Her smile widened. 'But I showed promise today. Dr Matheson would be proud of me. By the way, I hope it's okay that Gordon and I are staying here tonight. The boat's up on the hard, and who wants to sleep on a boat in dry dock? Besides, staying in a palace is kind of fun.'

Kind of fun... He gazed into the opulent supper room, at the impassive staff, and he thought...*kind of fun*?

'So I can stay tonight?' she prompted.

He raked his hair. 'I should have had Señor Rodriguez organise airline tickets.'

'Señor Rodriguez has better things to do than organise my airline tickets. I'll organise them when I'm ready. Meanwhile, can I stay tonight?'

'Of course, but Jenny, I don't have time...'

'I know you don't,' she said sympathetically. 'Señor Rodriguez says these first days are crazy. It'll get better, he says, but I'll not add to your burdens tonight. I hope I never will.'

Then, before he could figure how to respond, a servant appeared to remind him he was late for his next briefing. He was forced to leave Jenny, who didn't seem the least put out. She'd started chatting cheerfully to the maid who was clearing supper.

To his surprise, the maid was responding with friendliness and animation. Well, why wouldn't she, he told himself as he immersed himself again into royal business. Jenny had no baggage of centuries of oppression. She wasn't royal.

She never could be royal. He could never ask that of her, he thought grimly. But, as the interminable briefing wore on, he thought of Jenny—not being royal. He thought of her thinking of the palace as fun, and he almost told the suits he was talking to where to go.

But he didn't. He was sensible. He had a country to run, and when he was finally free Jenny had long gone to bed.

And there was no way he was knocking on her door tonight.

He missed her at breakfast, maybe because he ate before six before commencing the first of three meetings scheduled before ten. He moved through each meeting with efficiency and speed, desperate to find time to see her, but the meetings went overtime. He had no time left. His ten o'clock diary entry was immovable.

This appointment he'd made three months ago. Four hours every Wednesday. Even Jenny would have to wait on this.

Swiftly he changed out of his formal wear into jeans, grabbed his swimmers and made his way to the palace garages. He strode round the rows of espaliered fruit trees marking the end of the palace gardens—and Jenny was sitting patiently on a garden bench.

She was wearing smart new jeans, a casual cord jacket in a pale washed apricot over a creamy lace camisole and creamy leather ballet flats. Her curls were brushed until they shone. She looked rested and refreshed and cheerful.

She looked beautiful.

She rose and stretched and smiled a welcome. Gianetta.

Jenny, he told himself fiercely. This was Jenny, his guest before she left for ever.

A very lovely Jenny. Smiling and smiling.

'Do you like it?' she demanded and spun so she could be admired from all angles. 'This is the new smart me.'

'Where on earth…?'

'I went shopping,' she said proudly. 'Yesterday, when we finally escaped from that mob. Your security guys kindly escorted me to some great shops and then stood guard while I tried stuff on. Neat, yes?'

'Neat,' he said faintly and her face fell and he amended his statement fast. 'Gorgeous.'

'No, that won't do either,' she said reprovingly. 'My borrowed ball-gown was gorgeous. But this feels good. I thought yesterday I haven't had new clothes for years and the owner of the boutique gave me a huge discount.'

'I'll bet she did,' he said faintly.

She grinned. 'I know, it was cheeky, but I thought if I'm to be photographed by every cameraman in the known universe there has to be some way I can take advantage. She was practically begging me to take clothes.'

'Gordon said you were upset.'

'Gordon was upset.'

'I should have been there.'

'Then the cameramen would have been even more persistent,' she said gently. 'But I have clothes to face them now, and they're not so scary. So…I pinned Señor Rodriguez down this morning and he says you're going to see Philippe. So I was wondering…' Her tone became more diffident. 'Would it upset you if I came along? Would it upset Philippe?'

'No, but I can't ask you…'

'You're not asking,' she said and came forward to slip her

hands into his. 'You're looking trapped. I don't want you to feel that way. Not by me.'

'You'd never make me feel trapped,' he said. 'But Jenny, I can't expect…'

'Then don't expect,' she said. 'Señor Rodriguez told me all about Philippe. No, don't look like that. The poor man never had a chance; I practically sat on him to make him explain things in detail. Philippe's your cousin's son. Everyone thought he stood to inherit, only when his parents died it turned out they weren't actually married. According to royal rules, he's illegitimate. Now he has nothing.'

'He's well cared for. He has lovely foster parents.'

'Sofía says you've been visiting him every week since you got here.'

'It's the least I can do when he's lost his home as well as his parents.'

'He can't stay here?'

'No,' he said bleakly. 'If he's here he'll be in the middle of servants who'll either treat him like royalty—and this country hates royalty—or they'll treat him as an illegitimate nothing.'

'Yet you still think he should be here,' Jenny said softly.

'No.'

'Because this is where you were when your father died?'

'What the…?'

'Sofía,' she said simply. 'I asked, she told me. Ramón, I'm so sorry. It must have been dreadful. But that was then. Now is now. Can I meet him?'

'I can't ask that of you,' he said, feeling totally winded. 'And he's the same age your little boy would have been…'

'Ramón, can we take this one step at a time?' she asked. 'Let's just go visit this little boy—who's not Matty. Let's just leave it at that.'

So they went and for the first five miles or so they didn't speak. Ramón didn't know where to take this.

There were so many things in this country that needed his

attention but over and over his thoughts kept turning to one little boy. Consuela and Ernesto were lovely but they were in their sixties. To expect them to take Philippe long-term…

He glanced across at Jenny and found she was watching him. He had the top down on his Boxster coupe. The warm breeze was blowing Jenny's curls around her face. She looked young and beautiful and free. He remembered the trapped woman he'd met over three months ago and the change seemed extraordinary.

How could he trap her again? He couldn't. Of course he couldn't. He didn't intend to.

Yet—she'd asked to come. Was she really opening herself up to be hurt again?

'I can't believe this country,' she said, smiling, and he knew she was making an attempt to keep the conversation neutral. Steering away from undertones that were everywhere. 'It's like something on a calendar.'

'There's a deep description.'

'It's true. There's a calendar in the bathroom of Seaport Coffee 'n' Cakes and it has a fairy tale palace on it. All white turrets and battlements and moats, surrounded by little stone houses with ancient tiled roofs, and mountains in the background, and just a hint of snow.'

'There's no snow here,' he said, forced to smile back. 'We're on the Mediterranean.'

'Please,' she said reprovingly. 'You're messing with my calendar. So, as I was saying…'

But then, as he turned the car onto a dirt track leading to a farmhouse, she stopped with the imagery and simply stared. 'Where are we?'

'This is where Philippe lives.'

'But it's lovely,' she whispered, gazing out over grassy meadows where a flock of alpacas grazed placidly in the morning sun. 'It's the perfect place for a child to live.'

'He's not happy.'

'I imagine that might well be because his parents are dead,' she said, suddenly sharp. 'It'll take him for ever to adjust to their loss. If ever.'

'I don't think his parents were exactly hands-on,' Ramón told her. 'My uncle and my cousin liked to gamble, and so did Maria Therese. They spent three-quarters of their lives in Monaco and they never took Philippe. They were on their way there when their plane crashed.'

'So who took care of Philippe?'

'He's had a series of nannies. The palace hasn't exactly been a happy place to work. Neither my uncle nor my cousin thought paying servants was a priority, and I gather as a mother Maria Therese was…difficult. Nannies have come and gone.'

'So Philippe's only security has been the palace itself,' Jenny ventured.

'He's getting used to these foster parents,' Ramón said, but he wasn't convincing himself. 'They're great.'

'I'm looking forward to meeting them.'

'I'll be interested to hear your judgement.' Then he paused. 'Gianetta, are you sure you want to do this? Philippe's distressed and there's little I can do about it. It won't help to make you distressed as well. Would you like to turn back?'

'Well, that'd be stupid,' Jenny said. 'Philippe will already know you're on your way. To turn back now would be cruel.'

'But what about you?'

'This isn't about me,' she said, gently but inexorably. 'Let's go meet Philippe.'

He was the quietest little boy Jenny had ever met. He looked just like Ramón.

The family resemblance was amazing, she thought. Same dark hair. Same amazing eyes. Same sense of trouble, kept under wraps.

His foster parents, Consuela and Ernesto, were voluble and friendly. They seemed honoured to have Ramón visit, but not so overawed that it kept them silent. That was just as well, as their happy small talk covered up the deathly silence emanating from Philippe.

They sat at the farmhouse table eating Consuela's amazing strawberry cake. Consuela and Ernesto chatted, Ramón answered as best he could, and Jenny watched Philippe.

He was clutching a little ginger cat as if his life depended on it. He was too thin. His eyes were too big for his face.

He was watching his big cousin as if he was hungry.

I feel like that, she thought, and recognized what she'd thought and intensified her scrutiny. She had the time and the space to do it. Consuela and Ernesto were friendly but they were totally focused on Ramón. Philippe had greeted Jenny with courtesy but now he, too, was totally focused on Ramón.

Of course. Ramón was the Crown Prince.

Only Ramón's title didn't explain things completely, Jenny decided. Ramón was here in his casual clothes. He didn't look spectacular—or any more spectacular than he usually did—and a child wouldn't respond to an adult this way unless there was a fair bit of hero worship going on.

'Does Prince Ramón really come every week?' she asked Consuela as she helped clear the table.

'Every week since he's been back in the country,' the woman said. 'We're so grateful. Ernesto and I have had many foster children—some from very troubled homes—but Philippe's so quiet we don't seem to get through to him. He never says a thing unless he must. He hardly eats unless he's forced, and he certainly doesn't know how to enjoy himself. But once a week Ramón…I mean Crown Prince Ramón… comes and takes him out in his car and it's as if he lights up. He comes home happy, he eats, he tells us what he's done and he goes to bed and sleeps all night. Then he wakes and Ramón's not here, and his parents aren't here, and it all starts again. His Highness brought him his cat from the palace and that's made things better but now…we're starting to wonder if it's His Highness himself the child pines for.'

'He can't have become attached to Ramón so fast,' Jenny

said, startled, and Consuela looked at her with eyes that had seen a lot in her lifetime, and she smiled.

'*Caro*, are you telling me that's impossible?'

Oh, help, was she so obvious? She glanced back to where Ernesto and Ramón were engaged in a deep conversation about some obscure football match, with Philippe listening to every word as if it was the meaning of life—and she found herself blushing from the toes up.

'We're hearing rumours,' Consuela said, seemingly satisfied with Jenny's reaction. 'How lovely.'

'I…there's nothing.' *How fast did rumours spread?*

'There's everything,' Consuela said. 'All our prince needs is a woman to love him.'

'I'm not his class.'

'Class? Pah!' Consuela waved an airy hand at invisible class barriers. 'Three months ago Philippe was Prince Royal. Now he's the illegitimate son of the dead Prince's mistress. If you worry about class then you worry about nothing. You make him happy. That's all anyone can ask.' Her shrewd gaze grew intent. 'You know that Prince Ramón is kind, intelligent, honourable. Our country needs him so much. But for a man to take on such a role…there must be someone filling his heart as well.'

'I can't…'

'I can see a brave young woman before me, and I'm very sure you can.'

All of this was thoroughly disconcerting. She should just shut up, she thought. She should stick with her new found serenity. But, as she wiped as Consuela washed, she pushed just a little more. 'Can I ask you something?'

'Of course.'

'You and Ernesto… You obviously love Philippe and you're doing the best you can for him. But if Philippe wants to be at the palace… Why doesn't Ramón…why doesn't His Highness simply employ you to be there for him?'

The woman turned and looked at Jenny as if she were crazy. 'Us? Go to the palace?'

'Why not?'

'We're just farmers.'

'Um…excuse me. Didn't you just say…?'

'That's for you,' Consuela said, and then she sighed and dried her hands and turned to Jenny. 'I think that for you, you're young enough and strong enough to fight it, but for us…and for Philippe…the lines of class at the palace are immovable.'

'Would you try it, though?' she asked. 'Would you stay in the palace if Ramón asked it of you?'

'Maybe, but he won't. He won't risk it, and why should he?' She sighed, as if the worries of the world were too much for her, but then she pinned on cheerfulness, smiled determinedly at Jenny and turned back to the men. Moving on. 'Philippe. His Highness, Prince Ramón, asked if you could have your swimming costume prepared. He tells me he wishes to take you to the beach.'

Football was abandoned in an instant. 'In your car?' Philippe demanded of Ramón, round-eyed.

'In my car,' Ramón said. 'With Señorina Bertin. If it's okay with you.'

The little boy turned his attention to Jenny and surveyed her with grave attention. Whatever he saw there, it seemed to be enough.

'That will be nice,' he said stiffly.

'Get your costume, poppet,' Consuela said, but Philippe was already gone.

So they headed to the beach, about five minutes' drive from the farmhouse. Philippe sat between Jenny and Ramón, absolutely silent, his eyes straight ahead. But Jenny watched his body language. He could have sat ramrod still and not touched either of them, but instead he slid slightly to Ramón's side so his small body was just touching his big cousin.

Ramón was forging something huge here, Jenny thought. Did he know?

Maybe he did. Maybe he couldn't help but know. As he

drove he kept up a stream of light-hearted banter, speaking to Jenny, but most of what he said was aimed at Philippe.

Did Gianetta know this little car was the most wonderful car in the world? Did she know he thought this was the only one of its kind that had ever been fitted with bench seats—designed so two people could have a picnic in the car if it was raining? Why, only two weeks ago he and Philippe had eaten a picnic while watching a storm over the sea, and they'd seen dolphins. And now the bench seat meant there was room for the three of them. How about that for perfect? And it was red. Didn't Jenny think red was great?

'I like pink,' Jenny said, and Ramón looked as if she'd just committed blasphemy.

'You'd have me buy a pink car?'

'No, that'd be a waste. You could spray paint this one,' she retorted, and chuckled at their combined manly horror.

Philippe didn't contribute a word but she saw him gradually relax, responding to their banter, realizing that nothing was expected of him but that he relax and enjoy himself.

And he did enjoy himself. They arrived at the beach and Ramón had him in the water in minutes.

Jenny was slower. Señor Rodriguez had told her they often went swimming so she'd worn her bikini under her jeans, but for now she was content to paddle and watch.

The beach was glorious, a tiny cove with sun-bleached sand, gentle waves and shallow turquoise water. There were no buildings, no people and the mountains rose straight from the sea like sentinels guarding their privacy.

There'd be bodyguards. She'd been vaguely aware of cars ahead and behind them all day and shadowy figures at the farmhouse, but as they'd arrived at the beach the security presence was nowhere to be seen. The guards must be under orders to give the illusion of total privacy, she thought, and that was what they had.

Ramón had set this time up for Philippe. For a little cousin he was not beholden to in any way. A little boy who'd be miserable at the palace?

She paddled on, casually kicking water out in front of her, pretending she wasn't watching.

She was definitely watching.

Ramón was teaching Philippe to float. The little boy was listening with all the seriousness in the world. He was aching to do what his big cousin was asking of him. His body language said he'd almost die for his big cousin.

'If you float with your face in the water and count to ten, then I'll lift you out of the water,' Ramón was saying. 'My hand will be under your tummy until we reach ten and I'll count aloud. Then I'll lift you high. Do you trust me to do that?'

He received a solemn nod.

'Right,' Ramón said and Philippe leaned forward, leaned further so he was floating on Ramón's hand. And put his face in the water.

'One, two three…ten!' and the little boy was lifted high and hugged.

'Did you feel my hand fall away before I lifted you up? You floated? Hey, Gianetta, Philippe floated!' Ramón was spinning Philippe around and around until he squealed. His squeal was almost the first natural sound she'd heard from him. It was a squeal of delight, of joy, of life.

Philippe was just a little bit older than Matty would be right now. Ramón had worried about it. She'd dismissed his worry but now, suddenly, the knowledge hit her so hard that she flinched. She was watching a little boy learn to swim, and her Matty never would. Everything inside her seemed to shrink. Pain surged back, as it had surged over and over since she'd lost her little son.

But something about this time made it different. Something told her it must be different. So for once, somehow, she let the pain envelop her, not trying to deflect it, simply riding it out, letting it take her where it would. Trying to see, if she allowed it to take its course, whether it would destroy her or whether finally she could come out on the other side.

She was looking at a man holding a little boy who wasn't

Matty—a little boy who against all the odds, she was starting to care about.

The heart swells to fit all comers.

It was a cliché. She'd never believed it. Back at the hospital, watching Matty fade, she'd looked at other children who'd come in ill, recovered then gone out again to face the world and she'd felt…nothing. It had been as if other children were on some parallel universe to the one she inhabited. There was no point of contact.

But suddenly, unbidden, those universes seemed to have collided. For a moment she thought the pain could make her head explode—and then she knew it wouldn't.

Matty. Philippe. Two little boys. Did loving Matty stop her feeling Philippe's pain?

Did loss preclude loving?

How could it?

She gazed out over the water, at this big man with the responsibilities of the world on his shoulders, and at this little boy whose world had been taken away from him.

She knew how many cares were pressing in on Ramón right now. He'd taken this day out, not for himself, but because he'd made a promise to Philippe. Every week, he'd come. Affairs of State were vital, but this, he'd decreed, was more so.

She thought fleetingly of the man who'd fathered Matty, who'd sailed away and missed his whole short life.

Philippe wasn't Ramón's son. He was the illegitimate child of a cousin he'd barely known and yet…and yet…

She was blinking back tears, struggling to take in the surge of emotions flooding through her, but slowly the knot of pain within was easing its grip, letting her see what lay past its vicious hold.

Ramón had lost his family and he'd been a loner ever since, but now he was being asked to take on the cares of this country and the care of this little boy. This country depended on him. Philippe depended on him. But for him to do it alone…

Class barriers were just that, she thought. Grief was another barrier—and barriers could be smashed.

Could she face them all down?

Would Ramón want her to?

And if she did face them down for Ramón's sake, and for hers, she thought, for her thoughts were flowing in all sorts of tangents that hardly made sense, could she love Philippe as well? Could the knot of pain she'd held within since Matty's death be untied, maybe used to embrace instead of to exclude?

Her vision was blurred with tears and it was growing more blurred by the second. Ramón looked across at her and waved, as if to say, *what's keeping you; come in and join us.* She waved back and turned her back on them, supposedly to walk up the beach and strip off her outer clothes. In reality it was to get her face in order—and to figure if she had the courage to put it to the test.

Maybe they didn't want her. Maybe her instinctive feelings for Philippe were wrong, and maybe what Ramón was feeling for her stemmed from nothing more than a casual affair. Her heart told her it was much more, but then her heart was a fickle thing.

No matter. If she was mistaken she could walk away—but first she could try.

And Matty…

Surely loving again could never be a betrayal.

This was crazy, she told herself as she slipped off her clothes and tried to get her thoughts in order. She was thinking way ahead of what was really happening. She was imagining things that could never be.

Should she back off?

But then she glanced back at the two males in the shallows and she felt so proprietorial that it threatened to overwhelm her. My two men, she thought mistily, or they could be. Maybe they could be.

The country can have what it needs from Ramón but I'm lining up for my share, she told herself fiercely. If I have the courage. And maybe the shadows of Matty can be settled, warmed, even honoured by another love.

She sniffed and sniffed again, found a tissue in her bag, blew her nose and decided her face was in order as much as she could make it. She wriggled her bare toes in the sand and wriggled them again. If she dived straight into the waves and swam a bit to start with, she might even look respectable before she reached them.

And if she didn't…

Warts and all, she thought. That was what she was offering.

For they all had baggage, she decided, as she headed for the water. Her grief for Matty was still raw and real. This must inevitably still hurt.

And Ramón? He was an unknown, he was Crown Prince of Cepheus to her Jenny.

She was risking rejection, and everything that went with it.

Consuela said she had courage. Maybe Consuela was wrong.

'Maybe I'm just pig-headed stubborn,' she muttered to herself, heading into the shallows. 'Maybe I'm reading this all wrong and he doesn't want me and Philippe doesn't need me and today is all I have left of the pair of them.'

'So get in the water and get on with it,' she told herself.

'And if I'm right?'

'Then maybe serenity's not the way to go,' she muttered. 'Maybe the opposite's what's needed. Oh, but to fight for a prince…'

Maybe she would. For a prince's happiness.

And for the happiness of one small boy who wasn't Matty.

They swam, they ate a palace-prepared picnic on the sand and then they took a sleepy Philippe back to the farmhouse. Once again they drove in silence. What was between them seemed too complicated for words.

Dared she?

By the time they reached the farm, Philippe was asleep but,

as Ramón lifted him from the car, he jerked awake, then sobbed and clung. Shaken, Ramón carried him into the house, while Jenny stared straight ahead and wondered whether she could be brave enough.

It was like staring into the night sky, overwhelmed by what she couldn't see as much as what she could see. The concept of serenity seemed ridiculous now. This was facing her demons, fighting for what she believed in, fighting for what she knew was right.

Dared she?

Two minutes later Ramón was back. He slid behind the wheel, still without a word, and sat, grim-faced and silent.

Now or never. Jenny took a deep breath, reached over and put her hand over his.

'He loves you,' she whispered.

He stared down at their linked hands and his mouth tightened into a grim line of denial. 'He can't. If it's going to upset him then I should stop coming.'

'Do you want to stop?'

'No.'

'Then why not take him back to the palace? Why not take him home?'

There was a moment's silence. Then, 'What, take him back to the palace and wedge him into a few moments a day between my appointments? And the rest of the time?'

'Leave him with people who love him.'

'Like…'

'Like Consuela and Ernesto.' Then, at the look on his face, she pressed his hand tighter. 'Ramón, you're taking all of this on as it is. Why not take it as it could be?'

'I don't know what you mean.'

'Just try,' she said, figuring it out as she went. 'Try for change. You say the palace is a dreadful place to live. So it is, but the servants are terrified of your title. They won't let you close because they're afraid. The place isn't a home, it's a mausoleum. Oh, it's a gorgeous mausoleum but it's a mausoleum for all that. But it could change. People like Consuela and Ernesto could change it.'

'Or be swallowed by it.'

'There's no need to be melodramatic. You could just invite them to stay for a couple of days to start with. Tell Philippe that his home is here—make that clear so he won't get distraught if…*when* he has to return. You can see how it goes. You won't be throwing him back anywhere.'

'I won't make him sleep in those rooms.'

And there it was, out in the open, raw and dreadful as it had been all those years ago. And, even worse, Jenny was looking at him as if she understood.

And maybe she did.

'You were alone,' she whispered. ' Your father brought you to the palace and he was killed and you were alone.'

'It's nothing.'

'It's everything. Of course it is. But this is now, Ramón. This is Philippe. As it's not Matty, it's also not you. Philippe won't be alone.'

'This is nonsense,' he said roughly, trying to recover some sort of footing. 'It's impossible. Sofía saw that even before I arrived. Philippe's illegitimate. The country would shun him.'

'They'd love him, given half a chance.'

'How do you know?' he snapped. 'He was there for over four years and no one cared.'

'Maybe no one had a chance. The maid I talked to this morning said no one was permitted near except the nursery staff, and Philippe's mother was constantly changing the people who worked with him. He's better off here if no one loves him at the palace, of course he is. But you could change that.' She hesitated. 'Ramón, I'm thinking you already have.'

He shook his head, shaking off demons. 'This is nonsense. I won't risk *this*.'

'This?'

'You know what I mean.' His face grew even more strained. 'Gianetta…'

'Yes?'

'I hate it,' he said explosively. 'The paparazzi almost mobbed you yesterday. The threat from Carlos… How can anyone live in that sort of environment? How could you?'

Her world stilled. Her heart seemed to forget to beat. *How could you?* They were no longer talking about Philippe, then. 'Am I…am I being invited?' she managed.

'No!' There was a long silence, loaded with so many undercurrents she couldn't begin to figure them out. Through the silence Ramón held the steering wheel, his knuckles clenched white. Fighting demons she could hardly fathom.

'We need to get back,' he said at last.

'Of course we do,' she said softly, but she knew this man now. Maybe two weeks of living together was too soon to judge someone—or maybe not. Maybe she'd judged him the first time she'd seen him. Okay, she hardly understood his demons, but demons there were and, prince or not, maybe the leap had to be hers.

'You know that I love you,' she said gently into the warm breeze, but his expression became even more grim.

'Don't.'

'Don't say what I feel?'

'You don't want this life.'

'I like tiaras,' she ventured, trying desperately for lightness. 'And caviar and French champagne. At least,' she added honestly, 'I haven't tasted caviar yet, but I'm sure I'll like it. And if I don't, I'm very good at faking.'

'Jenny, don't make this any harder than it has to be,' he snapped, refusing to be deflected by humour. 'I was a fool to bring you to Cepheus. I will not drag you into this royal life.'

'You don't have to drag me anywhere. I choose where to go. All you need to do is ask.'

'Just leave it. You don't know… The paparazzi yesterday was just a taste. Right now you're seeing the romance, the fairy tale. You'll wake in a year's time and find nothing but a cage.'

'You don't think you might be overreacting?' she ventured. 'Not everyone at the Coronation ball looked like they've been locked up all their lives. Surely caviar can't be that bad.'

But he wasn't listening. 'You're my beautiful Jenny,' he said. 'You're wild and free, and I won't mess with who you are. You'll always be my Jenny, and I'll hold you in my heart for ever. From a distance.'

'From how big a distance? From a photo in a frame?' she demanded, indignant. 'That sounds appalling. Or, better still, do you mean as your mistress on your island?'

He stared at her as if she'd grown two heads. 'What the…?'

'That's what Sofía said we should do.'

'I do not want you as my mistress,' he said through gritted teeth.

'So you don't want me?' His anger was building, and she thought *good*. An angry Ramón might just lose control, and control had gone on long enough. She wanted him to take her into his arms. In truth she wanted him to take her any way he wanted, but he was fighting his anger, hauling himself back from the brink.

'I want you more than life itself, but I will not take you.' He took a deep ragged breath. 'I could never keep you safe.'

'Well, that's nonsense. I know karate,' she retorted. 'I can duck and I can run and I can even punch and scratch and yell if I need to. Not that I'll need to. Perpetua says Carlos is all bluster.'

'Perpetua…'

'Is a very nice lady with an oaf for a husband and with very old-fashioned ideas about royal wives shutting up. Ideas that I don't believe for one minute. You'll never see me shutting up.'

'It doesn't matter,' he said, exasperated. 'I want you free.'

'Free?' She was fighting on all fronts now, knowing only that she was fully exposed and she had no defence. All she had was her love for this man. 'Like our whale?' she demanded. 'That's just perspective. Our whale's free now to swim to Antarctica, but she has to stop there and turn around.

A minnow can feel free in an aquarium if it's a beautiful aquarium.'

She hesitated then, seeing the tension on his face stretched almost to breaking point. She'd gone far enough. 'Ramón, let's not take this further,' she said gently. 'What's between us…let's leave it for now. Let's just think of Philippe. Is his room still as it was at the palace?'

'No one's touched the nursery.'

'So you could go in right now and say, *Philippe, what about coming back to the palace for a night or two?* Tell him maybe if it works out he could come for two nights every week. See how it goes.'

'Jenny…'

'Okay, maybe it is impossible,' she said. 'This is not my life and it's not my little cousin. But you know him now, Ramón, and maybe things have changed. All I know is that Philippe's breaking his heart in there, and if he returned to the palace there's no way he'd be alone. Consuela is looking out the window and I wouldn't mind betting she knows exactly what we're talking about. She's bursting to visit the palace, even if she's scared, and if you raise one finger to beckon she'll have bags packed and Bebe in his cat crate and you can still reach your three o'clock appointment. And, before you start raising quibbles like who'll look after their alpacas, you're the prince, surely you can employ half this district to look after this farm. So decide,' she said bluntly. 'You've been making life and death decisions about this country. Now it's time to make one about your family.'

'Philippe's not my family.'

'Is he not? It might have started with sympathy, Ramón Cavellero, but it's not sympathy that's tugging him to you now. Is it?'

'I don't do…love.'

'You already have. Just take the next step. All it needs is courage.' She hesitated. 'Ramón, I know how it hurts to love and to lose. You've loved and you've lost, but Philippe is going right on loving.'

'He can't,' he said but he was looking at the window where Consuela was indeed peeping through a chink in the curtains.

And then he was looking at Jenny—Gianetta—who knew which?—and she was looking back at him with faith. Faith that he could take this new step.

'*You* can,' she said.

'Gianetta,' he said and would have taken her into his arms right then, part in exasperation, part in anger—and there were a whole lot more parts in there besides, but she held up her hands in a gesture of defence.

'Not me. Not now. This is you and Philippe. Do you want him or not?'

He looked at her for a long moment. He glanced back at the farmhouse, and Philippe was at the window now, as well as Consuela.

And there was only one answer to give.

So, half an hour later—Ramón would be late for his meeting but not much—his little red Boxster finally left the farmhouse, with Philippe once again snuggled between Ramón and Jenny. There was a cat crate at Jenny's feet. The Boxster was definitely crowded.

Behind them, Consuela and Ernesto drove their farm truck, packed with enough luggage to last them for two days.

Or more, Jenny thought with satisfaction. There were four big suitcases on the back. For all she talked of class differences, Consuela seemed more than prepared to take a leap into the unknown.

If only Ramón could join her.

CHAPTER ELEVEN

THE moment he swung back into the palace grounds affairs of State took over again. Ramón couldn't stay to watch Philippe's reaction to being back at the palace. He couldn't stay to see that Consuela and Ernesto were treated right.

He couldn't stay with Jenny.

'We can do this. Go,' Jenny told him and he had no choice. He went, to meeting upon interminable meeting. Once again he was forced to work until the small hours.

Finally, exhausted beyond belief, he made his way through the palace corridors towards his personal chambers. Once again he passed Jenny's door—and he didn't knock.

But then he reached the nursery. To his surprise, Manuel was standing outside the door, at attention. The footmen were posted at the top of the stairs. Had a change been ordered? But Manuel spoke before he could ask.

'I'm not permitted to move,' the man said, and it was as if a statue had come to life. 'But the little boy and Señorina Bertin… I thought you wouldn't wish them harm so I took it upon myself to stay here.'

'Good idea.' He hesitated, taking in the full context of what the man had said. Reaching the crux. 'Señorina Bertin's in there?'

'Yes, sir,' Manuel said and he opened the nursery door before Ramón could say he hadn't meant to go in; he was only passing.

Only of course he had meant to go in. Just to check.

Manuel closed the door after him. The room was in darkness but the moon was full, the curtains weren't drawn and he could see the outline of the bed against the windows. It was a truly vast bed for a small child. A ridiculous bed.

He moved silently across the room and looked down—and there were two mounds in the bed. A child-sized one, with a cat-shaped bump over his feet, and a Jenny-shaped one, and the Jenny-shaped one spoke.

'You're not a Hun?' she whispered, and he blinked.

'Pardon?'

'Manuel's saving us from the Huns. I thought you might have overpowered him and be about to…plunder and pillage. I'm very glad you're not.'

'I'm glad I'm not a Hun either,' he said and smiled down at her, and he could feel her smile back, even if he couldn't quite see it. 'What are you doing here?'

'Shh. He's only just gone back to sleep.'

He tugged a chair forward and sat, then leaned forward so he was inches away from Jenny's face. Philippe was separated from them by Jenny's body but he could see that her arm was around him. The sight made him feel…made him feel…

No. There were no words to describe it.

'This is Consuela's job,' he managed.

'She was here until midnight. The staff put Consuela and Ernesto into one of the state apartments, and it's so grand it's made Ernesto quiver. Ernesto seems more frightened than Philippe so I said I'd stay.'

She said she'd stay. With a little boy who was the same age as her Matty. In this room that he'd once slept in. He looked at her, at the way Philippe's body was curved against hers, at the way she was holding him, and he felt things slither and change within him. Knots that had been around his heart for ever slipped away, undone, free.

'Gianetta…' he whispered and placed his fingers on her lips, wondering. If she'd found the courage to do this…

'Shh,' she said again. 'He woke and he was a little upset. I don't want him to wake again.'

'But you soothed him.'

'I told him the story of the whale. He loved it. I told him about his cousin, the hero, saviour of whales. Saviour of this country. We both thought it was pretty cool.'

'Gianetta…'

'Jenny. Your employee. And Manuel is out there.'

'Manuel can go…'

'Manuel can't go,' she said seriously. 'Neither of us is sure where to take this. You need to sleep, Ramón.'

'I want…'

'I know,' she said softly and she placed a finger on his lips in turn. 'We both want. I can feel it, and it's wonderful. But there's things to think about for both of us. For now… Give me my self-respect and go to your own bedroom tonight.' She smiled at him then and he was close enough to see a lovely loving smile that made his heart turn over. 'Besides,' she said. 'Tonight I'm sleeping with Philippe. One man a night, my love. I have my reputation to think of.'

'He's not Matty,' he said before he could stop himself.

'Philippe's not Matty, no.'

'But… Jenny, doesn't that tear you in two?'

'I thought it would,' she said on a note of wonder. 'But now… He fits exactly under my arm. He's not Matty but it's as if Matty has made a place for him. It feels right.'

'Jenny…'

'Go to bed, Ramón,' she said simply. 'We all have a lot of thinking to do this night.'

He left and she was alone in the dark with a sleeping child. She'd given her heart, she thought. She'd given it to both of them, just like that.

What if they didn't want it?

It was theirs, she thought, like it or not.

Bebe stirred and wriggled and padded his way up the bed

to check she was still breathing, that she'd still react if he kneaded his paws on the bedcover.

'Okay, I can learn to love you, too,' she told the little cat. 'As long as your claws don't get all the way through the quilt.' Satisfied, Bebe slumped down on the coverlet across her breast and went back to sleep, leaving her with her thoughts.

'They have to want me,' she whispered in the dark. 'Oh, they have to want me or I'm in such big trouble.'

And in the royal bedchamber, the apartment of the Crown Prince of Cepheus, there was no sleep at all.

Once upon a time a child had slept alone in this palace and known terror. Now the man lay alone in his palace and knew peace.

He woke and he knew, but he couldn't do a thing about it.

It'd take him a week, Señor Rodriguez told him, this signing, signing and more signing. He had to formally accept the role of Crown Prince before he could begin to delegate, so from dawn his time was not his own.

'I need two hours this afternoon,' he growled to his lawyer as he saw his packed diary. 'You've scheduled me an hour for lunch. Take fifteen minutes from each delegation; that gives me another hour, so between one and three is mine.'

'I've already started organising it,' his lawyer told him. 'We all want you to have time with the child.'

'All?'

'I believe the staff have been missing him,' the lawyer said primly. 'It seems there are undercurrents neither the Princess Sofía nor I guessed.'

He didn't say more, but they agreed a message would be sent to Jenny and to Philippe that he'd spend the early afternoon with them. Then Ramón put his head down and worked.

He finished just before one. He'd have finished earlier only someone dared ask a question. Was he aware there were up to fifty students in each class in the local schools, and didn't he agree this was so urgent it had to be remedied right now?

He did agree. How could he put his own desire to be with Jenny and Philippe before the welfare of so many other children? Señor Rodriguez disappeared, leaving Ramón to listen and think and agree to meet about the issue again tomorrow. Finally he was free to walk out, to find the whereabouts of Philippe…and of Jenny.

'They're by the pool, Your Highness.' It was the maid who normally brought in his coffee and, to his astonishment, she smiled as she bobbed her normal curtsy. 'It's so good to have him back sir. There's refreshments being served now. If you'd like to have your lunch with them…'

Bemused, he strolled out the vast palace doors into the gardens overlooking the sea.

There was a party happening by the pool, and the perfection of the scene before him was marred. Or not marred, he corrected himself. Just changed.

The landscape to the sea had been moulded to create a series of rock pools and waterfalls tumbling down towards the sea. Shade umbrellas and luxurious cream beach loungers were discreetly placed among semi-tropical foliage, blending unobtrusively into the magical garden setting.

Now, however… At the biggest rock pool chairs and tables had been hauled forward to make a circle. There were balloons attached around every umbrella. This wasn't tasteful at all, he thought with wry amusement. The balloons were all colours and sizes, as though some had been blown up by men with good lungs, and some had been blown up by a five-year-old. They were attached to the umbrellas by red ribbons, with vast crimson bows under each bunch.

And there were sea dragons floating in the rock pool. Huge plastic sea dragons, red, green and pink, with sparkly tiaras. Sea dragons with tiaras? What on earth…?

Jenny was in the water, and so was Philippe and so was…Sofía? They were on a sea dragon apiece, kicking their way across the water, seemingly racing. Sofía was wearing neck to knee swimmers and she was winning, whooping her elderly lungs out with excitement.

There was more, he thought, stunned. Señor Rodriguez was sitting by the edge of the pool, wearing shorts, his skinny frame a testament to a life spent at his desk. He was cheering Sofía at full roar. As were Consuela and Ernesto, yelling their lungs out for their foster son. 'Go, Philippe, go!'

There were also servants, all in their ridiculous uniforms, but each of them was yelling as loudly as everyone else. And another woman was cheering too, a woman who looked vaguely familiar. And then he recognised her. Perpetua. Carlos's wife! What the…?

He didn't have time to take it all in. Sofía reached the wall by a full length of sea dragon. Philippe came second and Jenny fell off her dragon from laughing.

It felt crazy. It was a palace transformed into something else entirely. He watched as Philippe turned anxiously to find Jenny. She surfaced, still laughing, she hugged him and his heart twisted and he forgot about everything, everyone else.

She saw him. She waved and then staggered—holding Philippe with one arm was a skill yet to be mastered. 'Welcome to our pool party, Your Highness,' she called. 'Have you come to try our sausage rolls?'

'Sausage rolls,' he said faintly, and looked at the table where there was enough food for a small army.

'Your chefs have never heard of sausage rolls,' she said, clambering up the pool steps with Philippe in her arms and grinning as Sofía staggered out as well, still clutching her sea dragon. 'Philippe and I had to teach them. And we have fairy bread and lamingtons, and tacos and tortillas and strawberries and éclairs—and I love this place. Philippe does too, don't you Philippe? We've decided it's the best place to visit in the world.'

Visit. He stood and watched as woman and child disappeared under vast towels and he thought…*visit*.

'Oh, and we invited Perpetua,' Jenny said from under her towel, motioning in the general direction of the pallid little lady standing uncertainly under the nearest umbrella.

Perpetua gave him a shy, scared smile. 'You know Carlos's wife? And Carlos, too.'

'And Carlos, too?' he demanded. Perpetua's smile slipped.

'I told him to come,' she whispered. 'When Gianetta invited us. He said he would. He just has to…he's been making silly threats that he doesn't mean. He wants to apologise.' Her voice was almost pleading. 'He'd never hurt…'

And maybe he wouldn't, Ramón thought. For Carlos was approaching them now, escorted by palace footmen. The footmen were walking really close. Really close.

'He's not going to hurt anyone,' Perpetua whispered. 'He's just been silly. I was so pleased when Gianetta rang. He needs a chance to explain.'

'Explain what?' Ramón said and Perpetua fell silent, waiting for Carlos himself to answer.

Ramón's gaze flew to Jenny. She met his gaze full on. She'd set this up, he thought.

One of the maids had taken over rubbing Philippe dry. The maid was laughing and scolding, making Philippe smile back. She was a servant he'd thought lacked emotion.

Had the servants turned to ice through mistreatment and fear?

What else had fear done?

He looked again at Carlos, a big, stupid man who for a few short weeks, while Ramón couldn't be found, had thought the throne was his. For the dream to be snatched away must have shattered his world.

Maybe stupid threats could be treated as they deserved, Ramón thought, feeling suddenly extraordinarily light-headed. And if threats weren't there…

'We invited both Carlos and Perpetua,' Jenny was saying. 'Because of Philippe. Philippe says Perpetua's always been nice to him.'

'He's a sweetheart,' Perpetua said stoutly, becoming braver. 'I worried about him whenever I stayed here.'

'You used to stay in the palace?' Ramón asked, surprised again. What had Señor Rodriguez told him? Perpetua was a nice enough woman, intelligent, trained as a grade school teacher, but always made to feel inferior to Carlos's royal relatives.

'A lot,' Perpetua said, becoming braver. 'Carlos liked being here. Philippe and I became friends, didn't we, sweetheart. But then Carlos said some silly things.' Her gaze met her husband's. 'I used to believe…well, I'm a royal wife and a royal wife stays silent. But Gianetta says that's ridiculous. So I'm not staying silent any longer. You're sorry, aren't you, dear?'

Was he? Ramón watched Carlos, sweating slightly in a suit that was a bit too tight, struggling to come to terms with this new order, and he even felt a bit sorry for him.

'I shouldn't have said it,' Carlos managed.

'You said you'd kill…'

'You know how it is.' Carlos was almost pleading. 'I mean…heat of the moment. I was only saying…you know, wild stuff. What I'd do if you didn't look after the country… that sort of thing. It got blown up. You didn't take it seriously. Please tell me you didn't take it seriously.'

Was that it? Ramón thought, relief running through him in waves. History had created fear—not fear for himself but fear for family. His family.

A family he could now build. In time…

And with that thought came another. He wasn't alone.

Delegation. Why not start now?

'Perpetua, you used to be a grade teacher,' he said, speaking slowly but thinking fast, thinking back to the meeting he'd just attended. 'Do you know the conditions in our schools?'

'Of course I do,' Perpetua said, confused. 'I mean, I haven't taught for twenty years—Carlos doesn't like me to—but I have friends who are still teachers. They have such a hard time…'

'Tomorrow morning I'm meeting with a deputation to see what can be done about the overcrowding in our classrooms,' he said. 'Would you like to join us?'

'Me?' she gasped.

'I need help,' he said simply. 'And Carlos… How can you help?'

There was stunned silence. Even Philippe, who was wrapped in a towel and was now wrapping himself around a sausage roll stopped mid-bite and stared. This man who'd made blustering threats to kill…

How can you help?

Jenny moved then, inconspicuously slipping to his side. She stood close and she took his hand, as if she realized just how big it was. Just how important this request was.

Defusing threats to create a future.

Refusing to stand alone for one moment longer.

'I can't…' Carlos managed at last. 'There's nothing.'

'Yes, dear, there is.' Perpetua had found her voice, and she, too, slipped to stand beside her man. 'Sports. Carlos loves them, loves watching them, but there's never been enough money to train our teenagers. And the football stadium's falling down.'

'You like football?' Ramón asked.

'Football,' Philippe said, lighting up.

'I…'

'You could give me reports on sports facilities,' Ramón said, thinking fast, trying to figure out something meaningful that the man could do. 'Tell me what needs to be done. Put in your recommendations. I don't know this country. You do. I need help on the ground. So what do we have here? Assistant to the Crown for Education. Assistant to the Crown for Sport.'

'And I'll be Assistant to the Crown for New Uniforms for The Staff,' Sofía said happily. 'I'd like to help with that.'

'I can help with floating,' Philippe said gamely. 'But can I help with football, too?'

'And Gianetta?' Perpetua said, looking anxious. 'What about Jenny?'

'I need to figure that out,' Ramón said softly, holding his love close, his world suddenly settling in a way that was leaving him stunned. 'In private.'

Philippe had finished his sausage roll now, and he carried the loaded tray over to his big cousin.

'Would you like to eat one?' he asked. 'And then will you teach me to float some more?'

'Of course I will,' he said. 'On one condition.'

Philippe looked confused, as well he might.

No matter. Sometimes a prince simply had to allocate priorities, and this was definitely that time. He tugged Jenny tighter, then, audience or not, he pulled her into his arms and gave her a swift possessive kiss. It was a kiss that said he was pushed for time. He knew he couldn't take this further, not here, not now, but there was more where that came from.

'My condition to you all,' he said softly, kissing her once more, a long lingering kiss that said, pushed for time or not, this was what he wanted most in the world, 'is that Señor Rodriguez changes my diary. This night is mine.'

The car came to collect her just before sunset. She was dressed again as Gianetta, in a long diaphanous dress made of the finest layers of silk and chiffon with the diamonds at her throat. Two maids and Sofía and Consuela and Perpetua had clucked over her to distraction. Sofía had added a diamond bracelet of her own, and had wept a little.

'Oh, my dear, you're so beautiful,' she'd said mistily. 'Do you think he'll propose?'

Jenny hadn't answered. She couldn't. She was torn between laughter and tears.

Ramón's kisses had promised everything, but nothing had been said. Mistress to a Crown Prince? Wife?

Dared she think wife?

How could she think anything? After a fast floating lesson Ramón had been swept away yet again on his interminable business and she'd been left only with his demand.

'A car will come for you at seven. Be ready.'

She was ready, but she was daring to think nothing.

Finally, at seven the car came and Señor Rodriguez handed her into the limousine with care and with pride. The reverberations from this afternoon were being felt all around the country, and the lawyer couldn't stop smiling.

'Where's Ramón?' she managed.

'Waiting for you,' the lawyer said, sounding inscrutable until he added, 'How could any man not?'

So she was driven in state, alone, with only a chauffeur for company. The great white limousine was driven slowly through the city, out along the coast road, up onto a distant headland where it drew to a halt.

Two uniformed footmen met her, Manuel and Luis, trying desperately to be straight-faced. There was a footpath leading from where the car pulled in to park, winding through a narrow section of overgrown cliff. Manuel and Luis led her silently along the path, emerged into a clearing, then slipped silently back into the shadows. Leaving her to face what was before her.

And what was before her made her gasp. A headland looking out all over the moonlit Mediterranean. A table for two. Crisp white linen. Two cushioned chairs with high, high backs, draped all in white velvet, each leg fastened with crimson ties.

Silverware, crystal, a candelabrum magnificent enough to take her breath away.

Soft music coming from behind a slight rise. Real music. *There were real musicians somewhere behind the trees.*

Champagne on ice.

And then Ramón stepped from the shadows, Ramón in full ceremonial, Ramón looking more handsome than any man she'd met.

The sound of frogs came from beneath the music behind him. Her frog prince?

'If I kiss you, will you join your friends, the frogs?' she whispered before she could help herself and he laughed and came towards her and took her hands in his.

'No kissing,' he said tenderly. 'Not yet.'

'What…?' She could barely speak. 'What are we waiting for?'

'This,' he said and went down on bended knee.

She closed her eyes. This couldn't be happening.

This was happening.

'This should wait until after dinner,' he said softly, 'but it's been burning a hole in my pocket for three hours now.' And, without more words, he lifted a crimson velvet box and held it open. A diamond ring lay in solitary splendour, a diamond so wonderful…so amazing…

'Is it real?' she gasped and he chuckled.

'That's Jenny speaking. I think we need Gianetta to give us the right sense of decorum.'

Gianetta. She took a deep breath and fought for composure. She could do this.

'Sire, you do me honour.'

'That's more like it,' he said and his dark eyes gleamed with love and with laughter. 'So, Gianetta, Jenny, my love, my sailor, my cook extraordinaire, my heart…I give you my love. The past has made us solitary, but it's up to both of us to move forward. To leave solitude and pain behind. You've shown me courage, and I trust that I can match it. So Gianetta, my dearest love, if I promise to love you, cherish you, honour you, for as long as we both shall live, will you do me the honour of taking my hand in marriage?'

She looked down into his loving eyes. Then she paused for a moment, taking time to gaze around her, at the night, at the stars, the accoutrements of royalty, at the lights of Cepheus glowing around them. Knowing also there was a little boy waiting as well.

Her family. Her love, starting now.

'I believe I will,' she said gently and, before he could respond, she dropped to her own knees and she took his hands in hers.

'Yes, my love and my prince, I believe I will.'

A ROYAL MARRIAGE OF CONVENIENCE

BY
MARION LENNOX

CHAPTER ONE

'ROSE-ANITRA, we have a surprise for you.'

Rose sighed. In her experience surprises from her in-laws were like surprises in a fairground ghost-train: 'Surprise!' followed by green slime—or worse. Rose had spent the evening on a windswept scree, delivering a calf which had taken one look at the outside world and elected to stay put. It had taken her hours to persuade it to change its mind. She'd been up before dawn and she hadn't stopped since. More than anything else in the whole world, she wanted to go to bed.

There was also the issue of the letter. The stiff, formal communication had arrived, registered mail, in the midst of a bunch of condolence cards. She'd read it briefly, then had stuffed it in her overall pocket to try and make sense of later. She'd like to think about it now, but Rose knew better than to try and deflect her in-laws. So she perched on the edge of an overstuffed chair in their overheated sitting room, she clasped her hands obediently, and she braced herself.

'It's a wonderful surprise,' Gladys said, but for once she sounded a bit nervous.

'You'll be really pleased,' Bob said, and Rose cast him an uncertain glance. Ever since her husband Max had died two years ago, Rose suspected Bob empathised with her a little. But only a little. Not so much that he'd stand up to his wife.

'You know, it's the anniversary of Max's death today,' Gladys said, casting a quelling glance at her husband.

'Of course.' How could Rose have forgotten? Yes, she still grieved for the man she'd loved, but maybe it was a little over the top that her veterinary clinic had been filled with as many flowers today as it had been two years ago. Max had been a loved son of the village. His memory would be kept alive for ever.

'We waited until now to tell you,' Gladys said. 'Because Max asked us to wait. He said we were to let you get the worst of your grieving over, for you couldn't have coped with a child until now.'

'I… What are you saying?' Rose's fingers clenched involuntarily into her palms. Of course she couldn't have coped with a child. Not when she'd been fighting to earn her way though vet school. Not when she and Max had been battling his illness. And not now, when she was struggling to earn enough for this tiny vet clinic to support them all.

'But now it's time,' Gladys said, and she smiled.

'Time?' Rose managed. 'For what?'

'It's his sperm,' Bob said, and the elderly man's voice was eager. 'It's Max's sperm, Rose. When he first got sick, years and years ago, he was naught but a lad, but they told us that the treatment might make him infertile. Even then we thought who'd inherit this life? Who'd take this place forward?'

Who indeed? But Rose wasn't asking the question. She was staring at them in dawning horror.

'So we had it frozen,' Gladys said. 'And we wanted it to be a surprise. It's his two-year anniversary present. From Max to you. Now you can have his babies.'

* * *

Five hundred miles away in London, in the illustrious international law firm Goodman, Stern and Haddock, another surprise was being played out.

Nikolai de Montez, barrister-at-law, was staring at the elderly man across his desk in stunned silence.

He'd walked in five minutes before the scheduled appointment he'd made a week earlier, neatly dressed, stooped with age, and with hands that trembled. The card he'd handed over had said simply: *'Erhard Fritz. Assistant to the Crown.'*

'My question is simple, really,' Erhard said without preamble. 'If it meant you were to inherit a throne, would you be prepared to marry?'

As partner in this internationally renowned law firm, Nick was accustomed to listening to all sorts of outrageous proposals, but this was one to take the breath away.

'Would I be prepared to marry?' he said now, really carefully, as if his words alone could make the situation explode. 'May I ask…marry who?'

'A woman called Rose McCray. You might know her as Rose-Anitra de Montez. She's a veterinarian in Yorkshire, but it seems that she might also be first in line to the throne of Alp de Montez.'

How could she walk away? She couldn't, but for the last two days Rose had felt like she was walking in a nightmare—the nightmare that was the remains of her husband's life.

Everywhere she went she was surrounded by memories. She woke and Max looked down on her from the framed photograph beside their wedding bed. Gladys had collapsed in hysterics when Rose had wanted to give away his clothes, so Max's shirts and trousers still hung in the closet. Max's coats still hung in the entrance hall, his boots still stood on the back porch. 'I'll not be forgetting our Max,' she said fiercely when anyone challenged her.

Rose's grief over the death of her husband had been as deep as it had been sincere, but now it was starting to overwhelm her. She felt like she was living in a perpetual shrine to Max—and now they wanted her to have Max's child.

The request had been playing over and over in her head for the last two days—along with the contents of the letter. She was so weary she was about to fall over, but one truth was starting to emerge: this couldn't go on. Max had been dead these two years. If there'd been the money she would have moved out to a place of her own, but her income paid the upkeep on this place. She couldn't leave. Unless… Unless…

The proposal outlined in the letter was crazy, but so was this situation. The proposal was almost like a siren song. Alp de Montez…a country she loved. She lifted the photograph that had come with the letter, a picture of one Nikolai de Montez. He was long, lean and darkly handsome. His Mediterranean good looks were stunning.

He was about as different from Max as it was possible to get, she thought, reading the letter for the tenth time and then putting it firmly away. No. It was stupid. The letter was a lunacy, a crazy escape-clause with no guarantees that she wouldn't be worse off.

This was Max's community. She had to give it one last try, no matter how trapped she was feeling. If only they'd back off about the baby.

She walked into the sitting room, determined to say what had to be said. They were waiting for her. Bob was pouring her a sherry.

'We've been thinking,' Gladys said before she could say a word. 'We're so excited about the baby, but you need to hurry. There's enough sperm for you to have more than one, and you're almost thirty. If you don't have a boy first, then we...' She caught herself. '*You'll* want another. Rose, we've made an appointment for you with the specialist in Newcastle tomorrow, and Bob's arranged for a locum so you can go.'

'That's good,' Rose said faintly, but she didn't take the sherry. Gladys smiled her approval.

'Good girl. I told Bob no alcohol. Not if you're pregnant.'

'I'm not pregnant yet.'

'But you will be.'

'No,' Rose said faintly, and then more forcibly. 'No. If you'll excuse me...' She took a deep breath. 'It's good that you've organised a locum. I need to go to London for a couple of days. I've received a letter.'

'A letter?'

'It came registered post to the surgery,' she said, knowing full well that any post out of the ordinary that came via the private letter-box was likely to be steamed open. 'You remember my family has royal connections?'

'Yes,' Gladys said, stiffening in disapproval.

'It seems someone came here to see me a week ago,' she said. 'Someone from Alp de Montez. You told him I was away?'

'I...' Gladys looked at Bob and then she looked at the carpet. 'He said he had a proposal for you,' she muttered, defensive. 'What would you be wanting with a proposal?'

Rose nodded. Two proposals in two weeks. The one facing her here made the other one seem mild in comparison.

But what Gladys had just said firmed things for her. If she agreed to have a child, a daughter would never be enough. If she finally had Max's son, then the child would be a living memorial to Max. What crazy reason was that to bring a child into the world?

'It seems I'm needed,' she said, thinking it through as she spoke. 'I mean...needed by someone other than you. By someone other than my dead husband's family and his community. When I first read the letter I thought it was crazy, but it seems as if it's not crazy after all. Or no more crazy than this. Either way, I'm going to find out. I'm going to London to see if I've inherited a crown.'

CHAPTER TWO

THE restaurant Nick had organised as a rendezvous was a good one. It was old-fashioned, full of oak wainscotting, linen table-cloths, and individual booths where people could talk without struggling to hear or worrying about being heard.

He walked in and Walter, the head waiter, met him with the familiarity of an old acquaintance. 'Good evening, Mr de Montez.' He looked at Nick's casual Chinos and cord jacket and he smiled. 'Well, well. Holiday mode tonight, then, sir?'

Holiday. Yeah, maybe this was his holiday. Nick hardly did holidays at all, so he might as well term this one. Oh, every now and then he'd fly back to Australia to see his foster mother, Ruby, with whom he kept in touch and phoned every Sunday without fail. He skied now and then with a few important clients, but mostly Nick lived to work. He was on holiday tonight because he'd donned casual clothes. That'd do him for while.

He was led over to the booth he generally used. Erhard was there already, and Nick appraised him more thoroughly as he rose to greet him. The old man looked thin, wiry and frail, with a shock of white hair and white bushy eyebrows. He was dressed in a deeply formal black suit.

'I'm sorry I wasn't here when you arrived,' Nick said, and

he looked ruefully down at his clothes, regretting he hadn't opted for formal. 'And I'm sorry for these.'

'You think Rose-Anitra might be uncomfortable with formality?' Erhard asked, smiling.

'I did,' he confessed. Some time in the last few days, as Erhard had talked him through the situation, he'd handed over a photograph of Rose, taken a month ago by a private investigator. Rose had been working—the shot had her leaning against a battered four-wheel-drive vehicle, talking to someone out of frame. She was wearing dirty brown dungarees, Wellingtons and a liberal spray of mud. She was pale faced, with the odd freckle or six, and the only colour about her was the deep, glossy auburn of the braid hanging down her back.

She was a good-looking woman in a 'country hick' sort of way, Nick had conceded. The women in his world were usually sophisticated chic. There was no way this woman could be described in those terms, but she'd looked sort of...cute. So when dressing tonight he'd decided formal gear might make her uneasy.

'You may be underestimating her,' Erhard said.

'She's a country vet.'

'Yes. A trained veterinarian.' Still the hint of reproof. 'My sources say she's a woman of considerable intelligence.' And then he paused, for Walter was escorting someone to their table.

Rose-Anitra? The woman in the dungarees?

Nick could see the similarities, but only just. She was wearing a crimson, halter-necked dress, buttoned at the front from the below-knee hemline to a low-cut cleavage. The dress was cinched at the waist in a classic Marilyn Monroe style, showing her hourglass figure to perfection. Her hair was twisted into a casual knot, caught up with soft white ribands, and tiny tendrils were escaping every which way. She was wearing not much make-up—just enough to dust the freckles.

Her lips were a soft rose, which should have clashed with her dress but didn't.

She was wearing stilettos. Gorgeous red stilettos that made her legs look as if they went on for ever.

'I believe I had it right,' Erhard said softly to him, and chuckled and moved forward to greet their guest. 'Mrs. McCray.'

'Rose,' she said and smiled, and her smile lit up the room. Her pert nose wrinkled a little. 'I think I remember you. Monsieur Fritz—you were assistant to my uncle?'

'I was,' Erhard said, pleased. 'Please, call me Erhard.'

'Thank you,' she said gravely. 'It's been almost fifteen years, but I do remember.' She turned to Nick. 'And you must be Nikolai? Monsieur de Montez.'

'Nick.'

'I don't think I've met you.'

'No.'

Walter was holding out her seat and Rose was sitting, which hid her legs. Which was almost a national tragedy, Nick decided. What was she about, disguising those legs in dungarees? He surveyed her with unabashed pleasure as Walter fussed about them, taking orders, offering champagne. 'Yes, please,' Rose said, and beamed. When the champagne arrived she put her nose right into the bubbles and closed her eyes, as if it was her first drink for a very long time.

'You like champagne, then?' Nick said, fascinated, and she sighed a blissful smile.

'You have no idea. And it's not even sherry.' She had a couple more sips, then laid her glass back on the table with obvious reluctance.

'We're very pleased you were able to come,' Erhard said gently, and looked at Nick. 'Aren't we, Nick?'

'Yes,' said Nick, feeling winded.

'I'm sorry it took a while to contact me,' Rose told them,

glancing round the restaurant with real appreciation. 'My family has an odd notion that I need protection.'

'You don't?' Nick asked.

'No,' she said, and took another almost defiant sip of champagne. 'Absolutely not. This is lovely.'

It was, Nick thought. She was.

'Maybe it'd be best if I outline the situation,' Erhard said, smiling faintly at Nick as if guessing his degree of confoundment. 'Rose, I'm not sure how much you know.'

'Not much at all,' she admitted. 'Only what you told me in the letter. The whole village seems to have been playing keepings off, from telling you I was away when you called, to refusing to pass on phone messages. If Ben at the post office hadn't been a man of integrity I might never have heard from you at all.'

'Why would they be worried about Erhard?' Nick asked, puzzled.

'My in-laws know I'm the daughter of minor royalty,' she said. 'My husband used to delight in it. But since he's died anything that might take me away from the village has been regarded with suspicion. I gather Erhard came, looked dignified and spoke with an accent. That'd be enough to make them worry. My in-laws have a lot of influence, and they don't like strangers. I'm sorry.'

'It's not your fault,' Erhard said gently. He hesitated. 'At least you're here now, which means that you may be prepared to listen. It might sound preposterous…'

'You don't know what preposterous is,' she said enigmatically. 'Try me.'

Erhard nodded. It seemed he was prepared to do the talking, which left Nick free to, well, just look.

'I'm not sure how much you know already,' Erhard said. 'I've talked the situation through with Nick this week, and I did outline this in the letter, but maybe I need to start at the beginning.'

'Go ahead,' Rose said, sipping some more champagne and smiling. It was an amazing smile. Stunning.

Nick was stunned.

Erhard cast him an amused glance. He was an astute man, was Erhard. The more Nick knew him, the more he respected him. Maybe he should look away from Rose. Maybe what he was thinking was showing in his face.

What the heck? Not to look would be criminal.

'I'm not sure if you know the history of Alp de Montez,' Erhard was saying, smiling between the pair of them. 'Let me give you a thumb sketch. Back in the sixteenth century, a king had five sons. The boys grew up warring, and the old king thought he'd pre-empt trouble. He carved four countries from his border, and told his younger sons that the cost of their own principality was lifelong allegiance to their oldest brother.

'But granting whole countries to warlike men is hardly a guarantee of wise rule. The princes and their descendants brought four wonderful countries to the brink of ruin.'

'But two are recovering,' Nick said, and Erhard nodded.

'Yes. Two are moving towards democracy, albeit with their sovereigns still in place. Of the remaining two, Alp de Montez seems the worst off. The old Prince—your mutual grandfather—left control more and more in the hands of the tiny council running the place. The chief of council is Jacques St. Ives, and he's had almost complete control for years. But the situation is dire. Taxes are through the roof. The country's on the brink of bankruptcy, and people are leaving in the thousands.'

'Where do you come into this?' Nick asked curiously. He knew much of this, and not all of it was second hand. Several years ago, curious about the country where his mother had been raised, he'd spent a week touring the place. What he'd seen had horrified him.

'I've been an aide to the old Prince for many years,' Erhard said sadly. 'As he lost his health, I watched the power shift to Jacques. And then there were the deaths,'

'Deaths?' Rose asked.

'There have been many,' Erhard told her. 'The old Crown Prince died last year. He had four sons, and then a daughter. You'd think with five children there'd be someone to inherit, but, in order of succession, Gilen died young in a skiing accident, leaving no children. Gottfried died of a drug overdose when he was nineteen. Keifer drank himself to death, and Keifer's only son Konrad died in a car crash two weeks ago. Rose, your father Eric died four years back, and Nick, your mother Zia, the youngest of the five children, is also dead. Which leaves three grandchildren. Eric's daughters—you, Rose, and your sister Julianna—are now first and second in line for the throne. You, Nikolai, are third.'

'Did you know all this?' Nick asked Rose, and she shook her head.

'I knew my father was dead, but I didn't know any of the ascendancy stuff until I had Erhard's letter. My mother and I left Alp de Montez when I was fifteen. Have you ever been there?'

'I skied there once,' Nick admitted.

'Does that mean you can inherit the throne?' she asked, smiling. 'Because you skied there?'

'It almost comes down to that,' Erhard said, and Nick had to stop smiling at Rose for a minute and look serious. Which was really hard. He was starting to feel like a moonstruck teenager, and he'd only had half a beer. Maybe he'd better switch to mineral water like Erhard.

But, regardless of what he was feeling, Erhard was moving

on. 'We need a sovereign,' he said. 'The constitution of the Alp countries means no change can take place without the overarching approval of the Crown. I'd love to see the place as a democracy, but that's only going to happen with royal approval.'

'Which would be where we come in, I guess,' Rose said. 'Your letter said you needed me.'

'Yes.'

'But I'm not a real royal. Eric really wasn't my father.' She touched her flame-coloured hair and winced in rueful remembrance. 'Surely you remember the fuss, Erhard? Eric called my mother a whore and kicked her out of the country.'

'Not until you were fifteen. And you went with her,' Erhard said softly.

'There wasn't a lot of choice.' She shrugged. 'My sister—my half-sister—wanted to stay in the palace, but my mother was being cut off with nothing. There wasn't a lot of love lost between me and Julianna even then. My sister was jealous of me, and my father hated my hair. No. That's putting it too nicely. My father hated *me*. I had no place there.'

'He acknowledged you as his daughter until you were fifteen,' Erhard said. 'Yes, there was general consensus that you weren't his, but the people felt sorry for your mother, and they loved you.'

'And my grandfather wanted my mother in the castle,' Rose said bluntly. 'My grandfather didn't care about the scandal which had produced me. He knew his son was a womaniser, and he knew my mother's affair happened through loneliness. My mother was kind, in a family where kind was hard to get. It was only after Grandfather became so ill, and he wasn't noticing, that my father was able to send her away.'

'To nothing,' Erhard said bleakly. 'To no support.'

'We didn't care,' Rose said, sounding defiant. 'At least…it would have been nice at the end, but we got by.'

'So you left the throne for Julianna.'

'I didn't,' Rose said, sounding annoyed. 'My mother and I assumed Keifer and then Konrad would inherit. We weren't to know they'd die young.'

'So you've never officially removed yourself from the succession?'

'I didn't think I had to. If I'm not real royalty…'

'You *are* real royalty,' Erhard said, emphatic. 'You were born within a royal marriage.'

'I have red hair. No one in my extended family has red hair. And my mother admitted—'

'Your mother admitted nothing on paper.'

'But DNA…'

'If DNA testing were done, half the royal families of Europe would crumble,' Erhard told her. 'Your mother married young into a loveless marriage, but such things aren't unusual. Your parents are dead. There's no proof of anything.'

'Julianna looks royal.'

'You think?' Erhard asked, with a wry smile. 'There's no proof of that either, and no one dare suggest DNA. So we turn to the lawyers. There's an international jurisdiction—legal experts chosen for impartiality—set up by the four Alp principalities for just this eventuality. They decide who has best right to the crown. Rose, I told you in the letter, Julianna has married Jacques St. Ives and they're making a solid play for the crown. Their justification is that Julianna is the only one of the three of you who lives in the country, and moreover she's married to a citizen who cares about the place. You, Rose, walked away almost fifteen years ago. Regardless of your birth, your absence by choice sits as an implacable obstacle. The panel will decide in Julianna's favour, unless they're given an alternative.'

He hesitated. He looked as if he didn't want to continue—

but it had to be said, and they all knew it. 'Rose, if there are questions about your parentage there are also questions about Julianna's,' he said softly. 'Regardless of DNA testing, the panel acknowledge that. Your parents' marriage was hardly happy. You remain the oldest. And behind you both there's Nikolai, whose mother was definitely royal. I've thought and thought of this. The only way forward is for the two of you to present as one. Together you must outweigh Julianna's claim. A married couple—the questioned first and the definite third in line—taking on the throne together.'

Whatever Erhard had said in his letter, Rose must have been forewarned, Nick thought, as she was showing no shock. The idea had stunned him, but she was reacting as if it was almost reasonable. She sat and stared at the bubbles in her glass for a while, letting things settle. She wasn't a woman who needed to talk, he thought. The silence was almost comfortable.

'A marriage of convenience,' she said at last, as if the thing was worthy of consideration.

'Yes.'

'That's what I thought you meant after I read the letter. I guess it's why I came. It seemed that this way I might be able to help. But…' She smiled up at Walter as he delivered their meals, and she nodded absolute affirmation when he offered her wine. 'Are you sure Julianna and Jacques won't make good rulers?'

'I'm sure they won't,' Erhard said.

'Don't you know your sister?' Nick asked, curious.

'We were friends when we were little,' she said, sounding suddenly forlorn. 'Julianna was pretty and blonde and cute, and I was carrot-headed and pudgy. But despite that the old Prince liked me. He indulged me. He'd call me his little princess, and Julianna hated it. So did my father. It got so that

I hated it too, and when it all blew up I was glad to go. I got to stay with my mother, my great-aunt and six crazy cats in London, while Julianna got to be a princess.' She gave a rueful smile. 'So she got what she wanted. But she never answered my letters or returned my calls. It was like she and my father just wiped us. You say she's married?'

'Yes,' Erhard said. 'To Jacques, who wants control of the throne.'

'I see.' She gave herself an irritated shake. 'I guess I expected no less. But how can I believe what you say of her intentions?'

'I can verify them,' Nick told her, feeling it was time he helped out. Erhard was looking so strained he looked like he might collapse. 'I've spent the last week researching the place. Alp de Montez is in serious trouble, and it will take a sovereign to help. There's never been the slightest interest in ruling the country properly from either Jacques, the presiding council, or from Julianna herself. Corruption is everywhere.'

'Oh,' Rose said in a small voice. She swallowed, and then suddenly seemed to make a conscious effort to shake off dreariness. 'This food is wonderful.'

It was wonderful. Nick had chosen steak, and somewhat to his surprise Rose had too. He was accustomed to women ordering something like grilled fish with a salad—or just a salad—and then not eating most of it, but there was none of the dainty eater about Rose. She tucked into her steak with enjoyment. There was a bowl of roast potatoes to share, fragrant with rosemary, and she reached for the last one before he did.

'Ladies first,' she said, and she smiled at him again, and the odd warmth he was feeling intensified.

Erhard, who had been the one to settle on grilled fish,

chuckled quietly at the pair of them. 'This could be some match,' he said.

Hey, hold on. Nick jerked back to the issue at hand. He needed to put his hormones to one side and concentrate. 'We're far from deciding here,' he retorted. 'The thing seems a fairy tale.'

'None of us believe it's impossible, or we wouldn't be sitting here,' Erhard said smoothly. 'Rose thinks so too.'

'Rose isn't committing herself,' Rose retorted. 'I only said I'd meet him.'

'And you have met him, and he makes you smile.'

'Just because I beat him to the last potato. That's hardly a basis for a marriage.'

'Shared intelligence is a basis of a marriage,' Erhard said calmly. 'And shared compassion. Now I've met you both, I believe the thing might be possible.'

'Is there really no other way?' Nick said cautiously. But he wasn't feeling cautious. Ever since Erhard had walked into his office, a bubble of excitement had been growing inside him that refused to be suppressed. At first it had been the idea of having some say in turning around the fate of a nation. But now…

He'd never thought of marriage. Why should it be suddenly immensely appealing?

'Let's get this straight,' he said. 'Why not just Rose?'

Erhard nodded. He'd obviously prepared his responses very carefully.

'On the upside she's first in line, and once upon a time the people loved her,' he said. 'The downside is that as soon as the old Prince was unable to react Eric shouted from the rooftops that Rose wasn't his. Rose and her mother left the country fifteen years ago and never looked back.'

'Why not just Julianna, then?'

'On the upside, Julianna lives in the country and the people know her. But they don't like her. Or they don't like her husband, and Julianna does what her husband says. The inference that Rose isn't royal must also taint Julianna's claim. There's no proof. And Rose is older.'

'Why not just Nick, then?' Rose demanded.

'He's an unknown,' Erhard said flatly. 'I didn't know him myself until a week ago. He's been to the country as a tourist, but nothing else. The people will never accept him.'

'Maybe I could support Rose's claim without marriage,' Nick heard himself say, albeit reluctantly. There was a crazy voice in the back of his head saying 'take her and run'. He suppressed it with an effort. He had to be sensible. 'As someone in line myself, even if further away and the child of a royal daughter and not a son, I can surely add weight to Rose's position?'

'So can the President of our Council,' Erhard said bluntly. 'He supports Julianna. Julianna is a citizen of Alp de Montez, and she's married to another citizen. Rose was a people's favourite in the past. The press loved her, portraying her as a natural, friendly kid who always had a stray animal attached. But that knowledge of Rose has faded, and her father's vitriolic denunciation of her stands in her way. It will take a huge factor to swing the thing in Rose's favour. The only thing that will do it is your marriage.'

'And you?' Nick said, turning to Rose, puzzled. There was so much about this woman he didn't understand. 'You'd seriously consider marriage to gain a throne?'

She froze at that. She'd been smiling, but now her face stilled.

'Whoa,' she said. 'Let's not paint me a gold-digger.'

'I never said…'

'Yes, you did,' she said bluntly. 'So let's get things clear. Erhard's letter made me think. I'm not the least bit interested in playing the Crown Princess—that was always Julianna's preferred option—but there's not so many times in your life that you're presented with an option that just might be for the greater good.'

Then she smiled up at Walter, who was clearing the plates from the main course. 'Do your puddings match your mains?'

'They certainly do, miss,' Walter said, and he beamed.

'I'd like something rich and sticky.'

'I believe we can accommodate that, miss.' Walter was smiling down at her like an avuncular genie. It was as if she had him mesmerised. Well, why not? Nick thought. He was feeling pretty mesmerised himself.

'Pudding for you, too?' Walter said, beaming still, and Nick nodded before thinking about it.

What was he doing? He seldom had pudding. He had to get his mind back into gear. Now.

'I don't know the first thing about you,' he said weakly to Rose as Walter headed off to fetch puddings for all. 'How can we think about marriage?'

'Are you worried?' she asked. 'I'm not an axe murderer. Nor a husband beater. Are you?'

He ignored the question. 'Erhard says you're widowed.'

'Yes,' she said in a voice that suddenly said 'don't go there'.

'There's no impediment to marriage,' Erhard said, stepping into the breach.

'Except that I don't much want to be married,' he said. Or he didn't think he did. He *hadn't* thought he did. There seemed to be two strands of thought here. The strand that he'd had before meeting Rose, and the post-Rose strand. Actually the 'post-Rose' was a really convoluted knot.

'Neither do I,' said Rose. 'Isn't that lucky? We wouldn't need to stay married, would we, Erhard?'

'Of course not,' Erhard said. 'This isn't a happy-ever-after scenario I'm demanding of you. The idea is that you marry almost immediately. I'll put the necessary paperwork in train, and then we present you to Alp de Montez as the Jacques-Julianna alternative. I've had private words with the committee. Nick, you stay in Alp de Montez for a few weeks, until things seem settled. Maybe a month. Then you use the excuse that you don't want to give up your profession and return to London. Rose then stays in Alp de Montez until we can get things in train to get a decent government sorted. When affairs are under control, you can quietly divorce.'

'You'd depend on Rose to get the affairs under control?'

'You're the international lawyer,' Erhard said shrewdly. 'I'm willing to wager you know exactly what can be done.'

He did. He'd been thinking about it all week. The chance to make a difference....

He'd never belonged. His mother, Zia, had left Alp de Montez as a troubled teenager. She'd ended up in Australia, addicted to drugs, pregnant with him. His childhood until he was eight had been a struggle to survive, lurching from fleeting intervals living with his increasingly erratic mother, to extended periods in a long string of foster homes.

Then Ruby had found him. She'd plucked him off the streets of Sydney, and from then on his base had been with Ruby and her tribe of foster sons. Ruby had given him security, but still he felt rootless.

At some really basic level Erhard's proposition left him breathless. What had Rose said? An option 'for the greater good'. It just might be the chance to make a difference.

He thought back to the frightened girl who'd been his mother. She'd want this. He knew she would. She'd been desperately homesick for Alp de Montez but there was no way her increasingly disgusted family would have funded her to go home.

He could go home on her behalf now. With this woman by his side.

Marriage. It wasn't such a frightening thought if it was done for the right reasons. But were Rose's reasons right? How could a woman like this want to marry a complete stranger?

She was his cousin.

No. She wasn't even that, he thought. She was the product of his aunt-by-marriage's affair with someone they knew nothing of.

It didn't matter. She was gorgeous.

'What about Julianna?' he asked, looking for catches. 'You can't convince her to do the right thing?'

'Julianna won't speak to me,' Erhard said.

'But you?' he asked Rose. 'You're her sister.'

'She doesn't speak to me either,' Rose said sadly. 'I know it's dumb, but there it is.'

'So this really is a serious proposition.'

'It seems like it.' She smiled ruefully into her empty wineglass. 'You know, I swore I'd never marry again.'

'That'd be a waste.'

'Says you, who's never married at all,' she retorted, suddenly sounding angry.

'I'm sorry.' But his thoughts were elsewhere. 'I wouldn't need to stay in Alp de Montez,' he said slowly.

'You would for a few weeks,' Erhard said. 'Could you use a holiday?'

A holiday. Strange concept. With Rose?

She really was the most extraordinary woman. Stunning.

'Maybe I could,' he said. 'And you?' he queried Rose. 'How long would you have to be away from your vet practice?'

'A year,' Erhard said, answering for her. 'At least. Maybe longer. I'm sorry, Rose, but it'd be more your commitment than Nick's. You'd rule jointly, but it's you who's first in line. Unless anything happened to Julianna…'

'Which isn't going to happen,' Rose said, and shivered.

And then braced herself. 'No matter. I'd have to close my doors anyway, and there are…reasons why that's not such a terrible idea.'

'I guess the idea of playing princess for a year would be fun,' Nick ventured, and she frowned.

'Now you're being insulting,' she retorted, and he paused.

Maybe he was.

There's not so many times in your life that you're presented with an option that just might be for the greater good.

She met his look with calm indifference, almost scorn. His gaze fell to her hands. Here was another difference—a huge difference—from the women he dated. This woman's hands wouldn't have looked out of place on a woman twenty years older. Work-worn hands, not something he saw a lot of.

But she was looking down at his hands, and he suddenly realised she knew exactly what he was thinking. His hands were those of an international lawyer. There was not a lot of work wear there.

If she was to have fun for a year, maybe there were reasons she deserved it, he thought. She'd lost a husband…

On the far side of the restaurant, a band struck up. It was a simple quartet, playing softly enough to not disturb the diners on this side of the restaurant. There was a small dance-floor, and a couple of diners rose and started dancing.

To Nick's surprise Erhard rose. But not to dance.

'No,' he said as Nick rose as well. 'I'm sorry.' He sighed. 'I'm not…completely well. If you'll excuse me for a moment…' He looked across at the dance floor, almost wistfully. 'Maybe you could dance while I'm away.'

'I don't—' Nick started, but Erhard shook his head.

'You do. My informants say you do. And so does Rose.' He gave an uncertain smile at them both, but there was discomfort behind his eyes. 'Excuse me. You go on.' And he pressed his napkin to his lips and headed towards the rear of the restaurant.

Rose watched him go in concern. 'He seems a nice man,' she said. 'He's ill. I wonder what—'

'He's probably doing this to manipulate us,' Nick retorted, and she smiled, but absently, still looking concerned.

'I don't think so. Even if he is, he's doing it for the right reasons, and there is something wrong. I think.'

The silence stretched on. Behind them the band launched into a lively Latin-swing number.

Nick was already standing. He went to sit down again but then thought it seemed surly.

The woman before him was beautiful.

'You don't look like a country vet,' he said, and he must have sounded accusing because she smiled again.

'I'm not manipulating,' she said gently. 'I promise.'

But any woman who looked like she did tonight was making a statement, he thought, whether it was manipulative or not. And maybe his thoughts were transparent, because her smile gave way to a flash of anger.

'Stop looking like that. I have the right to wear what I like.'

'Of course you do.'

'My husband bought this for me on our honeymoon,' she said, still angry, and he stilled.

'So it is a sort of statement.'

'I guess it is.'

'A statement that you're available?'

The flash of anger stilled and her eyes were suddenly ice. 'I don't think I want to be married to you,' she snapped. 'Of all the boorish comments… If you wear a nice suit, is that an advertisement of availability as well?'

'No,' he said, horrified. He was suddenly way out of his depth. How could he have asked her such a question? As well as being insulting, he'd also hurt her. He could see it in the way she'd withdrawn.

'Rose, I'm sorry,' he said. 'I have no idea why I said that, but it was way out of line. Hell, marriage or not, we seem to have crossed some sort of barrier that's launched me somewhere where I'm not sure of the rules any more. I know that's no excuse. But please—I'm sorry.'

Her face softened—just a little. 'It does seem crazy,' she admitted. She glanced down at her dress ruefully. 'But maybe this is some sort of a statement. Maybe that's why you've made me angry. You know, this dress has sat in a camphor chest in my parents-in-law's house for the last five years. It's been like...well, I was locked up with it. Tonight I did wear it as a kind of declaration—not that I'm available, but that I'm free. If that makes sense.' She shook her head. 'No. It barely makes sense to me. But the last thing I want is more attachments. I've done family for life. I *am* free.'

'Diving into the royal goldfish bowl of Alp de Montez is scarcely freeing yourself,' he said cautiously.

'It all depends on what your prison has been,' she said. 'Are you going to ask me to dance?'

'I...' What the hell? 'Yes.'

'Excellent,' she said, and she smiled, rose and took his arm, altogether proprietary. It seemed as if he was forgiven. 'If I'm going to get the camphor smell out of this dress then I need to swirl it round a bit.'

She didn't smell of camphor.

Rose was an intuitive dancer, light and lovely on her feet. Nick had been taught the rudiments of dance by his determined little foster mother, and he'd always enjoyed it. With great music and a good partner one could almost lose oneself in dance.

But not tonight. He didn't want to lose himself when he was dancing with Rose.

The Latin music gave way to a gentle waltz. Erhard had still not returned to their table so suddenly Nick was holding her close, steering her around the dance floor, feeling her body mould to his in perfect time with his steps, in perfect time with him.

And she didn't smell of camphor. She smelled of Rose.

What was she doing? She'd brought this dress with her on a whim, walking out of the house feeling as if she'd betrayed everyone. She hadn't been worried about what she was wearing. But as her mother-in-law's weeping had increased, as her father-in-law had wrung his hands and said, 'Rose, you can't leave. We love you. You're our daughter. What would Max think?' she'd abandoned her distress as too hard and she'd let anger hold sway.

She'd lifted the lid of her camphor chest and had retrieved the dress and shoes that had lain there for what seemed almost a lifetime.

And then, before she'd closed the chest again, she'd taken Max's photograph from her bedside table and put it where her dress had been.

And had closed the lid.

Then she'd walked out of the house. Free.

No, not free. Still guilt-ridden. Seemingly obligated in some weird way to a country she'd left with the royal family's scorn following her.

But she wasn't going back to Yorkshire except to finalise things. No family. No ties. Nick's question as to her availability couldn't have been more wrong. If ever anyone else told her they loved her then she'd run a mile.

But she was in this man's arms.

Yes, and that was great, she told herself as she let him swirl her round the dance floor with an expertise that made her feel wonderful. Erhard's long letter had filled her in on who Nick was. A loner who'd pulled himself up the hard way. A man whose intelligence was extraordinary. A man with an Aussie accent overlaying his smooth French-Italian native tongue, and a laid-back charm that could knock a girl sideways. Nick was a sophisticated international lawyer who'd come from a background even more dysfunctional than her own.

He was a man who knew where his boundaries were.

So it was fine. Yes, she could marry him to keep Alp de Montez safe, and she could keep her independence. It would finally make her free.

Please.

Five minutes later Erhard returned to the table. The musicians took a break. There was no reason to stay on the dance floor, but as Nick led her back to the table he was aware of a sharp stab of regret.

Only because he loved dancing, he thought. Only that.

Erhard was smiling, watching them weave their way through the tables to join him. The strain had eased from his face a little.

'Two wonderful dancers,' he said softly as they sat down again. 'You see, this thing becomes possible.' He settled back into his chair and took a long sip of water. 'Well?'

Nick looked at Rose and found she was watching him. Intently.

It seemed a decision needed to be made. Now. Did that mean Rose had already decided?

'You need to trust me,' Erhard told him softly. 'This is a big ask. We need to trust each other.'

'It's fine,' Rose said, suddenly sounding impatient to move on. Sounding as if she was annoyed. 'I'm willing to take a chance, so it's up to you, Nick. If you don't choose to take part, then say so now. Let Erhard go into damage control and see if there's another solution.'

'There's no other solution,' Erhard said flatly, and they both went back to watching him.

She'd flung her hat in the ring, just like that. She'd agreed to marry him after knowing him only a matter of hours.

His foundations were shaken, he thought, and it wasn't just this crazy proposition that was shaking them. It was the way he'd felt, dancing with Rose. The way she'd felt…

He needed a cold shower, and then some good legal advice.

'You're holding a gun to my head,' he snapped, and the old man shook his head.

'That's what we're hoping to avoid. Guns.'

'You're serious?'

'I'm serious,' Erhard whispered, and the grey look flooded back. How ill was he?

'So tell us,' Rose said to Nick directly, with a sideways glance of concern towards Erhard. 'Are you in or are you out?'

'I need to do a little more research…'

'Fine,' she said. 'Research away. I spent a week on the internet myself. But if you come up with the conclusion I came up with—as you will—are you ready to have a go at fixing things?'

'You're seriously asking me to marry you?'

'I thought you were asking me to marry you.'

'I guess it's mutual.'

'Only I've said yes, and you haven't,' she said. 'Go on. It might even be fun.'

'I don't do fun.'

'Neither do I,' she snapped. 'Not for years. So we're perfectly compatible. I'm willing to take a risk on the rest. What about you? Yes or no?'

And there it was. Not a gun pointing at his head, but just possibly a chance to make a difference.

Rose was waiting for him to come to a decision, her grey eyes calmly watchful.

Erhard was waiting too. Two people he instinctively trusted who were trying to do good.

So what was a man to say?

'Yes,' he said, and there was a moment's stunned silence, and then they both beamed.

'There it is, then,' Rose said. 'Proposal accepted. Congratulations to us all, and here comes pudding. Do you think I might have some more champagne?'

CHAPTER THREE

ROSE finished an excellent pudding, but it signalled that the night, for Rose at least, was over. She excused herself without waiting for coffee.

'I was up before dawn, and I need to walk a bit before bed after all that champagne,' she told them. 'No, I don't want company. I need head-space to plan the next few weeks. There's so much I need to do. Finding someone to take care of a thousand square-miles of farm animals is the least of it.'

'If there are no hitches then you can marry in four weeks,' Erhard said. 'Marrying in Alp de Montez is the wisest course. Can you be ready then?'

'I'll do my best,' Rose said. She hesitated, and then she stooped and kissed the old man gently on the forehead. 'You take care of yourself. Please. For me.'

And she left without another word.

Nick watched as she wove through the tables, smiling as a waiter paused to let her pass, smiling at the doorman as he opened the door for her, smiling as she went out into the night.

'She's some lady,' Erhard said gently, and Nick came back to earth with a jolt.

'Sorry. I was just thinking.'

'She's worth thinking about.'

'I don't...'

'No, you don't, do you?' Erhard said. 'I've had you thoroughly checked. The longest you've ever dated one woman is nine weeks.'

That took him aback. 'You know that?'

'The investigative agency I hired is very thorough.'

'So you know all about me.'

'It wouldn't have been worth my while to approach you if I'd found you were another Jacques. But the reputation you have in legal circles is for integrity. You try to select cases where there's moral imperative, as well as financial. Also, the woman who fostered you since you were small—Ruby—says that you're honest, kind and trustworthy. As a reference I thought that was the best.'

'How the hell did you get Ruby to talk about me?' he demanded, and Erhard gave a small smile.

'The investigative agency has an operative who enjoys macramé,' he confessed. 'She infiltrated your foster mother's macramé group.' His smile broadened at Nick's astonishment. 'Desperate times call for desperate measures. Ruby seemed to be the best person to give a character reference, but she'd never have answered an official request with such honesty.

'As it was, she told our operative that you went through eight foster homes as your mother agonised whether she could keep you. That you grieved for your mother, even though she was...impossible. That once you joined Ruby and her family of foster sons you were fiercely loyal to every one of the family members. That you learned early to be a loner, but you were generous to a fault. There's an Australian children's home—Castle, at Dolphin Bay?—that you contribute to in any way you can. That if any of your foster brothers are in trouble you're there before they ask.' His smile deepened. 'I read the report and I thought, yes, you'll do.'

'Ruby's macramé group.' He was still feeling winded. Rose was out the door now, and the room was dreary for her going. Well, then. Erhard and his 'operatives' had to be good for something. 'Rose?' he queried. 'What did you find out about Rose?'

'I've told you most of it.'

'Tell me again,' he growled. He hadn't listened properly the first time. He hadn't been as interested as he was now.

'She's had it hard too,' Erhard said gently, with only a faint smile to tell he'd guessed at Nick's reactions. 'Maybe almost as hard as you. Her mother had rheumatoid arthritis and couldn't work, and after she left the palace Eric simply ignored both of them. Rose worked her way through vet school. She met and married a fellow student—Max McCray. Max was an older student—he'd missed schooling because of time spent recovering from cancer. Max was the only son of a veterinarian in the Yorkshire Dales. Rose was embraced into Max's family, and when Rose and Max graduated they took over the family veterinary practice. Then the disease recurred. Rose cared for Max devotedly—as well as running the vet practice—until Max's death two years ago. She's running it still.'

'But she's agreed to leave.'

'You know, I suspect there's almost an element of relief,' Erhard said honestly. 'The village she's been living in is tiny, and she's very much Max's widow. Everywhere we asked we were told how wonderful Rose is, and how noble it is of her to carry on her husband's work. There's a large veterinary conglomerate based in a nearby town that would buy them out in a flash, but her parents-in-law won't hear of it. So she's stuck dealing with lots of farm work—horses and cattle—which her father-in-law and husband loved, but it's hard physical work for one so slight. There's also been a huge money problem. Max's illness put her in debt, and she'd borrowed to put herself through vet school. Max had no family money.'

'You know…' He hesitated. 'This isn't a standard private-investigative report, but the firm I use is good—very good. Their brief is to compile character assessments of people in line for top jobs, so they give more than facts. Our investigator talked to one of the nurses who cared for Rose's husband. The nurse's assessment is that Rose is stuck in her husband's life.'

'But she *is* leaving.'

'We've given her a huge moral imperative to leave,' Erhard said. 'A whole country depending on her instead of just a village. She can walk away without Max's ghost dragging her back.'

'So you're expecting me to walk away from my profession like you're expecting Rose to?'

'No one's expecting anything of you,' Erhard said patiently. 'Apart from a few weeks of your time and a name on a marriage document. There's no need for you to stay in Alp de Montez. There's no need for your life to change very much at all. Simply take a few weeks off work, marry Rose, wait until the fuss about the succession has died down and then take over your life again. Yes, you'll be part of the royal couple, but apart from the coronation itself—and the wedding—your attendance is optional. Your interest is optional, and when Rose's position is established you can divorce. Rose seems willing to put in the hard yards.'

'You said she's working too hard as it is,' Nick said, frowning.

'I'll take care of her,' Erhard said. 'She won't be delivering calves in icy paddocks at midnight.'

'That's what she's doing now?'

'That's what she's doing. Living with her parents-in-law. Stuck in the grief of her husband's loss.'

There were so many facets of the woman, he thought. A cheeky imp. A beautiful, sophisticated woman. A magical dancer. A workhorse.

'I guess I can,' he said, and Erhard smiled.

'There are worse women to marry than Rose,' he said.

It seemed the thing was decided. By the time he turned up at work the next morning, Erhard had already initiated the first steps towards the royal wedding. Nick took a deep breath and quietly talked to the firm's senior partners. To his relief, the partners saw nothing but benefit. Even Blake, Nick's foster brother who also worked for the firm, was enthusiastic.

When Nick told him, Blake stared at his foster brother in amazement, and then quietly gone away and done the same research Nick had. Even to Blake the plan looked solid. 'It's your birthright, after all, and you'd be crazy not to,' Blake told him. 'There's enough stability in the country for your marriage to be received with relief. You get in there and support Rose-Anitra for all you're worth.'

'But marriage…' he said to Blake, and Blake grinned.

'Yeah, well, maybe this is the only sort of marriage that can work for the likes of us,' he'd said. 'It's not like you want a real marriage. Why not in name only?'

Why not? *Because it wasn't quite true.*

Marriage, for Nick, had always seemed something others did. From the time he first remembered, it had been as if he was on the outside looking in. Happy families? How did you go about achieving that? He had six foster brothers and they'd all come from disasters—partnerships that had imploded. Even Ruby, his beloved foster mother, had suffered tragedy.

He'd dated many women—of course he had—but the step toward commitment had always seemed insurmountable. But this…

'You're only committing for a month, right?' Blake asked.

'The general idea is that we stay married for as long as we need to. Minimum a month. Once Rose is firmly entrenched, there's no need for me to stay.'

'But the thought of helping get the country on its feet again turns you on?'

'It does, yeah,' he admitted.

'And the thought of being married to Rose?'

He grinned and didn't answer. But the bubble of excitement was becoming a tidal wave. This was a challenge. It was potentially beneficial for a whole country. And he'd be marrying Rose. If it worked out…

See, *there* was the scary bit. For some dumb reason, that was the thing that gave him pause. The way he felt about her.

She was gorgeous. Her smile made him gasp. She felt…

She didn't feel anything. What had she said? 'The last thing I want is more attachments. I've done family for life. I am free'.

That should make him feel better about the whole deal. Instead, it only made him feel more uncertain.

The thought of taking on a country's direction didn't worry him. The thought of marrying Rose did. Or, it didn't worry him as much as unsettle him. It made him feel like he was teetering on the edge of something he didn't understand.

But Blake didn't see that. No one did. He himself decided it was dumb, and as a week passed without seeing Rose he thought, okay, he was being a romantic fool. This was hardly a romantic wedding. It seemed more like a military operation, and he had to treat it as such.

Erhard was on the phone constantly, organising every tiny detail—when they'd arrive, when the wedding would take place, accommodation, transport, meetings with the council to take place as soon as the wedding was over, the ascendancy claim. The legal documents Erhard faxed for signature made even Nick's eyes water.

What was Rose thinking? But he couldn't know.

'I have a mountain of organisation to get through before I leave,' she'd told him in their one brief phone-call. 'I'm dealing with mass hysteria here. You sort the legal stuff. I know it's dumb, but I'll sign whatever needs to be signed. I have to trust you on this, Nick. You and Erhard.'

A later phone call elicited a bit more background. Instead of Rose, his call was answered by her mother-in-law.

'You have no right to do this,' the woman hissed down the phone. 'The whole town depends on her. She's saying the district will have to join the vet co-operative in the next town. She says with the money they pay we'll be well off, but we don't want money. My poor son would turn in his grave. How dare that man tell her she has no choice? How dare…?'

She became almost venomous, and in the end Nick had put down the phone, and thought he could understand another of Rose's conditions. She didn't want any press release until she was out of the country.

Erhard agreed with that reluctantly, but Nick thought that was fine. The juggernaut that was royal ascension rolled on.

Then, in the last few days before he and Rose were due to fly out, Nick's contact with Erhard had faltered. There was one stilted phone-call. 'Nikolai, things are in place for you to take over. I need to fade into the background. Good luck to you and to Rose.'

He didn't explain, but by the sound of his voice Nick thought that his health was probably a factor. Erhard had launched them, and was depending on them to take it from here.

Good luck to you and to Rose.

That caused another of those moments when panic seemed

to overwhelm him. But there was no reason for panic. No logical reason.

A royal marriage of convenience. Why not?

So he went on planning for this strange wedding, and the world didn't crash on his head.

But on that last day, when he walked out of his office before taking a month off, and he found the whole of the office decorated with bridal nonsense, he was forced to see this for the reality it was. It was Saturday. The office should have been deserted, but people had obviously come in especially. Obviously Blake and the partners had decided that today they'd break their silence. Champagne was flowing. The girls from the typing pool were handing round wedding-cake. Blake had found a picture of Rose in a local newspaper's weddings column, detailing Rose's wedding to Max years ago. Someone had blown her image up to banner size. Posters of a grainy, bridal Rose were plastered from one end of the office to another.

'She's gorgeous,' everyone agreed, and even Rose, laughing down from every wall, seemed to concur.

Rose's image unsettled him as nothing else could. This was a Rose without the care lines around her eyes. Rose before… life?

It felt weird that he could think of marrying this woman, he decided, trying to smile as he accepted congratulations. It even seemed dangerous. But he'd gone too far to back out now, and finally he escaped, under a shower of confetti and good-natured banter.

'There goes the groom to collect his bride. Or the prince to collect his princess,' they called after him, and he had to smile and concur.

'You'll be the second of Ruby's foster sons to get leg-shackled,' Blake said as he walked with his foster brother to the firm's car-park. He and Blake had gone through a lot together. They'd come from similar dysfunctional backgrounds, ending up under Ruby's care. They'd both been ambitious, and they'd made it through law school together. Nick had started work with this firm first, and Blake had followed the year after. They were about as close as brothers could be, which gave Blake the right to say what he liked. Which he intended to do right now.

'You're not looking happy,' he said thoughtfully. 'Bridal jitters getting to you?'

'You know this isn't a real wedding,' Nick growled, unnerved, but Blake smiled and shrugged.

'You make the vows. It's all the wedding the likes of us can do. What have you told Ruby?'

'That I've agreed to be married for a month in order for Rose to ascend the throne. That it's business only. That she needn't worry about anything, and I'll come over and pay her a visit when it's all over.

'And she said?' Blake said cautiously.

'She…um…sounded a little irate. I thought she might have phoned you.'

'When did you tell her?'

'This morning.'

'You have to be kidding.' He and Blake were pushing their way through a crowd of photographers on the pavement. The press had arrived seemingly out of nowhere. Someone must have told them what was happening, and they were now documenting every step. 'She'll probably have tried to phone me twenty times already.'

'Just assure her it's business,' Nick said. 'She shouldn't worry about it. It's nothing.'

'Nothing.' Blake stopped dead, his face a picture of incredulity. 'You want me to explain to Ruby you're marrying a princess but it's *nothing*? I'd be lucky to get off with burst eardrums.'

'Then don't. Ruby's agreed to do some babysitting for Pierce and his brood for a couple of weeks, so she won't have time to think about it.'

'They do have news services in Dolphin Bay,' Blake said with asperity. 'Australia's not so far away as you'd think when it comes to royal weddings. I seem to remember they even have newspapers. You're inviting guests to this wedding?'

'Only dignitaries. You can tell Ruby that.' He gave a rueful grin. 'I tried, but she wouldn't stop yelling.'

'You're seriously getting married without involving family?'

'I don't do family. You know that.'

'Yeah, but does Ruby? She'll be over here like a flash, taking Rose into the bosom of our peculiar family, finding out her sweater size, making a macramé spread for the marital bed, maybe even starting on a few booties.'

'See, that's what we don't want,' Nick said bluntly. 'If I let Ruby near Rose, Rose would run like a scalded cat. This is business.'

'A marriage made in heaven,' Blake said wryly.

'It's the only sort Rose will consider,' Nick told him, and didn't notice when Blake gave him an odd look. They'd reached his car now. The photographers were still at it. Somehow they had to be ignored.

Problems needed to be ignored. Meanwhile he gripped his brother's hand in a gesture of farewell. 'Thanks, mate,' he told him. 'Keep my place here warm for me.'

'You might not still want it,' Blake said, still looking at him strangely.

'Of course I will. This marriage is for a matter of weeks. That's all it's for. I'll be back.'

'Yeah,' Blake said and shook his hand back. 'Right. Just you be careful boyo, of marital threads as well as political ones.'

So what was the problem? Why did Blake sound dubious?

And where had those photographers come from? Surely they wouldn't spread this news as far as Ruby in Dolphin Bay?

Maybe he should have given Ruby a few more details. Maybe even invited her to the wedding.

But Ruby at his wedding? She'd sob, he thought. She'd hug them both. She'd make it incredibly, intensely personal.

Which would scare Rose.

And him.

In the comparative privacy of his BMW, heading for his Kensington apartment to collect his baggage, Nick had time to think, and the more he thought the more he felt like he was heading into trouble. To hurt Ruby by not inviting her…

He couldn't invite her. And he'd specified it was just business.

But it had his foot easing from the accelerator, thinking maybe even now it wasn't too late to draw back.

His mobile phone rang. It answered automatically on the hands-free base. If it hadn't, maybe he wouldn't have answered. His need for solitude to get his head right was starting to be overwhelming. But the voice came on the other end of the line before he could prevent the connection. 'Nick?'

'Rose.' She sounded as spooked as he was. 'It's good to hear from you,' he managed.

'There are photographers here,' she said. 'Everywhere. They arrived an hour ago and there's more arriving by the minute. My mother-in-law's weeping so hard she's making herself ill. The phone's ringing off the hook. I think…is this a disaster?'

So he wasn't alone in feeling overwhelmed. 'I guess it's what we had to expect,' he said cautiously, insensibly reassured that she was feeling the same as he was.

'I hadn't thought…'

'Neither had I.'

'It's not too late to back out,' she whispered.

'Do you want to back out?'

'I don't know,' she said. 'It seemed so easy when it was just fantasy. But now…'

'What would you do if you backed out?' he asked.

There was a long silence. 'Stay here, I guess,' she said, sounding unsure.

'You don't want to stay there?'

'No.' That was unequivocal, at any rate. Then, 'We did decide to do this for the right reasons, didn't we, Nick?'

He had to be honest here. 'Yes.'

'It will make life better for the people of Alp de Montez?'

'I think so,' he said reluctantly. 'My law firm is heavily geared to international disputes. We have people on the ground all over the world. The consensus is that we really can make a difference.'

'We don't have a choice then,' she said heavily.

'There is a choice, Rose,' he said. He'd pulled up at traffic lights. They'd turned green, but he wasn't shifting. There were horns blaring behind him but he thought, no, he had to concentrate. 'You can walk away.'

'I can't walk away,' she said. 'Unless I have an alternative.'

'You can stay where you are.'

'That's what I meant,' she whispered. 'Alp de Montez is my alternative.'

He didn't understand. 'Look, we can call the whole thing off.'

'Do you want to?'

'Hold on a minute,' he told her, and moved forward before the motorists banked up behind him got out of their cars and thumped him. He steered into a bus stop and stopped. 'Rose, this is up to you,' he said gently. 'You're the one first in line. I'm the supporting role here.'

'I guess.' She took a ragged breath. 'But you will support me?'

Five minutes ago he'd been thinking he couldn't. But now… It was only for a month or so, and it would make a difference. Rose was taking this on for much, much longer.

If she was prepared to do it, how could he say no?

'Of course I'll support you,' he said gently. 'We're in this together.'

'For a month.'

'And then I'll be on the end of the phone. I won't leave you isolated. We'll set up supports.'

'But you'll stay involved?'

He took a deep breath. 'Yes.' Where had that come from? The Nikolai de Montez mantra was 'never get involved'. But this was different. This was for a country.

This was for Rose.

'Yes,' he said again. 'I'll stay as involved as you want.'

'Then I guess I can cope with the press,' she said, still sounding shaky. 'The plane's due to pick me up in Newcastle at two. You swear you'll be on it?'

What was a man to say to that? Despite misgivings. Despite Ruby.

'Yes,' he said, and he was committed.

CHAPTER FOUR

THE plane was fitted out like something out of a James Bond movie. Nikolai was accustomed to first-class international travel, but this was mind boggling.

He couldn't cut and run now, leaving Rose to face the consequences, but he felt like it. He buckled his seat belt with grim resolution. *Let's get this over with.*

For the first part of the flight he was alone, apart from a dark-suited, elderly attendant who spoke in monosyllables. Somewhere up front there'd be a flight crew, but he never saw them. Erhard had made the arrangements. He just had to trust Erhard. Only, why hadn't Erhard answered his calls for the last few days? How sick was he?

What was Nick walking into?

Rose was due to catch the flight in Newcastle. He'd committed. To marriage.

Yes, to marriage, and it seemed weird. He sank into the luxurious upholstery and let his thoughts go where they willed. They asked questions he couldn't answer. Things like, would Rose get cold feet? What if Erhard's illness wasn't the reason for his withdrawal? How alone would they be?

It wasn't an uncivilised country they were going to, he told himself, his unease deepening with every mile they drew further from London. The worst that could happen was that he and Rose were asked to leave. Or refused permission to land.

The plane was in the air. His escape was cut off. Next step Rose.

'Would you like refreshments? A beer?' an expressionless fight attendant—Griswold, according to his name badge—asked him, and Nick shook his head.

'No, thank you.' He didn't need a beer. He needed to keep every faculty crystal-clear.

The attendant, a sober-suited man in his sixties, gave him a searching look. Nick smiled; the man seemed anxious and the last thing Nick wanted to do was make the locals nervous. But Griswold simply bowed briefly and left him alone.

And then they were landing at Newcastle. Griswold appeared again and told him there was no need for him to stir. 'The Princess Rose-Anitra is in the terminal,' he told him. 'It's raining outside. I'd advise you to stay put.'

The Princess Rose-Anitra. The name took him aback.

The Princess Rose-Anitra, boarding the official plane of the royal family of Alp de Montez. To join her future husband.

The fantasy had begun.

And here came the bride. Right—*not*. This wasn't your normal vision of a royal bride. Rose was running across the rain-soaked tarmac. An airport official was holding an umbrella over her head, trying to keep up with her. She was dressed in jeans and an ancient duffel coat. She was carrying a shabby holdall.

She was also carrying a dog. Some sort of terrier.

His feeling of unreality took a step back. Rose grounded this thing in practicality, he thought, and the craziness seemed possible again as he watched her run.

Seemingly ignoring the rain, she smiled at Griswold at the foot of the stairs, and Nick found himself smiling back. This wasn't fantasy. Rose was a country veterinarian with a scruffy looking dog and clothes past their use-by date.

She just looked like…Rose.

She stepped into the cabin, laughing at something Griswold said behind her, speaking in a language Nick recognised.

She saw him and she stopped short. Her smile faded, and she looked suddenly uncertain. Maybe even a little scared.

'Um… Hi,' she said.

'Hi.' As a response to the occasion it lacked a certain sophistication, but for the life of him he couldn't think of a more intelligent response.

'You don't mind sharing a cabin with Hoppy?' she asked.

'Hoppy?'

'Because of the leg,' she said kindly, as if he was a bit thick. She smiled down at the little dog in her arms and then checked out the plane. She seemed almost overwhelmed by its opulence, swallowing a couple of times like she was trying to dredge up courage. But somehow she made her voice light and smiley. 'Wow,' she whispered. 'I've hardly ever flown before. Surely they can't all be like this?'

'No,' Nick said. They certainly weren't. The two double settees that were the airline's only passenger seats were more luxurious than any seat he'd ever been in. They were fitted with seat belts, but that was their only concession to airline strictures. There was white shag-pile carpet. There were tiny side-tables with indents to hold wine glasses—all carved from the one magnificent piece of mahogany. A partition at the rear led to a bedroom—he could see a magnificent bed set up, ready for use. The entire interior was painted white with muted pinks, with soft hangings disguising the harsh outer casing of the airline's metal cabin.

This was definitely not cattle class.

But Rose had moved on, shrugging off her discomfort with her coat. She placed the little dog on the seat beside him. Griswold—who'd spoken hardly at all since Nick had come aboard—took her coat and smiled down at Hoppy.

'Le chien a faim? Peut-être il voudrait un petit morceau de biftek?'

'Hoppy would very much like a *biftek*,' Rose said, and beamed at the man. *'Moi aussi. Oui. Merci beaucoup.'*

'Et pour la madame, du champagne?'

'Ooh, yes. *Oui. Merci, merci, merci.*' She lifted her dog back into her arms, sank down into the seat beside Nick and giggled. 'Isn't this fabulous?'

The dog only had three legs. Hoppy. Yep, he had it. He was right on the ball today. If only she didn't smile so much.

'Do you suppose there'd be caviar if I asked for it?' she said, and he decided to stop the fatuousness and try and be serious.

'I thought the plan was to stop extravagant spending by the royal family.'

'Oh,' she said, and her face fell. 'Does that have to start today? I thought maybe we could have a little bit of fun first.' Her laughter disappeared as if he'd reprimanded her. She sank back into the sumptuous upholstery, clipped her seat belt and hugged her dog.

He felt bad. He hadn't meant to stop her smiling.

She stayed looking defensive. He went on feeling bad. And more.

More? Yes, more. Because suddenly he was hit with this really dumb urge to kiss her better.

Or just to kiss her.

Which was really dumb, he told himself, startled by the intensity of his urge as well as the unexpectedness of it. That would be really stupid.

As was her reaction, he thought, struggling for an even keel. She was acting like he'd slapped her. He was starting to feel like he was always apologising to this woman. She made him feel he was permanently on the back foot.

But if he was going to apologise he might as well get it over with.

'Maybe I was out of order,' he conceded. 'I'm sorry.'

'There's a concession,' she said. 'But of course you're right. This is a serious business. A marriage of convenience. There's not a lot to smile about in that.'

They didn't speak again as the plane took off. The two settees-cum-airline-seats were forward facing, set in a V, so up to four occupants could talk together. There was a silk-hung divider in front which hid the service compartment and the entrance to the cockpit, but they were essentially alone.

They were sitting side by side, and he felt…weird. She was very close.

But not for long. The plane rose smoothly and the seat-belt sign clicked off. The moment it did Rose gathered Hoppy, unclipped her seat belt and moved herself sharply across the aisle to the other double seat. To the furthest side of the far seat.

It was like she'd slapped him. Even Hoppy was looking balefully across at him, like he'd offended the dog too.

'I have offended you,' he said, frowning, and she shook her head.

'No. I just decided you're right. It's formal, the stuff we'll be doing, so I may as well start being formal now.'

'You could have caviar if you want. If it's aboard.'

'I don't really want it.'

'But you asked…'

'I just thought maybe it'd be fun to play the princess a little,' she said, and then looked ruefully down at her faded jeans and her three-legged dog. 'But I'm not princess material. I never have been.'

'Cinderella before the godmother?'

'Yeah, well, the godmother's the money thing,' she said. 'Bane of my life.' Griswold came through, bearing a tray carrying one crystal flute, the champagne bubbling deliciously. She looked at the champagne with regret.

'Do you think I should ask for it to be put back in the bottle?'

'I don't think it can be,' he said weakly. Hell, how to make a man feel bad…

'You mean I just have to drink it?' She cheered up. 'To save its life? Hooray.' Griswold smiled as she buried her nose in bubbles. 'Are you having one?'

'I'll have a glass of wine with my meal.'

She raised her eyebrows. 'And more than one never touches your lips?'

'I believe it'd be good if at least one of us kept our wits about us.' *Um…* He hadn't meant to say that. It was just that she made him feel *old*. No. Defensive, he decided, but he didn't know why.

And she seemed to agree with him.

'Of course,' she said, and raised her glass in his direction. 'How very wise. You stay on watch. You keep all your wits while I stick my nose into champagne.'

Why had he said that?

He sounded about a hundred. Talk about a killjoy…

He thought of what Erhard had told him about this woman. She'd had it tough for the past few years. No wonder she'd been talked into accepting her heritage. No wonder she wanted to escape to a little fantasy.

He glanced across to the other seat. In between sipping champagne she was hugging her little dog to her like a shield. She looked about ten years old.

'I'm really sorry I was mean,' he said, and she flashed him a suspicious look.

'Lawyers don't apologise. If you acknowledge fault, then I get to sue.'

So maybe she wasn't ten years old.

'Tell me about your dog.'

'He's Hoppy.'

'We've done that. I was hoping for a little more information.'

She looked at him suspiciously over the rim of her champagne glass.

'Hoppy's two years old,' she said at last. 'He got squashed by a tractor when he was five weeks old. I was helping deliver a foal, and the farmer was driving his tractor through the yard. Mud everywhere. This little one darted out to meet me, and went straight under the tractor wheel. When the tractor moved on we couldn't see a sign of him. Then thirty seconds later I found him buried completely in mud. One leg was broken so badly it had to come off, but otherwise he was perfect. He even wiggled his tail when I patted him, smashed leg and all.'

'So you bought him?'

'I was given him. The farmer's reaction to the accident was that it was a shame he hadn't been killed outright. Hoppy's so small he's useless for ratting. That's why he'd been bred. So I have my semi-useless, non-ratting Hoppy, and I love him to bits.'

'And you can take him into Alp de Montez?'

'Sure I can,' she said defensively. 'I'm a princess. Hoppy's out for adventure, and so am I.'

He stared at her for a moment while she finished the last of the champagne. And then stared regretfully into the empty glass. In a flash Griswold was out from behind his screen with a refill. The elderly man was now smiling, Nick saw. He hadn't smiled at him.

'I shouldn't,' Rose was saying.

'I'll be the wit-keeper,' he told her. 'Relax.'

'I'm not too sure I can trust you.'

'Aren't we almost cousins?'

'Cousins, if my mother hadn't played fast and loose. But, even if we were, family doesn't necessarily mean trust. Look at me and my sister.'

'Yeah, I don't understand that. Were you close when you were small?'

'When we were very young, yes. But my father thought Julianna was great, and he used to take her with him when he travelled. He travelled a lot, and I think it used to amuse him, to have such a gorgeous little girl calling him Papa. My mother and I stayed behind. Then we were booted out. I didn't mind,' she said diffidently. 'Much.' Then she shook herself. 'No. That sounds iffy. My mother and I had some really good times after we got out of the royal bit. We stayed with my Aunty Cath in London. The three of us always dreamed of going adventuring together, but Mum had rheumatoid arthritis and Aunty Cath owned six cats. That's a bit of a restriction where adventuring's concerned.'

'When did your mother die?'

'When I was twenty. Two years after Aunty Cath. A year after the last cat.'

'And then you met Max.'

'So I did,' she said diffidently. 'And he was great.'

'But an invalid?'

'Not when I first knew him. We had almost a year when he was in remission—we thought he was cured.'

'Did you marry him because you loved him?' Nick asked before he could help himself. 'Or because you felt sorry for him?'

Somewhat to his surprise, she answered seriously. 'You

know, it was a whole lot of things,' she said. 'Max was twenty-six, and seemed older because he'd been ill. He was so pleased to be well again. It was just lovely—he wanted to try everything, do everything. And his family… We'd hardly even been a family, and after Mama and Aunty Cath there was no one. We went up to Yorkshire the first Christmas after we'd met, and it was such a welcome. The whole town, one big family. It was like coming home again. It was only afterwards that I felt…'

'Felt what?'

'Look, if Max had lived it would have been fine,' she said, sounding defensive again. 'But Max was larger than life. He had to be, he had too much living to do. The village had pooled together to get him the best medical treatment money could buy. As a community it was a huge commitment, and they loved him. When he died, well, there was only me, and they sort of transferred their loving to me.'

'And you're tired of loving?'

'A little bit,' she admitted, and sipped her champagne and smiled ruefully. 'I wouldn't mind a bit of adventuring. Me and Hoppy.'

He smiled back. Her smile was infectious even when it was rueful.

'And you,' she said curiously. 'What about your childhood? Erhard told me you're devoted to your foster mother.'

'Ruby's great.' But his words were curt. He didn't like people enquiring into his background. The knowledge that Ruby's macramé class had been infiltrated gave him an odd feeling. Like he was exposed.

'Hey, if we're going to be married I need to know stuff about you,' she said. 'And you asked first.'

'So what do you need to know? How I like my toast buttered in the morning?'

'Butter your own toast, big boy,' she said, but she chuckled.

'No, but you know the sort of thing. I'd hate to find out that you have a fiancée and twelve kids.'

'No fiancée. No kids,' he said a bit too hastily. 'I'm sure Erhard would have told you if I had. But what about you? Did you and Max want kids?'

Her face closed, just like that.

'No.'

'I'm sorry. I didn't mean to pry.'

'That's three sorries in as many minutes from a lawyer,' she said, awed, and he thought she was changing the subject.

He went along with it though.

'I guess three sorries mean I'm at your mercy.'

'You know, I'm very sure you're not.' She smiled, but absently, and went back to hugging Hoppy. And looking out the window. Conversation over.

He left her to it, if reluctantly, retiring into a pile of documents he needed to study. Even though he was taking a month off there were things he couldn't delegate. And time on planes was work time.

So he studied. Or he tried to study. Rose's nose stayed against the window. It was a very cute nose.

'What are you looking at?' he asked at last, but she didn't look around.

'Mountains.'

'Surely you've seen mountains before?'

'I used to see these peaks from the distance when I was a child.'

'You never went there?'

'Mama was an invalid. And my father…' She shrugged. 'He took Julianna.'

'But you've travelled?' he said, startled, and she shook her head.

'Only when we came to London. My mother was English,

you see, so when my father sent her away she went to Aunty Cath. Then we were a bit stuck. But then, when I was twenty, Aunty Cath had a life-insurance policy—not very much, but enough. She'd stipulated I use it to travel. Mum seemed well, and the cats were all dead.'

Then she grinned. 'Hey, don't look sympathetic yet—we had some truly weird cats, and their collective age when they died was about a thousand. Anyway, Mum only had herself to look after and she was enthusiastic that I go. I had ten weeks' university holiday. Every holiday since I was fifteen I'd worked, trying to help. But this time it all seemed to fit. So I took a deep breath and flew to Australia, intending to backpack along the east coast. But the airline contacted me before I even reached Sydney. My mother had had a heart attack. Apparently she'd been having chest pain and hadn't told me. She'd seen specialists and still hadn't told me. She was dead before I got home. I used the last of Aunty Cath's nest egg to bury her and went back to university.'

He felt his own chest tighten. 'Didn't your father help?'

'You're kidding?' she said harshly. 'Of course not. He and Julianna stayed far away. Anyway…' She took a deep breath and moved on. 'How about you? How did you get to be an international lawyer?'

'Hard work.'

'If there was no money, you must have wanted it a lot.'

'I did.'

'Why?'

'I'm not sure,' he said, hesitating. She had him off balance. He'd not been questioned in such a personal way since… Well, since Ruby had sat him down after his secondary school results had come in, looked him straight in the eye and said, 'Tell me you don't want to be a lawyer because of the money?'

Was Rose asking the same question? Maybe she was.

'I don't really know,' he said, with the same reluctance he'd shown when Ruby had asked. But he'd been seventeen then. Now he was thirty six, and he'd had time to think his response through. 'I suspect it was a lot to do with my childhood. I felt helpless then—being taken from foster home to foster home. So I wanted security. Yes, I wanted a job where I could be in control. But there was also the issue of who my mother was. I knew about her royal background. It fascinated me. The only thing I had was a knowledge that the royal family of Alp de Montez was somehow my family. International law... Well, my job's helped to answer questions and make me feel as if the world is a smaller place.'

'Good answer,' she said, and she smiled.

'And vet science?'

'I always wanted a dog,' she said. 'And I was really fond of Aunty Cath's cats, even though they were collectively insane. Maybe that's a dumb reason for choosing a career, but there it is. I didn't have any wish to link internationally—even with Alp de Montez.'

'You've kept the language up?'

'I practiced with Italian and French language tapes while I was at university—just for fun, because it seemed a shame to lose it. How about you?'

'My mother must have spoken the language when I was tiny. I hardly know how I got it, but it's there. I learned French and Italian at university as well. I gather the language of the Alp countries is a mishmash of both, so it seems we've both kept a little of our backgrounds.'

'Yeah, we're both royal,' she said absently. 'Um, there's snow on these mountains. And dots. Lots of colourful dots. Ski slopes?'

'These are the best ski-slopes in the world.'

'Do you ski?'

'Yes.'

'On these mountains?'

'Sometimes, yes.' International ski-fields were a good base for meeting the people he needed to know.

'Goodness,' she said faintly.

'Lots of people ski,' he said, knowing he sounded defensive, but not being able to stop himself.

'Not in my world they don't. They trudge round digging out livestock and swearing at the snow in general.'

'You've never skied?'

'I suspect there's a whole lot of stuff I've never done.' She turned to face him. 'Including marrying someone who skies in places like these.' She shook her head and hugged her dog again. 'It's a whole new world.'

'Do you know what you're letting yourself in for?'

'No,' she said honestly. 'I know the people. I know there was lots that I loved. But I don't know the political set-up. Do you?'

'I've researched this well, yes.'

'It's more than I have,' she conceded.

'You just jumped.'

'That's right. Ran, more like.'

'It does sound appealing,' he said. 'Playing princess.'

'I don't expect I shall play princess,' she said absently. 'As you said, it's dumb to eat caviar. I guess if I have authority then I'll start by doing things like selling this ostentatious aeroplane.'

But it seemed she'd said the wrong thing. The screen in front of them was put aside with a decisive click. The man who'd been serving them, Griswold, was staring at them in consternation.

'You must not,' he said in his own language. And he sounded desperate.

Rose frowned, confused by his sudden interjection, slipping effortlessly into the language that matched his. 'We mustn't sell this aeroplane?'

'No. I… Not yet.'

'I guess it's your job,' she said, confused.

'It's not my job,' the elderly man told her. 'Or not very often. I'm sorry. This is none of my business. I shouldn't have said. Your dinner is almost ready.'

'So tell us why we shouldn't sell the plane,' Nick asked, moving easily into the language as well.

'We need you to be the royal couple,' Griswold said simply. 'Nothing else will save the country.' And he flicked back the screen and went back to work.

No more was said until the meal was served—magnificent beef steak, which spoke heaps of Griswold's skill in cooking in confined spaces. No pre-packed airline food this.

There was chocolate mousse to follow, and espresso coffee. Finally as he cleared the coffee cups away Griswold's severe face relaxed a little. But as he reached for Rose's cup she took his wrist and held.

'Tell me what you mean about wanting us to be a royal couple,' she said.

'*Madame*, I can't.'

'You can't do what?'

'I…' He shook his head. 'There's orders.'

'From who?'

'From Monsieur Jacques. The husband of your sister.'

'Orders to do what?'

'To tell you nothing,' he said miserably. 'To let you do this mock-marriage thing.'

'It's not a mock marriage,' Rose said, frowning more. 'It's a real one.'

'It's not,' Griswold said simply. 'I've been overhearing.

What Julianna and Jacques have been telling the people is right. That this is a marriage of convenience.'

'It's still a marriage.'

'Yes, but there's more,' he said unhappily. 'Reports are that this marriage is a sham, and so is any goodwill you might have towards our people. You're outsiders. You'll sign the right papers and then disappear again. No wrongs will be righted. Taxes will continue to be bled from the people and sent overseas. Our country will be worse off.'

'That's not why we're here,' Nick said, frowning as much as Rose was. 'Erhard Fritz—'

'Erhard Fritz is being discredited by the government-controlled press,' Griswold said. 'There's been a smear campaign. The press is portraying you both as upstart outsiders. You, *monsieur*, with vaguely sinister intentions and you, *madame*, as a greedy widow.'

'Why are you telling us this?' Rose said slowly, her eyes not leaving Griswold's face.

'Maybe…because of the dog?' he said unhappily. 'I know that sounds nonsense, but my daughter has a dog such as this one. I listened to you telling *monsieur* how you took in the dog, and I thought this can't be a woman such as the press describes. I remembered the stories of you as a child. The press was fairer then, not controlled by the Council. You were always described as a tomboy, more interested in animals than in learning society manners. Then the way you both gave thanks. Little things, but…I heard you talking about a marriage of convenience, and I thought "it doesn't fit".'

'It's a way of repairing the damage,' Nick said. 'We can set in place reforms.'

'Not if the people rise up against you,' Griswold said. 'Which they will if they think you're here for your own gain.

If you sell this plane straight away, they'll think it's a first act to siphon money. Things have been said, dreadful things.'

'I've heard nothing of this,' Nick snapped.

'Jacques and his friends are too clever to use the main newsprints to spread the worst of the rumours,' the man said unhappily. 'But rumours have been sweeping the country nevertheless. And people like Erhard, people of sense, have been effectively silenced.'

'There's not a lot we can do about it,' Rose said doubtfully. 'We were told it would be simple.'

'You need to get the people on side,' Griswold said. 'People like me. Working people. All of us. I do have some English. All the time I've been cooking, I've been listening to you. You both can speak our language. That's wonderful. *Madame*, the people were fond of you once, as a child. They'll remember that. You have the little dog. As you walk out of this plane, you need to look happy to be in the country. Happy to be home. You need to speak to as many people as possible. Ordinary people. You need to see and be seen. And you need to hold hands all the time. Speak to each other as a married couple. Don't appear to have heard a single thing that I've just told you. And…'

'And?'

'And let the people know that you mean well. And that you're not trying to deceive them. Let them know that you're about to enter into a marriage.'

CHAPTER FIVE

THEY landed soon after, questions unresolved. 'I think that my wife's cousin will be driving the royal car,' Griswold told them as the plane came to a standstill. 'He will wish you well. As I do.' But his contact with them was over. He stayed aboard, unhappily disappearing into the background as they emerged onto Alp de Montez soil.

They weren't sure what to expect when they arrived. After Erhard's silence, Nick had been contacted by someone calling himself the palace Chief of Staff, telling them he was taking care of the arrangements for their arrival. 'There'll be some form of official reception,' he'd told them, and when they stepped off the jet that was exactly what happened.

There were a couple of dozen military officers standing to stiff attention, and a middle-aged man in hugely decorated dress-regalia stepped forward to greet them.

'Good afternoon,' the man said in stiff English. 'Welcome to Alp de Montez, Your Royal Highnesses. Do you wish to inspect the guard now?'

'No,' Nick said before Rose could open her mouth. Then he looked at Rose. 'We don't want to inspect the guard, do we, sweetheart?'

Sweetheart?

Rose blinked. And then she got the message. What Griswold had said on the plane was that these people were expecting a marriage of convenience, a marriage designed to fleece the country. Somehow they had to change that image.

She swallowed, then grabbed Nick's hand and held tightly. 'We might,' she said. Then, 'I can't tell you how pleased we are to be here,' she said, in a voice that carried across the tarmac to the assembled troops, speaking in the Italian-French mix that was the country's own dialect. 'I loved this country as a child,' she said. 'I needed to leave with my mother when I was fifteen—you know my parents were separated?—and Nick was orphaned early. That's left us ignorant of what we should know of our heritage. So you'll need to excuse us as we find our feet. You'll have to teach us, but we're here to learn.'

Then she smiled sweetly at the greeting official, who was looking stunned, and just a little bit horrified. 'Thank you so much for meeting us,' she said, and before he knew what she was about she'd handed Hoppy over to him, then kissed the astounded man on both cheeks. 'I was sure we'd be welcome,' she said. 'You're truly kind.'

Then, before the official could say a word, while Nick stood on the tarmac with the warm evening breeze adding to his sense of unreality—even though it was late spring it had been freezing back at Heathrow—Rose grabbed his hand and towed him over to the assembled troops. She smiled at the first soldier and asked his name. Before Nick knew it, they were working their way down the line, greeting every soldier individually, taking their hands and shaking them. Forcing them to lower their guns as they did. And Rose was giving each of them her very nicest smile.

By the time they'd finished Nick was feeling gobsmacked. Maybe they all were. The line didn't look nearly as formal, and the stiff, unsmiling faces were, well, trying not to smile, but smiling for all that.

'So who do we meet next?' she asked, still beaming, returning to the official and Hoppy. She took Hoppy back from the stunned officer, thanking him with a smile.

'Your limousine's waiting to take you to the palace,' the man said stiffly.

'I don't know your name,' Rose said.

'I'm Chief of Staff,' the man said.

'But a name?' Rose said gently, smiling some more, and the man stared at her like she was speaking gobbledegook. 'I'm Rose,' she said, giving him an easy example. 'This is Nick.'

'Sir. Madam.'

'Yes, but we have names too,' she said, fixing him with a smile that took Nick aback even further. This wasn't some wilting violet. This was a woman determined to make her point. A woman starting her adventuring.

'Jean Dupeaux,' the man muttered, and she smiled some more.

'It's lovely to meet you, Jean. If you're our Chief of Staff, then I guess we'll see lots of you. This is my dog, Hoppy. Are you coming with us in the limousine?'

'I… No.'

'That's a shame,' she said brightly. 'I guess we'll see you at the palace, then. Does the driver know where to go?'

'Of course.' He seemed offended.

'I'm so sorry. Of course he does. You'll have to forgive us a lot as we learn our way round,' she told him. 'I have so much to remember. But don't worry. We're here for the long haul, and we'll get it right in the end.'

They didn't speak for the first couple of minutes in the limousine. It was as if both needed to catch their breath. Certainly Nick did. What had just happened seemed extraordinary. A salute of arms to start with, and then Rose's performance.

'Griswold was right,' she said at last, staring out the window at the passing scenery. They were less than a mile from the airport, travelling towards the nearby city, but the towering, snow-capped mountains were breathtaking. In the fields beside the road the farmers were gathering in the hay, forming bales in the way farmers had done for a thousand years.

'It seems we've been made enemies before we even arrived,' she said slowly. 'How did that happen?'

'Maybe we should have expected it,' he said.

What else should they have expected? The looks they'd been given by the troops before Rose's impromptu greeting session had been aloof and disdainful. This was a tiny segment of the army, and the army must be powerful. Where did the army come into this?

Rose was looking as thoughtful as he was. And there was a trace of fear behind her eyes.

Hoppy was on her knee. He wriggled off, crossed the gap in the seat between them and put a paw tentatively on Nick's knee.

'He thinks you need a hug,' Rose said.

'I don't need a hug,' he said, stunned.

'I might,' she said diffidently.

'I'm not sure that's wise.'

'Right,' she said, and lifted Hoppy back into her arms and hugged him. 'Sorry.'

Why couldn't he have hugged her? Why did she have him so off-balance? They were in trouble together. It made sense to be able to give each other comfort.

But if he hugged her now…

Don't go there.

'We need to do some fast footwork,' he said, trying desperately to move forward. Past the emotional. 'Rose, we know nothing. Where the hell is Erhard?'

'I was sure he'd meet us,' she said.

His legal mind was trying to sort things. Things other than how close Rose was sitting to him. Important stuff.

Only he was having a huge amount of trouble persuading his mind to think past her. She was messing with his equilibrium in a way he didn't understand.

Think. Think!

Back in London this succession had seemed reasonable—even sensible. Now it seemed fraught. Two people in a strange land, threatening those in power.

'Maybe we need to bail out for a bit and rethink,' he said dubiously. 'Damn, I didn't foresee this. I had my people—'

'My people?'

'My colleagues. I'm not an international lawyer for nothing. They checked this place. There's never been armed insurrection in any of the Alp countries. There didn't seem a threat. But now…'

'I'm not going home,' Rose said.

'We might have to.'

'I'm not going home,' she said again, and hugged Hoppy tighter. Hoppy gave a doleful canine sigh—he was obviously accustomed to being an emotional squeeze-bag. 'I might be persuaded to treat Hawaiian animals, or something similar, but no more in Yorkshire.'

'What's wrong with Yorkshire?'

'Too much family,' she muttered. 'Alright if you want a career as a battery hen. And, by the way, that includes you,' she said, glaring as he gazed at her in astonishment. 'I don't think I said, but you try and protect me and I refuse to be responsible for my actions. No matter that we're getting married—name only. No family. No ties. And I want to get this place sorted. Right. What's next?' And she looked so fierce that he held up his hands in mock surrender.

What a statement! His desire to hug her should have stopped right there. Only for some dumb reason it intensified. He had to fight to make himself agree.

'Sure,' he managed. 'That's how I feel too.' Or was it?

'Just so you know,' she said, still glowering. 'But, even if I didn't feel like that, I still wouldn't run. Yes, I got concerned when I didn't hear from Erhard this week, and I was spooked when the press arrived, but I've cut my ties now and I'm over it. So move on. We'll get some plans in place and do what Erhard wanted. Now.'

She looked so fierce that he smiled. But he was thinking hard. What lay ahead seemed much more of a challenge than it had seemed back home, but maybe he, like Rose, was glad to move on. For different reasons. She was leaving family. He was leaving a vacuum.

No. Just boredom. He wanted a challenge.

And it didn't hurt that he'd face this challenge with Rose beside him. He just had to resist the desire to…hug.

No. What he really wanted to do was kiss her until her toes curled. Or his toes curled.

What he really needed, on the other hand, was a cold shower. If he did anything so dumb she'd slug him into the middle of next week.

'We need to get meetings in place straight away,' he said slowly, managing to think a bit further. 'We'll get the armed-forces chiefs to the palace. Let them know what we intend. Figure out where they stand. We need to speak to each individual councillor.'

'So you will stay?' she said, and he glanced at her in surprise.

'For as long as it takes, Rose, yes. I promised, and I'll keep my word.'

'It's only…I'm aware that it's me who's supposed to be sovereign,' she muttered. 'But I don't have the skills.'

'I suspect neither of us have the skills. But no one else does either, so it's fight through it or run. You've said you won't run, and neither will I.'

'Thank you.'

He smiled. 'You know, from all accounts, prince consorts never had such a bad time of it in the past,' he said. 'All that wheeling and dealing behind closed doors. I'll be the one who'll tell you whose head to chop off, you do the dirty work, and then you get the flack and not me.'

'Oh, great.'

'I'm truly noble,' he said, and he managed to grin.

She tried not to smile. She failed.

She looked enchanting, he thought. The more he looked at her the more enchanted he became. She was still huddled in her oversized duffel coat—not because she needed its warmth, he suspected, but because she found the familiar smell of it comforting. Hoppy certainly did. The little dog was huddling against her, under her coat, only his nose exposed in quivering anxiety.

Me and my dog against the world.

'I don't think this'll work if you're prince consort,' she said softly.

He thought about it for a moment. 'That's what the whole idea is.'

'No, it's not. I don't think we should be crown and deputy.'

'I'm sorry, but—'

'Hey, you know I'm really not royal,' she said, interrupting him. 'My mother was married and then left to fend for herself. My father married her on a whim, tired of her within a year and then, as far as I can tell, never touched her again. He went from scandal to scandal, while my mother stayed in the castle and cared for the old Prince. There were visitors, and I was born with red hair, and I'll not be judging her for it. She must have been unbearably lonely.' She touched her flaming head and grinned. 'So there you are. I was born royal but I'm not really royal, whereas you… Your mother really was a princess.'

'Yes, but…' He was getting distracted. By her hair.

'But what?'

'It's the way it has to work,' he said with difficulty. 'It's you who's in line for the throne.'

'But you want it,' she said thoughtfully. 'You're aching to get in there and do stuff. You can't do that if you're not a full partner.'

'I don't think you can devolve authority until you have it,' he said, striving to keep it light.

'I guess not,' she whispered, and then her voice firmed a little. 'I guess I have to take it on. I can cope. I have before.' He watched her face became more resolute.

David aiming his slingshot?

They were reaching the outskirts of the city now. It was Saturday at twilight, the light just starting to fade.

'Where does everyone here go on a Saturday night?' she asked suddenly, and then as Nick looked blank she reached forward and slid back the glass partitioning them from the driver.

'If you and your family were wanting a fun night out tonight,' she said to the driver, 'Where would you go?'

'Madame?' the driver said, confused, and she repeated her question.

'What's a good local drinking place in the heart of the city?' she said. 'Maybe with a band playing. Is there somewhere like that?'

'The army officers use Maison d'Etre.'

'No, not the army,' she said, while Nick stayed as confused

as the driver. 'You. Or the farmers we just saw. Where do most people go?'

'I live just two miles from here,' the man said dubiously. 'It's Saturday night. It's harvest time and the weather's good. The time-honoured local tradition at this time of year is to gather down at the river bank not far from here, or at other picnic spots round the country.' He hesitated. 'There's not the money for families to go to pubs any more. Taxes are terrible. The army and the politicians use the restaurants and pubs, but most of them, well, they've closed for lack of patronage.'

'And down at the river?'

'That's where we go,' he said simply. 'Each district has its own meeting place. We go there or we stay home.'

'But the young ones, they go to the pictures and things?'

'If you're in a well-paid job. But there are few well-paid jobs.'

'So if we wanted to meet the people…'

'Maybe you could go on the television,' he said doubtfully.

'We don't want to do that,' Rose said. 'Not yet.' She visibly swallowed a gulp. 'I don't think I'd be very good at television.'

'So what are you thinking?' Nick said uneasily, watching the set of her face. This was a woman who, having decided to do something, went for it. Even facing television.

'I'm not going back to Yorkshire,' she said. 'Not for a lack of gumption on my part.'

'No one's making you.'

'Yes, but the main reason I can come here is that I have an imperative,' she said. 'I have an imperative here, but I also have an imperative back in Yorkshire. I haven't told you what that imperative is, but believe me facing a firing squad at dawn looks pretty good in comparison. No. We get proactive. Did you have to wear a suit?'

'Did you have to wear a duffel coat?'

'A duffel coat's more appropriate than what you're wearing,' she retorted. 'Lose the tie. Do you have a jacket in your baggage?'

'I'm not sure where our baggage is.'

'It's being brought separately,' the driver said, bemused, watching them through the rear-view mirror.

'If we wanted to go to your picnic…' Rose said slowly, looking ahead and behind at their convoy. There were twelve uniformed army-officers in front of them on motor bikes. There were twelve behind. 'Do you suppose they'd arrest us if we stopped down at the river?'

'Madame, we can't stop.'

'Yes, we can,' she said.

'My orders are to take you straight to the palace.'

'And whose orders are those?' she asked, and all of a sudden she was haughty. The driver stared at her in astonishment—and so did Nick. Then the eyes of the two men met. A small moment of male empathy. Two male shrugs, and the driver gave a small smile.

'You want to go to our picnic?'

'We need to meet the people,' she said. 'This is the fastest way to do that, right?'

'I guess.'

'Then our escort can come too. But we don't have food for a picnic. I won't be a freeloader.'

'The people will share.'

'I'm not going to my first picnic in Alp de Montez as a freeloader,' Rose said. 'My fiancé agrees with me.'

'Do I?' said Nick.

'Of course you do—darling,' she said. 'Now, what can we do?'

'If I might make a suggestion…' The limousine driver was looking at her as if she had two heads. So was Nick.

'Suggest away,' she said.

'If you were to produce, say, a keg or two of beer… Beer's expensive and rationed.'

'Beer's rationed?' she said incredulously.

'Do you have maybe a Diner's Card?'

'I bet my fiancé does.'

'Do you, sir?'

'Eh?' Nick said, getting more startled by the minute. This was a seriously startling woman.

She grinned. 'My fiancé will pay you,' she said. 'Erhard told me you're seriously rich. I'm not, but I'm working on it. Soon I'll be a princess, but I'm waiting on my first wages. I need a loan of a keg until pay-day.'

It was too much. They were sitting in the back of a royal limousine, escorted by armed troops, heading to a palace with who knew what reception, and she was calmly negotiating a loan of a keg or two of beer.

He chuckled. The driver chuckled. Nick delved obediently into his wallet and produced his Diner's Card.

'So how will this help?' Rose asked the driver.

'The husband of my wife's cousin works as a delivery driver to one of the army hotels,' the driver said, moving into the spirit of the thing with enthusiasm. 'If I radio your card details he can organise a keg to be here within the hour.'

'Two kegs,' Nick said, deciding he could be expansive too. 'And lemonade for the kids.'

'A keg of lemonade?'

'I don't have a clue how it comes,' Nick admitted. 'We'll leave that to your wife's cousin's husband. Tell him to bring what he thinks a gathering will need. I guess you know the numbers. Though how we know we can trust you…'

'There are very few people in the higher echelons you can trust,' the driver said flatly. Then he smiled again. 'But we're not accustomed to seeing our royalty in overcoats that smell a little like the farmyard. And while you were inspecting the troops Griswold told me we might hope. Things are desperate here. We're willing to take a chance on you.'

'You won't get sacked if you deviate?' Rose asked.

'By the time our escort has time to respond, we'll be there. I'll be following your direct orders. Maybe you organised this with Erhard long since, no? Not with me.'

'Not with you,' Rose said firmly.

The driver looked at her again for a long minute in the rear-view mirror and then he gave a decisive nod. He picked up his radio and spoke fast, quoting Nick's Diner's Club card number, ordering his supplies. Then he handed back Nick's card.

'Thank you both.' He smiled at Nick via the rear-view mirror. 'There's a jacket under the front seat you can borrow,' he told him. 'It's not as disreputable as your fiancée's, but it will have to do. Hold on please.'

With a squeal of brakes the car turned at ninety degrees and proceeded calmly down to the river bank, with Nick wondering what he'd got himself into. And it wasn't just the situation that was startling him. It was this woman beside him. And how he was starting to react to her.

Rose. Potential princess. Potential wife.

Up until now he'd hardly thought about the wife bit. It hadn't seemed relevant.

Now, though, when he should be thinking a thousand other things, that was the word that was drifting around his head, like a chink of light through clouds, a tiny glimmer of possibility.

Wife.

CHAPTER SIX

THERE had to be argument from their minders. Of course there did. There was a moment's peace, before their escort of motor bikes reassembled, veered off the highway and roared after them. Then the head of the squad—Jean Dupeaux—came alongside their limousine and gestured angrily for the driver to pull over. Nick's errant thoughts were dragged back to the here and now with a vicious jolt as the bike nosed sharply in front of the car, causing their driver to brake and veer onto the verge.

But not stop. The driver was starting to look as determined as, well, as determined as Rose.

The bike jerked back so it was driving alongside. Rose let down her window, put out her head and yelled, 'Our driver's following our instructions, Monsieur Dupeaux. We just want to see the river.'

'You must pull over,' Dupeaux shouted, and Rose smiled happily, waved and closed the window.

What was the Chief of Staff doing, riding motor bikes? Nick thought. And then, more nervously, *what is going on here*?

Dupeaux veered in front of the car again. The driver skilfully pulled out and overtook him.

What the outcome would have been if they'd had to go

further Nick couldn't tell, but they were already turning to where the cliffs along the river-bank formed what seemed almost a natural amphitheatre. Willows hung over the slow moving river. There were ruins of some ancient castle high on the cliffs. A few cars were parked under the trees, but mostly there were horses and carts. And people.

There was real poverty in this country, Nick thought. Horses and carts might look picturesque, but these weren't men and women using their horses and carts for pleasure. These horses were workhorses, and every single man and woman—and even the adolescents—looked as if they'd spent a long, hard day in the fields. No luxury of going home to a long, hot bath and a change of clothes, but still they'd assembled to enjoy the evening.

The people turned as one at the arrival of the limousine, with its trailing queue of motor bikes. Their jaws dropped in astonishment.

And then displeasure. Nick saw the moment their surprise turned to resentment as they recognised the coat of arms on the limousine, as they realised what the outriders represented.

They shouldn't be here, he thought, his astute mind working things through fast. If there was antagonism to royalty, how would they react to the surprise visit of two rank outsiders?

But, before he could stop her, Rose was out of the car. He climbed out afterwards, but was called back. 'Sir!' The driver sounded insistent. He was handing him a shabby leather-jacket.

'I'll get it back from you some time,' he said diffidently. 'Just don't lose it.' And then he smiled. 'By the way, the lady said lose the tie.'

Lose the tie. Right. He hauled his tie off, undid a couple of buttons, shrugged on the jacket and rounded the car to join Rose.

'Hi,' she was saying as the people stared at her.

The uniformed motor-bike riders were coming in now, gathering in a cluster around the car. But they didn't kill their engines. The noise was overpowering. And there were horses…

Nick saw the danger. 'Kill the engines. Now!' he ordered, but the damage had been done.

One of the horses—the one nearest the bikes—was shifting sideways in its traces, clearly panicked. It reared once and then grounded, backing. Its eyes were rolling, nostrils flaring.

There was a child in the cart behind it. *No!*

But Rose had seen. Closer than Nick, she could get there faster. She dumped Hoppy unceremoniously on the ground and strode swiftly forward to grab the horses bridle. She steadied it, then tugged it sideways, hauling its head around so it was forced to yield the force in its hindquarters.

Even Nick, who scarcely knew one end of a horse from another, could see this was an expert. In one swift movement she'd defused a potentially deadly situation.

'Hush,' she told the horse into the sudden stillness, speaking in the local dialect. 'Quiet, now. Hush.' Then, as the horse settled, she spoke to the people around them. 'I'm sorry. I should have known there'd be horses here. I forgot the bikes would follow.'

As the child's mother darted forward to retrieve her daughter from the cart, Rose took her time, soothing the big horse, scratching behind his ears, whispering reassurance, waiting until the flare of panic faded from his eyes. Nick could only watch, entranced. Every moment he spent with this woman meant he saw another facet of her. She was amazing. She took all the time she needed to settle the big animal, then handed the bridle over to his owner.

Hoppy pawed at her leg in some indignation. She picked him up and stroked him behind his ears as well.

She had the absolute attention of every person there.

'I'm so sorry,' she told the people around them. 'Nick and I have just come from the airport. I'm not sure if you know, but I'm Rose-Anitra. I left here when I was fifteen, but I was never able to leave the palace grounds very much before then, so I don't know you. This is my fiancé, Nikolai de Montez. Son of the old Prince's daughter, Zia. We've been told that we stand to inherit the throne. We're here to talk it through, and we want to meet some of the locals. Don't we, Nick?' She turned and smiled at him, and he walked forward until he was by her side. It was what she seemed to want.

Which suited him. This was a woman to be proud of.

A wife to be proud of?

Equal partners? The thought was suddenly seductive for all sorts of reasons.

'I'm a veterinary surgeon,' she told the assemblage, tucking her hand confidingly in Nick's—a gesture of intimacy which jolted him still further. 'So we should know better than to scare your animals. This was just a whim, to stop here.'

'You have no business being here,' Dupeaux shouted. 'These people don't want you.'

That might have been a foolish thing to say, Nick decided, watching the faces of the crowd around them. Rose looked a chit of a thing in her too-big jacket and holding her lame dog. She'd just quieted a massive horse. She had the advantage of looking a bit of a stray herself.

Dupeaux was big and uniformed and brusque. Authority personified. 'Get back in the car, woman,' he snapped, and there was a visible ripple of dissent. 'Leave these people be. They don't want you here.'

With one harsh order, this man had made Rose an underdog, and from all he'd seen so far Rose wasn't anyone's underdog.

'Erhard Fritz told us that we were wanted here,' Rose said

gently but firmly, stating something that was out of her control. 'Erhard said this country needed us.'

'We don't need royalty,' someone shouted from the back of the crowd, and Rose faltered.

Time to lend a hand, Nick thought. He couldn't stay being a complete wimp.

'Rose and I never thought there was any need for us to be in this country,' Nick said, loudly, urgently, speaking as Rose had spoken in the native tongue. 'You know, we never thought we'd inherit the throne. We don't understand what your problems are. But Erhard came to find us. He's shown us what's being done in your neighbouring countries—Alp d'Azur and Alp d'Estella. He says a sympathetic royalty could make that happen here. We could organise things so the country could self-rule as a democracy. Erhard's convinced us to try. Of course, if we're wrong, if we're truly not wanted, then we'll go.'

Silence. Not a man, woman or child moved.

Behind them, the troops shifted uneasily. These riders were the same men who'd greeted them at the airport. Rose had charmed them.

Here she'd done it again. Maybe.

Rose's grip on his fingers tightened. It felt good, he thought. It felt…right.

'What's your dog's name?' a little boy called out from the front of the crowd, and Rose smiled.

'He's Hoppy. Because of his leg. He can hop better than any dog I know.'

'He doesn't look like a royal dog.'

'I tried to get him to wear a tiara,' Rose said, and grinned. 'But Hoppy thought he looked like a sissy.'

Amazingly there was a ripple of laughter.

'Can he play with my dog?' the little boy asked. He

motioned to a half-grown collie, thin and straggly but wagging its disreputable tail with the air of a dog expecting a good time.

'Of course,' Rose said, and put Hoppy down.

The two dogs eyed each other warily, and then proceeded to sniff the most important part of their anatomy.

The shock and sullen resentment of the crowd was turning to smiles.

'Are you really a prince and princess?' someone called.

'We're the son and daughter of the old Prince's children,' Nick replied. 'We haven't been in direct line to the throne, so until we come into succession we've no title. Rose-Anitra is first in line to the throne before her sister, Julianna, and I come after her. If our claim to the throne succeeds, then Rose would be Crown Princess and I'd be…' He hesitated. 'You know, I'm not sure what I'd be.'

'Mr Crown Prince?' someone called, and there was more laughter.

'Crown Consort,' someone else called. 'You'd be Crown Consort, and Earl de Montez as well. I think you already are. There's no one else to inherit the title.'

'What about Julianna's husband?' someone else called.

'He's not royal,' someone else snapped. 'No matter what airs he might give himself.'

'Will you get back in the car?' Dupeaux snapped, and he sounded furious. He took a step towards Rose which might or might not have been menacing, but suddenly Nick was standing in front of Rose. He wasn't alone with his protective instincts. In a flash there were half a dozen burly men between Nick and the officer.

'It's you and your bullies who aren't wanted here, Dupeaux,' someone called to the officer in charge, and the man's face darkened in fury.

'Look, this is a private party,' Nick said, speaking quickly, knowing he had to deflect confrontation. 'Rose and I don't have a right to be here unasked. We've ordered a couple of kegs of beer and a few other things, to make the evening a bit more fun for you. They'll be here any minute, whether or not we stay. No matter. We just wanted to say hello. Now maybe we should leave.'

'But we'd like you to stay. And you can share our picnic,' someone called.

'And ours.'

'And mine.'

'These men are our escort,' Rose said, taking courage again, holding Nick's hand tighter and smiling towards the men on bikes. 'Can they stay too?'

'No,' Dupeaux snapped. 'They're on duty.'

'Then isn't it lucky we're not?' Rose said, and tugged Nick forward to where an elderly lady had unpacked her basket on a rug on the grass. 'Are they chocolate éclairs? My favourite.' She turned back to the officer and smiled her sweetest smile. 'If you leave us the limousine, we'll make our own way home. Thank you for escorting us so far.'

Dupeaux had no choice. There were a couple of hundred people gathered here, and more arriving every minute. To use force would escalate the situation in a way he might not be able to control. So he and his men disappeared in a roar of diesel engine that had the horses rearing again. Almost as soon as they'd gone, a battered truck turned into the clearing.

'Two kegs of beer, crates of lemonade, and wine for the ladies,' the man driving the truck said. 'Pierre said you were ordering for a party so I took the liberty…'

'Brilliant,' Rose said, beaming. Only the way she was still holding tight to Nick's hand let Nick know that underneath this outward show of bravado she was more nervous than he was. But she wasn't letting on. 'We have a party.'

And a party they had.

It would have been a good party anyway, Nick thought as the evening wore on. Anyone who could play any sort of instrument had been dragged into the toe-tappingly good band. The food seemed generous and plentiful—great home-cooking. The beer and lemonade and wine flowed plentifully. And Rose worked the crowd.

Actually, they both did. Nick had been in enough international situations to know how to make small-talk, to ask the right questions, to keep things flowing smoothly without treading on sensitivities. He'd been trained to do it. Rose did it naturally.

It almost felt as if he was back at work, Nick thought as he moved among the crowd, but there was a huge difference here. For whoever he spoke to in this gathering was trying desperately to find out about him, to gauge his interest as being genuine or not, and to discover whether Rose felt the same. He and Rose had spent so little time together that he could only hope they were now presenting a united front. They were forced apart—there were too many people wanting to talk to them to allow them to stay as a couple—but he was aware that people were talking easily to her, laughing with her, enjoying her presence.

As he was. She had style, he thought, the sort of style that couldn't be taught. They'd had people come into the firm who'd lacked people skills, and no amount of training had given it to them. It required genuine interest in the person they were talking to. It could never be feigned.

'She's a lovely young woman,' an elderly man said to him, and he realised that he'd turned to glance at Rose and maybe watched for longer than he'd intended. Well, why not? The farmer was watching her too, and his face showed he was as appreciative as Nick was.

'She's a damned sight more attractive than her sister,' the old man said, and that brought Nick up with a start. There were factors here that he hadn't yet met—threats? Their escort had disappeared. The powers that be would be uncomfortable with what was happening right now, he thought. What would they do?

'Please…' It was a young man, just arrived on a shabby motor-scooter. He had a camera slung around his neck. Beside him was an intense-looking young woman with pad and pencil.

'We had a call,' the young man said. 'To say you were here.'

'Lew and his friends run a newspaper,' the old man said.

'It's supposed to be illegal,' someone else said. 'Only the government can't shut it down because they don't charge. It comes out as two or four pages every month.'

'With things the government don't want us to know,' someone else added.

So he and Rose were interviewed, a professional, insightful interview that Nick realised was sympathetic to the people's cause. The journalist wasn't interested so much in Nick and Rose as what they intended to do. She was interested in them as a means to lessen the plight of the men and women around them.

As was everyone else. As the interview progressed, the crowd around them fell silent. Someone signalled the musicians to put aside their instruments. Every ear was tuned to what they were saying. As Nick outlined the changes in Alp d'Azur and Alp d'Estella—their neighbouring principalities—and their hopes that the same changes could be made here, there was a ripple of approval through the crowd.

Finally the reporter tucked her notebook in her jacket, smiling her approval. Interview over. Now for the photographs.

'Dance,' someone called. 'That'll make a great photograph.'

The musicians obediently struck up again, but not in the lively folk music they'd been playing. They played a slow waltz so the photographer would have time to focus.

Once more Rose was in his arms.

'We're doing okay,' he murmured into her hair as he led her round the grassy makeshift dance-floor. No one else was dancing—all eyes were on them.

'I know,' she said, but she sounded uncomfortable.

'So what's the problem?'

'I'm thinking… It feels weird.'

'The whole situation?'

'Dancing with you.'

He paused, lost his timing, made a recovery. The youth with the camera was moving around them, taking shots from all angles.

'It feels okay to me,' he said cautiously. 'You're not a bad dancer.'

'Thank you,' she said, but she didn't smile.

'So what's weird?'

'Nothing.'

'You just said…'

'I know what I said,' she snapped, and concentrated on the dance for a little. But she didn't need to concentrate.

'Um…Rose?'

'Yes?' She sounded seriously annoyed.

'I'm not sure what I've done wrong here.'

'You haven't done anything,' she said crossly. 'That's the trouble.'

'Right.'

'It doesn't make any sense to me either.'

'No.'

There was a moment's silence. Another circuit of the dance ground.

'You're very good,' she said at last, stiffly, and he thought about that for a bit, aware that it behoved him to tread cautiously.

'At dancing?' he asked at last.

'At this,' she said. 'At the political bit.'

'I was thinking the same thing about you.'

'No, but you're smooth,' she said. 'You do it like a professional. I don't know how much it means.'

'I don't understand.'

'It's occurred to me that I'm not really sure who you are,' she said. 'You're like a piece of veneered furniture, polished on the outside, but what's underneath?'

'Wormwood,' he said promptly, and felt her smile.

'I don't think so. But you're so…smooth.'

'And that worries you?'

'You see, I find you incredibly attractive,' she said.

As dance conversation that was a real show-stopper. His feet faltered.

'Do mind your steps,' she said kindly. 'The photographer's documenting your every move.'

'I've never been told before…'

'That you're incredibly attractive? I find that hard to believe.'

He was back in step now, and found himself smiling, responding to her laughter. 'It's a guy's line.'

'A pick-up line,' she agreed. 'That's why I thought I ought to say it.'

'You're trying to pick me up?'

'The opposite.' They turned right by the youth with the camera, and she beamed into the lens. 'It just occurred to me, then, watching you.'

'Watching me dance?'

'No, watching you talk to everyone. Watching you make people smile. Watching you make people believe that you're sincere and that you have their best interests at heart.'

'That's a problem?' he said cautiously, and she nodded. 'Yes.'

'You want to tell me why?'

'Because I'm starting to believe you. And it doesn't help that you dance so well.'

'You want me to dance badly?'

'I don't know what I want. All I know is that we're being forced to spend time together as a couple and it's starting to scare me. And because you'll be used to dating and I'm not…'

'I'm losing the thread here,' he said, and she looked exasperated. How they could be holding a personal conversation in the midst of such an audience was beyond him, but Rose was speaking to him as if they were completely alone. As if whatever she was talking about had to be said urgently. It had to be said now.

'I met Max in second year of vet school. I was just turned twenty and my mother had just died. Max was my second-ever boyfriend. My first was a guy called Robert who I fell for because he had a really cool sportscar. But that's it, my dating history, so brief you could write it on a postage stamp.'

'I'm still not following,' he said cautiously.

'You don't have to follow,' she said, and sighed. 'That's it. I just want to make it clear that I'm not the least bit interested in a relationship, so even if I do laugh at anything you say, and even if I do find you attractive, then it's up to you to call a halt. Use a bucket of cold water if necessary, but please, let's not let this relationship go any further than it already has.'

'No,' he said blankly. 'Right.'

'Yeah, and I can tell you think I'm forward,' she said. 'Or scatty, which is just as bad. But I do need to say that I'm not the least bit interested in a relationship. I'm not saying never—that'd be extreme, and I might want to stick my toe in the water in later life. But not for at least five years. I want freedom. Absolute freedom.'

'Just so I know,' he said.

'Yes.'

'For my information.'

'Yes.'

'So no hitting on anyone, then?'

'You can hit on anyone you like. Just not me.'

'But we are getting married, right?'

'Yes, but that's got nothing to do with the rest of it. I'm sorry,' she said, suddenly contrite. 'I'm sure you don't have the slightest intention of showing interest in me, so I sound really dumb and really gauche, and totally out of order. So I'll shut up.'

'Um…right.'

So what was that all about—the chemistry between them, the way she felt in his arms?

Was she feeling this too—almost overwhelmed?

Maybe it was a good thing to bring it out in the open, he thought cautiously. He didn't want relationships either.

Did he?

They danced on, but they were now no longer alone. The cameraman had finished, and the makeshift dance-floor was filling as other couples joined them. The last of the light had faded, but lamps had been hung in the trees, making the setting incredibly beautiful—the warmth of the late-spring night, the rippling of the river, the moon rising over the cliffs.

Incredibly romantic.

He should dance with someone else, he thought as they danced on. It was a bad thing only to dance with Rose. It went against everything she'd just warned him about. But she felt so…

So indescribable.

It was okay to dance with her, he told himself almost fiercely. She hadn't suggested changing partners. She wasn't wanting a relationship, so he could relax. He could marry her with no fear that she'd cling, and he could hold her right now, just as he was doing, without her fearing that he was making a move. He could savour the soft, yielding curves of her body. He could smell the citrusy fragrance of her hair.

He could…lose himself?

But he didn't. Of course he didn't. This was a weird interlude before reality raised its ugly head again—and here it was. Reality in the form of sirens, many sirens, the gentle lamplight overpowered by a score—maybe a hundred—vehicle lights.

Motorbikes and cars. A convoy.

Armed men.

The music and the dancing stopped. The men went swiftly to their horses, and the women ushered their children behind them, back to their individual modes of transport. Moving into protection mode.

A chauffeur climbed out of the leading car—a magnificent Rolls Royce—and ushered out its occupants. A man in a severe army-uniform. And a woman.

Julianna. There was enough about her to tell him this was Rose's sister, but where Rose looked what she was—a country vet—Julianna was a blonde beauty, a city sophisticate.

Rose was still held loosely in his arms. They were standing in the midst of the abandoned dance area. He felt her stiffen as Julianna appeared.

'It's Julianna,' she confirmed for his benefit only. 'I'd guess this must be Jacques.'

The big guns. The opposition.

'Let's do this optimistically,' he murmured into her hair.

'This is your sister. Go and tell her how exciting all this is. Don't pre-empt trouble by expecting it.'

But trouble was already with them. 'Julianna,' Rose said, smiling, taking his advice and moving forward with her hands outstretched in greeting. She was forcing a warmth Nick knew she was far from feeling.

Julianna didn't smile. The woman was magnificently groomed, in cream linen-trousers, a cream silk-blouse mostly hidden by a luxurious fur jacket, and with magnificently groomed blonde hair caught into an elegant chignon. As Rose approached her, Julianna held out exquisitely manicured hands—not in welcome, but as if to ward her off.

'You're not welcome,' she said flatly, and Nick thought she sounded worried. Frightened, even. 'I don't want you here.'

'Erhard said we're very welcome,' Rose said, forcing her voice to stay light. 'He said this country is in trouble and Nick and I can help.'

'This is none of your business,' Julianna snapped. 'Our father didn't want you here, and neither do I. Jacques says you've entered the country illegally.'

'We entered this country on the royal jet.'

'Which was appropriated by unprivileged persons,' Julianna snapped. 'Jacques says you need to go back where you came from.'

'And me?' Nick asked, and stepped forward to hold Rose gently by the arm in a gesture that was as protective as it was proprietary.

Jacques moved then, holding his wife's arm in a similar gesture to Nick's, but where Nick's hold was gentle there was a hint of underlying violence in Jacques' grip. He was a big man who looked accustomed to getting his own way, both within his own household and without.

'Enough,' Jacques said roughly. 'The succession is already

decided, and any attempt by you to come here is seen as an attempt to undermine the throne. We tried to stop the flight, but Erhard…' He shrugged. 'No matter. His authority is at an end. My people will hold you in protective custody until we can arrange for your deportation.'

There was a shocked hush. The crowd drew a little bit closer, as if to better see what was happening. Two couples facing off—a big man in a uniform designed to intimidate, and his beautifully manicured wife. And Nick, without a tie, in the driver's borrowed jacket, flushed from dancing. Rose in her faded jeans and a soft cotton shirt that was threadbare from too many washes. Her hair escaping from her braid. A princess?

Deportation…

'You have no right to hold us in protective custody,' Nick said lightly, but with a hint of underlying strength. 'My papers are in order, as are those of Rose. There's no reason to hold us.'

'Hey, maybe it's just my sister's way of being polite,' Rose said, standing so close to him she seemed to be using his body as support. 'Julianna,' she said, forcing her voice to stay light. 'It's great to see you. Julianna's my sister,' she told the assemblage, as if she was proud of the fact. 'Does protective custody mean you're promising to look after us, Julianna?'

'I…' Julianna looked astounded. 'You…'

'You're taking us to the palace?' Rose asked.

'Would protective custody mean a palace?' Nick asked.

'It might,' Rose said. 'Protection doesn't mean dungeons.'

'There's dungeons in the palace,' someone called.

'Your sister surely wouldn't put us in a dungeon?' Nick said, forcing his words to sound lightly amused. 'That's hardly a family thing.'

'We're not a very close family,' Rose said, sounding dubious.

'Look, failing to send Christmas cards hardly deserves dungeons,' Nick said. 'Does it, Julianna?'

'I'm the Princess Julianna,' Julianna said, but she sounded worried.

'And I'm going to be your brother-in-law,' Nick said, sounding astonished. 'Surely we don't have to be formal in the family? You don't want to call your sister Princess Rose-Anitra, do you? Which you'd have to if we wanted to be formal, as she's just as much a princess as you are. Maybe even more as she's the Crown Princess.'

Whatever Julianna and Jacques had expected, it wasn't this. The conversation included the crowd. There were cameras, and the journalist was taking furious notes. The journalist was backing into the crowd as she wrote, and the crowd was closing in around her, cutting her off from sight.

The photographer was still shooting, and there were a few other cameras in view as well. This was being documented, whether Jacques willed it or not.

And Jacques didn't like it one bit. 'This is a fiasco,' he yelled, staring round him in impotent fury.

'No, it's a picnic,' Rose said, clinging to Nick's hand proprietorially. 'These people have been really welcoming. But if you have other plans for us…'

'Take them,' Jacques growled, and the uniformed men moved in, surrounding them as if ready to seize them—or stop them escaping.

'Hey, we're coming, Julianna,' Rose said, still sounding amused. 'There's no need for your men to make an effort on our behalf. Coming, Nick? I think we're expected to go in that car.'

And before anyone could stop her she'd tugged Nick forward and slid into the Rolls Royce.

Nick slid in beside her. He was bemused, but his mind

worked fast, and he was totally appreciative of what she'd done. With one swift movement she'd given Jacques and Julianna an invidious choice. They could haul Rose and Nick bodily from their car and toss them into one of the black cars that had been following—where they'd been clearly intended to go.

They could join them in the Rolls, intensifying the impression of family.

Or they could use one of the black cars themselves.

Nick sank into the soft leather of the Rolls, looked out and saw indecision on Jacques' face. And fury.

This was no game. They were playing for huge stakes here. Did Rose have any idea what she'd just done?

The stakes were upped about a millionfold. Jacques was being forced to state his case right now. Should he treat them as undignified prisoners, when Rose had just reminded the crowd that Julianna was her sister? Should he treat them as equals by climbing into the car with them? Or should he follow calmly behind?

Jacques looked apoplectic.

'Come,' Julianna said uncertainly, and tugged her husband forward towards the Rolls.

'No,' Jacques said, and sneered, slapping his wife's hand away. 'Let them go. Take them straight to the palace, as they said. Let them have their delusions of grandeur before they leave this place for ever.'

And he slammed the Rolls' door after Nick.

'Hoppy,' Rose said urgently, realising too late that her dog was still outside the car. 'Please...Hoppy!' she yelled.

'Take them away,' Jacques growled, and then, as Hoppy dived forward from where he'd been snoozing after a surfeit of sausages, Jacques drew back his booted leg and kicked him. Hard.

'Drive,' he yelled, and the car moved forward.

* * *

'You realise we're in trouble,' Nick said. They'd driven in silence for three minutes, and it seemed he was the first to have found his voice again.

'Hoppy's in trouble,' Rose whispered, sounding close to tears. 'He kicked him.'

'Yes, but he's okay.' He'd twisted and seen as they'd left the clearing. 'The little boy with the collie pup was picking him up.'

'He was alright?'

'Yes,' he said, although he couldn't be sure.

'He hates us,' Rose said in a small voice, and all the bravado had gone. All of a sudden she looked small and vulnerable, and…afraid? No, not afraid. Just sad. 'They both do. Julianna's my sister, and they both do.'

'I'm not sure that Julianna does. Jacques, yes, for what you represent.'

'Which is?'

'A threat to his future.'

'You think we should go home now?'

He smiled but it was a tiny smile. What had they got themselves into?

There was no friendly driver here. Their driver was in the same uniform as Jacques, albeit with less bars on his sleeve. He looked grim and businesslike, and there was no way they could talk to him through the sealed glass-partition.

The car was speeding northward into the city. Nick glanced behind them to see a stream of official cars. Black ones. There were outriders on motorcycles.

'Yorkshire's looking good,' he confessed, but at that Rose firmed and looked behind them and out at the outriders, and she set her face.

'No. No, it doesn't.'

'Hell, how bad was it?'

'You ever delivered a calf in a sleet storm in Yorkshire in February?'

'Um…no.'

'Dungeons are okay,' she said. She took a deep breath. 'They're a sight better than being a breeding mare.'

'A breeding mare?'

'Never mind,' she said flatly. 'That which doesn't kill us makes us stronger.'

'My foster mother used to say that about toothache,' he muttered. 'And I'm dead scared that what's in front of us isn't toothache.'

'Hey, you're not supposed to scare me,' she said, still subdued but trying to sound indignant. 'You're the diplomat. Talk your way out of this.'

'I'm not exactly sure that's possible,' he said. 'I can't talk us out of this Rolls. Let's see where they put us next before we test my talking powers.'

She subsided back against the leather cushions. Her behavior back at the river had been brilliant, he thought. Yes, he was supposed to be the diplomat, but her diplomacy—and sheer effrontery in staring her sister and brother-in-law down—had been amazing.

But she was paying for it now. Reaction was starting to set in. Her face had paled, and when he glanced at her hands he saw she was clenching them together to stop them shaking.

He swore and moved across and tugged her against him.

She froze. 'We… We're not play-acting now,' she muttered.

'You mean I don't have to act like your husband? No,' he said grimly. 'But I do have to act like we're two people in trouble and I should have known something like this would happen.'

'How should you have known?'

'I'm a big boy. I just gave Erhard the benefit of the doubt—he said there wouldn't be major problems, and I—'

'Of course there would be major problems,' she said, astounded. 'We're trying to wrest the throne.' Then she paused. 'But you aren't thinking major problems in the way I'm thinking major problems, are you? Major problems to me are being escorted to the airport and told to leave.'

'I guess there are more major problems than that.'

'Like imprisonment.'

'Yes.'

She didn't relax, but he felt her body edge closer to his, gaining comfort in the nearness of him. As indeed he was gaining comfort from her.

'You think someone will look after Hoppy?' she whispered in a small voice.

'Of course they will.'

'Not Jacques' men.'

'No, but there were people sympathetic to our cause. I'm sure they'll take care of him.'

'But he's been kicked.'

'He'll be okay,' he muttered, and found his fingers had clenched into fists. To kick this woman's dog…

And his reaction was for Hoppy too, he thought with a start. How had that happened?

Early in life Nick had learned to be independent. His foster brothers were like him—taught early to be loners. Ruby, their foster mother, had done everything in her power to teach them to love, and maybe they did love her. But to extend that loving…

Nick had never really thought of it until he'd met Rose, and here he was realising that after only hours' acquaintance he'd go to quite some trouble to make sure Hoppy was safe. For Hoppy's sake. Just for the way the dumb dog had wriggled his tail in ecstasy when dinner had arrived on the plane. Then, as he'd realised the two plates were meant for Rose and Nick, he'd transformed, crouching low on his haunches, covering his nose with his front paws and then looking mournfully over—a lost orphan dog who no one had fed for the last month but far too polite to ask…Until Griswold had brought him his own steak.

'You're smiling,' Rose said, staring at him, and he brought himself back to the present with a start. They were being hauled off to goodness knew where and he was thinking about a dog.

'I was thinking that if anyone can survive Hoppy will.'

'Yeah,' she agreed, and managed a rueful smile in return. 'I guess.'

'I'm sure of it.'

'You think maybe we should worry about us first?'

'Maybe it'd be sensible.' She was huddled against him and he welcomed her warmth. He wanted to hug her closer, hold her tight, but he wasn't sure how she'd take it. He thought back to the words she'd spoken while they'd been dancing. *No more relationships.*

Like him. So they were fine.

'So you're thinking, maybe, firing squad at dawn?' she asked, in a tone that said she suspected the direction his thoughts were taking and it was time he got back to matters of import. Like firing squads. Right.

But at least he could reassure her there. 'Rose, they can't,' he said, quelling the sudden urge to kiss her lightly—just as a reassurance. But she was withdrawing, moving slightly away from him as she regained control, and so must he.

'These people aren't criminals,' he told her. 'The people in charge here are out for their own gain, but to bankrupt the country and leave themselves nowhere to run would defeat their purpose. Every member of the Council has homes in places like the south of France, or Capri or, well, places where they can enjoy swanning round with their wealth. If we were to disappear without trace, they'd be international criminals.'

She thought that through. 'You checked?'

'I checked,' he said. 'And I do work for a huge international law-firm. I'm not too keen on the assassination bit, but opinion was unanimous that we'd be safe. So let's not worry, and see where they take us.'

'To the palace?' she said, trying to sound hopeful.

'Five-star luxury coming up,' he said, and grinned. 'Let's count on it.'

CHAPTER SEVEN

THEY were indeed going to the palace. The car pulled up in the forecourt of a building that brought Rose's memories flooding back. The grand palace of the royal family of Alp de Montez.

'I'd forgotten it was so grand,' Rose whispered, staring up at gleaming white turrets, battlements, fountains in the forecourt two stories high, marble steps leading to an entrance that took up an area the size of a tennis court. 'My mother was never given an independent allowance. So here we stayed. I was tutored here, and we hardly left the place. But I'd forgotten…'

It looked like something out of a fairy tale. Could she really be a princess?

And then the car door was hauled open by men in uniform, and the fairy tale evaporated like the bursting of a bubble.

'Out,' someone snapped, and a hand grabbed her arm and tugged so hard she fell out onto the gravel.

But she had a protector. In seconds Nick was on her side of the car, lifting her to her feet, pushing the uniformed thugs aside as if it was he who was in charge and not these people. He set Rose firmly before him, and placed a hand strongly on each shoulder. He smiled at her, a 'we're in this together' smile. And then he faced Jacques. The black car that had drawn up right behind them had disgorged Jacques and his lady. Julianna.

'If you lay a finger on the Princess Rose, you'll be facing enquiries from the international community,' Nick said in a carrying, commanding voice he must have perfected in years of work as a lawyer. Now he deepened his voice, making it louder, as if wanting to carry his words as far as possible.

'Princess Rose-Anitra and I—Nikolai de Montez—have been escorted to the Imperial Castle of Alp de Montez against our will,' he said strongly, loudly, to the world at large. 'The date is… The time is… We're being held in custody by Jacques and Julianna de Montez. Jacques and Julianna are here right now, in my sight, with direct authority over the people holding us.'

What was he doing?

'At any moment my mobile phone will be taken from me,' he continued. 'I will then stop transmitting, but this message is recorded. Blake, you know what to do.'

There was a moment's taut stillness—and then a roar of fury from Jacques as he realised what Nick had just done. The man who'd done the talking back at the river and at the airport—Dupeaux—snapped a curt order. Nick was summarily searched and a mobile phone tugged from his shirt pocket.

'It's still transmitting,' Nick said blandly as Dupeaux handed it to Jacques. Again he raised his voice. 'The phone's been forcibly removed from me.'

Jacques threw the phone on the ground and ground it with his heel.

'I'd guess it's stopped transmitting now,' Nick said and smiled, tugging Rose tight against him. 'But it's been transmitting to my foster brother, Blake, partner in the international law-firm Goodman, Stern and Haddock. I commenced recording back at the river, and what I just said has been transmitted as well. If Blake—and my friends at almost every international embassy in London—don't hear from us soon they'll know where to look. Wouldn't you say?'

He smiled again. But Jacques wasn't smiling.

'Take them away,' he snapped, staring down at the ruined phone as if it was a live scorpion.

But… Julianna?

'Julianna?' Rose asked, turning to her sister. Julianna seemed almost stunned with what was happening. Surely the transmission thing hadn't been necessary. Surely in this day and age…

'You're threatening us,' Julianna whispered, and her face was white with shock.

'You're threatening this country,' Rose said.

'We're not. Jacques isn't.'

'Ask the hard questions, Julia,' Rose told her, but she had to yell her last two words over her shoulder. They were being hustled away.

To…a dungeon?

Not quite.

They passed through three thick doors, hustled so fast they hardly had time to be aware of their surroundings. Then they were unceremoniously shoved through a final door, and the clang of metal against stone echoed solidly as they were left alone.

Breathless with shock, Rose stared around her in dismay. By this time she'd almost been expecting to see a torture chamber. She'd never seen such a thing when she was a child, but circumstances now made her fear the worst.

It wasn't a dungeon. Not even close. It was an austere room, whitewashed with a concrete floor, and she recognised it as one of a number of windowless storerooms under the castle. Two single beds were simply made with white coverlets. A small, wool mat lay between each bed, a solitary concession to comfort. Through a door on the other side of the room she could see simple bathroom facilities.

Austere, but not scary.

'So much for me wanting to be a princess with tiaras and everything,' she whispered, and she couldn't keep her voice steady.

'Rose…'

'It's alright. It's still better than Yorkshire.'

Nick was right. This was her choice, she told herself. There'd had to be some imperative to give her the moral strength to walk away from Max's life. Well, this was surely a moral imperative. And a physical imperative. She couldn't return if she tried.

She touched the door, tentatively, putting pressure on the handle.

'It's locked,' Nick said unnecessarily.

'I guessed.'

'Hell, Rose…'

'It's okay,' she whispered.

'Would you mind very much if I hugged you?' Nick asked.

'I…'

'You see, I don't much like enclosed places,' he confessed. 'I think I'm claustrophobic.'

'You think?'

'I need a hug,' he said, and he turned and took her into his arms.

He was claustrophobic?

She didn't believe it for a minute. He was just saying it because he thought she needed a hug herself.

He was absolutely right. This was deeply, deeply scary. And where, *where*, was Hoppy?

She let herself be drawn against him. Again. She was getting almost accustomed to it, she thought as she let him tug her into his arms, and then she forgot to think.

He needed a hug to drive away fear? Well, maybe he was right at that, for a hug from this man did drive away fear. It drove away everything. The strength of him, the sheer arrant maleness of him… This man had a reputation as a womaniser and she was starting to see why. What woman wouldn't react to Nikolai de Montez exactly as she was reacting now?

He was gorgeous. And she was afraid. For all her bravado, for all his assurances of her long-term safety, she'd seen the look on Jacques' face, and it had been hatred. She was being held a prisoner.

She'd lost Hoppy.

The last was the worst. She shuddered and he tugged her closer, his fingers raking her hair with gentle reassurance.

'Hey, it's okay. It's okay, Rose. This is just a hiccup. We'll get out of here, you'll see.'

'It's you who's supposed to be afraid,' she retorted, but she didn't pull away. Not when he was raking her hair, just as it should be raked.

'Someone will take care of Hoppy,' he said, and she froze against him.

'I'm a vet,' she whispered into the muffling anonymity of his shoulder. 'Hoppy's had a couple of his lives already. I shouldn't care so much.'

'If you didn't care so much you wouldn't be you,' he told her. 'Did you have to stay with your in-laws for so long?'

She frowned, but she was frowning against the warmth and strength of his shoulder. She had no intention of pulling away just yet.

'What's that got to do with the price of fish?' she managed, and she felt rather than saw him smile.

'Nothing. But we're in prison. We might as well fill the time socially.'

'By cuddling.'

'And talking,' he said gravely. 'Saving me from claustrophobia.'

'You're not really claustrophobic.'

'Let go of me and I'll start climbing walls. And hollering. You want to see a grown man turn into a caged animal?'

She smiled, but she did manage to pull away. Just a little.

A lock of his hair had fallen over his eyes. He did look anxious. But there was a hint of laughter behind his dark eyes that belied the anxiety he was expressing. This man was dangerous, she told herself. This whole situation was dangerous, but the most dangerous thing of all was that she was locked in a single cell with Nick.

'You're on your own,' she said, broke away and went to sit on the far bunk. She sat with the expectation that there'd be a bit of spring in the bed. There wasn't. Her backside hit with a solid thud.

'Ouch!' Nick said, seeing the way her body reacted.

'Hard as nails.' Then as he made to sit beside her she slid along further so the area he'd attempted to sit on was blocked. 'Bounce on your own bed.'

'What fun is that?'

'There isn't any fun in what's happening.'

'Let's assume there is,' he said. He sat down on the other bed, seemingly obedient, and smiled at her with a smile that wasn't the least bit obedient. 'Just to stop me being claustrophobic.'

'Cut it out with the claustrophobia,' she told him.

'Telling someone to cut it out isn't exactly a tried and true therapeutic approach to the problem. Whereas my idea—distraction—is much more likely to work.'

'So how long do you think they'll keep us here?' she demanded, and he shrugged.

'This is unknown territory, Rose.' His voice was suddenly serious. 'But we've done all we can. We've presented our case to as many people as we could. As long as that message isn't able to be suppressed, then things will happen. Erhard said this country has been suppressed for so long that it's a powder keg waiting to blow.'

'With us in the middle.'

'No, because we're an alternative to blowing,' he said, still serious. 'The people here don't want anarchy—you just have to look at how long they've put up with dreadful rulers to see that. So with us they don't have to change the status quo. All they have to do is insist on the application of the law.'

'So how are they going to do that—ask Julianna and Jacques politely to let us take over?'

'I have no idea.'

'You've gone into this as blindly as I have.'

'Maybe not quite,' he admitted. 'I did have the reassurance of almost everyone else on the staff. And my brother.'

'Your brother,' she said, thinking things through and not able to work it out.'

'I have six foster-brothers,' he told her. 'One of whom is Blake, who's in the same law firm as I am. He was on the other end of the telephone. "If in doubt, ring and I'll record"—that's what he told me as we left. I did. So everything we've said since we landed has been recorded.'

'So Blake will come with a battalion of armed SAS agents.'

'It won't come to that.'

'Are you sure?'

'No,' he admitted.

'And Blake doesn't have an army, does he?'

'Um, no.'

'And my dog's wandering the country, friendless.'

'He won't be.'

'I think I'm going to bed,' she said, giving her hard bed another tentative poke. 'My conversation with you is getting me nowhere.'

'You'll sleep?'

'It's almost midnight,' she said. 'So maybe I will. You don't think if we asked nicely they might give us our luggage?'

'Um…'

'You don't know that either,' she said, and sighed. And then brightened. 'Hey, but I'm set.'

'You're set?'

She tugged off her duffel coat and foraged in an inner pocket, then triumphantly produced a battered-looking toothbrush and a half-empty tube of toothpaste. She held it up like it was the crown jewels.

'Bet high-flying lawyers don't carry toothpaste on their persons,' she said smugly.

'Um…no. Can I ask why?'

'I keep getting stuck,' she told him. 'I'll go to a calving and it'll be four in the morning, and as I finish the farmer will say can I hang around until his pig farrows or his neighbour's cow calves. It's too far to go home, so I kip on the couch and keep going. Hence the toothpaste.' She smiled. 'I'll lend you toothpaste, but you'll have to use your finger cos I'm not sharing toothbrushes. Even if we are going to be married, which I'm starting to seriously doubt.'

And she smiled, took herself to the bathroom and closed the door behind her.

She slept.

He was quite frankly astonished. To have the ability to close her eyes and sleep… It was a gift.

He wished he had it. Even as a kid he'd never been able to sleep. Bad things happened when you slept…

Where had that come from? The weird background of his past, where his mother was a shadowy figure moving in and out as life's events lurched around her.

'She was a frightened kid,' Ruby had told him when he was old enough to respond to his foster mother's deep concerns about his nightmares—where people had come and gone in the dark, and sometimes his mother had wept, sometimes she'd disappeared with the shadows, and when he'd woken she wasn't there. 'Your mother had nightmares of her own,' Ruby had told him. 'They didn't let her grow up properly. The trick is—the thing we have to do—is to take charge of your nightmares and see if we can find you a way to live through them.'

She was a wise woman, Ruby. His one true thing. He and his six foster-brothers had been blessed by her taking charge of their shattered lives.

Ruby had been sensible enough to know he could never escape completely from the nightmares. Just learn to live around them.

So, dredging up a Ruby lesson from the past, he didn't try to sleep now. He lay and watched the ceiling as he'd lain and watched the ceiling, countless nights in his past, not trying to sleep, just letting his thoughts go where they would.

But the ceiling wasn't interesting. There was a light on through the other side of their prison's thick doors, and he could see faintly by the chink of light it permitted in.

He could watch Rose.

Brave, he thought. Brave and lonely. But so practical. So accustomed to moving through grief.

She'd lost her dog this day. He knew already how much Hoppy meant to her, but had she wept or made a fuss?

There was nothing she could do about it. He'd been watching her eyes as she'd spoken of Hoppy and he knew how much it had hurt, how much she'd wanted to be out looking.

But there was nothing to be done, so a fuss hadn't been made. There was nothing to do, so she'd settled for sleep.

She was some woman. A woman in a million. Like Ruby.

Ruby would love her, he thought, and then thought maybe, just maybe, he should have told Ruby more of what was happening. He'd described this marriage to his foster mother as a political move, nothing more. She'd been horrified, for she wanted so much more for her beloved sons.

Maybe Ruby was wiser than he was, he thought ruefully, for there was nothing political about how he was thinking of Rose.

He watched on. An hour. Two. This place was cold. They'd been given one blanket each. He was still wearing all his clothes, bar his shoes. The room was chill and getting colder.

'I'm cold,' Rose said into the silence, and he jumped about a foot.

'I thought you were asleep.'

'I was,' she said. 'But I just woke up. One blanket isn't going to cut it.'

'You've got your duffel coat.'

'I have,' she agreed equably. 'So my top half is cosy. My bottom half is jealous. Do you only have one blanket?'

'I… Yes.'

'Could I trust you if I said you were welcome to share my bed?'

That took his breath away. 'You're proposing we sleep together?' he asked cautiously.

'Not in the metaphoric sense,' she said lightly. 'In the literal sense.'

'You mean sleep as in *sleep*.'

'Take it or leave it,' she said. 'It's a once-in-a-lifetime offer.'

'Never knock a lady back,' he said, and two seconds later he was spreading his blanket over her and then diving under the covers as well.

'I have another suggestion,' she said before he could attempt to settle.

'Which is?'

'My feet are freezing,' she said. 'We've both got jackets on. If I spread my nice woolly duffel over our feet, you could put our limousine driver's jacket over our tops. Note that this is a major concession on my part,' she said before he could move. 'Because my duffel is very, very warm, and your leather jacket won't be nearly as warm, not to mention that it's really been lent to both of us. So I could be within my rights to keep my duffel just for me, but insist that your leather jacket goes over our feet. But I'm magnanimous,' she said in a truly magnanimous voice.

He chuckled.

They spent a convivial couple of minutes arranging their bed. Two blankets. The duffel spread-eagled over the bottom half. The leather jacket over the top. Then they were both under.

She was in her jeans and a cotton shirt. He was in his trousers and linen shirt. His tie was still in his pocket.

Sleeping in her jeans would be uncomfortable. They now had sufficient coverings that taking off their outer clothes would be sensible, but he wasn't about to suggest it.

The bed was too narrow for them to lie apart. Their bodies touched, side by side. He lay rigid.

This was impossible. They were two mature people, and…

'This is crazy,' she said. 'We're never going to sleep like this.'

'So what do you suppose we do about it?'

'Relax,' she said. 'If I lie on my side and you lie on the same side, you'll curve round me and keep me warm. I'm a widow. I know.'

'I…I guess,' he said doubtfully, trying to figure how this could stay a nice, platonic sharing of beds—and she was *so* close.

'And you're not a widower, but I'm betting you know as well that people can sleep together without wanting sex,' she said. 'So stop lying there like you're standing at attention, only lying down. Relax.'

'Yes, ma'am.'

'That's better,' she said, and he felt rather than saw her smile as she turned on her side, waited patiently for him to do the same and then wriggled until her spine was curved against his chest.

Unbidden, his arms came round to hold her.

She stiffened—just for a moment—and then she relaxed again.

'See, it's not just me coming up with the ideas,' she said. 'Excellent. Now, relax and go to sleep. Unless you're worried about being taken out at dawn and shot. But we have Blake to stop that happening, right?'

'Um, right.'

'Then what else is there to worry about?' she said. 'Apart from Hoppy, and there's nothing I can do about him until they let us out of here. So we might as well sleep. Sleep!'

'Yes, ma'am.'

And he did. He closed his eyes, and when he opened them again to his unutterable astonishment he'd slept for hours.

Rose was still deeply asleep, curled against his breast as if she belonged there. He was still holding her, his left arm underneath her, tugging her tight against him even in sleep. His right arm was resting lightly on her shoulder. He had to move slightly to see his watch, but she didn't stir.

She must have been exhausted, he thought. Damn, he should have researched her background further. He wanted to know…

He did know.

He'd never lain with a woman like this. Never. She felt different, amazing, exciting…warm, and…as if she belonged.

She did belong, he thought, with a sure knowledge starting deep within. It had started that first night he'd met her, and it had grown deeper last night as he'd watched her work the crowd with an intuitive empathy he'd never seen in his years of working in the international legal community. Then last night, tossed into prison with a man she hardly knew, losing a dog she obviously loved deeply, thrown into an uncertain future…

She'd been brave beyond belief. She'd been upbeat and courageous, laughing whenever she could, refusing to be intimidated, treating the situation as something to be faced with optimism.

She stirred a fraction in his arms and his hold on her tightened.

This woman was affianced to be his wife, he thought with something approaching incredulity. His wife.

In name only.

But now things had changed. What was inside him had changed.

Had he fallen in love?

The thought was so startling that he must have moved or gasped—or maybe she could feel the sheer force of what he was thinking. She lay motionless in his arms, but he could feel that she was awake.

He didn't speak, letting her make the first move. If she wanted to wake up slowly, well, she'd earned the right. She'd earned the right to do whatever she wanted, he thought. Rose…

'What's the time?' she whispered, and he knew she didn't want this time to stop.

'Seven.'

'Do you think they'll feed us?'

As if on cue the door swung open. A tray was put on the floor and shoved forward, and the door was slammed shut before they could see who their jailer was.

'I guess the answer to that is yes,' he said, and as she stirred he reluctantly released her and sat up. It was unbelievable what he was feeling about her right now. His world had changed.

'Don't look like that,' she said, suddenly getting business-like, sliding to the end of the bed so she could get out without pushing past him.

'Like what?'

'I don't know. I don't know what you're thinking, and I don't intend to ask,' she said briskly. 'I bags the bathroom first, and don't you dare eat all the toast.'

There wasn't toast. There was cereal and long-life milk, tepid water and instant coffee.

'Not what I had in mind when I decided to be a princess again,' Rose muttered. 'Is this a good time to tell you I'm addicted to good coffee and if I'm deprived I'm scary?'

'Me too,' Nick said.

'So what do we do now?' Rose asked, finishing her coffee resolutely, even though wrinkling her nose in distaste.

'I guess we wait.'

'How long do you reckon?'

'Twenty years?'

'They'll have to give us a pack of cards, then,' Rose said, seemingly unperturbed. 'Otherwise I'll write a letter to the United Nations.'

He smiled. Things firmed even further.

They sat down to wait.

If anyone had told Rose that she'd tell her complete life story to a man she'd met once almost a month ago, she would have said they were crazy. Nuts. She wasn't an extrovert. She'd married Max, but even Max had needed time to coax her out of her shell. Finally she'd learned to trust him, but that trust had landed her into a mess over her head. Her privacy had become the shared concern of Max's family. Everything she told him his family had known too, as well as the whole village. So she'd learned once more to shut up.

Yet here she was, handing out private information like it was free.

Why? Maybe it was because Nick didn't really want it, she told herself. He was asking because he was bored and there was nothing else to do. When this whole fiasco was over, no matter how it ended, he'd head back to his city law-firm and she'd be isolated, just as she desperately wanted.

So he was asking questions, and there was no pack of cards, and she didn't want to spend time thinking about all the various fates in store for someone who tried to take the crown—so what was a girl to do, but answer his questions honestly and ask questions herself and pretend to be interested in the answers?

Actually she *was* interested, and that was the problem. It was a little like a game of snap, she thought. They'd both had bleak childhoods—their legacy from their connection to this ill-fated royal family. They'd learned to be independent, which was only a tiny factor in their shared passions.

'Do you play tennis?'

'No, but I love hockey. I was hopeless, as I didn't play until I got to England, but I love it now. I still play. Or, until last week I played.'

'You're kidding. I played hockey for my university.'

'Forward?'

'Centre-forward mostly. You?'

'Mostly right full-forward,' she said. 'I hit harder to the left.'

'If we had a couple of sticks now we could have a battle.'

'If we're stuck in this place much longer we could pull the

bed apart and use the planks,' she said. 'So let's delay the hockey match till tomorrow. Meanwhile, what about ice cream? What's your favourite flavour?'

'I'm a chocolate man.'

'With choc chips?'

'Ugh, no. I like my chocolate melted in, triple or quadruple-strength chocolate, and no crunchy bits to deflect the taste.'

'Yum,' she said, feeling suddenly hungry. 'When do you reckon lunch will arrive?'

'I think our chances of ice cream for lunch are minimal. What about swimming?'

'Five strokes and then I go under,' she said. 'This place never ran to a swimming pool. Maybe it has one now. Here's hoping. What about you?'

'My foster mother's cottage just outside Sydney had a dam in the back paddock. We all had to learn to swim across it before we were allowed out of Ruby's sight.'

'So Ruby taught you?'

'Ruby taught me everything.'

'Lucky you,' she said.

'For having a foster mother?'

'I…I guess. Sorry. Dumb comment.'

'No, it's okay. But you—when we get to live in this luxurious palace with an Olympic-sized swimming pool…'

'Then we buy me some floaties and don't let photographers near. Nick, what do you think is happening outside?'

'I don't know.'

They'd been aware of the noise since just after breakfast. At first it had sounded like a faint far-off rumble, as if maybe they were not too far away from a sports pavilion. It wasn't so much individual sound—more a steady murmur, slowly building. But it was building. In the last few minutes it had become so close they could hear individual voices.

'It's well over time for lunch,' she said nervously. 'Maybe we should complain.'

'Let's not,' Nick said. 'I have a feeling whoever's on lunch duty might be distracted.'

They listened for a while longer. The shouts became louder. Whoever it was, they weren't going away.

'How are you at singing?' Nick asked, and Rose thought about singing and then thought, no, this sound was getting too loud to permit distraction. It was definitely loud. It was definitely close.

'You know, if this is a revolution, the age-old way to depose monarchy is to do a bit of head chopping,' she whispered.

'The Russians were the last,' he said, obviously distracted too. 'But royalty's been ousted efficiently since, with nary a bruised neck to show for it. Look at the women's magazines. There are prince and princesses all over the place, minus thrones, but necks nicely intact.'

'Nick…'

'I know,' he said. He'd crossed to the door, trying hard to hear individual noises from the background din. But there'd been need in her voice. She'd heard it, but there wasn't anything she could do about it.

This was supposed to be an adventure. How could it suddenly have got so serious? And where was Julianna? Her sister.

And Hoppy…

'Nick,' she said again, not even trying to disguise her need this time. And he reacted. In three long strides he'd crossed the room and hugged her close.

'We're in this together,' he whispered, and his lips brushed the top of her hair.

That should make her feel safer. It did—sort of. It made her feel as if she could face anything with his arms around her for support, but that was scary all by itself. The feeling that she was starting to depend on him.

This man was an international businessman—a jet-setter who'd agreed to a marriage of convenience.

What had she done? A normal woman would have listened to Erhard's proposition and treated him like a very polite madman. To leave her home and come halfway across Europe to claim a throne—to threaten her sister, to involve herself in a power struggle where she had no idea who the players were, much less how to deal with them…It was like she'd stepped into a James Bond movie, but it was real.

She'd guessed there'd be risks. At some subliminal level she'd figured that this couldn't be as easy as Erhard had suggested—arrive here, say 'move over' to Julianna, and become a princess. Yet things had been closing in on her so tightly at home that she'd come regardless. And the really frightening thing now was that although she should be terrified of outside factors—like a crowd of what sounded like thousands gathering in the castle surrounds—she hugged tight to this man and she still thought that it was okay. Better to go down fighting with this man by her side than to stay for ever in Yorkshire and keep calmly on living Max's life.

'We're in this together,' he whispered into her hair, and that was terrifying as well. She'd have to do something about it. He was holding her as if he loved her.

As if he loved her…

She hadn't slashed one set of silver chains to be caught by another, she told herself fiercely. No more emotional baggage. Ever.

Except right now she couldn't pull away from Nick's arms. Right now she lacked the strength to be independent, so she held on while the noise from outside grew to an ear-shattering roar. There was a sudden burst of gunfire, and that made her cling tighter, and it made Nick hold her closer. What was happening—a revolution outside their prison door? What? *What?*

The gunfire stopped as abruptly as it had started. There was a sudden lull, and then a vast, roaring cheer of approval.

It went on and on, but finally it grew muted. The roar subsided and sounds of confusion took its place. People yelling. Individual voices growing closer.

Was this what war was like? Rose had stopped thinking about how close she was holding Nick. If he tried to pull away now she'd fight him. And by the feel of his arms he was feeling exactly the same as she was.

The shouts grew louder. People yelling to each other. Jubilant yells. But why jubilant?

They stared at the locked door as if it was a time bomb. The minutes ticked by.

And then a shout of approval from just through the door. Men's voices, shouting, demanding. The sound of a key in the lock.

The door swung inward, and a crowd of people stood in the doorway.

Facing them was the earnest young reporter who'd interviewed them the night before. Behind her was the cameraman, his camera raised over his head, flash flaring.

And pushing through was a child—the boy with the scraggy collie from the night before. There was a man holding the child by the shoulders, trying to make him stay back a little, but he was still pushing through.

'Let him through,' the man said earnestly as the door swung wider still and people started surging in. 'The boy has the lady's dog.' He pushed hard, the reporter gave way and the child burst into the room.

He was holding out Hoppy. Rose gasped. And then she smiled.

'Hoppy!' she said, and knelt and held out her arms. 'Oh, Hoppy. I might have known I'd be rescued by a dog.'

CHAPTER EIGHT

HER wedding day dawned as the day most brides dream of. It was a perfect spring day. When the maid pushed back the drapes, she turned to Rose and she beamed her approval.

'Happy is the bride who the sun shines on.'

'Yeah?' Rose groaned and thrust back her covers. Revealing Hoppy. This was a huge and scary palace, and Hoppy had decided his mistress needed round the clock protection.

There really was no need of it. The murmurings of dissent had grown to a full-throated roar the night of their arrival. The population had arrived at the castle to voice their dissent. Hundreds had turned to thousands. There'd been one burst of gunfire over the head of the crowd, to try and stem the rush, but they'd still kept coming.

Jacques and Julianna had disappeared, their heavies with them, only agreeing because they were forced to that the succession be decided by the international panel. The panel had yet to meet, but there seemed little chance that Erhard would be proved wrong. As long as this marriage took place, the throne would go to Rose.

Was it too good to be true? Maybe. Rose was still uneasy, as was Nick, but there was nothing that could be done but continue what they'd planned.

A wedding. Today.

'Prince Nikolai breakfasted before you, ma'am,' the maid said, beaming romantically. 'For a groom to see the bride before the ceremony is bad luck.'

Well, we wouldn't want that, Rose thought. Not now.

For this was going exactly as planned. Nick would marry her today. The succession would be organized. Nick would be free to leave her, and return to his career.

So why wasn't she happy?

It was just… Well, living happily ever after as reigning sovereign was starting to feel a bit empty. What would she do?

'The hairdresser will be here in an hour,' the maid told her. 'And your dress will be ready at twelve. Photographers at two.'

See, that was the problem. She hadn't factored in the 'princess' stuff.

Nothing to do but reign.

Without Nick.

Her mother had been a royal bride, and she'd been isolated for ever. Was that what she was condemning herself to?

Yeah, but… *Yeah, but…*

'I wanted to be by myself,' she told Hoppy as the maid left, but Hoppy gave her a quizzical look, leaped off the bed and trotted to the bedroom door. They'd been here only a week, but already Hoppy knew and approved of her routine. Breakfast with Nick. A couple of hours in the office working through the reams of paperwork, trying to get her head around stuff that Nick understood better than she did. But he wouldn't be here for ever to help her. Then maybe a long hike in the woods. With Nick. A swim with Nick—yes, as the old Prince had lost authority his son had installed a pool. A magnificent pool. Nick was teaching her, and already she could dog-paddle.

Then maybe a picnic.

Then dinner and conversation long into the night. And then…

Bed alone.

He is going to be your husband. A little voice had been saying that over and over to her in the past week. It wouldn't hurt to…

But it would hurt.

'I'm getting the happy-ever-after without the prince,' Rose told her dog, firmly stifling the doubts. 'And the last step I have to take before I can start my happy-ever-after is to marry.'

So get on with it.

He stood alone at the end of the aisle of the palace chapel. This chapel was no grand architectural statement. Unlike the rest of the palace it had been built with love—making it a place where humans could seek sanctuary from troubles surrounding them. It seemed almost intimate. Apart from the crowd of dignitaries filling the chapel to almost bursting. And the television camera broadcasting their union to the world.

Rose entered the church—and she paused.

Up until now it had seemed a dream. An escape. She'd been running from a situation that had threatened to overwhelm her. From the time she'd walked in to the restaurant five weeks ago things had moved in fast motion, a blur of things that had had to be done. Organisation. The chaos of arriving here. The fuss associated with this royal wedding.

This dress alone; the royal dressmakers had spent hour upon hour with the heirloom wedding gown, altering the fragile lace, fitting it so that it seemed like a second skin. The people wanted a fuss. The people were desperate for a royal bride. That's what she'd been told over and over since she and Nick had been let out of their underground prison.

'The news that you are here has inspired the country as nothing else could. A clean sweep without bloodshed—oh, my dear, how wonderful. And you and Prince Nikolai… You're such a romantic couple. There won't be a dry eye in the country.'

She'd blocked that comment, expressed by the chief dress-maker but seemingly echoing the sentiments of the populace. But now, as the organ was swelling into the first chords of the bridal march, she paused and took a breath.

What was she doing?

The last time she'd heard this music, she'd been in a tiny church in Yorkshire and Max had been waiting for her.

Now Nick was waiting for her. The whole sweet trap.

And it rose up to catch her. She caught her breath in panic. Her feet refused to move.

Nick was at the end of the aisle, but he was a blur, seen through misting eyes, too far away to see her panic, too far away to help.

An elderly man rose from the pew beside the door. He placed a hand on her arm, and she turned in shock.

Erhard.

She hadn't seen him for five weeks. She'd been told he was convalescing from illness. He'd made a couple of organisational phone calls but he'd stayed away. She and Nick had both worried, but he'd refused to let them see him.

For him to be here now seemed almost magic.

He'd shrunk a little, but in other ways he'd expanded. He was wearing full military uniform. Tassels and braid everywhere. A dress sword. And he was smiling.

'Nikolai isn't the same as Max,' he said softly, and his grip on her arm was surprisingly strong. 'You know that.'

She looked into his face for a minute and he met her look, unflinching. How had he known?

'He's waiting for you,' he said.

She turned to look towards Nick. Panic cleared.

Nick was concerned. She could see that even from here. He was watching, waiting, but there was a slight furrow in his brow that said he knew she was troubled.

How did he know that? How could he tell that from here? And how could she know that he knew?

He looked fabulous. He was wearing the same uniform as Erhard, rich, deep, deep blue, with red and gold braid, tassels, a golden sash slashing across his chest, and a dress sword hung by his side.

Nikolai de Montez. A prince coming home. He looked the part.

He should be sovereign and not me, she thought, starting to feel hysterical. He looked fabulous. He looked royal. He looked so far apart from her world that she felt giddy.

The whole chapel was waiting for her to start walking. To go to her bridegroom. But Erhard's pressure on her arm wasn't insistent—he was waiting for her to decide. Letting her take her time.

Nikolai was waiting.

And then Nick smiled. He stooped and lifted something from the floor.

Hoppy.

She'd left Hoppy in the care of one of the palace gardeners. The little dog had made friends of everyone here, so much so that Nick had suggested the reason for the country's insurrection was that Jacques had kicked the dog. It was a tiny thing in the scheme of things, but it had been caught on camera, and Jacques had not been seen in public since. Hoppy, however, had been in demand. For every photo call there had been the request: 'and the little dog?'

Rose had thought he had no place here today in this most

formal of ceremonies. But Nick obviously had had other ideas.

The furrow of worry had disappeared from Nick's brow. He was smiling. Hoppy was tucked under his arm, and then, maybe lest she thought it was some sort of enticement for her to come to him, Nick set the little dog on his three feet.

He'd been washed and brushed until he shone. He looked almost regal. There was a gold and blue riband stretched around his chest, matching Nick's to perfection.

He waved his tail like a flag, seemingly aware that the eyes of the world were upon him, lapping up the attention.

'Go to Rose,' Nick said.

The bridal march was still playing. Hoppy looked up at Nick enquiringly, then gazed around the church while all the dignitaries, officials and palace staff held their collective breath.

Hoppy had watched her dress. He knew that this confection of white-and-cream lace and ribbon was his mistress. His disreputable tail gave another happy wag and he set off down the aisle at full tilt.

Hop-along Hoppy.

Rose giggled and bent down to greet him. Hoppy reached her and bounded up into her arms, wriggling all over. She gathered him to her, then straightened and looked ahead at Nick. He was still smiling.

And suddenly this was as far as it was possible to be from that long-ago wedding to Max. She remembered it—the tiny church in Yorkshire, Max waiting looking thin and gaunt and anxious, and his parents sitting by him, fretting that everything was as it should be.

The bride's guests sat on the left, the groom's on the right. That was the way it should be, and Max's mother had strictly enforced it. 'Are you Max's friend?' she'd directed the ushers to ask, and if the friend said yes, regardless of the fact that she and Max shared many friends, then they'd been directed to the right as well.

So she'd walked into the church and there'd been three lone stragglers, friends who'd defied her mother-in-law's rules and sat on her side regardless.

It had been Max's wedding. It had been nothing to do with her.

It had been Max's life.

But here both sides of the church were crowded, even if it was with strangers. Erhard was beside her, calmly smiling, giving her all the time in the world. Hoppy was trying to lick her face.

Nick was smiling.

This was *her* life. That flash of certainty she'd had when Erhard had first put this proposition to her, when she'd sat across the dinner table from Nick and looked at the way he'd talked to Erhard, courteous, kind, sensitive…

There were no strings here. This was no golden net waiting to catch her, hold her, as it had held her mother. Nick was doing this to free this country. Sure he'd kissed and held her, and he'd been her rock during the past few days, but there were no conditions.

She could marry him and he'd walk away and leave her to it.

He was watching her, hopeful but uncertain. The whole church was watching her uncertainly. What was she doing? Having second thoughts in front of the world's press? Giving Erhard and Nick heart attacks? If Julianna and Jacques were watching her now they'd beam with delight. Or say really loudly to the nation, *see, she's vacillating*.

It was only the thought of marriage that had her vacillating.

'Are you right to go?' Erhard whispered, and she managed a smile.

'I like to make my bridegrooms sweat,' she said, and his old face wrinkled into a smile of delight. He looked along the aisle to Nick and she intercepted that look again: *women—we don't understand them but we love them anyway!*

'It's not a real marriage,' Rose whispered, tucking her hand securely into Erhard's. 'This is Nick. Love 'em and leave 'em Nick. I can do this. Let's get this ceremony on the road.'

It wasn't a real marriage. The problem was, though, that it was starting to feel like one. They were standing in church and Nick was making vows that felt…right.

Do you take this woman…?

Rose was beautiful. Not just now, he thought, though beautiful would certainly describe her almost ethereal appearance as she made her vows beside him. The first night in the restaurant she'd taken his breath away. He knew now what lay behind the façade, and it was with almost stunned disbelief that he heard her responses

'I, Rose-Anitra, take you, Nikolai…'

It was mockery. Make believe. *Til death do us part?* No, only until divorce.

But it surely didn't feel like that, and for once he let himself go.

Forget the control. Forget the isolation bit.

He took Rose's hands in his and he held them. Erhard looked on from the sidelines. Hoppy looked on from underneath. And he spoke the words.

'I, Nikolai, take thee, Rose-Anitra… Forsaking all others, keeping myself only unto you, as long as we both shall live.'

It didn't matter, Nick thought almost triumphantly as he kissed her tenderly on the lips in front of the whole congregation. It didn't matter what had been said before or what had been planned for the future

No matter. Things had changed.

He, Nikolai de Montez, was a married man.

* * *

The formalities of the wedding were tedious. Signing, signing and more signing, made longer because Nick decreed there wasn't one document to be signed without checking the wording. Then photography and more photography. And then…

Fun.

A great dance out on the front lawns of the formal palace. At Erhard's suggestion, made by telephone from his convalescence bed, their guest list for the party comprised representatives from every walk of life, from every corner of the country. As many people as were safe to fit squeezed into the grounds, and the festivities were beamed out over the country to where similar celebrations were taking place over and over. The locals looked at their television sets, toasted the bride and groom and allowed themselves to hope. Nick and Rose were dancing their hearts out in each other's arms. This seemed a turning point for this desperately poor principality—it was a new beginning for them and a new beginning for all the country.

Then, as the late hours turned to the small hours, as Rose sagged in exhaustion until all that was holding her up was her husband's arms, the bride and groom were escorted back into the castle and cheered every step as they made their way up the vast marble staircase to the bedchambers beyond.

Nick and Rose. Alone. Even Hoppy had retired long since, sneaking off to find a warm kennel with the kitchen dogs. Tomorrow he'd have Rose to himself, and a dog had to have some beauty sleep.

So for now Nick had Rose all to himself. As they reached the first landing she tripped slightly on her train, and before she knew what he was about he'd swept her up into his arms and carried her the rest of the way. She squeaked in protest, but there was a roar of approval from the crowd below.

'Say goodnight to our friends,' Nick ordered, smiling

wickedly down at her and swinging her round so they could both look over the balustrade to the people below. 'Wave.'

She was too dazed to do anything else. She waved.

Nick grinned, swung his bride around and pushed open the first bedroom door.

His.

The door swung closed behind him with a resounding slam.

Another cheer from below, which was just as well, as it disguised the squeak of indignation and the imperious, 'Put me down. Now!'

He put her down. It behoved a man to tread warily when he thought he was married but he wasn't sure where the woman was in the equation. *The earth hadn't moved for her, then?*

'I thought separate bedrooms might be frowned on tonight,' he said.

'By who?'

'By everyone downstairs. You know both our doors are visible from the entrance hall.'

'Then we'll wait until everyone goes away and go to our own rooms.'

'Right,' he said, still cautious. 'You know, you look beautiful.'

'You look pretty gorgeous yourself,' she retorted. 'Gold tassels and a dress sword. Wow.'

'I did scrub up well,' he admitted, and thought fleetingly that if his foster brothers had been here they would have looked at the dress sword and given him a very hard time. But Blake and his brothers had been told not to come—not to a mock wedding; that would have been crazy.

But thinking of his foster family was for later. For now he had to placate his bride—who showed every sign of retreating to her own bedroom.

'I need to go,' she said. 'Even if people see me.'

'It's not a good look—bride bolting for her own room.'

She glowered.

'It was a very nice wedding,' he said, striving to keep his voice normal.

'It was.'

'You don't have to look at me like that,' he complained. 'I'm not about to jump you.'

'You'd better not.'

'Why would you think I'd want to?' he asked and that obviously set her back. The suspicion on her face gave way to confusion.

'You don't want to?'

'Not if you don't.'

'I don't.'

'Not even a little bit?' he asked, and she gasped.

'No. I…'

'I just thought,' he said, seemingly innocent. 'I mean, you've been a widow for a long time, and there are some things… Well, you might be missing sex?'

'That's none of your business.'

'No, but I really enjoy sex,' he said softly, wickedly, thinking well, why not? She was gorgeous. And she was his wife. 'I'd hate to think of my wife as being deprived.'

She gasped again and took two steps backwards.

'Don't you dare.'

'You really don't want…'

'This marriage is a marriage of convenience.'

'So it is. But I think you're beautiful and you think I'm gorgeous.'

'Just your tassels,' she said. Breathlessly.

'You want to see me without my tassels?' he asked, and started unbuttoning his dress coat.

She yelped.

His hand stilled. 'You don't want me to undress?'

'No. No!'

'So this marriage stays unconsummated.'

'Yes,' she said, but suddenly her voice was a little unsure. She was looking at his throat. Why?

She wasn't looking at his face.

'Rose-Anitra.'

'Yes?'

'Have I ever told you that's a beautiful name?'

'Rose.'

'But you're not English,' he said. 'You're a princess of Alp de Montez. You're my wife.'

'You don't have any rights,' she said.

'I know I don't,' he said gently. 'I would never want you to do anything you didn't wish. But if you wished…'

'I don't wish.'

'No.'

He nodded. This room was massive. It was a suite, really, a vast sitting room with an opulent bedchamber attached. He'd been bemused when he'd seen it. 'The master of the castle always uses these rooms,' he'd been told, and he thought he'd better go along with it. But it really was over the top.

There was a vast four-poster bed draped with crimson velvet, edged with gold. Gold tassels a hundred times as large as the ones on his uniform. Gilt furniture, overstuffed. A couple of gilt lions on either side of the blazing fireplace.

'I guess your patients back in Yorkshire wouldn't recognise you now,' he said gently, and she did look at him then and managed a smile.

'No.'

'Your parents-in-law didn't come to the wedding?'

'What do you think?' she said bitterly. 'I asked them, but no. I've betrayed them.'

'How did you betray them?'

'I abandoned Max.'

'Max died,' he said, frowning. 'Two years ago.'

'I didn't have his baby.'

'I see,' he said cautiously, but of course he didn't. 'And the reason you don't want to sleep with me?'

'I'm not in love with you.'

'No, but if you were?' he said, probing something he suddenly sensed was important. She was so lovely. His bride.

Rose's dress was a family heirloom. The palace housekeeper had produced it the same day that the country had installed them in this castle.

'We hid it,' she'd said as she'd presented it to Rose. 'We hid it from your sister because she's not the right one.'

The dress was maybe a hundred years old, exquisite: a clinging bodice and flowing skirt, white silk with gold embroidery, a soft gold underskirt; there was enough color for everyone to decide it was suitable for a widow's remarriage.

'I can't be in love with you,' she said, still breathless. 'Not and be free.'

'I'd never tie you to me.'

Her brow creased into a furrow. 'That sounds almost like a proposal.'

'No, but I was just thinking…' he said, wondering as he said it, what was he thinking? He wasn't sure. It was just… She was so lovely. And she was right here before him, her brow creased with just that little furrow. And he'd made those vows, and suddenly they seemed not so stupid after all. Not so scary.

But she was frightened. She took a step back. 'Nick, we're taking this no further.'

'No.'

'I'd get pregnant,' she said.

Yeah? 'That could happen,' he said cautiously. 'But I read something at the back of a very dark bookstore, somewhere in my deep and murky past, that suggested it might just be possible to prevent it.'

'The only sure contraception is a two-foot-thick brick wall.'

'Have you been talking to my foster mother?' he demanded, but she wasn't smiling.

'I could never have a child.'

He frowned. Up until now he'd felt that this situation right now was light. Fun, even. No, she didn't want to go to bed with him, and he'd never force her. But a bit of light-hearted dalliance after the romance of the day had seemed okay, and if it had led further…

He wouldn't have objected at all. The more he saw of Rose the more desirable she became. Today had been fantastical. They'd been transported into a fairy tale, a make-believe that was for now only. But why not let it run its course? What harm would it have done?

But suddenly the mood had changed. There was bleak heaviness in her voice. *I could never have a child.*

'Is there something wrong?' he asked, aware that he was intruding, but there was such bleakness in her eyes that he felt compelled to.

'There's nothing wrong,' she said.

'But you can't have children?'

'I…No.'

'You and Max tried?'

'No!'

'Oh,' he said. Then, 'You know, this is one thing we haven't thought of.'

'What?'

'The succession.'

'Why would we worry about the succession?'

'If you died then Julianna would inherit.'

'Erhard said we can put changes in place. Permanent changes. This country will never be so dependent on its sovereign again.'

'No,' he said, doubtful.

'Don't you dare tell me it's my duty to have a baby,' she spat, and her voice was suddenly so laced with fury that he stared.

'Hey,' he said, and held his hands up in mock surrender. 'I didn't.'

'You inferred it.'

'I just said it might be fun to learn about how *not* to have babies.' He was trying to make her smile again, but she wouldn't be persuaded.

'Nick, leave it.'

'I'll certainly leave babies,' he said, still rattled. 'I certainly don't want them myself, and if you can't have them then—'

'Then the discussion's ended.'

'Right,' he said, and drew his sword.

'What are you doing with that?' She sounded nervous.

'Hey, Rose, I'm not about to ravish you at sword's point. I thought I might hang it on the hook behind the door,' he said. 'It occurred to me that if I'm promising not to ravish my bride I'd better put down my weapons.'

'All your weapons,' she said.

'There's only my sword.'

'Stop smiling too,' she said, and he paused. Carefully he hung his sword and turned back to her.

'Does my smile do to you what your smile does to me?'

'I… What?'

'You see, there's the problem,' he said. 'There's the crux of the whole mess. Because you're standing there looking absolutely fabulous and you look amused, and then you look angry, and then you look frightened, and you know what? Every single expression you use makes me want to kiss you senseless.'

'Which…which would be a mistake,' she stammered, and her voice wobbled.

'I can see that. But I'm damned if I know what to do about it.'

'I'm sure I can go to my room now.'

'Listen,' he told her. From below came the sound of laughter, many voices settling in for the long haul. 'Did we have to invite so many people?'

'They'll go home soon. I could sneak—'

'Oh, sure. Open the door really, really silently, checking every inch of the way that there's no one in the hall. Crouch on all fours so you're below the level of the balustrade. Crawl slowly along, hoping no one looks up. Oh, and may I remind you that we have guests staying on this floor? Foreign dignitaries from all over. Any one of them could chance along and meet the royal bride crawling bedroom-wards. Wouldn't look good.'

'No,' she agreed, and she smiled, resigned. Damn it, there was that smile again. 'So what do we do?'

'Read,' he said. 'I have a legal brief or six somewhere.'

'Sleep's probably a better idea,' she said. 'I'm exhausted.'

'Me too,' he said, and looked hopefully through the door at the four-poster bed.

'You go to bed,' she told him. 'I'll use the settee.'

The settee was huge. It looked very, very comfortable. Nick looked at it, sighed and knew what his duty was.

'I'm an honourable man,' he said.

'So?'

'So you use the bed and I'll use the settee.'

'But—'

'Don't say it,' he said, and held up his hands in mock surrender. 'I know. Hero is my middle name. Just toss me out four of those feather pillows and two of those duvets, and I'll suffer in silence right here while you wallow in my rightful princely bed.'

She giggled.

He smiled. He'd made her giggle. There was so much about her that he didn't understand. He wanted desperately more and more to kiss her, to get closer to her, to see if, just if, this relationship might go a little further. He'd always been wary of marriage—attachments—but slowly Rose was creeping under his skin in a way he hadn't felt possible.

He'd suggested seduction this night and she'd refused. But instead of feeling wounded he wanted to know why, not for him, but for her. And he liked that he'd made her giggle.

There was something in the baby thing, he thought. He'd get to the bottom of it eventually. But for now he'd brought the laughter back into her eyes and he was quitting while he was ahead.

'Goodnight, my bride,' he said and he took her hands and tugged her forwards and kissed her lightly on the tip of her nose. God only knew how hard it was to leave it at that, but he did. 'Sleep well,' he told her. 'Sleep in your royal bed while your knight errant guards your sleep.'

'My knight errant?'

'I have no idea what that means,' he confessed. 'But it sounds great. It's me. It means I get to go to sleep with my sword.'

When I'd far rather be sleeping with my lady, he added under his breath. He wanted the laughter to stay.

He wanted this lady to smile.

CHAPTER NINE

SHE lay in his too-big bed, dressed in the soft chemise that had been her underskirt during the day. The silk was soft against her body. The feather duvet was so luxurious—so far away from the heavy blankets she'd been used to in Yorkshire—that she felt she was floating.

She was married. *Remarried*, she reminded herself. She'd been married once before, and now she'd made those marriage vows again. Only she had not. She'd lied.

She lay there in Nick's big bed and felt small. And lost. And lonely.

Hoppy was down in the kitchens. She should get up and go find him.

Right—the royal bride padding down through the ancient corridors calling Hoppy, Hoppy, Hoppy…

It'd probably make headline news.

See, that was what she hadn't counted on. This interest. The realisation that this marriage wasn't just between the two of them—it was a marriage for the country. She'd wanted freedom, but what dumb reasoning had had her thinking she could have freedom as a royal bride?

And if she succumbed to Nick's sexiness, the blaze of desire she saw in his eyes every time he looked at her… Where would her freedom be then?

And a child… A baby…

It was closing in on her. Nick was too close, just through the door in the shadows, sleeping. She hoped he was sleeping. The thought that he was awake—as she was—was almost unbearable.

'Nick', she wanted to call, but she didn't.

Think of something else. Think of the good things she could do here. Erhard had been with them tonight, pleased but frail. 'I'm proud of you,' he'd said, and that had been something to hold onto. For some strange reason he almost felt like family. Erhard had known her mother and he'd known her as a child. She remembered him as a solicitous attendant to a sick old man.

He was a link to the past.

Julianna hadn't been here today.

That worried her. Rose should have been accustomed to the loss of her sister by now, but she probably never would be. And the whole set-up worried her—that Julianna thought of her as the enemy. She hadn't thought it through enough. There were repercussions she hadn't thought of, and she lay there and tried to think of them now, but couldn't, and she felt like…

Like padding out and saying to Nick, 'Move over, I want to share your settee'.

She didn't. How could she?

But sex is fun.

What sort of irresponsible thought was that?

It wasn't a bad thought, she conceded, and she found herself smiling wistfully into the night. She was married. Yes, sex with Nick could be more than fun. But…

The only true contraceptive was a brick wall.

Or a bed and a settee in different rooms.

She sighed again, rolled over and buried her head in her pillows.

A royal bride on her wedding night. Without even her dog to keep her company.

Nick stayed awake for longer than she did. He wasn't a good sleeper—four or five hours usually did him, and tonight even this eluded him. So he was awake when the door opened.

He was drifting, letting his thoughts go where they willed. Which was right through the door to Rose. So at first he thought he dreamed it.

The settee was on the far side of the sitting room, facing the fireplace. The fire had burned down, so there was only a soft glow of embers. Nick sensed rather than heard the door open; the soft creak of moving hinges was barely audible.

Rose must be up and moving about. But why? Had she passed him? Was she leaving the suite to fetch her dog, or returning to her bedroom?

But then the door closed again, and whoever it was hadn't left. He or she was still in the room. Footsteps went slowly past him, so muted that if he wasn't straining he would never have heard them.

Not Rose. He knew that with a certainty that had nothing to do with logic but everything to do with self-preservation. If it had been Rose going to get her dog he would have heard her go out, and there'd have been no need for her to creep back through the room with stealth. She knew him well enough to accept he wouldn't jump her. Surely.

But if it wasn't Rose, then who?

The settee he was on was ancient, down-filled, a great, squishy, luxurious pile of feathers. No modern springs here to squeak as he moved. So he did move, inch by cautious inch, away from the end of the settee closest to the fire so as he edged around he wasn't in line of sight.

One of Nick's foster brothers, Sam, was in the SAS. From

the time Sam had come into Ruby's care as a battered nine-year-old, he'd been intent on joining the armed services. Sam had lived and breathed action comics, James Bond movies, superheroes, and by the time he had been in his mid-teens he was reading how-to manuals that were deadly serious.

There'd never been any money living with Ruby. The boys had been expected to entertain themselves, but they'd never had to think how when Sam had been around. He'd had them organised into Boys' Own adventures every minute he could persuade them to leave off cricket or football.

And Sam's semi-serious instructions came back now: never put your body between an opponent and the light. Never move until you're sure of what you're doing. They'd played tag in the back yard, creeping up on each other, touching and winning by stealth alone.

Boys' fantasies. All of a sudden serious. All of a sudden imperative to remember.

For whoever it was meant no good. Whoever it was, he or she had almost reached the bedroom door. Nick was used to the dim light, and he could see the shadow now. One man, he thought, one man with his back to him. One man, slowly lifting the latch to the bedroom beyond.

The bedroom door opened slowly, slowly.

Hell, he needed a weapon.

The fire-iron. He slid forward, and the cold steel of the massive poker slid soundlessly into his grasp. He moved back, still crouched behind the settee, waiting.

His heart felt as if it had stopped beating. *Sam, where the hell are you?*

Whoever it was had opened the door fully now. There was an almost-full moon. The curtains in the sitting room were drawn but Rose must have opened hers, letting the moonlight flood her as she slept. As the bedroom door opened wide,

Nick had a clear, full view of the man's silhouette. Long and lean and all in black. One hand on the door handle.

The other… The other holding a gun.

How he moved, he didn't remember afterwards. The man's arm was raising. He was moving inside the bedroom, intent, concentrating fiercely on his target. His hand came up further…

And Nick's poker smashed down with all the force he could muster.

He must have made a sound, slight but a sound for all that, for the man jerked to one side so that the poker didn't smash down on his head but hit him hard, sickeningly, where neck met shoulder, then slid down, still with force, smashing into his gun-arm, causing the gun to drop and skid and spin across the room.

And Nick had him, hauling him round, bringing his knee up, fighting foul as he'd learned to fight with six brothers. Ruby had hated their fighting, but they'd all been brought up tough and they knew the ways of the world. They'd practised constantly. Every single one of Ruby's boys had learned the hard way that you could never depend on others to defend you.

But the man whirled and smashed back. Nick was too close to raise the poker again. He punched with all the power he had.

'Rose!' Nick roared as the man staggered against the wall, and he powered in again. 'Get the gun.'

'Wha…?' Wakened from deep sleep, it took Rose all of two seconds to snap to wakefulness. 'The gun?' she said blankly.

'Under the bed, your side!' Nick yelled, and hit the guy again. If this guy knew any martial arts, Nick was in big trouble. Nick was a lawyer. Yeah, he'd learned to fight, but he hadn't fought for years. But he wasn't giving the guy room to do anything, punching him against the wall, hitting him, hitting him until the guy lashed out again…

'Move one muscle and I'll shoot.' Rose's voice rang out clearly over the moonlit room. The nightlight snapped on.

She must have been brought up in the same school as him, Nick thought approvingly, for she'd flicked the bed-lamp on and moved away up to the back of the bed so *she* could see but was in the shadows.

All the same, he could see enough to know she had the gun.

He moved back, which was a mistake. The guy lurched forward and his hand suddenly glinted in the light.

A knife…

The gun fired, a heavy, dull pop into the stillness. And everyone froze. For a moment.

The black figure cursed, grabbed his shoulder and lurched backwards. The knife, a wicked-looking stiletto, clattered onto the bedroom floor and slid harmlessly away.

'I'll shoot again,' Rose said in a voice devoid of all inflection. 'I'd advise you to keep very still indeed.'

The guy did. So did Nick. This seemed dream-like. Like a game with his brothers. But it was no dream. He was wide awake now and he felt sick.

Hell, she'd shot the man…

'Back against the wall,' Rose said, still in that cold, dead tone, and she jumped lightly from the bed and flicked the overhead light on. Nick grabbed the huge gold tassel of the bell-pull and pulled for all he was worth.

The bell pealed out so loudly that you could have heard it in the middle of next week. Not a nice, discreet, 'hear it only in the butlers pantry' bell. If the old Prince had wanted something he'd wanted the whole castle to know about it. The man made an involuntary lurch towards the door.

'Still,' she snapped. 'I will shoot.'

'Rose…'

'Get right away from him,' Rose said.

He couldn't believe it. She was standing in her chemise, barefoot, her hair tousled from sleep, her face deathly pale. She was holding the gun in both hands and she was aiming it straight at the intruder.

The intruder had frozen. And why wouldn't he? The man was young, thickset, dressed all in black with a balaclava covering his face. He was holding his arm, and blood was dripping slowly onto the polished floor.

And then there were people in the doorway. An elderly liveried manservant. A couple of dignitaries who were staying in the castle, in their nightwear. And behind them, blessedly, one of the castle security-guards. The man edged through the crowded doorway and stopped dead in astonishment.

'He came to kill us,' Nick said.

Rose hadn't moved. She was still pointing the gun directly at the man before her. 'Can I put it down?' she whispered.

'Let's get back-up first,' Nick said, and looked expectantly at the security guard, and the guard took a shocked look at Rose and moved into action. He spoke urgently into his radio.

And suddenly things were out of their hands.

The next hour passed in a blur. The security guards took their intruder down to one of the main sitting-rooms, where those who had no direct cause to be present could be closed out.

Nick called Erhard. The old man was a guest this night in the castle. Nick didn't want to disturb him, but faced with what might have happened, faced with the evil he'd seen tonight, he needed to be sure who he could trust.

Erhard arrived in bathrobe and carpet slippers, looking pale, old and shaken to the core, but still retaining the aura of dignity that he'd carried from the first.

'I'm so sorry,' he told Rose, his voice trembling. 'I would never have asked you if...'

'It's alright,' Rose said, but she wasn't moving from where

she was. Which was tight against Nick. From the moment Nick had lifted the pistol out of her hands, she'd started trembling and the trembling hadn't stopped. Nick had wanted her to be put to bed, for the doctors here to give her something to help her sleep, but she'd reacted with anger, and momentarily the trembling had stopped.

'Someone tried to shoot me, so I'm supposed to take a sleeping tablet and go calmly to sleep without getting it sorted? You must be out of your collective minds.' Then as Nick had held her she'd subsided against him and let him do the supporting. 'I have a husband,' she said with dignity. 'When he goes to bed, I go to bed, and not before.'

She'd held to that line, as more onlookers had spilled from the surrounding bedrooms, as every member of the castle staff had seemed to find some excuse to see for themselves what was happening.

Little was happening. The security guards had held their prisoner until Erhard had arrived.

'These men can be trusted,' Erhard told Nick, nodding to each of the four security-guards. 'I know each of them. But I don't understand how—'

'There was a disturbance on the far side of the castle grounds,' one of the guards told Erhard, sounding appalled and apologetic at the same time. 'The fence was slashed and a group of youths tried to break in. They were young and drunk and foolish, but we all attended.' He hesitated. 'There's only been the old Prince here for so long,' he said. 'There's been no interest in the castle. My officers have been lax.'

'There's been little need for security in the past,' Erhard said gravely. 'But there is now. What chance these youths were paid to make a distraction?'

'I'll find out,' the senior guard said grimly. He looked at the man they were holding. Rose's bullet had clipped his skin, a surface wound. One of the guards had roughly bandaged it to stop it bleeding. The man stood now between two guards, grim-faced, silent. 'As we'll find out who this is.'

'And who's paying him,' Erhard said heavily. 'Can you triple your numbers here tonight, using trusted people only? I want people outside and in the corridors.' Then he turned to Rose. 'I'm so sorry,' he said again. 'We weren't prepared. You'll be safe now.'

'I had Nick,' she said.

'Yes.' The old man's eyes met Nick's. 'Without you…'

'It was Rose who did the shooting.'

'Thank you both,' he said grimly. 'My two…' He hesitated, and appeared to think better of what he'd been about to say. 'We'll keep you safe,' he said roughly, and turned and walked away, signalling the guards and their prisoner to follow.

They were left alone.

'I think we should go fetch Hoppy,' Nick said, and as they walked out of the sitting-room door they had to walk past two burly security guards.

Two more appeared from nowhere and escorted them to the kitchens.

They retrieved Hoppy. Their guards followed at a respectable distance as they made their way upstairs again.

'Not your room,' Rose said urgently, hugging Hoppy close, and Nick nodded.

'Okay, sweetheart,' he said. There'd still be blood on the floor. He could understand. 'But I'll walk you to your door.'

'Not…' She took a deep, shuddering breath. 'I meant *both* of us not to your bedroom. I thought maybe you'd come to mine?'

The security guards behind them had paused. They stayed, impassive. Maybe they didn't follow English, Nick thought hopefully.

'Of course,' he said. It was totally understandable that she didn't want to stay in the bedroom by herself, he thought. So why his heart should lurch…

'Thank you,' she said simply, and they didn't say another word until they were in her suite with the door locked behind them. Securely, with a key, and the key stayed on the inside of the door, with a bolt besides.

Rose placed Hoppy on the floor. Hoppy looked up at his mistress, and gave a sleepy wag of his tail; it was four in the morning, after all, and a dog had need of beauty sleep. He hopped through to the big bed in the next room, leaped lightly up onto the pillows and proceeded to go back to sleep.

'Great watchdog,' Nick said, and smiled.

'I think we're safe tonight,' she said.

'Yes.'

'It'll have been Jacques.'

'Probably,' he said.

'And Julianna.' She was still deathly pale. Dressed only in her chemise, she was shivering. It was warm enough, and the fire made it more so, but still she shook. 'Julianna's my sister,' she said, distressed. 'I never dreamed…' She shuddered. 'She must hate me. I never thought. Back home this seemed so simple, but how did we ever think we could do it, take over a throne just like that? You know, somehow, because Julianna was planning to do it herself, it seemed possible. Feasible, even. Marry you. Have the great adventure. Save a country. It's the stuff of storybooks where there are happy endings and everything's resolved by…I don't know kissing a frog.'

She hiccupped on a sob and he reached for her and tugged her against him, holding her, simply holding her as she sobbed and sobbed. The front of his shirt grew wet from her weeping, but still she wept, great, shuddering sobs that wracked her whole body.

He held her for as long as it took. But finally she cried herself out. He felt her body go limp. He was half-supporting her. She felt so… So…

So much his wife.

That was what it felt like. It felt like he had all the time in the world. It felt that indeed this was his wedding night, or more, that this was his wedding moment. He'd sworn never to fall in love, but he had, he had. If she'd been killed tonight…

He kissed her gently, wonderingly, on the top of her head, and maybe he shuddered himself for she drew back a little and looked up at him in the firelight.

'I'm s-sorry,' she said, hiccupping slightly as she tried to find her voice. 'I don't cry.'

'I can see that about you.'

'No, really,' she said, and somehow she made her voice firm. 'I don't. I don't know what I'm about tonight.'

'You shot a man,' he said gently. 'How you did that…' He felt his gut clench at the thought of what she'd done. 'How the hell did you do it?' he asked, thinking it through. 'To wake up and get the gun and actually fire the thing?'

'I'm a vet,' she said simply.

'I'm not sure that that explains it fully.' He tugged her close again, not because he needed to—oh, fine, yes, he needed to—but not for comfort. Just because this was Rose.

His wife!

'I deal with big animals,' she said.

'And?'

'And I had to learn to deal with firearms. The first time I ever needed to… Well, there was an injured bull. There was no way I could get near it, but I couldn't leave it. The farmer handed me his gun and expected me to use it.'

'He handed *you* the gun?' What sort of wimp had this guy been?

'Farmers get attached to their animals. It's hard to put them down.'

'So you did.'

'Not that time,' she said. 'I couldn't. I… Well, the farmer had to do it, and it took him two shots and he cried. I went home that night and said I couldn't do it, and my father-in-law said he'd take the practice back over for a week while I did a firearms course.'

'He what?' Hell. 'Where was Max in all this?'

'Ill. He was only well for a short time.'

'So you had to do the shooting?'

'Not often.' But he could hear it in her voice—too often.

'Did you want to do big-animal stuff?'

'I'd started vet school wanting to look after dogs,' she said, and sniffed. 'And cats and canaries and kids' tortoises. Cases where sheer strength isn't an issue when an animal's in pain.' She was hugged against him as naturally as if she belonged there. 'But the family needed me.'

'Max's family. And now your family's trying to kill you,' he said. 'You've had a rum deal.'

'No.' She hugged him a bit closer while she thought about it. Which was fine with him. More than fine. 'I asked for this,' she said at last. 'But it's been a shock…that Julianna would…' She hesitated. 'Maybe she didn't know.'

'Maybe she didn't. Maybe it wasn't even Jacques.'

'Do you think whoever it was really meant to kill us?'

'Yes.' There was no point in lying to her. The man behind the gun hadn't hesitated, he had aimed at the figure in the bed with one thought in mind. He'd have been expecting there to be two in the bed. Maybe the far side of the bed had been in shadow, but he'd had six bullets in the chamber. He'd come to kill. He'd even brought a knife as a back-up, to finish the job if he had to.

Rose knew it as well as he did. He felt her shudder and held her tighter.

'Julianna's my sister,' she whispered bleakly. 'My family. There's no one else.'

He couldn't bear it. 'There is someone else,' he said, pulling her hard against him so strongly that he could feel her heartbeat against his. 'You have a husband. As of today. It's time someone took care of you. It's time.'

'You're only here for four weeks or so.'

'I'll stay for as long as you need me.'

'I don't… I don't think…'

'You don't need to think. Leave thinking for the morning, sweetheart,' he told her. 'You're done.'

'I am.' She hesitated. 'Hoppy's asleep on the bed.'

'So he is. You want me to shift him to the settee?'

'I… No. It seems a shame to shift him.'

Right. Rose's suite was the same as his. A living room with fire. Bedroom through the farther door. From where he stood her bed looked vast. Far too big for one. There was plenty of room for Rose to sleep and not disturb the dog. But…

'Nick?'

'Mmm?'

'You wouldn't like to share the settee with me?'

There was a moment's pause while he thought about it. Her heartbeat was synchronised with his, he thought, and it felt fine. It felt right.

Share the settee. To sleep. But the way he was thinking of her… 'If we did that,' he said cautiously, 'we might just…'

'Yes,' she said, and it was an answer to a question he hadn't asked.

'Yes?'

'Yes,' she said again, and she smiled.

He put her at arm's length, searching her face in the moonlight. Astounded. 'Rose, are you sure?'

'Yes.'

'But you were so sure we shouldn't.'

'Yes, but things have changed,' she whispered. 'For tonight, it's not the same. I don't want to be an adventurer for tonight. What I'd really like is to be a wife.'

'You are my wife,' he said.

'Yes.'

'And you're sure?'

'Yes.' And she smiled again.

He kissed her then, softly, sweetly. Wonderously. She melted into his kiss, and her arms wound round his neck and held.

'Yes,' she said again. 'Nick, I need you. Please, I need you in my bed. You're my husband, Nick, and I want to be your wife.'

And then, suddenly, before any more of these stupid scruples could get in the way, she tugged her chemise over her head. Underneath she was wearing scant lacy knickers. Nothing more. With her eyes not leaving his face, she slipped them down and let them fall, stepping out of them and taking a step back.

Standing before him in the firelight. Gloriously naked.

His wife.

Her auburn curls, loose and floating round her shoulders, almost seemed to be dancing in the firelight. Her eyes were too big in her too-pale face. Yet she smiled, tremulously, as if she wasn't sure what she was offering was wanted.

How could she doubt that?

He caught her hands and held her out from him, glorying in her nakedness. Glorying in the fact that this could be happening. That such a woman could want him.

That such a woman could be his wife.

The words he'd spoken this afternoon came back to him, and they seemed so right. How could he ever have thought he'd never marry? He hadn't understood until tonight what it was. Marriage. The joining of man and woman, making one.

But he needed to be sure. He wouldn't take this woman unless she understood…

'Rose, there's the contraceptive thing.'

'There's condoms in my toiletries bag,' she told him, and he almost gasped.

'But you said…'

'I know what I said,' she told him. 'But I was coming here to be married to the world's sexiest man, and a girl would have to be crazy not to plan for all eventualities.'

The world's sexiest man…

He needed to put that aside. 'But if there's a baby?'

'There won't be.'

'Rose…'

'Okay, there might be,' she said. 'Slight chance. I'm risking it.'

'Earlier tonight you wouldn't.'

'Earlier tonight I was ten years younger than I am now. Nick, I need you. Are you saying no?'

'Not just for sex, Rose.' He shook his head, confused, but at some deep level understanding that he was in uncharted territory. This was important. A voice in the back of his head was hammering with dogged insistence, *get this right.*

He'd never felt like this about a woman, and he wouldn't mess with it for want of patience, or for want of restraint, no matter how much that restraint might cost. He wouldn't risk her waking in the morning and reacting with horror at what they'd done. 'This needs to be an act of love,' he said, and as he said it he knew that it was right. Something was changing inside him. Something he hadn't been aware could be changed.

She was smiling in the firelight, standing on tiptoes so she could kiss him. His hands dropped to her waist, and the feel of her silk-smooth skin…

If she was to move away she had to do it now, he thought, and his thoughts were getting a little blurred. He was offering her the chance to change her mind, but a man was only human. If she said no now…

She did no such thing.

She lifted one of his hands from her waist, lifting it high so the back of his hand was against her cheek. So she could feel the roughness of his skin against her. Then she moved his hand slowly down, gently guiding it so the palm of his hand was cupping her breast.

It seemed she had no doubts. For this night, she was his wife. For this night, their vows would hold.

The terrors of the night, overwhelming, appalling, out of their world, were slipping away now as if they'd been a bad dream. This was the reality, and only this. She put her hands up and touched his face gently, tenderly, never letting her eyes move from his.

'Nick.'

He bent and he kissed her.

And in that instant, her world readjusted. The awful tilting somehow righted itself. For this wondrous moment, the horrors of the night and the bleakness of the past few years made way for…

For Nick. For loving. For wonder. Nick's mouth was on hers, and he tasted wonderful. His hands were on her waist, tugging her against him. His hands were a man's hands, big, strong, but caressing with a tenderness that made her want to weep. But the time for weeping was past. She was tracing the contours of his cheeks with her fingers, feeling the roughness of the beginning of stubble, glorying in his sheer masculinity.

It had been too long since she'd held a man. Any man. She'd loved Max, but for years he'd been ill, and her touch had needed to be tender. She'd been the one doing the giving.

Not here. Not now. She could feel the strength in Nick, the unleashed power, and she wanted it, oh, she wanted it. But she'd never guessed until this moment how much.

He was deepening the kiss, and she gloried in it. Her lips parted, and her tongue did its own exploring. Her breasts were pressed hard against him, against the soft linen of his shirt, feeling the strength of his chest. Feeling…

All she was doing was feeling. All she wanted to do was to feel. He'd kept his trousers and his shirt on during all the troubles of this night, but she wanted them gone now. But to ask him to remove them—to remove them herself—was to break the moment. And how could she?

It was Nick who paused. It was Nick who moved back, just a little, holding her at arm's length so he could look into her eyes. His eyes were dark in the firelight, almost black, and when he spoke his voice was deep and husky with desire.

'This is love-making,' he said softly. 'Rose, what we're doing, it's because of love. I should say…'

She knew what he wanted to say. This was a marriage of convenience. A marriage for a month. He wanted no commitment, and he was an honourable man.

Too honourable. When she wanted this so much.

'We can be in love only for tonight,' she whispered, knowing it was what he wanted to hear. It was what she wanted herself—wasn't it? But she no longer knew and she no longer cared. Tomorrow was for tomorrow. 'For now, yes, I'm loving you. I just want you to love me. Please, Nick. Now.'

The 'now' didn't quite work. For she couldn't quite form the word before her lips were claimed again. Her mouth was being plundered by his, his hands were tugging her close, pulling her up against him, almost lifting her in a long, triumphant, loving kiss where the night dissolved around them and doubts were swept away, and there was only Nick in her world. And there was room for nothing else.

She closed her eyes, her whole body responding with sensual pleasure as he deepened the kiss. She was holding his face in her hands, aching for him to be closer, closer. His hands were in the small of her back, pressing her against him, sending shivers of ecstasy though her whole body. Nick… Her man.

Her hands slipped under the fine fabric of his shirt, tugging him against her, moulding to him, letting him take her weight as she gloried in the strength of him. For Rose, who'd had to be strong for so long, to let go now, to let this man take her…

This was some romantic fantasy that was suddenly, gloriously real. This was happening in truth and not in dreams. She'd married this man today. This was her husband. She had every right to demand that he take her, as he could demand that she surrender. Glorious surrender. Only it worked both ways, this surrender. She was plundering him as he was plundering her. As he was surrendering to her. He groaned softly into the night and she thought, yes, he was out of control and so was she, and this was their right.

His mouth was moving now. Still he held her against him so her feet were barely on the floor, but he had total control. He kissed her as she ached to be kissed. Her neck, her lips, her eyelids. She arched her neck and let him do as he willed, her body heating as she'd never known it could heat. Her whole world centred around the pattern he was making with his tongue.

He was lowering her now, to the rug before the fire, following her down, his hands, his mouth still conjuring their magic. But he was still in his clothes. She needed him closer.

She wanted his skin against hers. She wanted his body, and this man was her husband. She had the right.

She pulled back, just a little. The flickering firelight was lighting his face, shadows and contours, illuminating the strength of his bone structure, showing the passion deep in his eyes. A passion that she was sure was matched in her own.

He watched her, intent, tracking every expression as her fingers unfastened the buttons of his shirt. She was lying full-length against him, side by side, and she could feel his breathing deepening as she made her way downward. Button by button. Slow but sure. There was no rush. She had all the time in the world, and this was her man.

His shirt was gone now, and she couldn't think how. She didn't need to know how. She shifted downward a little and pushed him back, just slightly, so he rolled onto his back and she could lie her cheek on his chest. His fingers caressed her hair as she kissed his chest. She found his nipples, one after the other, tasted them in turn, teased them with her tongue and felt him groan again. He was at her mercy. Her man. Hers.

She pulled herself over him so her body lay full-length on his. She tugged his arms up, holding them, then lowering her mouth so she could kiss him as he needed to be kissed. Then her own arms were captured and he pulled her upward, lifting her higher. She lay motionless, gasping her pleasure as his tongue found her breasts. Slowly. Slowly. He explored each breast and kissed them in turn, taking her sensory awareness to a new plane, a place she'd never known was there…

He rolled her sideways then, so they were side by side again. Her lips cried out a protest, but this time it was needful. His mouth claimed hers again, but she felt his fingers fumble for the catch of his pants. Yes. Her fingers moved to help him and his kiss stopped, and he gave a low chuckle of pure, sensory pleasure.

'I can undress myself, Madam Wife.'

'Not fast enough—my husband,' she murmured, and she chuckled and tugged the zip down in one triumphant tug. Away. He'd have to do the rest himself, for as his trousers disappeared her hands stayed where they were.

She was going nowhere. This was what she wanted most in the entire world. There was nothing except this place, this time, this man. She'd made her vows and this was her right.

How could she have wanted this to be a marriage on paper only? How could she have denied herself this joy? Yes, this was for now. Nick had no want of an everyday wife, and she wanted her freedom. Or she *thought* she wanted her freedom. But that was for tomorrow and to deny herself this pleasure, this wonder, this sensation that she was where she most wanted to be in the world, that she had at last found her home…

'Where did you say this condom was?' he growled, and she came as near as a hair's width of saying 'no, no need', for to lose him now, to have him move away… But somehow sense prevailed; somehow she managed to whisper directions; somehow she made herself release him and wait and hold her breath in case the magic was lost…

But then he was back, sinking down onto the wonderful thick fireside-rug, smiling down at her in the moonlight and making love to her with his eyes.

'And now,' he whispered softly, in a slow, sensual whisper that made her body tingle with aching need. 'And now…'

He was above her, lowering himself with tantalising slowness. Skin against skin, not all at once but inch by glorious inch, until they lay full-length naked against each other.

Oh, the wonder of him. He was kissing her neck, her breasts, a rain of kisses, while his wonderful hands caressed her body, her navel, her belly and beyond.

He was so beautiful. He was…Nick.

The fire crackled, spitting out a tiny shower of sparks like an exclamation mark into the night. She could hear the fire, hear Nick's breathing, and she'd never felt so alive as she did at this moment.

'Nick,' she whispered.

'My love?'

'I want you.'

'Not half as much as I want you,' he whispered, and he shifted, pushing himself upward, holding her firm within the strong bounds of his thighs. She gasped with pleasure, with aching need, arched upward, aching to be closer, closer, closer.

Nick.

He was too slow. She held his hips and tugged him forwards but he leaned forward and kissed her, slowly, languorously, a foretaste of what was to come.

'My Rose,' he whispered. 'My wife.'

'I need you.' Her thighs were aching with need, her body was creating a flame all of its own, but still he resisted. He smiled at her, his smile a caress, and then he kissed her. He moved dreamily downward, tasting her, loving her, moving from lips to neck to belly and beyond, until she was ready to cry with frustration and pleasure and want, and aching, throbbing need.

This was no one-sided love match, she thought as her need took over. This was her man. Her husband. The last dreary years—the fear of Max's illness, a husband who had no strength to take her, a desolate widowhood—they had been far too long to wait a moment longer to take what she most wanted in the whole world.

Nick…

He was rising again, thinking where next his mouth should explore, but she was no longer interested in his mouth. With a fierceness that surprised him her hands moved to have, to hold, to centre him exactly where he needed to be centred.

'My love,' she whispered, and he was there. He was where she most needed him to be.

And he came down, deep, deep inside her, strong and gentle, plundering yet loving. She arched, wanting him deeper, deeper. She moved with him, moving sensuously on the fireside rug as he needed her to move, letting him take her where he wanted, but assuaging her own need, taking her to where she was meant to be.

She loved him. For this moment she loved him, and how could she not? She was wedded to this man, and that he could be her husband left her wide-eyed with wonder. Her husband. Her mate.

But then she stopped thinking as her body reacted in the most primeval of ways. This was meant to happen—a man taking a woman unto him and becoming one. That was how she felt, as if she was dissolving and becoming part of him, losing a part of herself and gaining him in turn. The warmth, the dark and the firelight, the terrors of the immediate past and the bleakness of the last few years, none of them could impinge on what was happening here—this wondrous fulfilment of passion that had her body taking its need, and causing the night around them to merge into a mist of heat and firelight and white-hot love.

It went on and on, blissfully, achingly, magically, and the moment the sensation eased another started to build. Over and over.

And when it finished, when finally they lay back exhausted, still she held him. Her Nick. Who knew what tomorrow held? But for tonight she was where she was meant to be. She was in her husband's arms.

They rolled until they were side by side. The fire was

warm in the small of her back. Somehow she found the energy to pull away, just far enough so she could kiss him tenderly on the mouth. So she could smile at him in the firelight and watch him smile back. She loved his smile. She loved the way his eyes crinkled at the corners. She loved *Nick*.

'Thank you,' she whispered.

'Thanks?' Surprise was mixed with the remnants of spent passion. 'You're thanking me? Rose, do you have any idea how beautiful you are? You're the most desirable woman.' He groaned. 'And how do you think I can walk away after that?'

Her thoughts clouded a little. Just a little, as reality returned.

But tomorrow was for tomorrow. She refused to let it cloud right now.

'We should go to sleep,' she whispered.

'Hoppy has the bed.'

'So he has.'

'Are you warm?' he asked, and she chuckled.

'You're really asking that?'

'I guess I'm not,' he said, and kissed her again. 'Do you really want to go to sleep?'

'I guess.'

'You *guess*?'

'Maybe not.'

'Good,' he said, and tugged her to him again. 'Good, my love. Hoppy has the bed and he needs his beauty sleep. But you don't need beauty sleep, for how could you be any more beautiful than you are right now? So, if you don't need beauty sleep, have you any more suggestions as to how we can fill the time?'

'I'm guessing here,' she said, smiling at him. 'Maybe twenty questions?'

'There is that,' he said with mock seriousness. 'Or "I spy".'

'Maybe we could find that pack of cards.'

'I have another suggestion,' he said, and lifted himself up

so his eyes were gleaming down at her in the firelight. 'It's a really good suggestion.'

'What…what is it?'

'That's for me to know and you to find out,' he whispered. 'Just lie back my love, think of England and let me show you.'

CHAPTER TEN

MORNING came too soon.

Or maybe it wasn't morning. Rose stirred where she lay. She was still before the fire, which was now a pile of glowing embers in the grate. At some stage of the night Nick had thrown on another log, and fetched pillows and a vast down-filled duvet, so as the fire had died they'd stayed warm. She was still cradled against his body, the small of her back pressed gently into the curve of his chest. As if she belonged there.

There was a soft knock on the door. Maybe that was what had woken her. She lifted Nick's wrist a little so she could see his watch—and she yelped.

But, instead of releasing her, Nick's arms held her tighter. He nuzzled her ear and she felt rather than heard his low chuckle.

'Going somewhere, wife?'

'The door…Nick, it's two in the afternoon.'

'Golly,' he said, and hugged her still tighter, and kissed the nape of her neck. She giggled and rolled sideways, sighed and reluctantly sat up. The sun was entering through the chinks in the drapes. Hoppy was sitting on the settee looking down at them with lop-sided concern.

The knock sounded again, gently insistent. The world wanted to come in. Whoever it was wasn't going away.

Nick reached for his trousers. 'Just roll away while I open the door,' he told her.

'Roll where?'

'Somewhere.' He smiled down at her. 'You want to be found naked on the sitting-room floor?'

'Hmm.' She smiled back up at him. Last night someone had tried to kill her, yet right now she felt light and free and deliriously happy.

'Roll,' he told her, and he leaned over, bundled the duvet round her and pushed.

She chuckled, and rolled behind the settee, and then wiggled a bit so she was obediently out of sight. Nick walked to the door, bare-chested. Rose peeked out from behind the settee—and there were her panties right where she'd stepped out of them the night before. 'Nick, wait…'

Too late. 'Yes?' Nick said, and opened the door.

It was a maid, one of the normally somber, uniformed staff who kept the wheels of domesticity turning. At the sight of Nick, naked from the waist up, she gasped.

'Can we help you?' Nick said politely.

'If you please, sir,' she said, but she ran out of words. She was gazing at his chest, then looking past him. Her mouth sagged open.

'Yes?' he said encouragingly, and she gasped again.

'I…Monsieur Erhard has asked me to tell you…'

'Mmm?'

She swallowed and made an Herculean effort to get things straight. 'He wants to see you. He says… He says he's sorry, but it's urgent. We told him you hadn't had breakfast, so he's asked us to serve croissants and juice in the conservatory.'

'I think we might have breakfast in our room,' Nick said.

The girl had spotted the panties now. Her lips were pressed together. Hard. In disapproval?

'I… No,' she said, and pressed her lips closed again.

'No?'

'Monsieur Erhard says you have company,' she said. Desperately. Clamping her lips tight together again.

'Company?'

'Monsieur Erhard himself. And the Princess Julianna, the Princess Rose-Anitra's sister. And a lady I don't know. She says she knows you and her name is Ruby.'

'Ruby,' Nick said blankly.

'If you please, sir, they're all in the conservatory, and Monsieur Erhard says maybe you could be down in half an hour, but if there was anything you needed before then… um… anything at all…'

'I believe we have everything we need,' Nick said, attempting to sound severe, and the girl's tight-lipped expression finally cracked.

'Yes, sir,' she said, and she smiled. And then she giggled. 'Yes, sir, I see that you do.'

'You realise discipline in this castle is shot to pieces?'

'Yes,' said Rose, chuckling more than the girl had chuckled, and hugging Hoppy as she rolled back out from behind the settee. 'I believe they're my knickers you're standing on, sir.'

He bent and picked them up. They were pink and white and lacy, with butterflies embroidered on them.

'My God,' he said with reverence. 'And I stood on them. Why didn't I notice these last night? Were these special for your wedding?'

'Of course,' she said, and then she giggled again. 'Nope. I tell a lie. I wear knickers like this all the time.'

'You're kidding me.' He held them to the light as one might hold up a piece of priceless art. 'You wear these? As a country vet?'

'I wear brown, grungy overalls and mud, and I smell like cattle,' she said. 'I have to be a girl some time.'

'It's a tragedy,' he said, awed. 'All that time they've been under brown overalls?'

'Um…' She choked back another giggle, then thought about what the girl had said and suddenly it was easy to stop laughing. 'She said Julianna was here.'

'And Ruby,' Nick said, in a tone of deep foreboding.

'Ruby?'

'If it's the Ruby I think it is, it's my foster mother.'

'Your foster mother.' She gathered her duvet round her and rose awkwardly to her feet. 'I didn't…' She frowned. 'You didn't ask her to the wedding?'

'I sort of did. I told her she was welcome but it was a political move, business only, and there was no reason for her to come. Did you ask your in-laws?' he retaliated.

'As a matter of fact I did,' she said. 'Not only did they know why I was coming here, I told them the date of the wedding, and I told them they'd be welcome. Gladys slammed the phone down on me. So why does Ruby's arrival make you sound scared?'

'Because.'

She grinned. 'You sound about ten years old. Because *why*?'

'Because she'll care.'

'I see,' she said cautiously. 'And this would be a disaster?'

'She'll hate that it's not a real marriage,' he said. 'She'll hate that it's a fraud.'

It was like a slap. Rose stilled.

'A fraud,' she whispered. 'I… Oh, yes. Sorry.'

'She's always wanted her boys to marry,' he said, not seeing her dismay as he concentrated on the possible consequences of Ruby's arrival. 'She married for love, and it's her ambition to see us fall in love just like her. She'd never understand why we did this. But Ruby knows I go my own road. Why she's here now…'

'And Julianna,' Rose whispered, pushing aside Nick's troubles in the face of her own. 'Why would she be here? She was invited to the wedding, but she didn't come either. I haven't seen her since that awful night.'

'And they're all waiting for us in the conservatory,' Nick said morosely. 'You think we ought to knot sheets and escape through the window?'

'It's hardly dangerous,' she said.

'If Ruby's mad at me it might be.'

'If Ruby's mad at you then you deserve something dire.'

'Hey, you're on my side.'

'Says who? Can I have my panties, please?'

'Are you going to put them on?'

'I think bluebirds today,' she said with dignity. 'Can I remind you—sir—that this is my bedroom, and all my clothes are here, and everything you own is in your bedroom down the hall? Therefore you should leave.'

'Right,' he said. Dazed. 'Bluebirds.' He almost visibly swallowed. 'But Rose?'

'Yes?'

'I'll wait for you at the head of the stairs,' he told her. 'I think we should go down together.'

'There's safety in numbers?'

'I hope there is,' he said.

Nick returned to his bedroom. The domestic staff had been before him. All evidence of the night's intrusion had disappeared. He showered and dressed as fast as he could, then returned to the head of the stairs.

Rose was already waiting for him. 'How the…?'

'You obviously take longer putting on your make-up than I do,' she told him, and smirked and started down the stairs.

She was wearing ancient jeans, an oversized sweatshirt and shabby sneakers. She'd tugged her hair back into a simple ponytail. Her face was scrubbed clean of all make-up. Anyone further from the elegant bride of yesterday he couldn't imagine.

But somewhere under those jeans were bluebirds. He stood at the top of the stairs and forgot to move, so she had to stop at the first landing and turn to him, exasperated.

'Coming?'

'Sure,' he said uncertainly, and she grinned.

'I couldn't find the bluebirds. It's bumblebees.'

He nearly tripped and fell all the way to the bottom. Somehow he kept his feet and managed to follow her through the maze of corridors to the conservatory. *Bumblebees.* They passed three of the domestic staff on their way, and each had a smile as wide as a house plastered on their faces.

This wasn't a house shocked to the core by news of an assassination attempt, he thought. Their movements since the intrusion had obviously been noted and were giving pleasure. Maybe news of the butterflies was winging its way round the castle right now.

But not the bumblebees. He was feeling decidedly proprietary about those bumblebees.

His mind was having trouble focusing on anything it should be focusing on, and it was almost a relief when they reached the conservatory and Rose pushed open the door. This was an orangery, a conservatory planned in the days when oranges had been an inconceivable luxury in a climate too cold for them. There were orange trees in beautifully ordered lines under the magnificent glass-roof. A truly royal tiled floor—a coat of arms in tiles—was magnificent enough to take the breath away.

But Nick scarcely saw it. There was a table in the bow window at the end of the long, glass-panelled conservatory. There were three people sitting at it.

Erhard. Julianna.

Ruby.

Uh-oh.

Maybe he shouldn't have told her, he thought nervously. But she'd have found out anyway. Ruby was a diminutive white-haired lady. She was dressed in her customary pastel twin-set, tweed skirt and sensible shoes. A string of pearls her foster sons had given her for her sixtieth birthday showed she'd considered this day worth dressing up for, but there was little of the celebration about her small person now. She looked very, very hostile.

She rose, and Nick had the same urge to run that he'd had when he'd been ten years old and she'd discovered him 'making lollies'—rolling dollops of butter in brown sugar and eating them with delicious abandonment. Half a pound of butter had disappeared before she'd found him.

'Nikolai Jean Louis de Montez,' she said now, in exactly the same voice as she'd used then. 'What do you think you're doing?'

He had an almost irresistible urge to hold Rose in front of him like a shield. Only the knowledge that Rose was staring at Julianna like she was seeing a ghost stopped him.

'I did say I'd fly you over if you wanted to come,' he said weakly, and Ruby stalked towards him with such determined anger that for an awful moment he was afraid she'd box his ears.

When had she ever, though? Even after 'the butter incident' she'd simply made him walk the two miles to the nearest dairy to buy some more, and then go without butter on his toast for a week.

But she was angry. Boy, was she angry.

'You told me,' she said icily, 'that you were marrying a European princess in name only so she could claim the throne. You said it wasn't a real marriage. A contract only, if I'm not mistaken. Two signatures on a piece of paper. Why would I want to come and watch that?'

'It was only supposed to be…' He shook his head, not knowing where to go from here. 'How did you get here?' he tried instead.

'Never you mind,' she snapped. 'Sam said I was never to tell anyone. Such nice soldiers. They had me here before breakfast.'

He might have known. Ruby had her own means of getting where she wanted, when she wanted. And he wasn't off the hook yet.

'I would have come before,' she said, darkly glowering. 'But I was babysitting Pierce's children. There I was, stuck with four kiddies, when I opened this week's *Woman's Journal*—it has the best macramé patterns—and there you were! And there was Rose, bending over a whole litter of piglets, and I knew the moment I saw her that this wasn't a paper contract. Then I had to wait for Pierce to get home and for Sam to organise transport before I could come. And I missed it.'

She fixed him with a look that said, 'stay right there; I'll deal with you later'. And she turned to Rose.

But Rose was facing her own demons. Julianna.

It *was* Julianna, but she was barely recognisable.

This wasn't the elegant young woman Nick had met the first night they'd been in the country. Julianna was dressed in quality trousers and blouse, as she had been that night, but that was as far as the elegance went. A savage bruise marred her left eye. Something had hit her hard. Her hair, twisted into an elegant chignon the last time Nick had seen her, was now a riot of unmanaged curls. Her face was blotched from weeping, and rivulets of mascara had edged down her cheeks. She looked much older than Rose, he thought. Drawn. Haggard.

'Rose, I never meant…' she was saying, while Rose kept staring at her like she was seeing a ghost.

'Never meant what?' she whispered.

'Last night. I swear, I didn't know. I thought…'

'What are you talking about?' Rose asked, and Julianna choked on a sob, reached for her sister's hands, but then seemed to think better of it. She retreated, backing against the table, holding to the table edge for support.

'I thought Jacques had given up,' she whispered. 'He said we'd go to Paris—he said we'd skimmed all we needed and the panel was never going to come down on our side. Rose, I married Jacques when I was seventeen. I know that's no excuse, and I could have left him, but I kept hoping things would be better. I thought I loved him. I never—'

'You wanted to rule,' Rose said bluntly, and Julianna blenched even further.

'From the time I was little our father told me it was my right. He said I was the one. He made it sound so wonderful, and I always felt the chosen one. But of course there was always Keifer and Konrad, and ruling seemed impossible. Only now it turns out Jacques knew Konrad would die young. Because—'

She faltered, then took a deep breath and continued, forcing every word out as if she could scarcely bear it. 'I swear I didn't know, but maybe our father knew. I think now that's why Jacques married me.'

'Oh, Jules.'

'What did your father know?' Erhard asked, but she shook her head. Whatever had to be said must be said in her own time.

'I knew by the time Konrad died that Jacques didn't love me,' she said, and she tilted her chin in a gesture that mirrored Rose's. 'I've been so miserable, I just stopped…seeing. When Erhard came to see me after Konrad was killed, I told him that

Jacques could do what he wanted with the country. I didn't care.'

They were all focused on her now. Ruby had turned from Nick and was looking at Julianna with a look Nick recognised. Ruby had raised seven foster-sons. When a new boy had arrived at her home, this was the look she'd used.

Here was a chick that needed a mother hen, her look said. But Julianna was in her late twenties.

'You sound like you have that depression thing,' Ruby said sympathetically. 'I had it after my husband died. It was like I was in a fog, and the fog was too thick to push through.'

'I did,' Julianna said, choking on a sob. 'I do. Last week, after that awful time with the crowd, we went to Paris. But then yesterday Jacques said we had to come back. He said we weren't coming to the wedding, but we had to be near.'

'Why?' Erhard asked, and she put her hands to her face again as if she couldn't bear to go on.

'He didn't tell me,' she whispered. 'He's stopped telling me anything. I think he's even stopped thinking I can hear. It's my stupid fault. It's just been easier to agree, to do what he says, to be left alone.'

'Only last night…' Erhard prodded.

'He was excited,' Julianna whispered. 'We were staying in one of the palace hunting-lodges, which was weird, all on its own. But I wasn't thinking. Or maybe I *was* thinking—of you, Rose, and your wedding, and how you were my sister and you were being married and I wasn't there.'

'You weren't either?' Ruby said, and sniffed her disgust. 'I might have known.'

'I went to bed,' Julianna said, too miserable to be deflected. 'But I heard him downstairs, pacing, pacing. And then I started thinking. The fog lifted a little. I heard him on the phone saying we were only twenty miles away and we could be at the palace in an hour. And of course there'd be suspicions, but the money transfer was impossible to trace and there was no proof. And hadn't he succeeded with Konrad? A car crash with a drunk driver, he said, and he sounded really pleased with himself. No proof at all. And then Erhard…'

She looked wildly at Erhard, as if she couldn't believe he could be here. 'He said to whoever it was, "But you should have done better with Fritz. The old man turned up today. You were meant to hit him so hard he'd never stick his nose into what's not his business again." He had you bashed. He…'

'He didn't,' Erhard said gently, reluctantly. 'His thugs came to my home two weeks ago. My wife's poodle raised the alarm. They killed our Chloe, but Hilda and I managed to escape.' He closed his eyes, remembering the terror, but then he looked directly at Rose and then at Nick.

'I'm sorry,' he said. 'I should have told you. I thought with all the publicity he'd never try to hurt you two. I so wanted this wedding to go ahead. I took Hilda out of the country because she was terrified. I reassured her. But I didn't think he'd try…I misjudged.'

'We all misjudged,' Julianna whispered. 'I never thought he would, but he did. Jacques did. "We'll get away with them both," he told the guy on the end of the phone. I knew what he was saying. He'd killed Konrad and he was going to kill Rose and Nick.'

There was an appalled silence. Julianna was staring blindly at Rose. 'You're my sister, Rose,' she whispered. 'I can't get away from that. When I thought of what he was planning…'

She swallowed, fighting for the energy to go on. 'Finally I went downstairs and asked him,' she managed. 'Even then I couldn't believe he'd go that far. But he just looked at me as if I was stupid, as if I was nothing. And then he hit me.'

'Oh, my dear,' Ruby whispered.

'He pulled me back up to the bedroom and locked me in,' Julianna said dully. 'He ripped out my phone extension. He said I was in it up to my neck, and if I said a word I'd go down first. And I couldn't get out. I tried and I yelled, but he laughed and told me to take a tranquillizer. Take five, he yelled. And then the phone rang downstairs. I heard Jacques say one word: "Well?" That's all. Then silence.'

She swallowed, and Nick could see the horrors of the night were still with her. 'I was sick,' she whispered. 'I thought it was over.' She took a jagged breath and looked at Rose as if she still couldn't believe her sister could still be alive. 'Then the front door slammed and I heard his car. The lodge-keeper came by this morning and let me out, but Jacques was gone. I rang here and they said you were safe, but I had to see. The lodge-keeper brought me here.' She shook her head as if trying to shake away a nightmare. 'Rose, I swear I didn't know what he intended. I'd never…I'd never…'

'I know you wouldn't,' Rose said softly. Ruby moved aside—as Ruby would; the woman had the most finely tuned intuition Nick had ever known—and Rose took Julianna's hands.

'Even last night, when Nick said it had to be Jacques, I still knew it couldn't be you,' Rose said softly. 'You're my sister.'

'Oh God,' Julianna said, and she pulled back and put her face in her hands. 'What must you all think of me? I don't want this. I hate it. I want to be out. I want to be ordinary. I want to go somewhere, breed horses, take in washing, anything but this. I don't want to be royal.'

'Taking in washing's a bit extreme,' Rose said, and Julianna choked on something between laughter and a sob.

'I don't care. But how can I do anything? Jacques will never let me.'

'No one owns you,' Rose said. 'I'm just figuring that out.

You need to do what you need to do. As for the royal bit—can't you resign?'

'You can't just resign.'

'Edward did,' Rose said. 'Back in England. With Mrs Simpson. Isn't that right? He was supposed to be king, but he signed something that said he was giving up his rights to the throne. Erhard, can't Julianna resign?'

'I don't know.' The old man looked grey. He groped blindly for a chair, and Nick pulled one forward for him.

There was too much emotion here, Nick thought. If he wasn't careful Erhard would collapse. He strode out through the conservatory doors to the sitting room beyond. There were decanters on the sideboard. He poured a generous brandy for the old man and carried it back.

Erhard hardly registered when he placed it in his fingers. 'I should have warned you of the dangers,' he whispered. 'I wanted this wedding to go ahead so much.'

'Drink a little,' Nick urged. 'And don't look like you've just confessed murder. We have our assassin from last night under lock and key, and everything else palls into insignificance.' He shook his head. 'And you've lost your dog. I suspect Rose will say there's nothing so dreadful.'

Erhard looked up at him, and Nick smiled. He put a hand on the old man's shoulder and squeezed.

'We're here now. We're alive. We'll find Jacques.'

'And you'll tell me the truth,' Ruby said. Nick's foster mother had been quiet for a whole five minutes now—almost a course record—but it seemed she'd been talking aside to Rose urgently. 'Rose tells me this wedding *is* a fraud. A marriage of convenience.'

'Rose?' he said helplessly, and Rose shrugged and tried to smile.

'Why not be honest? It is a fraud.'

'But…'

'That's what you called it this morning,' she said.

He had. But last night…Over and over the image played in his head. Rose standing in her bare feet and chemise, aiming her gun with her eyes filled with terror.

Rose against the world. Rose with bumblebees.

Rose in his arms.

But Rose was moving on. 'If Julianna is resigning, then I could too,' she said, attempting to sound brisk and business-like. 'I've just thought—if neither Julianna or I will take the crown, then Nick is Crown Prince. Which makes sense. My father wasn't really royal, and you want it, don't you, Nick?'

Did he want it? Suddenly they were all looking at him, and the question hung.

Of course he did. This had started as something that seemed exciting, almost as a Boy's Own adventure. But somewhere in there…

'My mother was a princess here,' he said slowly. 'She was so homesick. She'd want me to take it on..'

'There you go, then,' Rose said. 'You can do it.'

'But together,' Ruby said urgently, sensing trouble. 'Because you're married.'

'No.' Nick took a deep breath. 'Maybe it's time for Rose not to be married.'

Ruby sighed. She put her hands on her hips and surveyed him with care.

'Right,' she said at last. 'You know, I'm getting really muddled here. Didn't you just get married yesterday?'

'Yes, but Rose didn't want to get married,' he explained. 'She did it out of obligation. Rose has had too many obligations for too long. Like Julianna, she needs to be free. If Julianna's prepared to renounce her succession too, then it leaves Rose free to do what she likes. We can have the marriage annulled and she can renounce her succession too, if she wishes.'

'I have a feeling the people in this country are going to get very confused,' Ruby said darkly. 'If I'm anything to go by, they'll be very confused indeed.'

'Maybe they'll kick Nick out,' Rose said. The group seemed to be reviving now. Just a little. Rose's words contained just a trace of her old perkiness.

He loved that about her. He loved her to distraction. How could he let her go?

He could let her go, because he loved her.

'You know, they might,' Julianna said, breaking back into the conversation. She was suddenly tremulously hopeful. She'd faced the nightmare and come out the other side. 'The riot when we put you under house-arrest was frightening. I've never seen anything like it. Until then I hadn't realised... Maybe I still don't realise what power the throne has.'

'I can't see Nick taking on the throne alone,' Erhard said.

Ruby had been concentrating really, really hard. She still looked confused, but she wasn't prepared to be relegated to the role of mere onlooker yet.

'Nick will do whatever needs doing,' she declared. 'He's a very responsible boy.'

'Yeah?' That was Rose. She'd been hugging Julianna, but her attention was caught by that. Her eyes flew to Nick's. 'Responsible—is he just? Well, well. I'd never have thought it.'

And suddenly she smiled, then gave him a measured look which was suddenly all about who'd remembered the condom last night. It was like the sun had come out. After all this emotion, after all this fear, she was suddenly teasing him.

He'd never realised he could blush.

'Why don't you want the throne?' Julianna asked Rose.

'I suspect no one's asked Rose what she's wanted for a

very long time,' Ruby said, putting her oar in again. 'Did you know her mother- and father-in-law were trying to make her have babies with her dead husband's sperm?'

No one knew what to say to that. Especially Nick. He stared at Ruby. Then he stared at Rose. Appalled. 'Is this true?'

Rose nodded, her eyes suspiciously bright. 'Yes, but how Ruby found out…'

'I found out exactly the same way as Monsieur Fritz found out about Nick,' Ruby said with asperity. 'My friend Eloise at my macramé club told me she'd been talking to someone who was asking about you, Nick. So I did the same. I have a friend who lives in your district in Yorkshire, Rose, and I got an in-depth report of what you've been going through. You've been bullied into taking over your poor husband's life, and now you've been bullied into taking over this one. Enough.'

'I chose.' Rose ventured.

'The worst of two alternatives,' Nick said slowly, watching her. And suddenly things were clear. Or as clear as they could be in the circumstances. She should never have been asked to do this, he thought. In all of this, that she'd been asked to take on more responsibility….

'Why did you ask Rose?' he said to Erhard, and there was something in his voice that made them all turn to him. 'Rose's father thought Rose wasn't royal. You've inferred Julianna wasn't Eric's legitimate child either. You've said the DNA thing isn't an issue, but maybe it could be. You didn't go down that path. Why not? Shouldn't I have been the one to take responsibility?'

'But I didn't know you,' Erhard said bluntly.

'You didn't know Rose.'

'I did.' Erhard was still clutching his brandy glass as if he needed it, but a little colour had crept back. 'Rose was here until she was fifteen. She was always the reliable one. Her mother was ill. Her father was a drunk. The old Prince was failing. She took everything on her shoulders, worrying about everything. When I enquired about her, it seemed she'd kept right on doing that in Yorkshire. She was responsible, and that was what I wanted.'

'You wanted Rose to keep on taking the burden.'

'I didn't think.'

'No,' Nick said gently. 'We couldn't expect you to be thinking of Rose's welfare. You were frightened for your country and you wanted what was best. Rose is the best. We all know that. But it's time someone looked out for her interests. That time is now, and that someone is me.'

Rose was looking confused. He reached out and tugged her against him, feeling almost compelled to hold her close. But he wouldn't hold her. He mustn't.

He loved her too much.

'So here's the plan,' he said softly, feeling Rose mould to his body, loving the feel of her, but knowing he had to offer her freedom. 'Julianna, you abdicate. We'll do our best to find Jacques and put him in jail, but maybe for the time being you could go home with Ruby.'

He smiled at Ruby. 'I know. You're annoyed with me, but I'm asking for your help, and when have you ever refused it? Ruby lives in Dolphin Bay, which is the best place in the world to recuperate. Maybe, Erhard, you could go too. You're looking ill. There are two wonderful doctors at Dolphin Bay.' He grinned. 'And there are all sorts of weird and wonderful dogs. If you take your wife, I'll guarantee you come home with a new puppy.'

'And Rose?' Ruby asked, sounding wary. Not hostile to his plan, though, just thoughtful.

'I think Rose should go too,' he said.

'I'm not going anywhere,' Rose said, stiffening.

'You must.'

'Oh, sure. And leave you here to get yourself killed?'

'Well, that won't happen,' Ruby said, still sounding thoughtful. 'I've organised that.'

'You have?' Nick blinked.

'You're not the only one who can organise,' Ruby retorted. 'This is a mess. People going round at midnight shooting other people…I brought my boys up to be responsible citizens, which is why they're all flying in tonight.'

'All?'

'Pierce will be a bit longer because he's coming from Australia,' she said. 'Sam couldn't go back to fetch him. But when I got here this morning and found out about the shooting I said enough, I need all my boys. So they'll be here. Sam's taking security over right now—Monsieur Fritz has set it up for him, and Sam swears we'll have this Jacques person locked up by lunchtime. Blake's got the legal mind. Darcy can sort out the army. Between them they'll have this place sorted, and then it'll be time for Rose to decide whether she wants to come back again.'

'I don't…' Rose tried, but Nick smiled and shook his head.

'You're trying to argue with Ruby?'

'I'm not leaving you,' she said.

'You don't need to worry,' Ruby said. 'I realise Nick is a very good-looking boy, and he has a very nice smile, but he's got to give you time to think. Don't worry about him being lonely—his brothers will be here.'

'But I can't afford—'

'You can afford,' Nick said, feeling gutted, but knowing he had to let her go. 'I've looked into the royal exchequer this week. For all the poverty in the country, the royal fortune is practically obscene. I want to plough some of that into capital works to get the economy going, but there's more than enough to let you and Julianna spend the rest of your lives in comfort. You can take that trip around Australia you wanted to do. You can do anything you want. You have no responsibilities, Rose. Not one.'

There was a moment's stunned pause.

'So I'm free,' Rose said. 'When I said I could resign…' She swallowed. 'I didn't think. And I couldn't take Hoppy—or not straight away.'

'Who's Hoppy?' Ruby asked, and Rose motioned to the little dog who'd been standing in the background looking innocuous. As well he might. He'd come via the kitchens where he'd been given a rather large ham-bone leftover from the festivities of the day before. He was paying attention to the goings on—but only just.

'There's quarantine regulations in Australia,' Rose said. 'I can't leave my dog. So…' She took a deep breath. 'I do have a responsibility.'

'Nick will look after your dog,' Ruby said.

'Nick's not very responsible,' Rose retorted.

'You should know,' Nick said, and smiled. 'You're my wife.'

'You said it was a sham marriage,' Ruby said sharply, looking from one to the other.

'That was Nick,' Rose said.

'Do you want it to be?' Nick asked. 'Sham, that is?'

'I haven't learned to swim yet,' she said, and she was smiling tremulously, as if she was about to take a very large step and wasn't quite sure if it was in the right direction.

'So it's not sham?' Ruby said.

'Ask Nick what I have on my knickers,' Rose whispered.

'Bumblebees,' Nick said promptly.

'And my wedding knickers?'

'Butterflies.'

'There you go, then,' Rose said. 'How sham is that?'

There was a loaded silence. No one said a word.

'You know,' Ruby said finally, looking vaguely into middle distance, yet not looking at anyone at all. 'I could really use a brandy. It was very inconsiderate of Nick to bring one for Erhard and not for me. I'm a frail old lady and I need my sustenance. Julianna. Erhard. If you were to take an arm each, I might just be able to stagger feebly forth and find my own brandy.'

'You're sure they're safe to leave alone?' Erhard asked, but he was smiling.

'They're talking bumblebees and butterflies,' Ruby said. 'Unless you're interested in botany, I have a feeling this conversation is going to get really, really boring.'

CHAPTER ELEVEN

THEY were left alone. Apart from Hoppy, who'd gone back to bone munching.

Nick was aware that it behoved him to tread warily. *Very* warily. There was so much at stake.

He had to forget the bumblebees and start from scratch, he decided. Repeat the conversation they'd just had, and hope he got the same outcome.

Had he got an outcome? He found his heart was having trouble beating. Maybe because he was having trouble breathing. So much depended on these next few minutes.

'That was frivolous,' he said, and she nodded.

'Yes.'

'So we need to be businesslike.'

'Yes.'

'I'm not sure where to start,' he said, which seemed a good sort of start. It was the best he could do under the circumstances.

'Start by telling me that you still want this job,' Rose said, being brisk. Trying not to smile. 'And tell me why.'

He hesitated. 'Rose, I didn't think this through,' he admitted. 'Yes, it appealed, that I could do a bit of good. And it seemed an amazing offer—to be Prince Consort—to spend a few weeks here and get off scot-free.'

'But…'

'There's the "but",' he said. 'It had to happen and it has. I can't walk away now. I'm in too deep. The kid who rescued Hoppy is depending on us—on me—as are his parents, and his aunts and uncles, and his whole extended family. The country's a mess and it can be put to rights. I want that job, Rose, and I intend to take it.'

'So I really can walk away?' she said, wondering.

'It's up to you. I told you. There's more than enough money in the royal coffers to provide well for you and for Julianna. There's no need to be a princess to have a life of ease. You deserve the choice.' He smiled. 'Julianna won't have to take in that washing after all.'

'I don't want a life of ease,' she said.

'You wanted to travel around Australia. You told me that. I figure this gives you the freedom to do it. I'll be Prince Regent. When you've done with your travelling, maybe you can come back, decide whether or not to take on the throne, and I can leave or stay, whatever you wish.'

'But that puts your life in limbo.'

'No,' he said forcibly. 'I want this job, Rose. There's so much I can do. There are so many plans to make—so much to do to get the economy turned round. It's the most exciting job I've ever taken on—it's an honour to be asked to take it.'

'But…' she said.

'But?'

'I wouldn't mind helping.'

'You can at the end of the year. Or you can now. You can take over in your own right.'

'I'm not a legitimate princess.'

'You're the acknowledged daughter of a prince. You're my wife. You're legitimate in every sense of the word.'

'It was a fake marriage.'

'We signed all the documents,' he said. 'It felt real to me.' He smiled. 'And you've personally introduced your botany collection to the world. There'll not be one person in this castle who'll believe our marriage is sham now.'

'But you don't want me to stay…with *you*.' It was a soft whisper, but behind it… Was he imagining it, or had there been a tiny thread of hope?

'You want to be free,' Nick said, trying not to let his heart leap. She couldn't want him. He had to be imagining it. Theirs was a marriage of convenience.

But, damn it, he wasn't going to let her go without giving it a shot.

'Though I wouldn't mind,' he said softly. 'If you wanted to stay. I mean, freedom means freedom of choice, so there is that option.'

'Freedom does mean choice,' she whispered back. 'So if I chose, say, not to travel round Australia but instead maybe to travel, say, round the perimeter of this castle…With my dog and my companion.'

'What sort of companion?'

'Ooh. Maybe a husband?'

The world stilled. The world held its breath.

'What about that for an idea?' she said cautiously. 'In theory, are there things about it that might appeal to you?'

'There might be,' he said, just as cautiously.

'Like, um, what?'

'Sharing a tent is always fun,' he said.

The smile was returning to her eyes. It was the smile he'd fallen for.

He smiled back, and for Rose it was the same. Nick's was the smile that had lifted her from the bleakness of her past and propelled her into the future.

'There's probably room in the grounds of the royal castle

for a small tent,' she told him. 'But we'd have to get your brother's security forces to leave us be. Floodlights in the wee small hours sweeping our tent might not be as romantic as I'd like.'

'You'd like it to be romantic?'

'Wouldn't you?'

His smile died. The look he gave her was searching. He wasn't touching her. Why not? She wanted so badly to be touched.

She couldn't reach out to him. She wouldn't. A girl had some pride.

'Rose, your freedom.'

'What about your freedom?' she asked. 'You never wanted to be married.'

'I never wanted to be married to anyone at all until I met you. Now I never want to be married to anyone *but* you. But I won't hold you, Rose.'

'I want to be held.'

'You've never been free.'

'Freedom's got some downsides. It needs some inclusions.'

'Like what?'

'You.'

There it was. Out in front, for both of them to see.

And his smile didn't fade one bit. It changed, deepened, broadened, and the smile in his eyes was a caress all by itself.

'I love you, Rose,' he said simply, and her heart did that stupid stopping thing all over again. He'd said it. She looked deep into his eyes and saw immutable truth: love and wonder and need. But also a trace of bleakness—even fear—as though even now he felt like he was exposing himself. A child who'd been brought up in foster homes. Who'd struggled to be independent. Who'd struggled not to need, and who'd come to the same sweet conclusion that she had.

That need wasn't such a bad thing. In fact, need could be the most glorious thing in the world.

'How can you love me?' she managed, and he smiled.

'In a million ways. Far too many to count. But Rose, your freedom…'

'I am free,' she told him. 'I'm free to go wherever I want in the world. I'm free to leave the shadows of Max behind, and move forward without guilt or regret. You've given me that. I'm not sure how, and I'm not sure why, but you have. I'm free to be my own woman and I'm free to love. And I do love, Nick. I choose to love you.'

'You do?'

'Yes.'

Still he didn't move. It was like he couldn't believe what he was hearing.

'We'll have to live here.'

'Oh, no. A castle. In the most beautiful country in the world.' She smiled up at him, feeling dizzy with happiness. 'I'll try to bear it.'

'We'll be in the public eye. It's a goldfish bowl, royalty.'

'It might be fun,' she said, with a certainty that was becoming stronger by the minute. 'I felt claustrophobic here as a kid, but I'd have a lot more freedom now. Us in our tent on the front lawn…I expect we'd shock the socks off the tabloid press at least once a week.'

'I'll never ask you to have babies.'

She stilled. There was so much between them.

Why was he not holding her?

'You won't?' she whispered.

'Rose, to be asked to bear Max's baby…'

'It was different,' she said, thinking it through, trying to figure things out for herself. 'It was just… It just felt wrong. You know, Max had that sperm frozen when he was seventeen years old. He never discussed it with me. It was like a bolt from the blue. If I'd had a baby, it would have been like bearing a child that belonged to Max's past. And any baby I have I want to belong to the future. So if you and I wanted a baby…'

'I never thought I would,' he said softly, wondrously. 'I never imagined I could possibly want to bring a child into the world. But you know, with you…If we had a castle…'

'And Ruby as a grandma. She'd make a great grandma.'

'She will.' His smile was back now, with vengeance. 'And maybe we could even include Gladys and Bob. Just a little bit.'

'You'd do that?'

'I'll talk to them,' he said. 'If you want. They've been part of your life for so long that it might hurt if they don't give us their blessing.' He frowned. 'Maybe some of that independence money you've just knocked back could set up a fund for a veterinarian practice in the town—in Max's name.'

'Oh, Nick,' she said, awed.

'I know,' he said softly, and grinned. 'I'm wonderful.'

'And handsome and kind and clever.'

'And *humble*,' he said. 'Don't forget humble.'

'I'll give you humble,' she said and glowered, and her glower was so delicious that he chuckled.

'Rose?'

'Yes?'

'Most of all I want you,' he said.

'Nick?'

'Yes?'

'If you don't kiss me right this minute I might do something I might regret.'

'What might that be?'

'I might have to kiss you first,' she said, and it was a near thing. A very near thing. Who kissed who?

Rose didn't know. She didn't care. She fell into Nick's arms, and he kissed her until her toes curled.

While at the glass doors of the conservatory three people stood and watched this second wedding-ceremony. The joining of this man to this woman to become man and wife.

'I did get to see it after all,' Ruby said, and smiled and smiled.

'And there's the coronation to come,' Erhard said, deeply satisfied.

'And maybe…' Julianna smiled through the glass at her sister, and then turned to usher the two oldies away. After all, what was a sister for but to protect her sibling?

'Maybe there'll be the odd christening to come too,' she said softly. 'I think the succession to the throne of Alp de Montez is assured. And I think we can safely leave them to it.'